SHEAVES OF ZION

A Murder Mystery

E.W. Sullivan

THIS IS A TEN TALENTS BOOK
SELF-PUBLISHED BY E. W. SULLIVAN

ISBN *(soft):* 978-0-9887-5842-1

Editor: Dennis De Rose, MoneySaver Editing

Manufactured in the United States of America
First Edition

Dedication

For
My loving and supportive wife Anita,
without whom this would not have
been possible.

For
All who chose this path, who side-stepped
the potentates of the written word and
breached their defenses to the public's
literary ear.

PROLOGUE

He made a slit between the Achilles tendon and the ankle, taking care not to over incise the wound, the gambrel inserted, and proper contact ensured, the line tensioned, the freshly killed carcass lifted to the proper height. He used a short, pointed, stainless steel knife, slipping it into the slit made at the Achilles and cut circum the foot—cut out, not in. He left the tendons and muscles intact as they held the extremities in place.

His brute took hold of the blade, cutting through the bone where it met some resistance, the cortical, tough and well-made, did not break easily. This, however, did not deter him from his task. When his efforts to cut further proved futile, he pounded and crushed—a much less elegant undertaking. The trabecular posed no resistance and he soon breached the bone's defenses. He continued his assault, cutting, crushing and pounding until an unrecognizable heap hung before him with an untidy affair of blood and matter strewn and littered about. This was his first. His master grabbed the blade, teaching him that in order to disarticulate a body, he must start at the joints.

ONE

"You called about a body?" Marmaduke asked the reverend, waiting under the covered porch of a small, wood framed church, when Detective Chennault and he arrived.

"That's right, I did." His voice trembled. He fumbled through a large ring jingling with all manner of keys. "I'm still trying to figure out which one opens which door. I locked this—I didn't want anyone disturbing . . . ."

Finally Reverend Gainer, pastor of Bethel Primitive Baptist Church, found the key. He flung open the two wooden double doors and led the detectives into the sanctuary. Dim light filtered through the stained glass windows lining the grey walls. One wall, streaked with white paint, screamed through the sanctuary with images and symbols in red; along the floor of the chapel, the names "Zeus" and "Antiochus" blazed across the weathered wood.

"This is some mess," Detective Chennault said.

"That's not all." The reverend led them farther into the sanctuary. His bent back and limping gait, unstable like a rickety chair, slowed his pace to the podium. "I knew something wasn't right soon as I got the door to my study unlocked. Wasn't no power. No lights anywhere. I thought for sure it was that storm last night, took our power out. I was heading for the fuse box—right over there," he pointed to the back wall of the sanctuary. "Sure enough, there was a bad fuse. So when I got that all fixed and the lights came on . . . well, that's when I saw that . . . that evil coming out of the dark."

Behind the podium lay a gray trench coat draped over a large wooden chair. The reverend grabbed the coat's collar, lowering it enough to expose the face of a young man—dead. He looked back at Marmaduke and Chennault, their eyes locked on the body sitting in the chair.

"Are y'all praying men, Detectives?" He reached his dark, trembling hand back to remove the entire coat. His jaundiced eyes stretched wide at the sight. He perspired in a biblical way, grabbing a readied handkerchief to dry the sweat from his face. "I placed my coat over it. I didn't want anyone from my congregation seeing this by mistake."

The body wore a white sheet with one end tied across the left shoulder. The head glistened with gold paint and was adorned by a laurel leaf crown.

"Shit! What is this?" The reverend cut Marmaduke a harsh stare. "Excuse me reverend." He waved a flashlight over the silver painted arms and upper torso and the brass painted lower torso and thighs. The body's slit belly exposed the innards which spilled onto the floor. The smell overpowered the space. They pinched their noses together and breathed through their mouths. The feet pointed away from each other, twisting the legs in a strange way. An iron material encased the legs and part of the feet. The other part of the feet crusted over in red Georgia clay with spikes protruding from the ankles.

"What are those things where the arms should be?" Reverend Gainer asked.

Marmaduke shined the light where he pointed. "They look like pig feet. And this . . . ," he flicked the light to a stick with a hooked end, "some kind a makeshift staff." The arms were sewn onto the back like wings flapping. Written in the palm of the left hand was the word, "Sieg" and in the right, "Lieh".

Marmaduke saw Chennault's mouth agape—*poor sap*. "Bet you didn't see anything like this in Vice. You're sure you don't want to rethink that transfer to Homicide?" They stood, startled. Water dripped from their rain-soaked clothes, forming small puddles at their feet.

"So what do you think?"

"No idea. Been in Homicide for years and never seen anything like this."

"I been a pastor here near on thirty years and I ain't never seen nothing—nothing like this."

"Well, just leave it. We've got to get a crime scene team and the Medical Examiner in here." Marmaduke didn't look all that settled. He sweated like the reverend and squinted when gazing at the body.

"I'll make the call," said Chennault, dashing from the church. He disappeared behind the weathered doors, back out into the rain.

Within minutes, an army of uniformed officers and Homicide Detectives descended upon the small church, along with parishioners. They arrived for the morning services, a slow steady stream of gray-haired, half-bent, cane-bearing old folk, the stuff of this small church.

The congregation waited behind the crime scene tape stretched across the front of the churchyard, their faces drawn and anxious. The glaring lights and sirens boded something far more exciting than just their usual Sunday sermon. Reverend Gainer wobbled from the chapel and stood atop the stoop, watching his members gather at the road. He threw his hands in the air, waving at them.

"Everything's okay. Y'all gone back home now. Won't be no church today," he shouted from the stoop before officers took him away in a patrol car.

The parishioners parted like the Red Sea, headed for the vehicle carrying their pastor away. A light blue station wagon, a large sign on its flank, "DeKalb County Medical Examiner", rounded the same curve in the driveway. Marmaduke walked to the car, approaching the driver's side. A woman dashed forward from the crowd, hobbling on two bad feet.

"Officer! Officer! Where are y'all taking Pastor Gainer?" she cried.

"Lady!" Marmaduke yelled, barging up to her, "Hold it, ma'am, you can't come near here." He held onto her. She struggled. "This whole area is a crime scene!"

"Where is Pastor Gainer? Why won't y'all tell me what has happened to him?"

"Calm down, ma'am, calm down. Pastor Gainer is headed down to the station to answer questions about the body—"

"Body! What body? Oh Lord! Oh Lord!" the woman screamed. "Is Pastor Gainer okay?" Marmaduke clenched his teeth and threw back his head. He wanted to kick himself for his choice of words, upsetting the woman even more.

"Yes. Now if you will, this Detective," he grabbed Chennault by the arm, "will escort you back to your car."

"But what about the body?" She pointed to the church. Drops of rain pelted her glasses almost covering them.

"The body of evidence, ma'am. Now, please, go with the Detective." Chennault grabbed the old woman by the arm and led her down the drive.

"Detective Marmaduke."

"Shhhhiii! What is it now?" He stomped the ground, splattering mud and water over his pant legs and coat. "Damn!" He pulled a handkerchief from his pocket, brushing the mud away. Lightning flashed and thunder roared. Marmaduke ducked, shielding his head. He turned toward an outstretched hand. He looked up at it. He looked higher and back down again before rising and grabbing it.

"I'm Dr. DeGlorious, D.C.M.E. What do we have?" They walked toward the church, he in loafers and she in heels, skipping across the rain-soaked soil like a well chucked stone across a still pond.

"I'm not sure yet. What happened to Stan?"

"Dr. Witherspoon is no longer with the M.E.'s office. Is the body in here?"

"That's right. What do you mean he's no longer with the M.E.'s office? Where did he go?"

"Listen, if you want to know where Stan is, I suggest you check with human resources or call up his momma. Now are you going to show me where the body is or do I have to call on Jesus to raise me one from these graves here?" She pointed at the weathered headstones flanking the church. He looked at her, his brow raised.

"I see the Irish aren't the only ones full of ire."

"That's right. It comes in Puerto Rican too. Now where's my body?"

They walked the short distance through the pouring rain until they reached the church. Marmaduke showed Dr. DeGlorious the chair behind the podium, still draped with the reverend's coat. She rolled it off the body. Her squinting eyes lit up and her mouth hung open. She froze for a moment, holding the rolled up coat in her hands, saying nothing. Marmaduke cleared his throat, snapping her back to her duties.

She shined a penlight over the body. Starting at the head, she moved the light down along its length, circling the corpse resting upon the chair.

"This your mess?" she asked Marmaduke, seeing the puddle of water on the floor near the chair, shining her light on it and back to his feet. He said nothing, didn't have to. He stood on the weathered church

4

floor, water still dripping, the proverbial child with the ill-gotten cookie residue all over his face.

Dr. DeGlorious grabbed a camera from her case. She snapped pictures, capturing, in perpetuity, the gruesomeness of the crime. She examined under and around the arms, both pig and human.

"There is some lividity and both early and late stage decomposition between various parts of the body. There appear to be insects and insect larvae present. Time of death to be determined later. Cuts to the body, some hesitation, some clean, shows two distinct blade types, maybe more." She dictated into the recording device attached to her waist and collar. "The eyes are open with some petechial. The mouth is closed. Skin coloration varies. No blood is present at scene and there appears to be no additional trauma to the body." She went on to describe the appearance of the body and its manner of dress. "Was that coat with it?"

"No. It's the preacher's coat," Marmaduke answered.

"I need it bagged and sent to my office with the body."

"Have you ever seen anything like this?"

"No, can't say that I have." She removed the latex gloves from her hands. They popped, drawing the attention of the officers milling about.

"So when will we know something?"

"Well, the samples I'm collecting will need to go to the GBI; it might take me a couple of days to do the autopsy. So I'd guess by Thursday. Call my office."

Marmaduke watched as Dr. DeGlorious gathered her things and disappeared past him through the weathered church doors, back out into daylight.

He turned to Chennault. "She had no smell to her."

He nodded. "Neither did Stan, for that matter."

"Gets in the way of their senses I reckon."

The rain stopped pouring down, leaving the stain of red Georgia clay streaking over the ground. The sun peaked over the horizon, blazing through the thunderous clouds that had, a while ago, brought forth a deluge. A much stronger stench now filled the air, the smell of rotting flesh.

"What kind of sick SOB thought up a crime like this anyway?" Marmaduke asked.

Chennault turned toward the body. "The kind that wants to shock our senses." He covered his nose.

"Yeah, and perhaps kill our spirit. But why this place and why this type of crime?" Chennault shrugged. "Take a few blue suits with you. We need to canvass the entire area. Stop anyone who comes this way."

"All cars?" Chennault flipped open a pad, preparing to write.

"I don't care if they're riding, walking or rolling. I want everyone stopped. And get a list of all the members of this church from the preacher while he is down at the station. Also find out the last time he or anyone else was at the church. I want to know who had access to this place and when. Get the route sheet from that delivery service up the street, question all their drivers, those who had routes from last week until this morning. And those pig feet look fresh—check with local farmers for any missing or mutilated porkers."

"What about the power company? The preacher said that he had to change a fuse to get the lights back on. Maybe someone else called about the power outage and Georgia Power came out to check."

"Good idea. And you might as well check USPS while you're at it."

"Okay Marmaduke."

"And make sure this place is secured. I want a guard posted here twenty-four hours a day for the next couple of days."

"You've gotta get the okay from the Captain."

"I'll get the okay."

Marmaduke knew the urgency of solving this type of crime. The council grilled the Captain the last time a major crime went unsolved for too long. He needed resources allocated around the clock.

"Listen up!" Marmaduke shouted to the officers milling about. "We have a sicko on this one and the good citizens of DeKalb County won't wait patiently while we bump our heads together to figure this out. So let's earn those Christmas bonuses!"

Marmaduke slogged through the muddy ground, slipping and sliding, but avoiding a fall. He took in a big yawn, stretching his arms out to get in more air. He shook his head, trying to knock off the sleep. This crime started at the beginning of his shift and already the day waxed long. Crimes like these only happened in the big cities like New York, Chicago and L.A., not DeKalb County. Sure they loomed under the shadow of a big city, but up till now they eluded even Atlanta's major crime problem.

Marmaduke, now on firmer ground, turned toward Chennault. "In fifteen years as a Homicide Detective, I've seen stabbings, shootings, strangulations, even some bazaar ritualistic shit, but never anything like this."

His phone rang. Marmaduke scrambled to find it, patting himself all over. He dug his hand deep into his pants pocket, pulling the phone out. He flipped it open.

"Marmaduke here," he answered. "Another body! Where?"

TWO

Marmaduke and Chennault pulled into the church parking lot. Leaves and downed limbs covered the ground, nearly obscuring the "First Iconium Baptist Church" sign. The winds of this particular storm brought with them an evil that plagued the small, isolated churches of DeKalb County, but no conclusions could be made this soon.

"What kind of crazy bastard would run around leaving bodies in churches?" Marmaduke asked. "Look, only one body, that's local news. Two and we go national—I want the media kept back two hundred feet from the property lines."

"Shouldn't we tell them something?" Chennault asked. "They're not going away."

"We can't let them boogeyman this perp. The sign reads, 'County of churches, schools and homes', not 'Manson or Dahlmer country'." Chennault nodded in agreement. "Put the gag on your boys too; no one and I mean no one talks to the media. We don't need a media circus and the last thing we want is the media giving this bastard some cute nickname and letting everyone know we're taking too long to solve this shit." They walked toward the sanctuary, dodging the debris strewn about.

"What about the feds? Shouldn't we call them in?"

"Not yet. That's the quickest way for this to go national. Half of them fuckwits are on some newspapers' or TVs' payrolls. But you can contact the M.E., a Dr. Glorify, or some shit like that. Tell her two days it was going to take her for the first autopsy are out. I need it done in two hours."

"What do you want me to do with the deacon?"

"Who's the deacon?"

"Deacon Pike. The responding officer says he found the body.

He's eighty-nine years old, damn near gave him a heart attack. I called EMS. He's over there sucking up oxygen."

"Well, unless he's about to croak, I want him held here for questioning."

"Which one of you suits is Detective Marmaduke?" an officer asked.

"I am."

"Cap'n on the horn, he wants to speak with yah."

"Damn, just what I need." He tossed back the flaps to his trench coat, putting his hands to his hips. His sidearm poked from its holster.

Marmaduke followed the officer to his squad car. He sat in the passenger seat, but only half way, radio receiver in hand. He stared at it for a moment, shaking his head.

"I don't have a damn thing to tell him," he mumbled. He dropped the receiver back on the hook, hanging up. "Let me speak to the deacon," he told Chennault. They walked over to the EMS unit. The deacon, a slight man with salt and pepper hair, sat inside with an oxygen mask plastered to his face.

"Hello, Mr. Pike, I'm Detective Marmaduke. Can you tell me what happened, sir?"

"You got the first part right. It sure was hell! I don't know 'bout the 'o' though." He gasped for air, wheezing and coughing. His hand trembled, moving wildly all over, struggling to find the right place on his face. He jammed the mask back to his nose and gulped at the oxygen.

"Now calm down, Mr. Pike. Take it easy, go nice and slow," Marmaduke cautioned. "Do you need to give him something?" he asked the paramedic.

"I'z don't need a damn thing, 'cept for y'all to get that thing out our church. That ain't nothing but pure evil!"

"Can you tell me what happened, sir?"

Taking a big gulp from the oxygen, the deacon began to explain. "I'z come to open up the church 'cause Brother Nesmith took ill and couldn't do it. Now I'z tried to get Brother Barnes to do it but you can't get these young folk to do nothing now a days—"

"What about the body, deacon?" Detective Chennault interrupted.

"I'z gettin' to that. How old is you, son?"

9

"Take your time deacon, you're doing fine," Marmaduke reassured him.

"Thank yah. Anyway, I'z come into the church and there it was sitting in the pastor's chair looking at me, looking at it. Damn near scared me to death. And that's what happened."

"Thank you, Deacon Pike. I'm going to have an officer take some information from you and we'll get you to the hospital to make sure you're okay."

"Thank yah but that in there ain't nothing but pure evil." He placed the mask back to his face and closed his eyes. The paramedics secured him to the cot and loaded the gurney into the ambulance.

"I'm surprised he didn't piss himself," Chennault said. He and Marmaduke watched the EMTs drive off.

Marmaduke reached into his coat pocket for the nicotine gum his doctor prescribed him. He tried to quit before—this was his third time back on the wagon. He dug the gum from his pocket, opening it half way.

"Ah! I need a cigarette, damn it." He crushed the gum in his hand, tossing it to the ground un-chewed. "Let's go see what we have in here."

Inside the church, Marmaduke found the same graffiti painted over the wall and floor: the inverted pentagram, images of the sun, moon and stars, a singular large eye and an inverted 'V' intersecting a right angle at its legs. This time, however, the name 'Hadrian' in blood, dripped from the wall. A body posed and mutilated, similar to the first, sat at the podium of the pulpit.

"It sure isn't pretty," Chennault said.

"Murder never is, Detective. Murder never is."

THREE

Atlanta, like the bodies in those churches, sprang from the earth out of nowhere—a southern Stonehenge. The red Georgia clay birthed a city a hundred and eighty degrees different than the quaint, antebellum charm of its surroundings. A spaceship from Mars, landing in the middle of Piedmont Park, would seem less out of place.

In this city, old money met new vices, a tumultuous mix, like strong cocktails and fast women, who huddled on "good corners". Graying old gents wearing twenty-year-service gold Rolexes staggered from their favorite late night haunts, their bellies filled with Maker's Mark and their arms filled with twenty-year-old women with golden hair, out for a good time. The city fathers tried their best to curtail the revelry but good ole boys will be good ole boys.

Atlanta held many memories, recent and past. The flames of Sherman's march still smoldered here, as did the memories of little black boys lost and little pimped-out girls, of mayors and monsters and Jews strung up by their necks and taken for a whirl. Within this city of nostalgic novels and lost empires, from civil war reenactments to civil right marches, history flowed through its heart.

Now, a new tale demanded time spent in the collective conscience of the people of Atlanta. A story that, when written, would add more than just a footnote to the history of this metropolis. The scribes' pens awaited the ending, one that rested, for now, in the rumpled clothing and questionable habits of a man this place called a detective.

. . .

On its last ring, Marmaduke's phone startled him from a stupor. He had tossed in the hard chair all night trying to find a soft spot. He raised his head from his desk, wood-grain pattern imprinted on his face. He tried to sleep but after seeing those bodies painted up inside the churches, his mind raced, keeping him awake. He spun the computer monitor around on his desk and pecked away at the keyboard, the last entry on his screen read, "The Ripper Slayings of Nineteenth Century England". He had spent the night at the station, poring through endless police databanks, searching for a crime anywhere that came close to being something like these two. He had found none, but this didn't surprise him.

His phone rang again.

"Marmaduke here." He snatched up the phone. His hand came close to knocking over a dying potted plant resting near the edge of his desk. He scrambled to keep it from falling, leaping from his chair to grab it. He pressed the phone tight to his ear, trapped between his shoulder and head. His desk stayed cluttered with things: accommodation plaques from earlier years when he tried to impress the stripes, pictures of wives one, two, and three, the order of which he no longer remembered, and stacks of files he pored over when he wanted to look busy for the Captain. He hoarded things, fitting in amid other similarly cluttered desks.

"Detective, this is Dr. DeGlorious."

"What do you have for me?" He took a sip from a half a cup of coffee, the other half long gone, and took a bite from a sweet roll.

"It's what I have to show you that's important."

"What . . . that we have a Frankenstein running around the county?"

"What makes you say that, Detective?"

"I figured the way the bodies were painted up, our perp was trying to create his own version of a monster. At least that's my fifty-cents worth of analysis."

"You may want to pay yourself a little more than that, Detective."

"Don't I know it but what do you mean?"

"I'll explain when you get here."

Marmaduke dropped the receiver on the hook and headed toward his car. Puffs of smoke trailed him; he was back on the sticks, Marlboro Menthol, soft brown filters, the burn of the nicotine going down his throat was the only thing that worked, ridding him of the nausea he felt. His stomach churned, letting out an audible growl, hoping to hurl the pizza and beer from the night before. He was no rookie, but he had all the symptoms of one. Marmaduke rubbed his bloodshot eyes, held his belly tight and eased into his car. He snatched the eight-track tape from the slot, hit the power button on the radio and cranked up the volume. Beethoven's Moonlight Sonata blared from vibrating speakers, filling the car with sound.

Marmaduke reached beneath the front seat, feeling for the brown paper bag he stored there. He struggled to dislodge it. The tape he used to secure the bag resisted his every attempt. Marmaduke balanced the car in between the lines of his lane, unscrewed the top to the bottle in the bag, turned it up full tilt and chugged. The old Deuce and a Quarter veered to the left. He corrected, swerving to miss an approaching car, spilling none of the libation.

He drank Thunderbird, his favorite. For the past six months, he fell on and off the wagon. His counselors at Alcoholics Anonymous warned him that smoking again could cause him to drink. For this reason, he tried giving up the sticks.

"Fuck it." He turned the bottle upward again. "One more demon can't hurt."

Marmaduke's mouth dried despite the swigs from the bottle. He wiped beads of sweat, forming around his face, with his hand, drying his moistened palm on his pant leg. After finding the bodies, nothing more shocking, more disturbing or more evil seemed possible. Dead bodies showing up all over town happened once in a hundred years, if not longer. These crimes, unlike most killings he had investigated, carried a hidden, abstruse motive.

Marmaduke wheeled his Deuce and a Quarter up to the M.E.'s office, shifting into 'Park'. He struck a match and put the flame inside his wide-opened mouth, each exhale burned away the scent of alcohol. He rinsed with the Listerine he kept in the glove compartment, swishing the stinging liquid around in his mouth, gargling it as far down his throat as he could, without swallowing. He wrapped his lips around the now empty liquor bottle, spitting into it. Marmaduke grabbed a handful of peppermints. He popped two in his mouth, placing the rest in his coat pocket.

Just as he stepped inside the M.E.'s building, his phone rang again.

"Marmaduke," he answered.

"Marmaduke," the Captain started, his voice low and calm. "Does your momma love you?"

13

"I . . . ."

"WELL I HOPE SO, 'CAUSE YOU'RE GONNA NEED SOMEBODY AT YOUR FUNERAL TO CRY FOR YOUR ASS!" Captain Franklin yelled.

"But Captain . . . ."

"But Captain, my ass. Are you watching the news?"

Marmaduke turned to the startled-looking receptionist, flashing his badge. "Where can I find a TV?"

"Around the corner, down the hall and second door on the right." She pointed the way.

Marmaduke trotted down the hall, the phone still to his ear, the Captain still spewing words. He entered the small room. Others sat, eating and watching TV. He walked over and changed the channel.

"Hey!" someone shouted. Marmaduke ignored them. "Breaking News" flashed across the screen. Deacon Pike and Reverend Gainer had held a press conference.

"Damn!"

"Are you cussing me, Detective?"

Marmaduke closed the phone. He trotted back to Dr. DeGlorious' lab, his mood foul, having to change into a scrub suit, a mask and goggles didn't help any. He pushed through the double swinging-doors and entered the examination area. Steel tables lined the room everywhere, on each of them was a body. The death business was a good business.

Marmaduke sniffed the air, sterile, like a hospital. He placed his hands in front of his mouth to catch his breath. He smelled the mouthwash and the peppermint.

"Detective, over here," Dr. DeGlorious called him, arm in the air. He walked to a steel table where she was examining a body. "One of yours is over here, the other is on ice." She led him over to a table across the room. "This is the Bethel church body."

"The first site."

"And the cause of death was decapitation."

"Decapitation? But the head was connected to the body when we found it."

"Connected to 'a' body, not 'the' body. Grab that end." Marmaduke took hold of the legs. Dr. DeGlorious took the upper. They rolled it over onto its side, exposing the rear.

"What the . . . ." Marmaduke's voice went up an octave higher.

"In case you're curious, those are a perfect pair of D cups," the Doctor offered.

"What is this, some medical freakery? The head is a man."

"The head and torso are from different donors, male and female respectively. The head was severed from the one donor while he was still alive. I'm having the other body parts analyzed, but I suspect they are from different donors as well."

"How many?"

"Hard to say. But we know that we're looking at two for this body alone."

"So are you telling me that we have some sick bastard out there chopping people up and sewing them back together?"

"More like stitching. There is a difference."

"What about our second body?"

"Same thing. I'm having the DNA cross-matched to see if any of its parts match this one."

"And if they don't?"

"Then your two victims may go up to three, possibly four, or even more." She rolled the body flat on its back. "One more thing, Detective, the hands sewn onto the back had bite marks on the phalanges, like this." She removed her glove and bit down on her fingers to show him what she meant. "They could have come from the victim trying to free a restraint. I took pictures, so that we can compare dentals, if we end up with another victim. "Donny, we're finished here," the Doctor called over to her assistant, he rolled the table and the body away.

Dr. DeGlorious left Detective Marmaduke standing amid the dead bodies. He stared at the floor, thinking, his mind in a far-off place, trying to wrap itself around these crimes.

"Dr. DeGlorious," he called out to her, she was across the room. He trotted over. "So where do we go from here?"

The Doctor glanced at her watch. "It's time to quit, Detective Marmaduke. I'm going home." She turned and walked away again, her hands tucked inside the white lab coat she wore.

"I meant about these crimes, Doctor?"

"You're the detective, Detective. I only cut them up." Her words and the tap of her heels on the floor echoed from down the hall. He stood there, phone ringing, unnoticed by him. "Your phone, Detective!" Dr. DeGlorious yelled, now much farther away. He fumbled to answer it.

"Marmaduke."

15

"Detective Marmaduke." Ms. James, the Captain's secretary and sister-in-law was calling him. A woman, tougher than any man, she cursed and drank with the best of them. "The Captain wants to see you immediately, Marmaduke."

"Can't this wait until tomorrow? I'm trying to solve these cases." He listened to her breathing hard through the phone. Marmaduke tightened his body, expecting a hard verbal punch.

"If you don't get your narrow ass in here, Marmaduke, you're not gonna see the sun rise tomorrow. You—"

"Okay! Okay! I'm on my way." He flipped his phone closed.

He pulled out of the parking lot. The clock struck five—quitting time, right. Cars lined the roads end to end, filling every lane. A thick haze settled over the skyline, baptizing the city and everything around it in a cloud of smog. Marmaduke dashed in and out, but made no progress. Cars came to a stop, the popcorn and the movie were all that remained. Commuters left their nine to five's and headed home to their own little make-believe worlds in the suburbs. They used the city like a john used a whore, for momentary gratification and excitement. They detached and discarded it once they had satisfied themselves.

When he reached the Trinity Street station, James was sitting at the front desk, the one next to the Captain's office.

"Why, hello, Detective Marmaduke, nice of you to join us. Go right on in. The Captain's been waiting on you. I hope you've grown more ass since this morning because he's gonna bite another chunk out of what you have left." She smiled. He smiled back but said nothing. He opened the door to the Captain's office, just enough to stick his head in.

"Ah! Come in, Detective," the Captain said, seeing him. Marmaduke pushed through the door to enter. The Captain sat at his desk, speaking with another gentleman.

"Detective Marmaduke, say hello to Special Agent Mike Rose of the FBI." Marmaduke walked over to the stocky gentleman, now standing. He wrapped his fingers around the Agent's meaty hand.

"I was just talking to Agent Rose about your church cases and he may know someone who might be of some assistance. Tell Detective Marmaduke about your thoughts, Agent Rose."

"Wait a minute now, Captain. We've only been on these cases for two days and we're making some progress. This might be the wrong time to bring some fed psych-cop in to have us chasing boogiemen."

"Well, Detective, let me ask you this. Do you have any suspects?"

"No."

"Any witnesses?"

"No, but . . ."

"What about a motive or any forensic evidence?"

"No, but . . . ."

"Marmaduke, sit your ass down and listen." He pulled a chair out from against the desk and sat. "Excuse my detective, Agent Rose, go ahead."

"Well, I was telling the Captain here that, from the evidence I have seen, there may be a ritualistic motive associated with the two murders . . ."

"See, just as I thought, a boogieman."

"Detective!" The Captain stared at Marmaduke hard, showing his continued displeasure with his interruptions. "Continue, Agent Rose."

"Six months ago, we looked into recruiting a criminalist for our Behavioral Science Unit. He wrote an interesting paper on crimes with religious and symbolic overtones. Many of his theories seem to coincide with what's in the report the Captain provided. I think you should bring him in as a consultant on these cases."

"You're really bringing some book-head in on this?" Marmaduke grumbled.

"He has a Ph.D. in criminal psychology," Agent Rose replied.

"And you support this?"

"Not only do I support it but the Chief and Commissioner do as well."

"So I have no say so in this?" Marmaduke folded his arms, giving the Captain the worst side of his face. He sulked like a rejected suitor on prom night.

"Look, Marmaduke, it's still your case, I'm just giving you some assistance. Agent Rose, when can your man report?"

"I have to contact my deputy manager to make the arrangements but I think we can have him here in a day or so."

"Good. Detective Marmaduke will be your contact on this. Thank you very much, gentlemen." Agent Rose plopped his brown fedora on top his head and exited the office. Marmaduke remained seated.

"Captain . . . ."

"Marmaduke, get the hell out of my office."

Marmaduke leapt from his chair and left, disgruntled to find Agent

Rose still outside the Captain's office, getting contact information from Ms. James.

"Detective, your consultant's name is Thelonious Zones. He's presently employed with Drake and Associates . . . ."

"Whoa! I thought he worked for you?"

"No, we tried hiring him but we ended up rescinding our offer."

"So, this guy works for a private company. Does the Captain know this?"

"He's aware of it, yes." Marmaduke turned back toward the door of the Captain's office, puzzled.

He turned back to Agent Rose. "So, when do I get to meet this genius?"

"As a matter of fact, he is consulting down in Pulaski County. We could leave first thing in the morning. I'll pick you up here say around 7:30 a.m."

"See you at 7:30, Agent Rose."

. . .

The old Deuce showed its age, pulling into the parking lot of Mama's, a local pub. The glimmering gold-speckled paint was peeled and faded to a brushed tan. The pleather interior seat coverings were bursting at the seams. The once roaring V6 engine puttered and spewed trails of black smoke into the air. Marmaduke and his car led a hard life and lived on the down slope of the bell-curve, long past the help of any tune-up or treatment program.

He leaned gangster-style back in his seat, flipped open his phone and dialed. "What do you have for me, Chennault?"

"I got nothing from the canvass near the churches and no one from the delivery service or USPS saw anything suspicious. Georgia Power didn't send anyone out that night either."

"What about the church members? When was the last time any of them had access to their churches?"

"The members of both churches said Wednesday night's Bible study was the last night any of them were at their respective churches. Most of the members checked out, some had minor brushes with the law but nothing that said *crazed killer*."

"Well, get some rest and keep digging tomorrow. We're going to need a break to catch this guy. Unfortunately, I can't join you, Captain's got me meeting with some book-head in the morning."

"There is one other thing. I pulled the video from the gas station on the corner of our first crime scene. It showed a work van in the area around two o'clock that morning."

"Any details?"

"The van? The video was too grainy."

"Probably nothing. They work three shifts at that bakery on Panthersville Road. Wouldn't hurt to follow up though."

. . .

The small, dark pub brimmed with hard-drinking old men in ruffled shirts, dangling ties, worn-out fedoras, puffing on cheap cigars. Photographic memories of those who served and had served the city lined its walls—it was a cop bar.

"Dukie boy!" they greeted Marmaduke, holding their drinks in the air, some foaming over. He scowled, hating that name.

"A Johnny Lightening," he ordered, hunched in his seat over the counter. The barkeep concocted the mixture of Thunderbird and Coke—shaken, not stirred.

"Ain't ever gonna give up this cheap, bum's wine are yah, Dukie?" the barkeep asked, plopping the large, glass mug onto the counter. "That shit grows hair on my chest just from taking a whiff of it."

"Numbs the pain, my friend," Marmaduke quipped.

"Yeah, and if you keep drinking that stuff, it's gonna dull your senses. You won't feel nothing, you won't see nothing, you won't hear nothing, and you won't smell nothing."

"All welcomed deficiencies in the death business." He raised the glass above his head, lowered it to his lips and chugged it dry. He plopped the empty mug onto the counter. "Barkeep! Keep them coming."

Marmaduke drank himself into a blind stupor. He swished and swayed toward a small room at the rear of the pub afterwards, just like his father before him.

FOUR

The drive down to the maximum security prison along the South Georgia countryside waxed nostalgic for Marmaduke, a southern boy with no hint of a twang. Tobacco and cotton fields lined the two-lane highway and the rebel flag crackled in the breeze, flying high and proud above the open plains of the American Confederacy. Those who held dear these remnants of the gentile south put up a fuss to keep them relevant. The picture postcard settings and antebellum arrangements, kept and watched over by the Daughters of the Confederacy or other such southern patriots, grounded this southern hamlet in its past.

"I got a rain – bow. Unh! Tied—all a-round my shoul—der—Unh! I'm a-go-in' home—Unh! My—Lord I'm go-in' home," the shackled men sang, all decked out in pinstriped jumpsuits and black Brogans.

"Alright boys, let's cut it low!" a white guard on horseback yelled, his shotgun butt propped against his thigh, barrel pointed in the air. The prisoners cut weeds and high grasses with sling blades and busted rock with sledgehammers.

"The 'Brothers' sure do like the plantation life," Marmaduke quipped, as Agent Rose and he inched up to the prison gate.

"Does your Captain know about your penchant for off-colored remarks, Detective?" Agent Rose cut his eyes over at him. Marmaduke stared back into a pair of beady, black pellets poked onto a bulldog face.

"I'm just saying, even after emancipation and civil rights, there are still masters and there are still slaves. But I guess someone fresh off the boat, like you, wouldn't know anything about that. Besides, the Captain and James both dish it out as well as anyone."

"The south is still minting the currency of provenance and pedigree, I see."

20

He continued to stare at Agent Rose who faced straight ahead. "If you're referring to my ancestry, my family goes back to the founders of this country." Marmaduke unfurled a newspaper. He snapped the ends of it taut, making a crackling sound. His eyes moved between the paper and Agent Rose.

They reached the prison gates, passing through security. A guard led them to an observation room where Dr. Thelonious Othello Zones conducted counseling sessions.

"I love my mama and he should not have talked about my mama like that! I love my mama! I love my mama! I love my mama! That woman was a saint." Prisoner 2596, aka Marcus Tineman, aka Tiny, cried like a big baby, all six feet and five inches, two-hundred and seventy-five pounds of him. Marmaduke thumbed through his chart; it was left on a table in the observation room. Sentenced to life without parole and hard labor, for murder in the second degree, he sat shackled to a table in an interrogation room.

"I'm sorry that he said those things about your mother Mr. Tineman, but if you loved your mother so much, why did you stab her forty-five times?" Dr. Zones asked.

"Because the bitch deserved it! She talked about my daddy. I love my daddy! I love my daddy! She should not have said that about my daddy." He continued to cry and wrestle with his chains.

"Guard! Guard!" Zones called out. The door flung open and the guard stormed into the room. "Mr. Tineman is ready to return to his cell."

"Come on, Tiny, time to go bye-bye."

"Goodbye, Dr. Zones, I'll see you next week." The guard led Tiny out of the room. He took baby steps. The leg irons limited the length of his gait. He turned back to Zones, who remained seated scribbling in a pad. "Doctor," he called him, now calm. Zones looked up from his papers. "I love you, Dr. Zones." Tiny smiled.

"Thank you, Tiny—I think."

"Come on, mister sensitive." The guard pulled Tiny out of the door and led him back to his cell. The steel bars clanked when they opened and closed.

Zones turned his attention back to his papers. Another guard appeared at the door.

"Send in the next inmate, officer," he instructed him.

The guard turned to leave the room. "Oh yeah," he turned back to Zones, "there's an Agent Rose and a Detective Marmaduke here to see you, Doctor."

"In that case, officer, reschedule my other appointments and send in our guests."

"Okay, but Mama's Boy and Cry Baby ain't gonna like hearing it."

"I'm sure you'll find the proper words."

"Mama's Boy! Cry Baby! Back to your cells, no cuddle time for you today!" the officer shouted down the hall. Soon afterwards, Agent Rose and Marmaduke entered the room.

"Dr. Zones, I'm Agent Rose, FBI and this is Detective Marmaduke, DeKalb County P.D. We called your office and they told us we could reach you here. Do you have a minute?"

"Sure. They told me that you might be stopping by. Although, I must admit, I am surprised to be hearing from the FBI. What can I do for you?"

"Well, Doctor, I'm sure you've been following the church murders that have occurred within the last few days."

"Only what's been in the news."

"I've read your papers and think that your theories on crime scene analysis could be beneficial to our investigation."

"Have you also read the views of those who denounce those theories, Agent Rose?"

"I've read many theories that either denounced or supported other writings, not just yours. I'm willing to try whatever it takes to solve these murders before there are more bodies, even if it means having tea leaves read by an African shaman."

"There can't be many of you left at the Bureau."

"You'd be surprised, Doctor."

" . . . And what about you, Detective? You carry any tea leaves around with you?" Zones asked Marmaduke.

"I'm not as other-worldly as Agent Rose here, Doctor. I believe in good old-fashioned detective work. And for the record, I'm only here because the brass thinks, unlike me, that this isn't a colossal waste of time. While some sicko runs around out there carving up bodies, we sit around here talking head games."

"Um, Detective Marmaduke's skepticism aside, are you willing to help us, Doctor?"

Zones hesitated. Even though the Bureau rejected him months prior, forcing him to have to accept a position with his uncle's consulting firm, this might be the opportunity for him to prove his theories.

"Have you cleared everything with my boss, Sam Drake?"

"I asked, but he wasn't agreeable. Said FBI didn't pay enough."

"But you came anyway?"

"I read your theories on criminal exegeses and saw that you applied to the Bureau. I thought you may still have an interest in working with us."

"So, is this an offer of employment?"

"I'm afraid not, Dr. Zones, at least not now. The Bureau's budget is watched carefully these days. We are, however, offering our usual consulting stipend—and the southern hospitality ain't bad either."

"And I'll be working with Detective Marmaduke?"

"Yes. He's the lead on these cases."

"And who do you report to, Detective?"

"That would be Captain Franklin."

"And might I add that the Captain is one hundred percent in support of utilizing your unique investigative techniques, Doctor," Agent Rose added.

"Well, Agent, Detective, as you can see, my work here keeps me pretty busy." He tapped a stack of files piled on top the table. "When do you need my answer?"

"I was hoping to get one today."

"I'm going to need more time to think about it, Agent."

"While you're thinking, here's a copy of the autopsy, the photos and the crime scene report. If you find some time, let Detective Marmaduke know your thoughts." Agent Rose and Detective Marmaduke shoved back from the table, rising to leave. He tossed an envelope onto the table. Zones reached for it, then pulled his hand away. "We'll find our way out, Doctor."

Zones continued to look down at the brown envelope.

"Agent Rose," he called to him. "Why was my application rejected by the Bureau?"

The Agent reached behind his ears, stretching out the bend in his wire rimmed glasses. He removed them and cleaned the lenses with a kerchief plucked from his pocket. Agent Rose walked over to Zones, leaving Marmaduke at the door. Measuring his words, he leaned in close to Zones.

"Sam Drake called the Deputy Division Chief and had him rescind the offer."

Zones snapped his head up, closer to where Agent Rose stood. "Sam was behind my rejection?" Agent Rose nodded. "I should have known."

Zones snatched the envelope from the table, stuffed it into his briefcase. He tore past Marmaduke at the door and bolted down the hall.

FIVE

Zones yawned wide and rubbed his eyes red on the drive back to his hotel in Atlanta. He stayed in the city instead of one of the roadside motels that lined the highway to the prison. South Georgia's lack of a night life made staying outside the city unbearable—too "country" for him. The ghettos and barrios of New York and L.A boiled in his blood. His roots, however, sprang from the south. His grandparents migrated to the north from Mississippi and Georgia back in the fifties. The rural enclave of Pulaski County, however, seemed worlds away from the urban jungle of New York City. Zones craved its bright lights and nightlife, an addiction, one not easily satisfied.

. . .

He reached his hotel room, tossed his briefcase onto the bed and plucked the phone receiver from its hook. He dialed.

"Room service," the voice answered.

"Buttermilk biscuits smothered in gravy, please." He reclined back onto his bed, awaiting the delivery of his food. He turned the TV on, CNN came up. Breaking news on the bodies found at the churches flashed across the screen. Reverend Gainer and Deacon Pike stood outside their respective churches, talking about what they found one early Sunday morning. Zones lay there, watching as the two of them described their ordeal.

"The bodies were painted all up and wearing this sheet," one said.

"And there was writing all over the wall and the floor," the other added.

Zones paid less attention to them and more to the crowd that was gathered around. He knew that some perpetrators of these types of crimes tended to revisit the scene. No one, however, stood out.

"I'm Bishop Marren with the Inter-Faith Council." He stepped to the microphone. "Behind me are members of the Council. We all join our brothers, Reverend Gainer and Deacon Pike, demanding that the authorities lend every resource necessary to find the culprits in these crimes. Bishop Jackson," another man stepped forward, "will represent us on the civilian task force that Councilwoman Grudges has formed. Although this is a step in the right direction, we expect and hope to get more . . . ."

Zones studied the crime scene reports, flipping through the pictures, reading the autopsy. He listened to the men's account of the scene.

"Cryptic," he said. He placed the photos and reports back into the file, wanting to see and hear more about these crimes, a full stomach soon lulled him off into a deep sleep.

Zones awakened in the still-dark of late night. Restless, he slung off the bed covers, hopped to his feet, showered and threw on his clothes. He called the hotel valet for his car and cruised down Peachtree Street—surprisingly named, since more Bradford pear trees lined Peachtree Street than actual peach trees. He hoped to experience a little of Atlanta's nightlife. Patrons of the many bars and clubs he passed sat out on sidewalk cafes or spilled onto the street in drunken revelry. "Club Anytime", the sign read—a 24-hour dive. A line filled with young co-eds and preppies wearing their school jerseys stretched for one block.

"No guppies tonight," he said. He continued on. The Vortex, although the name sounded menacing, it played host to a rather tame crowd. He stopped at none of these, wandering around instead, searching for something specific, hoping to find his own brand of entertainment.

Zones pulled along the side of the road. He rolled down his window. "Where's the party?" he asked a man slumped on a bench.

"What's up, brother, what're you looking for?" He leaned against the car. Gold chains hanging from his neck swung back and forth, tapping the half–rolled down window. He peered over his shoulders at the sound of every noise he heard. "If you want straight, that's Downtown, gay and BSMD, that's here in Midtown. Brookhaven, that's Cleaverville and I don't see no children with you."

"That's it?"

"Man, what you want? This ain't New York!"

"You got that right." He pulled back out into the traffic.

Zones continued to drive, cruising the juke joints and seedy haunts of the city to satisfy what he never had—the feeling of belonging. Finding his mother lying on a cold, hard floor with a knife sticking out of her chest may have had something to do with that. He knew the psychosis of such a thing. No matter how much he wanted to, he could not deny the short leap from what he struggled with to leaving dead bodies in churches. He found his release one way, the perpetrator of those crimes found his release another way.

He turned down a side street. Leafless trees, with their limbs hanging low, clawed at unsuspecting passersby. A night darker than the one surrounding it beat back the light of the moon, sinking deep into the street's cracks and crevices. At the corner of Piedmont and Twelfth Street, he found his particular kind of sin.

The sign in front of the nondescript building read, "Heels". A picture of a woman's red high-heeled shoe emblazoned the face of the sign. Piedmont Park framed the scene, along with many eclectic shops that dominated this bohemian mix of lives and personalities. He parked on the street and walked along its narrow sidewalk up to the door of the building. The entrance, not well lit, hid in the dark. Those who visited this place already knew where to look.

Zones turned the door handle, finding it locked. He knocked, softly at first and then harder. The door opened. A man stood at the entrance, his tattooed arms folded over his belly. The two stared at each other. Zones followed his tattoos from his arms up to his neck, where they ended at his pierced face and baldhead.

"I'm here to play," Zones said.

"That'll be twenty-five cover." Zones took thirty dollars from his wallet, handing it to the man.

"I'll get your change." He moved to close the door. Zones grabbed the edge.

"Keep it." He forced his way past the man.

"Enjoy it while you can. We won't be here much longer. Some big shot's building condos. Boss wants everyone to know."

He pushed his way through the dark interior, illuminated by red strobe lights bouncing off everything. The smell of lavender, with a hint of plumeria filled the air, soft music, "Sexual Healing", played in the background. Forms and faces pressed tight against each other, giving away their anonymity. A well-formed man dressed in a revealing costume allowed himself to be paraded on the end of a dog collar and chain. A woman dressed in business attire led him. Other men and women strolled around with various body parts exposed.

"Fifty dollars to spank, one hundred to lick and two hundred to suck," they repeated. Zones pressed farther into the space, seeing many other strange things. He hesitated joining the investigation into the church killings officially, but the sights and sounds of this place brought them to mind. This place catered to damaged souls. Anyone of these people could be the murderer.

The club housed many rooms and in each of them, an erotic pleasure. Zones opened one of the doors. A lone figure stood in the corner dressed in all black leather from head to toe, obscuring his face. He drew close to Zones, his piercing blue eyes shattering the dimly lighted room. He led him over to a rack of ropes hanging on the wall. His thick, veiny hands attached to Popeye-like arms, grabbed one from the rack and placed it in Zones' hand, but said nothing. The room, more of a chamber, catered to bondage. Zones looked the rope over, running his hand along its textured surface, feeling the intricacies of its knot. He placed the rope back on the rack, moving to another that caught his eye. He lifted it from the hook. He never saw that type of knot before. An avid sailor, he noticed such things. Like the other, he placed this rope back on the rack.

"I'll have your specialty," he told a hostess as he exited the room.

"Follow me." She led him to a room in the rear, reached out and opened a door painted bright purple. A wide smile crept across his face. Shoes of all varieties lined a corner of the wall.

"Make your choice, sir," the hostess bade him.

His eyes grew large. A cold chill ran through his body. He began to tremble and sweat.

"Are you okay, sir?"

"They are all so beautiful." He chose the black stilettos with straps and open toes. The hostess led Zones away down a dungeon-like hall; a stable of women awaited him. He walked over to them, all lined up for his inspection, revealing their well pedicured feet. They offered them to him for closer inspection. He made his selection, a thick, light-skinned sister with a statuesque build and the biggest, prettiest legs one could imagine. His taste was ordinarily the darker hues, he chose her because he liked the contrast of the black stilettos against her light, mocha brown legs.

"I'm Mercedes, pleased to meet you." She stuck out her hand.

"Mercedes, I'm . . . José. The pleasure will be all mine." Zones grabbed her hand, raised it to his lips and kissed it.

She slipped her feet into the shoes, stretching out one toward him, twirling it around in the air. He watched, licking his lips while following the twirl of her foot.

"You like?" she asked him, a big smile on her face. "It's okay to taste."

Zones dropped to one knee and then the other, grasping her foot in his hands caressing it. He moved it close to his mouth, kissed and sucked it as if it were a woman's neck.

She reached down, placing her hand beneath his chin, lifting him to his feet. "Come with me," she said, leading him by the hand to a small alcove where she sat, her big, well-toned legs even more exposed from beneath the short, black sequined skirt. She crossed them, one over the other. She pulled a small plastic bottle from the shelf nearby and poured its contents onto the nave of her foot. With a slow viscosity, it moved down to the base of the shoe and along the neck of the heel, dripping freely and pooling onto the floor.

"I want to ravish you," he whispered.

"You're a naughty one."

Zones again knelt before her and began to taste the substance, allowing it to drip from the shoe heel onto his tongue—honey, sweet and sticky. He licked the honey from the long, spiked heel, following its flow up to her ankle. He loosened a strap from around her foot, removing the stiletto. Mercedes poured the honey; it dripped onto his face where she playfully smeared it.

"You need a sheet, before I paint your body all over with honey," she said, giggling.

"What did you say?" Zones popped his head up. "You said the body was painted and covered with a sheet."

"No! Your body—covered in honey."

"Oh!" He looked down at his sticky clothes.

Her foot, now bare, he kissed and licked it all over, the sweet, sticky substance coming to a partial rest as she cupped her toes. He parted them, engulfing each toe wholly into his mouth, sucking, starting with the largest, meatiest one.

She moaned and fondled herself. Zones sensed her pleasure and stopped. He removed the other shoe from her foot while she, in her euphoria, lay stretched out over the sofa. He leapt to his feet and dashed from the room, the black stilettos dangling from his hand. He did not stop until he reached his car. He searched for his keys, finding them in his pocket. He stuck the key into the car door lock and turned.

"Hold it right there, sir!" someone shouted. Zones turned, a bright light shined in his face. "Atlanta Police, get your hands up!"

Six

While the Captain answered questions from the media, Marmaduke spent his time trying to identify the victims. He thought it strange that two white corpses found their way into two black churches. He needed a break and he needed it now.

"Dr. DeGlorious? Detective Marmaduke. I'm calling to see if you have those tests back from the lab."

"I was just about to call you, Detective. Those results just came in." He heard the ruffling of papers followed by tearing and then silence. Finally she asked, "Are you a lucky man, Detective?"

"Not particularly."

"Then it hasn't changed. The DNA analysis shows the tissue samples came from five different donors."

"Five? But I thought you said that it could have been three at the most." Marmaduke sat up in his chair. A grim look grew over his face.

"What I said was three or possibly more. I based that on arms and legs coming from the same donor. Apparently we have multiple donors for these parts. And one other thing, at least one of the limbs had been frozen for some period of time."

"Frozen! For how long?"

"Hard to say, but the lab's best estimate is twenty-four days from the time of discovery."

"So that puts us around late May or early June. So we have five victims with one of them on ice somewhere."

"Not quite, Detective. Here's the strange thing, the frozen limb was on the body from our first site."

"The Bethel church location."

"It's matching limb was found on the body from our second

site. However, it shows no sign of ever having been frozen. In fact, microscopic analysis shows the tissue was freshly cut from the body while still alive, or at least while the heart was still pumping."

"What are you telling me Doctor? Do we have a dead body or not? And how could one limb be frozen twenty-four days ago and the other only hours old?"

"Those are the same questions I have, Detective. The only thing I can think of is that one limb was severed from the body and frozen and the killer removed the other at a later date."

"So the victim was kept alive for twenty-four days while parts were grafted from him or her?"

"Graft is a good word, Detective."

Marmaduke waved Detective Chennault over to his desk. He held the phone away from his face. "Check with missing persons to see if they have any reports within the last forty-eight hours, also check any reports around late May or early June."

"Detective, are you there?" Dr. DeGlorious shouted through the phone.

"Doctor, did the report say anything about their sex, age, etc.?"

"No, but two of the hands had fingernail polish on it—rose red, my daughter's favorite. I'm having a forensic anthropologist at the university examine them now. I should have something on that shortly."

"Very good, Doctor."

Marmaduke hung up, knowing now that his investigation had just significantly widened. He struggled to wrap his mind around this case. Nothing made sense. He had a task force meeting with the Captain in one hour and knew no more about solving these murders than when he first began. *Why had two white bodies shown up in two black churches?*

"Chennault, got anything?" He shouted from his desk.

"A woman reported her seventeen-year-old daughter missing on Saturday night, said she never returned home from a party. I heard you speaking to the M.E. so I also checked any missing reports for the last thirty days; there were exactly five within a thirty county area."

"Good work, Detective. Also, pull the property records: deeds, tax, legal disputes on both locations."

"Why? You think this has something to do with the land?"

"Let's just make sure we have covered all bases." Marmaduke stood to walk away.

"Where are you going?"

"I have a community task force meeting with the Captain. As soon as you have anything, call me."

. . .

"Damn, Detective! You look like shit!" James greeted Marmaduke when he arrived at the Captain's third floor office. "Back on the sticks again, are yah?"

"The elevators . . . they're out." Marmaduke bent over, trying to catch his breath. His heart pounded, legs burned, sweat poured from his brow.

"Oh yeah, gonna be out for a while, I hear. And—let's see." She opened the calendar on her desk, looking through it. "Yes, I have you scheduled to meet with the Captain in his office all this week." A quick smile came over her face. "Just say no, Detective. Just say no."

"I didn't know you cared." Marmaduke left her desk, still trying to catch his breath. He walked toward the large double doors of the Captain's office. They opened just as he reached for the latch.

"There you are, Detective. I was just coming for you." The Captain gave Marmaduke a look.

"I know, I know. I look like shit." He glanced back at James who laughed.

"Well, you said it. Come in and have a seat." Others sat around a small conference table, members of the council, their aides and select community leaders. "This is Detective Marmaduke. He's the lead on the case and he will brief us on its status, Detective." The Captain gave Marmaduke the floor.

"Thank you Captain, ladies, gentlemen. The M.E.'s office has confirmed that we are dealing with five victims. We're doing testing to determine their sex, age, and other characteristics and we have identified possible victims from missing persons which we are following up. We're also examining possible links between the two sites, other than the murders. Finally, we are also working closely with the FBI on leads of interest in the church arson and vandalism investigation. Are there any questions?"

"Yes, I have one, Detective," Councilwoman Grudges said, raising her hand like a first grader. "Has your investigation looked into a possible Ku Klux Klan involvement?" She stuttered.

"Well ma'am, not particularly. We have no direct evidence yet showing any Klan involvement."

"With all due respect, Detective, you have no evidence leading to any suspects. And given the nature and the targets of the crimes, they would seem as likely a suspect as any." She stuck her thumb in her mouth, securing the loose dentures slipping from between her lips.

"Well ma'am, until we have evidence . . . ."

"Councilwoman, the Detective will follow up on that, right, Detective?" the Captain interjected, bidding Marmaduke to move on with his eyes.

"Thank you, Captain," the councilwoman said, writing a note to herself.

"Any other questions?" The Captain paused a moment. "Yes sir . . . I'm sorry, but I don't have your name listed." He looked down at his task force members' list.

"Dr. Hyde. I'm representing the Inter-Faith Council."

"Oh! I was expecting Bishop Jackson."

"He was called away on an emergency. Detective, do you have any idea what is behind these crimes?"

"We're generating evidence as we speak, sir."

"So, I take it that's a negative. What other resources are you deploying to hasten the capture of these killers?"

"Well . . . ."

"We are getting specialized support from the FBI. We will have them fully deployed soon," the Captain chimed in.

"That should be interesting."

"What do you mean?"

"Nothing, let's just hope they send you their best and not try to short change you with some post-graduate student because we're a small town—you know, not Atlanta."

The Captain shot Marmaduke an ugly face. He looked away, not able to bear the Captain's menacing, cold stare.

"Now are there any more questions? Great, since there are no more, we'll let the Detective get back to work." The Captain gathered his papers, avoiding eye contact and ignoring any raised hands. "Thank you, Detective Marmaduke. My assistant will make sure each of you get the minutes."

Marmaduke left the room, not sure of what just transpired. He looked around for James, her desk was empty, sparing him any unkind remarks. He walked toward the stairs.

"Marmaduke." He turned. The Captain called to him. He walked back.

"Captain, you know damn well we don't have the manpower to go off chasing every ghost and boogieman there is."

"Shhhhh! Lower your voice, Detective," the Captain whispered, waving his hands around, peering back toward the door to his office. "That old biddy won't let the Klan angle go. Ever since they hanged her father in the fifties, she has seen their hand in everything from the cancellation of the Cosby Show to hurricane Katrina."

"So now we've got to chase down every crackpot theory she comes up with?"

"No! Now the councilwoman sits on the finance committee and on the appropriations committee. I have a budget before her that I would very much like to get passed. I have a department to run and that means looking at the big picture. So if I have to appease that old, slave-looking fart, giving her what she wants to hear, then so be it. But I will not have your pale white ass fucking up my system. Do I make myself clear, Detective Marmaduke?"

Marmaduke stood there, the Captain's face, with its mean disposition, only inches away. He reached up to wipe his face, now moistened by the saliva spewed from the Captain's mouth.

"So we're playing politics while some nut case is roaming around free?"

"Detective, you have exactly—" the Captain raised his watch to his face, not moving his head. He looked at it from the corner of his eye, still inches away from Marmaduke's face, "twenty-four hours to have your written report on my desk—'I's' dotted, 'T's' crossed and no grammatical errors. Do you hear me, Detective?"

"Yeah, I hear yah."

"That's yes, I hear you, sir!"

"Yes sir, I hear you!"

"Excellent! And I hope for your sake you didn't tell ole boy about me hiring a profiler in order to get it shot down. 'Cause if so, you think of the lowest possible job in the department and count ten rungs below it, that's where I'll stick your ass. I might not be able to fire you but I can make you smell shit until you retire or quit. Union can't save you there. Are we clear, Detective?"

Yea . . . ." The Captain tightened up his face, widened his eyes and stood a little taller over Marmaduke. "Yes sir," he said.

. . .

"Chennault, what do you have for me?" Marmaduke barked into his phone, not a minute later.

"I'm down at the county following up on that property info."

"And?"

"And we may have something. I traced the deeds of both properties back a hundred-fifty years and both were owned by the same person . . . a Colonel Bedford Crawford. After his death, the colonel deeded both properties to his slaves. Most of it has been sold to various individuals, except for where the churches now stand. And that's not all. It appears that the colonel's descendants waged a quiet war to have the properties returned to them."

"You never told me you were such a history buff, Detective."

"I'm not. One of the clerks here is a local historian and has been doing some research for the churches on it—to fight the lawsuit and all."

"Do you have names for these descendants?"

"One is Clinton Crawford and the other is Maggie Alford. Address, 1950 Bedford Forest Road, that's in Marietta."

"Got it. Now spread a little more of that big city charm and see what else you can find out, then meet me over at this address."

"No need. You'll be surprised what a pack of Camels can get you."

"I wouldn't know; I'm a Marlboro man myself. Good work, Detective."

SEVEN

Marmaduke drove, heading north for Marietta, another suburb of metropolitan Atlanta. The city avoided the spotlight more than an escaping convict. But for the sign designating it, one would be hard pressed to find this slice of once rural Georgia. Atlanta and Marietta, however, could not be any more opposite. If you wanted a taste of a small town struggling to remain unaffected by the woes of the big city, then Marietta offered plenty for you to dine on.

A civil war relic unto itself, with the town square at its heart, the city's fathers held on to the past like kinfolk coveted a family heirloom. Old battlegrounds, monuments to long dead soldiers and column-lined plantation estates, all remnants of the old south, still remained. Calls for secession still dripped from the lips and invaded the minds and hearts of the citizenry of Marietta today as if it was 1860 and Jefferson Davis had just stomped through the south with it as his presidential campaign platform.

Confederate flags lined the long, narrow drive to the home of Clinton Crawford and Maggie Alford, which sat far back on some fifteen acres of old farmland. A large wooden cross stood closer to the house, its burn patterns still visible, having been set on fire. "Dixie" blared from speakers mounted at two corners of the house. A white sheet and a pointed wizard's cap hung from what looked to be a granite statue.

Marmaduke and Chennault exited their vehicles. A bearded gentleman met them, dressed in a Confederate military uniform. His haggard appearance betrayed his relatively young age.

"Y'all gentlemen would do yourselves well by turning 'round and driving back out the same way y'all came in. This is private property as the sign reads at the entrance." He rested his right foot on the head of a black-faced jockey boy statue that guarded the front steps.

"We're with DeKalb County P.D." Marmaduke stepped toward the gentleman. He reached inside his coat to retrieve his identification, exposing his sidearm.

"Now y'all hold on there!" The man drew the saber dangling at his side. He shook it above his head.

Detective Chennault drew his gun, aiming it at the saber wielding man. In the distance, dust from a car coming up the drive filled the air. Marmaduke squinted and saw the local sheriff approaching in a black and white late-model Lincoln Town car. The car reached the house and the deputy leapt out while it was still rolling to a stop.

"Now, everyone just hold on!" the deputy demanded.

"You tell him to put that thing away!" Chennault yelled.

"The only place I'm gonna put this is right through yah yellow hearts."

"Sir, you have just threatened a peace officer."

"It's no threat, it's a promise."

"Listen here everyone. There ain't gonna be any shooting and there ain't gonna be no stabbing. Now Clinton, you put away that saber and Detective you put away your gun. I'm sure we can just sort this out peacefully."

Clinton lowered his saber back to his side and Chennault did the same with his gun. The deputy walked between them, his arms outstretched as if parting two prize fighters. Marietta, not being in his jurisdiction, Marmaduke had called the local law enforcement prior to his arrival to ask for assistance.

"Clinton, these Detectives have a few questions they would like to ask you. I told them that you would cooperate with them."

"I am on my way to the battlefield. I'm gonna be late standing 'round bumping my gums with y'all. What is it yah wants anyway?"

"Mr. Crawford, we would like to ask you about the recent murders in DeKalb County," Marmaduke told him.

"Aah, I knew it. I knew it. A few niggra churches have dead bodies in them and the first thing yah do is come 'round looking for the first Klansman yah could find. Well, what 'bout all us good ole white folk who those monkeys rob, steal and kill. Where are y'all then with yah suits and guns?"

"What about Mrs. Alford?"

"What 'bout her?"

"Is she in? May we speak to her?"

"She ain't in and she ain't had nothing to do with them bodies of those niggras or Afro-Americans or whatever they call themselves now."

"Then why are you trying to claim their land?" Chennault asked.

"Not claim, reclaim. The ole colonel owned that property, and he was my great-granddaddy. Them niggras ain't got no claim to it. Y'all need to check out their criminal asses, with their hippity-hoppity and gangster music. All of them are criminals and we need to round the lot of them up and ship them back to Africa."

"And just where should the Native-Americans send all us good ole white folk?"

"This is white man's country, and this is my property y'all standing on and I don't allow no nigga lovers on it. This conversation is over, gentleman. And John Walter," he looked at the deputy, "you have some nerves in bringing them 'round my property."

Clinton turned and went back into the house, mumbling as he walked. He slammed the door hard, rattling various items mounted on the wall of the house.

"I thought I asked y'all to wait for me before approaching him." the deputy said, turning to Marmaduke.

"You didn't tell me he was a Klansman either." Marmaduke looked around the property, filled with Klan relics.

"I didn't tell you he was a Klansman? Hell, most of the people around here have Klan affiliations, just like most of them have gang and drug affiliations; ain't no difference." Marmaduke and Chennault stared at the deputy.

"He called you John Walter."

"That's my name. What of it?"

"Not Deputy Riley or just plain deputy? You on a first name basis with all the people in this town—John Walter?" Marmaduke eyeballed him.

"If you have something to say, Detective, say it, otherwise, your business is done here." He squared up his shoulders.

"No, John Walter, I believe we have all the answers we need." Marmaduke turned back to the car. The slight wind shifted. "Wait, what's that stench?" He sniffed the air, following the odor to an old weathered barn. Chennault and Deputy Riley followed close behind. He drew near the structure, the smell intensified. The sound of snorting came from behind it. He rounded the corner of the barn and saw a herd of pigs corralled, and some pig parts littering the ground around the stall.

"Well, there're your porkers," Chennault said.

"What do you mean?" Deputy Riley asked.

"He means, John Walter," Marmaduke turned, getting in his face, "that your chubby little friend in their got some 'splainin to do. We need a warrant." They returned to their vehicle.

"It's Deputy Riley to you—Ass-hole!" Chennault stuck his hand out of the window, flipping Deputy Riley the bird. They drove off, gunning the engine, leaving a large plume of dust from the gravel drive behind them. They had their first suspect. The councilwoman may not have been wrong after all.

Marmaduke leaned low in his seat, but his mind rode high. His temporary euphoria would not last however. On the drive back to DeKalb County, a call from the precinct came in over the radio.

"Marmaduke," James said, "They found two more bodies."

EIGHT

In the cramped jail cell, Zones awaited his fate, along with all the other souls who had transgressed the law. With each guard's visit, he hoped for a quick hearing or better, a fast bail.

"Zones, Thelonious!" the guard yelled, giving away any hope of anonymity. He walked along the corridor of cells. "Zones, Thelonious!" he yelled again.

Zones rushed to the front of the barred room, shouting, "Here! Here!"

The guard turned and walked back to where he stood at the bars. He whipped out a picture, looked at it, then at Zones, then back at the picture. Zones knew criminals, convicted of much harsher crimes, often impersonated someone else to hasten their release.

"Okay, you're good." The guard opened the door to the cage allowing Zones out. Others tried to follow him through the door as well, but the guard pushed them back inside.

"Your bail has been met," the guard told him. He escorted Zones down the corridor and into a processing area, where his attorney met him.

"Jack, thanks for coming, man," Zones greeted him.

"Sure, no problem. Look, I read the charges and I'm not gonna even ask. The judge is a frat brother and I could probably get this thing squashed. Just a bit of advice though, this is the south and Atlanta isn't as tolerant as New York when it comes to gentlemen's activities."

"No shit. They scared the fuck out of me. I thought for a minute that Eyewitness News or some damn body was going to pop out. Damn! A brother can't have a little fun without five-o in his ass?"

"I suggest, next time, you get Creative Loafing and find yourself a private party."

"I hear you on that! Look, there's no need to let Sam know anything about this. He may try to use this to mess up my gig with the FBI."

"Don't worry; we'll consider this privileged information. Besides, I've gotten his fucking ass out of worse than this. Look, do you need a ride?"

"No, they towed my car here. I'll drive it."

"Okay then, I better be getting home. The wife was hard-pressed to believe that I've had clients to see at 6:00 a.m. in the morning for two days straight. Listen, call me. Maybe we'll get together."

"I'll do that, tell your wife I said thank you."

"Okay, Mr. Zones," the clerk interrupted, "please verify that all your contents are here, read and sign here please," she instructed him, handing him a plastic bag. He gave the items only a cursory review, but did notice fifty dollars was missing. He said nothing, however, writing it off as the cost of his transgression, assured that the hustlers, johns, pros and pimps they brought in got the same treatment.

"Is he the last one from the club?" an officer asked.

"No. Those three over there. May have to hold the dominatrix though, caught her with some illegal blades. Pretty sharp too, do a lot of damage," the clerk answered.

"Who owns that joint anyway? This is the second time this year we've busted it."

"Don't know, but it used to be a florist, until the old lady who owned it found two dead crack heads with needles still stuck in their arms sitting inside when she opened up. She sold it the next day. Putting up condos there soon, I heard."

"You three!" the officer called them over. They stood next to Zones at the counter.

Zones handed the paperwork back to the clerk. He turned, seeing a short, dumpy woman next to him dressed in red leather shorts and top, black fishnet stocking and high heeled shoes. She limped to the counter, her fat feet oozing between the straps of her shoes like dough. He did a double-take, disbelieving his eyes.

"What the fuck yah looking at coon? I'll make yah my slave," she growled, her face piggish.

. . .

42

From his window overlooking Peachtree Street, Zones watched party-goers make their last rounds to the bars and clubs that lined the street. The raid on the sex club earlier had been enough excitement for him, although he still could not sleep.

He looked over; his briefcase lay next to the bed. He flipped it open and retrieved the case file on the church murders, along with a pen and yellow legal notepad. He started with the crime scene photographs. He spread them out on the bed. They left the bodies in the churches and displayed them, requiring strategizing by the unidentified subjects. The staging of the scenes displayed both signs of fantasy—the whimsical images on the wall and floor and the mutilated body—and planning. On his notepad he scrawled, "high degree of premeditation. Methodical— highly organized."

Zones pored over the autopsy reports, focusing on the various knife wounds on the body. He wrote, "Learning process? Multiple perpetrators of varying skill? Knife = Affinity for victim? Personal motive?" Next he considered the premortem disarticulation of the victims and their subsequent articulation. He added to his notes, "classic signs of Dissociation Disorder." Finally, he considered the big M: Motive. The locations of the crimes gave the best evidence for it—a religious motive perhaps—choosing churches.

Once he made his initial notes, Zones set about formulating a profile and theory about the motive and the nature of the crimes. Hours later, he picked up his phone, ready to share his ideas with local law enforcement.

"Detective Marmaduke, this is Dr. Zones."

"Dr. Zones, the prison shrink? What can I do for you, Doctor?"

"I was just reviewing the case file on your homicides and would like to share some of my thoughts with you."

"Well, Doctor, while you've been psycho-analyzing case files, I've been running down leads on a possible suspect."

"A suspect, I would like to be there when you question him."

"Too late, Doc, I'm just leaving his place now. Besides, your ancestry is a little too far south for his taste. He would not have liked you being there."

"I'm from New York. So where's he from, Canada? Besides, what does where I'm from have to do with this anyway? Look, can we meet, Detective?"

"Well, Doc, I would like to oblige but right now I'm on my way to investigate two more bodies."

"Two more. Where?"

"Out at the old Indian sites. One is out near the prison. I'm on my way to the airport now."

"I'll meet you there. What gate?"

"We're leaving out of Peachtree-DeKalb, just come to the main terminal. I'm about twenty minutes away."

. . .

Zones watched a small plane glide to earth. Winds swirled all around, rocking it side to side. The aircraft's wings flapped in the gusts, fragile, like the bodies in the churches and now those awaiting them at some old Indian sites.

"Dr. Zones, I see you made it," Detective Marmaduke called from behind him.

"Detective, we meet again."

"This is Detective Chennault; he's working the case with me. And this is Dr. Zones," he turned to Chennault, introducing them both. "Dr. Zones is a criminalist with Drake and Associates. He's on loan to us as a consultant."

"Welcome, Doctor, we're gonna need all the help we can get."

"Thank you, Detective."

"Are we all ready to go?" Marmaduke led them out of the hangar and onto the tarmac where the pilot greeted them, the small plane's engine roaring as the propellers spun.

"We're not going in this puddle jumper, are we?" Zones asked.

"Why? What were you expecting, a 747?" Marmaduke poked Chennault in the ribs with his elbow, grinning.

Zones paused at the door of the aircraft, one foot inside and the other still firmly on the ground. He had not planned flying over Georgia in some crop duster. Over the roar of the engines, he heard an inner voice: Small plane crashes with four onboard—no survivors.

"Can we drive there?" Zones shouted over the engines.

"Doctor, there are over one hundred-fifty miles between the two sites. By the time we drive to both, the bodies will be maggot meat. This is it, Doc, you're either coming or staying!" Marmaduke shouted back.

"Come on, Doc, I'll take her up and set her down nice and easy for yah," the pilot cajoled.

Zones eased the other foot into the small craft, rocking it slightly.

. . .

"Damn it! I'm not getting back into that thing!" Zones shouted, pointing at the plane. He threw a paper bag filled with vomit onto the ground and kicked at it. He spit the remaining residue from his mouth.

"Well, Doc, there are no taxis out here. So unless you're planning to hitchhike back to Atlanta, your chariot will await you here." Marmaduke said smiling.

They drove toward the crime scene. "What is this place?" Zones asked their escort, a local law enforcement officer.

"This is the Kolomoki Mounds, a state park and historical site."

"And what are those?"

"Those are the burial mounds. There are seven in all, two burial, four ceremonial and one used as a museum. The mounds are thought to have been built by the Creek Indians who lived in this area. Some of the locals think this place is haunted and they don't dare set foot in here."

They rounded one of the mounds and came upon the body, displayed just like the first two. On the mound's side, painted in red, "Vespasian," marred the green lush grass.

"Have you ever seen anything like this?" the officer asked Marmaduke.

"Unfortunately I have, twice."

They walked closer to the roped off area where the body sat.

"Whoa! Whoa! You're in my crime scene, gentlemen. Officer, I asked you to keep everyone back," a detective shouted from across the field, his arm extended as he walked over to them.

"We're the detectives from DeKalb County. We had those other two bodies," Marmaduke yelled. "You mind if we take a look at this one?"

"Hell no, I don't mind. I was hoping that someone would know what the hell this is."

Zones tramped up the steep mound, following Marmaduke and

Chennault, careful not to disturb any possible evidence. The detectives had seen this before, for him the image of the body atop the mound flooded his senses like a brilliant light, a horrendous smell or a piercing shrill. Photographs did not compare.

"Extraordinary!"

"Calm down there, Doc. Don't get a hard-on," Marmaduke said, seeing his excitement. "This is some pretty gruesome shit aye, Doc?" Zones said nothing. "You're pretty calm for someone in the middle of this horror."

"This is such a peaceful place, Detective." Zones scanned the distance. The nausea from the plane ride had gone. He enjoyed being in the midst of the horror.

He retrieved a penlight, tweezers, gloves and a plastic bag from his case. He shined the light over the body, comparing it to the photographs from the other two sites.

"What are you doing, Doc?"

"Admiring the handiwork."

"No . . . really. I thought the sight of this would've scared the living bejesus out of you."

"Sorry to disappoint you, Detective, but this is where I want to be, chasing crazies, the damned in life."

"You make them sound like they're celebrities and you're their paparazzi."

"It's paparazzo. And unlike celebrities, these crazies serve a useful purpose."

"Now what good could these killers serve?"

"They rip wide open the pretty norms and mores of society, exposing the ugly underbelly it also birthed, but hoped to keep hidden."

"You sound as if you want to understand them more than you want them captured."

"Is that such a bad thing? Perhaps, in doing so, we could understand ourselves better."

The body sat perched near the edge of the steep mound. To see the front of it, Zones climbed along the slope, digging his feet and hands into the muddy soil. He clutched palms full of grass and kept his head down, watching every placement of his feet to keep from slipping. Soon, he stared directly into the corpse's eyes, barely a breath's distance between them. Zones moved the light along its head, that of a woman, her eyes glazed over, the blank stare of death on her face. He moved the light down along the sheet fashioned as a toga, stopping at a spot near the breasts. In one of the folds, he saw a grain of rice, its brown hull contrasting against the whiteness of the sheet. He plucked the grain from the fold with the tweezers. His hand trembled as he balanced himself along the slope. He placed the grain into the plastic bag and shoved it into his coat pocket—wanting to send it off to the lab personally.

Zones continued to look around the site, paying particular attention to the name scrawled on the side of the mound, "Vespasian", the twenty-third Emperor of Rome. The Iconium Church site had the name "Nero" scrawled on it, but, other than them both being Roman emperors, there didn't seem to be a connection. He moved over near the detectives and began to examine the area around the body. Footprints, from the many visitors to the park, covered the ground, but not much else.

"They teach you anything at that fancy university about stuff like this?" Marmaduke asked.

"Not about the crime, Detective, about the mind behind the crime."

"Well, my mind says that those behind these crimes wear sheets."

"What do you mean?"

"In due time, Doctor, in due time," he answered. "Well, I have all I need here. I say we go to the next site. Chennault, tell the detective to make sure we get copies of the crime scene report."

"One moment, Detective." Zones shined his light along the ground near the body. "When was the last time you got rain here?" he asked an officer.

"Yesterday, it ended sometime late last night."

"What is it, Doctor?" Marmaduke asked.

"These foot impressions, they are significantly deeper than any of the others in this area, and yet they contain no standing water like the others."

"This is clay, so you're thinking they were made after the rain ended? Most likely by our perp?"

"That and the size of the human being who made them."

"Let's get impressions and see if our next crime scene tells us anymore."

. . .

"So Doctor, what is your area of expertise?" Marmaduket asked, once they were back in the air, flying toward central Georgia.

"Criminal psychological exegesis."

"What the fuck is that?"

"It's the critical analysis of the criminal mind, in particular, crime scene symbolism. My focus is on crimes with an institutional motive—"

"Institutional!"

"Yes, religious and governmental primarily."

"So if some fuck wants to kill his whole family because he hates paying his taxes, they call your ass in?"

"Not quite, Detective." Zones took a deep breath, expelling it slowly. Talking kept his mind off the turbulence and the brown paper bag he held in his lap, just in case. "He would have to kill a few other families as well. You see, some criminologist believe that human criminal behavior has its origins in the genes, the 'bad seed theory' or the environment. I am of the belief that criminality has more of a psycho-institutional origin. The institutionalization of man, not mama and daddy, is the source of his criminal mind. And in the annals of human kind, there are no bigger institutions than religion and government."

"Is that what you see here in these crimes, some loser who butchers people because they don't like shit in society? Hell, they didn't need to call your ass in for that. I could have told them that shit for free my damn self."

"It's a little more complicated than that, Detective. For example, I think part of your killers' motivation is driven by religious conviction. Just look at the sites they chose—those two churches and now these sacred Indian mounds. The mutilations signal a sexual dysfunction, brought on by revulsion to, and at the same time, an attraction to a sexual act. The perpetrators' struggle with this is manifested in violence, in this case, mutilations. Even the positioning of the body has meaning. The perpetrators could have placed the body anywhere. Why there? Why facing in that direction? Muslims, for example, face toward Mecca to pray. Perhaps your perps' religion has a special affinity for a particular direction."

"Yeah, well, I just think it's a colossal waste of time like I told you before."

"When you are running out of time, you will come to appreciate my theories, Detective. I'm briefing the task force later. Perhaps it'll make more sense to you then."

. . .

The plane landed and they soon arrived at the next crime scene. Zones saw the body immersed in the warm waters of the Indian Springs, a mist of steam swirled about and "Caligula" painted faintly on the surface of the water surrounding the body. He felt something, a presence.

He joined Marmaduke and Chennault; they were already examining the body. The warm eddies gently brushed against the strange form. He scanned the surroundings, snapping his head around at every sound, unable to shake the feeling of being watched. Just then, a flash of something glistened in the distance; the movement of a shadow caught Zones' attention.

He backed out the spring and approached a wooded area. Something moved between the trees, concealed by the dewy mist. As he drew closer, it began to distance itself from him. Zones ran, trying to catch up to the shadowy form. "Stop! Stop right there!" he yelled, drawing Chennault and Marmaduke's attention, luring them into the chase as well. Zones darted in and out between the trees, trampling the ground, breaking low hanging limbs with his arms stretched out in front of him. He scattered insects and small creatures in his path, before coming to a clearing. The detectives crashed through the brush behind him, sliding and stumbling on the wet leaves and grasses covering the ground.

Through the field, the chase continued. Zones, without the obstruction of the trees, closed the gap until he could see a young boy ahead of him, zipping through the brush. Within inches of him, he reached out, grabbing and lifting him from his feet. The boy looked to be Native-American. He struggled with Zones, trying to free himself from his pursuer's grasp.

"Hold on there, son," Zones said. The boy yelled back in a tongue strange to him.

"That's some running, Doctor," Marmaduke said, winded, bending over trying to catch his breath.

"Yeah, where did you learn to run like that?" Chennault huffed.

"DeMathis High, four by one-hundred relay team, state champions." The two detectives glanced at each other. They shook their heads and gasped for air.

"Who do we have here?" Marmaduke pointed to the young boy.

"I don't know. I saw him watching us from the trees and thought he might know something. He wouldn't stop when I yelled, so I chased him."

"Has he said anything?"

"Yes, but I can't understand him. Maybe he's a Creek Indian."

"Who-Are-You?" Marmaduke asked the boy, pronouncing each word slowly. The young boy yelled, as before, but they did not understand the language. "Let's take him back and see if we can get an interpreter."

They turned to lead the boy away when men, dressed in Western wear, emerged from the surrounding trees. Marmaduke and Chennault immediately reached for their side arms. The men continued to approach. Zones scanned them, their dome-top Stetsons and high-heel boots with pointed-toes lengthened their stature above the tall weeds at the perimeter of the field. The few without hats wore their hair pulled back into a ponytail or allowed it to hang down their back and shoulders, kept in place by a kerchief tied tightly around their heads. They trudged out of the trees, each carrying a long-barreled shotgun slung over their shoulders or hanging low to the ground inches above the mud and grass. They moved together without making much of any noise. Their circle closed in until they surrounded Zones and the detectives, who tried to cover all sides at the same time. Zones held the boy tight. One of the men strode to them, grabbed the boy by the shoulder, and began to lead him away. Zones held tight to his arm.

"You hold on there!" Chennault shouted at the man. He pointed his gun at him. "He is a potential witness to a crime."

Another man, older, with long flowing gray hair, moved into the circle. His face, creased and weathered like the faded, sagging dungaree jeans he wore, held up by a wide leather belt and a large buckle, bore only a frown. He walked with a large stick fashioned into a staff. He limped, moving toward them, thrusting the staff into the ground ahead and pulling himself forward Moses-like.

"The boy knows nothing," the old man said in a rich, deep voice. He motioned the man to take the boy. Zones gripped him tighter, but then released him.

"Who are you people? And why are you on state property?" Marmaduke asked.

A chorus of shouts filled the air. The men surrounding them shouted and thrust their guns into the air. The detectives, though they could not understand them, sensed their hostility and prepared themselves. Their firearms still drawn, they aimed them back and forth. The old man raised his hand and the crowd quieted.

Zones: *How crazy is this?* He grew up an urban kid, used to concrete, blacktop and steel trees, where the smog, smoke and dust leaves drifted through the hazy air. He never saw a real life Native-American before. Growing up, he thought all the Indians were extinct, along with the dinosaurs. Now, here he stood at gunpoint, a virtual western standoff with the real thing, feeling all Custer-like.

"This land has been Creek land long before the white man. These are our sacred springs where once we healed our sick and these are our sacred woods where we once hunted, where the spirits once dwelled. One cannot trespass on what one owns. In truth, it is you who trespass. In truth, it is you who do not belong. In truth, it is the spirit of the Creek ancestors who are at home here and those who you bury wander without a resting place. Those who look like you," pointing at Marmaduke and Chennault, "defile the sacred springs with the carcass of a man. We must now prepare to perform the sacred ritual to cleanse and purify the springs."

The old man turned and walked away, in the same way that he approached them. The others followed him back into the woods. The boy turned back to them and yelled something that sounded to Zones like, "Rakke est-hvtke!" Then he turned back around and walked away with the others.

"What the hell was that all about?" Chennault asked, as he holstered his gun.

"I don't know. I didn't even know there were still Indians living around here," Marmaduke answered.

"Yeah, but it looks like one part of my profile has been confirmed. The perpetrators are white," Zones added.

"How do you figure?"

"When the chief spoke of those who defiled the springs, he pointed at you two."

"That's pretty weak, Doc. He could have been referring to the way we dressed."

"I doubt if he was referring to bad fashion, Detective Marmaduke," Zones quipped.

The three walked back toward the springs, still perplexed by what just occurred.

"Shit! Can you believe that?" Marmaduke asked, as he brushed the grass, leaves and other vegetation that stuck to him from his clothes. "Wait till I tell my boy I was in a standoff with real-life Indians," the seriousness that showed on his face moments ago now gone and in its stead a big, wide smile. "Do you think they know anything about the body in the water?"

"I don't think they had anything to do with these crimes, if that's what you're asking," Zones answered. He looked back toward where the natives had disappeared into the woods. "But obviously they saw something. I wonder where they come from? Sounds to me like they want to reclaim this land."

"That seems to be a familiar theme in all these crimes."

"What do you mean, Detective?"

"In due time, Doc, in due time."

Zones remembered that Marmaduke had said this once before. He was keeping something from him, but what? Perhaps he was waiting for some Perry Mason moment to spring it. These murders, however, did not fit into the neatly scripted word of Hollywood and, "In due time", did not conjure up a viable suspect. He figured the detective had his reasons for not sharing what he knew with him, so he didn't push the issue.

Zones wondered about the strange turn the case was taking and how it might affect his theory. No longer exclusive, dumping bodies inside churches with black congregations, now the perps dumped bodies in Native-American state parks—the only connection between the crime scenes being their unique disfigurement. The same perpetrator or perps committed the killings, but for what motive, if not religious?

"You gents need to look at anything else 'fore I take it away?" the Medical Examiner asked them when they got back to the spring.

"Nah, just make sure we get a copy of your report, especially the lab analysis on that paint in the water. Couldn't have been easy to do that without some special shit," Marmaduke answered. "Hey listen, you all know anything about a tribe of Indians still living around here?"

"You must've run into the Chief and his braves," one officer responded. "They moved in here 'bout six months ago, saying they weren't gonna let them take this land."

"Who was trying to take this land?"

"Don't know, but the Chief and his braves got pretty worked-up about it. The gov'ment been trying to get them out of here but, with affirm'tive action and everything, they can hardly do anything, being afraid and all. Not 'PC'," he made quotation marks in the air with his hands, "if you know what I mean." The officer winked at Marmaduke and spit out a stream of brown juice from the tobacco he chewed, making a popping noise with his lips.

"What the fuck does affirmative action have to do with Indians, you ass—" Zones began to shout toward the officer.

"Um, thank you, officer." Marmaduke interrupted. The officer turned, walking away, looking back at Zones.

"Are all of these Bubbas the same?"

Marmaduke's phone rang. "Marmaduke here—Yeah—Where?" He fumbled in his pocket, pulling out a small notepad and pen. He scribbled furiously, the phone propped between his ear and his shoulder. "Okay, bye." He closed the phone. "That was James. She's been trying to reach you, Doc. They need you at the prison. Something about a snitch and information about this case." He ripped a page from his pad, handing it to Zones.

"I better go." Zones shot toward the squad car. "Will I see you two later at the task force briefing?"

"I wouldn't miss it for the world." Chennault tried to follow. Marmaduke stiff-armed him in the chest. "Hold on. What was the name of that researcher down at the county?" He watched Zones dash toward the squad car.

"Bob Whitmore." Chennault fished a card out of his pocket, handing it to Marmaduke. "Why?"

"The good Doctor isn't the only one around here who has a theory."

"You're going to need these." Chennault flipped him a pack of smokes.

NINE

"He requested to see you personally." The warden ushered Zones into the inmate holding room, very similar to the room where he interviewed inmates.

"You always so generous with your prisoners?" Zones asked, taking a seat at the table.

The warden gave him a hard stare. "Well, look here, I don't normally give much credence to this kind of shenanigans but I saw the news about the mutilation case you're working—"

The door opened and two guards led a prisoner into the room; he was shackled and restrained.

"Well, I'll leave you to it." The warden backed out of the room.

Zones had not seen this prisoner before. Not many still slathered on the hair jell and looked like they traveled a hundred miles an hour down the freeway in a convertible. The guards sat him down hard at the table across from him. The inmate sat there, smiling as if he had this grand secret to tell, saying nothing. Prison life made him either complacent or discontented; he smiled and frowned at the same time, making it hard to tell. This confused the pencil-thin mustache resting on the ledge of his top lip. He sat there, looking all Don-like, still saying nothing. One of the guards gave him a nudge, trying to prod a conversation out of him.

"So you're the prophet's son," he began, still smiling, his voice raspy, his speech often interrupted with a cough of phlegm.

"The prophet? I don't know anyone by that name."

"Yeah, you're the prophet's son alright. You both do the same thing with your lips, turning them up like you done tasted something bitter." He coughed hard, bending over the table with his mouth open. He heaved, seemingly to force something out. A guard standing to his rear struck him on the back, trying to help.

"My Lord, you should be in a hospital, man. I hope whatever you have ain't catching." Zones pushed himself from the table and away from the prisoner, frowning in disgust.

"I'm okay, I'm okay," he said, catching his breath. "Your father is T.O. Zones, ain't it? He doing time up in Attica. Yeah, that's your old man. We called him the prophet cause he always running his mouth 'bout what's gonna happen if they didn't do this, that or the other. He gave old warden hell. You know, your father didn't kill his old lady, your mother."

"Did you call me down here for fables or do you have a real story to tell?"

"I looked into his eyes, boy, that's where you can see into a man's soul, know if he's telling you the truth or not. I know a killer when I see one. Look into my eyes, boy; I'm a killer, more than twice over. Your father is counting someone else's time." He coughed violently, his head low as if heavy weights hung around his neck. A much younger man than he seemed, his manicured face and hair could not hide the harshness of the years he spent locked up. Moments went by without a word spoken. The guard nudged him once again, bringing him back to reality; he seemed to drift in and out of it.

"You got a cigarette?" he asked Zones.

"I don't smoke and from the looks of it, neither should you."

"I know, I know. It's just that a cigarette would loosen my mouth up and make what I have to tell you come out a lot quicker and smoother."

"Are you conning me for a pack of smokes, man? Look, I don't have time for this." Zones rose from his chair and headed for the door.

"They desecrate holy places!"

"Information that's available on every TV station and Google!"

"With altars to Zeus." This caught Zones' attention as he reached out to open the door. The authorities had kept this information from the public. Only those close to the investigation would know this. *How could he, this convict, know of this?* He turned, looking back at him, still seated, as if he knew that Zones would not go anywhere upon hearing those words.

"The Bethel Church site." He closed the door and returned to his seat.

55

"Now, how 'bout them smokes, Doctor." He leaned back in his chair, crossed his legs and raised his chin in the air, confident he had sufficiently gotten Zones' attention.

Zones motioned for one of the guards to get him a pack of cigarettes, the universal currency on the inside. He knew inmates ratted each other out quicker than a southern belle could say no to a sexual proposition and with as much frequency. In fact, law enforcement relied on this jailhouse treachery, even promoting and fostering the conditions for it. They questioned the accuracy of the information, however.

The guard returned with a pack of cigarettes but before he could offer then to the inmate, Zones said,

"I'll take that, officer." He twirled the pack around in his hand. "I'm listening." The inmate watched Zones twirl the pack, but still said nothing. Zones opened the pack, tapping a single stick from it, lighting it, taking a drag, blowing puffs of smoke into the air.

"I thought you didn't smoke," the inmate said, licking his lips.

"I don't but there's no need to let a good pack of smokes go to waste." He took another drag from the cigarette. The inmate's mouth began to moisten. His head followed the rising smoke as Zones blew it into the air.

"A Gadianton Robber, that's who you're looking for," he began, breaking out into a slight sweat, unable to resist the cigarette's temptation.

"A Gadianton Robber. What's that?" He removed the cigarette from his mouth, placing it into the inmate's.

"Oh, they are a secretive bunch but that's all I'll say in public." He looked at the guards from the corner of his eye, hinting his discomfort with their presence.

"Officers, give us a minute please."

"Are you sure, Doc?" one asked. Zones nodded.

"We'll be right outside." They left, closing the door behind them.

"Okay, we're alone. Now, tell me what you know."

The inmate leaned back in his chair. The cigarette, already half smoked, dangled from his lips; its ashes tumbling onto the table. He squinted as the smoke rose in a cloud, hovering around his face. He cocked his head to the side as if trying to get a better look at Zones through the hazy cloud obscuring his vision.

"What's your religion, son?" he asked, snarling. "You look like a

Christian, sitting around waiting on some dead prophet to come back and save your ass while the rest of the world's getting fucked over."

"Are you going to tell me what you know about these killings?"

"Hinduism, now there's a religion. If your ass comes back as a cockroach, then damn it, it's because your ass fucked up in a prior life and not because some devil made you do it."

"Okay, have it your way. Guard!" Zones called out. The guards burst into the room.

"They are a secret society, Doctor!" the inmate shouted.

"Hold it, officers." They backed out of the room, closing the door behind them once again.

"Now, the next time they take you away."

"Can I have another smoke?" Zones lit another, placing it in his mouth. He took a few puffs, securing the cigarette in the corner of his lips, his voice rattling as he prepared to tell his tale.

"Now let's hear it."

"Joe Smith. You ever heard of him?"

"Is he an inmate here?"

"Ha! Ha! Ha! Doc, you funny." He coughed violently, but still gripped the cigarette between his lips. "No. I'm talking about the one who got run out of Missouri," he whispered, leaning in closer to Zones sitting across the table.

"I'm not following you, man. What are you saying?"

"He got run out of Missouri and now he's in Utah. He's rich now. Got a lot of businesses and everything. I also hear he's a preacher. Preach the word, brother! AAAAWOOOL!" He howled like a wolf, tilting his head in the air, shaking it back and forth, his greasy hair falling out of place wildly.

"Are you alright in there, Doc?" a guard shouted through the door.

The inmate quieted and lowered his head. He looked around the room, whipping his head from shoulder to shoulder, rolling his eyes around so fast they threatened to leave their orbits.

"Shhhhh! If we're quiet, they'll go away," he whispered.

"I'm calling for a Doctor." Zones pushed his chair back to leave, recognizing the inmate's decline.

"No! No! No! Now their temple with all the stars and the moon on the wall, they're gonna own their own too, like me."

"What do you mean?" Zones pulled his chair back to the table. He remembered the images of the stars, moon and sun painted at each of the sites. This could not be coincidental, psychosis or not.

"That's where they gonna live when they leave here. Some of their big men already have 'um, big men in the gov'ment. They're already saving up the food to move there. They got this big-ol' warehouse where they keep all the food. That's in Utah. Now, do you like beef? 'Cause down in Florida and up in Nebraska, they got all the cows in the world. They gonna take them with 'um too—unless Ted Turner tries to stop them."

"Ted Turner. What does he have to do with this?"

"He's trying to stop them and take their cattle for his stores."

"Ted Turner, trying to stop this Smith guy in Utah from taking his cattle to the planet he's going to own when he dies."

"Yep!" the inmate said with a straight face.

Zones shook his head. The inmate rocked back and forth in his chair, mumbling and singing words only he understood. Some details of his rant did catch his attention. How did the inmate know two unreleased details of the crime scenes?

"Let's go back to the stars and the moon. You say that's where they're going to live?" Zones now turned the interrogation into one of his counseling sessions.

"That's right, and me too. Now you can't come—until you lighten up a bit," he said with a hard swallow.

"Anything else you have to tell me?"

"Yes. They keep track of us—all of us. They know everybody in my family, dead and alive. They track you through your blood, and this tracker is put inside your babies when they're born too. That's how they know who to let in the church and who to give a planet to.

"I see. Tell me about the Gadiantons."

"Gadiantons? Shhhhh! Who told you about them? We're not s'posed to talk about them," he whispered.

"Joe—He told me they were helping him here in Georgia."

"Joe told you? Oh yeah, with the temple building, to bring about the second coming."

"And how would they go about doing that?"

"Joe didn't tell you? By defiling the Holy of Holies, of course. Do you see? Do you understand? Do you see? Do you understand?"

The inmate repeated these words over and over, working himself into a rage. The guards, hearing the shouting, knocked on the door.

"Are you okay, Doctor?" Zones did not respond. He stood, back pressed tightly against the wall, staring hard at the inmate, startled by his sudden outburst. The guards burst through the door and grabbed hold of the inmate, dragging him from the room. He continued to shout the same words.

Zones, not sure what to make of this, thumbed through his notes from the crime scenes, looking up, seeing the inmate being dragged away. *Delusional.* He didn't know if his delusion came from being confined too long or being the partaker of too many psychotropic drugs, which were in no short supply on the inside, or perhaps both. Regardless, he appeared to have intimate knowledge of the crime scenes.

"Sorry about that—he missed his med call. He didn't tell you about Joseph Smith and his Gadiantons did he, Doc?" a guard asked Zones as he left the room.

"Yes. Why?"

"He had Homeland Security in here after 9-11, telling them the same thing."

Zones walked past the guard who laughed. *A mad man, a colossal waste of time.* The inmate mentioned two components of the cryptic symbolism painted on the walls and the ground at the crime scenes. He needed to follow up on these.

TEN

Marmduke arrived at the county records office and met with Bob Whitmore, his office overflowed with papers and files within stacks of bound records. He greeted Marmaduke with an outstretched arm, bent at the elbow, the other secreted behind his back.

"These are for you." Marmaduke held out the pack of smokes.

"Not here." He led Marmaduke to a place in the stacks. He opened up the inside pocket of his coat and Marmaduke quickly slipped the pack into it. "What do you need?"

"I need a deed search on these properties." He handed him a slip of paper. Whitmore looked down at it, peering from behind Coke-bottle thick glasses and then back up at Marmaduke before leading him to a computer station.

"We only keep DeKalb County records in hard copy here. The property records for these counties can be accessed online." He logged on, bringing up the property records. "What exactly are you looking for?"

"You told my partner that you researched information for two churches regarding a lawsuit they had pending with the Crawford family. I want to know if the Crawford's have any ties to the two properties on that list as well."

Whitmore pecked away at the keyboard, scrolling through lines of information. A weasel-ish looking man, he sported a Hitler style mustache and a long comb-over.

"Ah! See right here?" He pointed at the screen next to the number 1859. "This goes back over a hundred years but it seems that Colonel Crawford owned both these properties as well. He deeded these two over to the government after he died. Let me check one more thing for you—I can access the court records from here as well and . . .

yes, it appears that the Crawford's have a suit filed against the federal government for the return of these properties."

"Thank you, Bob!"

Marmaduke bounced out of the county records office, feeling confident.

"Now, let's see you top this, Mr. two-hundred dollars an hour, psych-cop motherfucker," he said. "I deserve to reward myself."

. . .

Marmaduke, a little buzzed, pushed the door to the conference room open. The Captain rose to the podium and introduced Zones to the other task force members, all law enforcement personnel.

"Dr. Zones is a consultant on loan to us from Drake and Associates. We have asked him to help us profile the perpetrator or perpetrators and analyze our crime scenes. Dr. Zones."

Zones walked over to the podium at the front of the room. The officers and detectives scooted their chairs close together while others stood lined up along the walls, squeezed shoulder-to-shoulder. The number of people stuffed inside made the room look inadequate. They sat waiting, lined up in rows, their uniforms softening the hard chairs. The sun dipped below a distant line. Zones could feel, from the energy in the room, that many of them preferred to be on their way home, killer or not. He knew these guys had all used profilers before. He figured most of them welcomed the help, using them as a tool like any other. Others, the hard-boiled type like Marmaduke, held its practitioners as no higher than psychics and shamans.

"Ladies, gentlemen, other than the obvious—that you all have a crazy son-of-a-bitch on your hands—I would like to give you my profile of the type of persons you may be looking for. First, I'm certain you're dealing with two distinct personalities . . . ."

"You mean there are two perps?" Marmaduke interrupted from the back of the room.

"Absolutely, at least two. Perp one will possess an ectotonic personality, which centers on privacy and restraint. May I have the lights, please," he asked, turning a projector on remotely as the room went dark.

"Where's the popcorn, Doc?" Marmaduke quipped. "This is science-fiction, ain't it?" Laughter erupted. Zones ignored him.

"The symbols found at the crime scenes, seen here, hold a riddle within their meaning. Ectotonic personalities have a deep need to understand the riddles of life. These hold great meaning to him." Zones shined a laser pointer onto the images projected on the screen. "Perp one would not be the mastermind behind the crimes. He would be educated minimally and rely mainly on intuition, rather than logic and reasoning. And I can personally vouch for the whereabouts of Detective Marmaduke so you can take him off your list." Laughter cascaded throughout the room. Marmaduke rolled his eyes and scowled. "He knows the meaning behind the symbols and the imagery of the bodies. You understand the riddle, you understand perp one and his motive. They also tend to be introverts, which may explain why law enforcement or the media has not been contacted."

"You said his motive, not their motive. Are they not both the same?"

"Rarely are the master's and slave's motives the same, but in this instance they could be." Zones answered. "The other perp, or perp two," he continued, "possesses a mesotonic personality, which centers on physical action and ambition. The gruesomeness of the crimes betrays this personality type, which is very dark. I'd expect to find animal mutilations in his history as well as other criminality." Zones flipped through a series of slides showing the bodies displayed at the crime scenes. They gasped, even the seasoned cops, seeing images of the bodies for the first time. "The mesotonic personality would be a college graduate, highly intelligent; he may rely mostly on duplicity to advance his agenda."

"Which one would be the leader in this partnership?" Chennault asked.

"This personality, the mesotonic, is the dominant or lead personality. He does not, however, physically commit any of the crimes except by proxy. He controls, guides and instructs perp one, whose personality is too weak to object or, if he does, is easily beguiled or coaxed anyway. Perp two's personality type may also suffer from a Paraphilia, causing onanism, which could be the root cause of or help to explain the body mutilation. Lights, please." He turned off the projector as the lights came on.

"Okay Doc, explain this Parphile and omany, or whatever you call it. Sounds like more of your psycho-babble to me."

"Detective Marmaduke—" Captain started.

"It's all right, Captain." Zones smiled. "I understand I'm using awfully big words and an old cop like Marmaduke might never have heard them."

"You got jokes now, Doctor? A real Eddies Murphys," Marmaduke shot back, snarling.

"Paraphilia is sexual arousal to things not normative. It's typically brought on by sexual suppression by a dominant, usually a parent. But since the crimes seem religiously based, it's more likely that the dominant is connected with a religion—priest, nun, rabbi, and so on. This may explain the absence of any sexual trauma to the bodies."

"And Onanism?"

"Onanism is better known as jerking-off. Its name derives from Onan, son of Judah who spilled his seed on the ground rather than impregnating his dead brother's wife as ordered by his father. Genesis thirty-eight, I believe."

"Well, Doctor, if our perps jack-off, then they could be any of us in this room, except of course, for our female guests."

"It's not quite that simple, Detective. Whereas someone like yourself—" he began to explain, pointing at Marmaduke, "may partake for sexual gratification, this individual's ability to perform the act is inhibited by some moral or physical restriction. The frustration of his inability to relieve himself manifests itself in many violent forms."

"And the violent form in these crimes would be?"

"The mutilation of the bodies is a manifestation of self-mutilation or castration. He may want to castrate himself, but he is unable to, so he sublimates. Since the focus of his fixation seems to be religious places, I suggest that his onanism is rooted in religion. Most likely one that espouses the strongest aversion to masturbation but it could be any of them."

"Any thoughts on physical attributes and habits, Doctor," the Captain asked.

"Typically, our ectotonic personality, perp one, would have an ectomorphic body type—thin with lean muscle mass. The evidence, however, shows an endomorphic body type, that is soft and round with proportionately short, but powerful limbs. In other words, this guy is a fat bastard. My analysis is supported by the depression depth of the footprints found at our most recent crime scenes and by an eyewitness. What may explain—"

"Eyewitness! What eyewitness? No one has mentioned anything about an eyewitness. Detective Marmaduke!" the Captain raged.

"I have no idea what he's talking about, Captain."

"Allow me to explain, Captain, if I may. While at Indian Springs, we came upon a group of Native-Americans, one of whom was a young boy I saw observing the investigation from a wooded area. We gave chase and attempted to question him but, before we could, others from his tribe took him away. As the young boy was leaving, he spoke, saying, "Rakke est-hvtke", which I've translated at the university library to loosely mean, 'Fat white man'. Their chief also alluded to at least one of the perps being white.

"Did he say that he saw who dumped the body, Doctor?" the Captain asked.

"How do you explain the boy's description?"

"Description, what description? For all you know, he could have been referring to Detective Marmaduke here. Did you hear him say this, Detective?"

"The boy mumbled something but I couldn't tell you what he said."

"I don't know, Doctor, that's pretty weak evidence for us to go on. What about the other shit, the names and symbols written all over everything?"

"I haven't quite figured them out yet, Captain. Except for the fact that they refer to Roman emperors and a Greek pagan god, I have no other connection."

"Will they continue to kill, Doctor?"

"The crime scenes reflected the perpetrators' lack of regret and the feeling that the killings were justified. The scenes were staged exactly as the perpetrator would have it—grotesquely, but not in a taunting way. The staging was ritualistic. They will continue to kill until their objective is met or arrest is facilitated."

"Thank you, Doctor. Marmaduke, do you have any—"

"One other thing, Captain. There may be a third perp. Remember I said perp one would stereotypically be thin and muscular but the crime scene showed we've got a lard ass on our hands? What may explain this discrepancy is a serious overlap between the mind-body systems or a third perpetrator. He would most likely be white also. The perpetrators would look out of character and context in the area, non-African-American, or Native-American, but may have done transitional work in the community, such as contracting."

"What the fuck?" Marmaduke groaned. "Or this voodoo you're selling could be wrong," he quipped.

"You're killing me, Doctor," Captain said.

Zones just shrugged. "I'm just giving it to you straight, Captain. It's what you're paying me the big bucks for."

"Marmaduke, do you have anything to add? Besides another goddamned perp?"

Marmaduke leapt from his seat and raced to the podium, nudging Zones out of the way.

"Well, instead of using a Ouija board or hocus pocus, we ran record checks on the first two sites. It appears that the owner of both properties was Colonel Bedford Crawford. He deeded the lands both churches occupy to his slaves after his death. Some descendants of the colonel have been petitioning the courts to have the properties returned to the family. Today I checked the property records for the two recent sites and found that these properties were also owned by the Crawford family. They deeded them over to the U.S. government as a state park."

"All four properties? Have you spoken to these relatives?"

"One Clinton Crawford seems like he could be good for these."

"Get James to find a federal judge to sign a warrant. Tell him it's a hate crime. Bring Mr. Crawford's ass in for questioning and see what other relatives may have an interest in these properties. And take the state patrol with you. I don't want some local yahoo Barney Fifing the arrest. In the meantime, have the lab put a rush on processing the scenes. Let me know the minute you have anything. That's all, people. Let's keep plugging away at this. The council and the mayor are both in my ass about this so you can expect me to be in yours," the Captain admonished them as they dispersed.

Captain Franklin's phone rang. "Speak of the she-devil," hand held over his mouth. "Hello Councilwoman Grudges," he answered. "You have Dr. Hyde with you and would like an update. I see. Well, we do have a suspect and we're preparing a warrant now. No ma'am, I can't give you any more details . . . ."

"Is this the same suspect you mentioned earlier, Detective? Who is he?" Zones asked.

"You'll see him as soon as I get the warrant in my hand," Marmaduke answered, puffing his chest out, raising his nose in the air.

"I would like to be present when you interrogate him."

"I'm not sure that's wise, Doctor, suit yourself. Just stay out of sight. My suspect doesn't cotton to your kind."

"My kind? What do you mean?"

"Yeah, you Ph.D. types," Marmaduke said smirking.

"And how did you develop this suspect?"

"Well, it wasn't by reading it in a book. Good old-fashioned detective work, Doctor, something I'm sure wasn't taught at that fancy school you went to."

"I'll see you later then, Detective."

" . . . . As soon as we have something, I'll let you and Dr. Hyde know, ma'am. Good-bye. Shit!" the Captain said, finishing his conversation with the councilwoman. "Marmaduke, you go get this Crawford guy and twist him so hard that he tells you where all the slave money is."

Marmaduke dashed from the room, confident he had his man. He winked at Zones, wetted the tip of his finger, marking one stroke in the air, keeping score. So far, he led by one to Zones' psycho-babble zero. For Zones, the hard work still lay ahead. He knew he had to come up with a viable suspect or the Captain might lose faith in his analysis.

ELEVEN

"Clinton Crawford and Maggie Alford, this is Detective Marmaduke with the DeKalb County P.D.," he called out over the bullhorn, standing securely on the driver's side of a deputy's car. He knew firsthand the danger and volatility of the suspect and took no chances.

"I have a federal warrant to search the premises. Please exit the home with your hands in the air."

The sound of his voice blasted through the air, dominating the morning—the most excitement for this small hamlet since the great train robbery of 1862. The neighbors peeked through their windows, trying to see what disturbed their day. The locals knew the Crawford clan and their brand of politics. Clinton Crawford never retreated from an opportunity to espouse his viewpoint on everything, especially his heritage.

"Get off my property," he shouted from within the house.

"Now Clinton, you come out here. Let's not make this worser than it is," Deputy Riley shouted.

"Is that you, John Walter?"

"Yeah Clinton, it's me"

"Well y'all best leave. I ain't got no eyes on these bullets."

"Now ain't no need to talk about any shooting, Clinton."

"I'll stop talking with my mouth and let Winston speak for me." Clinton thrust his vintage Winston rifle out the front window.

"Now, Mr. Crawford, all we want to do is search your property and ask you and Mrs. Alford a few questions, that's all," Detective Marmaduke interjected.

"I ain't letting no feds rummage through my things. So y'all can just get on, or get comfortable, either way, I don't care."

"He's not coming out, damn it." Marmaduke considered his

options. He hadn't planned on a standoff, especially a loose cannon.

The SWAT commander approached. "Would you like us to take him down, Detective?"

"Take him down!" Deputy Riley said, eyes wide and mouth agape. "Now I know ole Clinton is a hell-raiser and all that and his politicking ain't what you liberals consider PC but he ain't in need of no taking down."

"Well, just what would you have me do, baby-sit him all day? Who knows what he has stashed in there. He could hold us off for days." Marmaduke looked hard at the deputy.

"You give the word, Detective, and we'll smoke him out," the commander added.

"Now, just wait a minute. I got an idea." The deputy took the bullhorn from Marmaduke, aiming it toward the house. He set off a loud squeal from the horn that irritated the ears of those close by. Marmaduke grabbed the horn.

"Here, let me help you with that." He held it, working various buttons. The deputy eased his lips close to the horn.

"Clinton, this is John Walt . . . Deputy Riley," he started, quickly glancing over at Marmaduke. "Is Maggie in there with you?"

"Is that you, John Walter? Stop talking through that thing and talk natural."

"Let me speak with Maggie," the deputy demanded, the horn now moved away from his mouth.

"She ain't her, haven't seen her in days. She might be gone to mamma's."

"Who has a phone?" Marmaduke pulled his phone from his coat pocket, handing it to the deputy. He dialed.

"Hello, mamma Crawford?"

"Yaas," a voice shouted back through the phone, loud enough so everyone within a stone's throw could hear.

"Mamma, this is John Walter . . . Yes ma'am. Is Maggie there with you? She's not. I'm over here at Clinton's and I need for him to go down to the station with me, but he won't come out the house. Could you call him and talk to him for me please ma'am . . . No, he ain't done nothing yet, we just need to talk to him."

Deputy Riley hung up the phone. "She calling him up, she says."

Sure enough, a phone rang in the distance, coming from the house. It rang strongly with the sound of an old style rotary phone;

like everything else, it was a relic from the past. Someone answered, cutting the phone off mid-ring. They heard a chorus of "Yes ma'ams," with a final "Yes Mamma" to end the conversation.

The door to the old antebellum home opened, but no one came out. It remained ajar. Marmaduke glanced at his watch and strummed the top of his car. He repeated this until he heard,

"I'm coming out. Don't shoot," Clinton shouted.

"Make sure you have your hands in the air, leaving any weapons in the house," Marmaduke shouted back. Clinton eased his rotund frame from behind the door, his arms were raised high in the air.

"Don't shoot," Clinton shouted again. He inched toward the edge of the sweeping front porch, his posture slightly bent backwards to keep him from tipping over.

"Keep those hands up," a shout came from the crowd of peace officers invading his property.

"I'm only going with you, John Walter, not with those stinking FEDs!" he demanded.

"Okay, Clinton, you'll ride with me." The SWAT team moved in, grabbing his arms, twisting them behind his back and pushing him to the ground. He landed with a muffled thump, screaming from the hard takedown.

"I can't breathe," he yelled, gasping for air, his face pressed into the dirt.

"Okay boys, not so rough," Deputy Riley insisted. They tried to lift him from the ground, but not all at once. Much of him remained as if stuck against the earth. Those who handled him struggled to secure their weapons and pull Clinton to his feet at the same time. They stuffed him in the back of Deputy Riley's car. A few minutes later the deputy drove off into the early morning with Clinton Crawford in tow.

"Okay boys, let's not overlook anything. It'll be hell trying to get back in here," Marmaduke instructed them. He climbed the porch steps, pulled open the screen door and paused. He stepped inside, taking in the clutter. "Well, holy hell. Talk about needing an intervention. Let's try to keep this stuff organized. Bag that thing with the star on it. I saw a drawing like that at our crime scenes."

"What about these knives?" Chennault asked.

"Bag those. And this thing looks like that upside down 'V' and angle, so tag it."

"Marmaduke, take a look at this." He stepped over the many boxes packed with junk. He passed pictures of Klan rallies and cross burnings hanging on the wall, reaching the next room. "Drawings of eyes." Chennault held up papers with the images on them.

"Good job, Detective."

"This is a freaking damn museum, Marmaduke. What are we supposed to be looking for?" another Detective asked.

"Anything that doesn't look right, Detective."

"Are you kidding me? I'm a black man, none of this shit looks right." He held up a white robe adorned with the insignia of a high-ranking member of the Knights of the Ku Klux Klan.

"Just look, Detective." Marmaduke tapped Chennault on the shoulder. "Let's head over to the station. I don't want to give ole Colonel Sanders a chance to concoct a story."

"Sounds good. Let me bag this up first."

"Have you heard from our friend?"

"Who, the good Doctor? No, why?"

"Oh, nothing. Just that he was right about one thing."

"Yeah, what's that."

"If Crawford is our perp, he sure is a fat fucker."

TWELVE

A lone figure squirmed in an isolation room. He grimaced as he tried to stretch his discomfort away. His body, enlarged from years of neglect, engulfed the chair where he sat.

"Hello!" he yelled. He got no reply. Marmaduke and Chennault observed him through a one-way mirror. They'd known for years that the art of isolation is a means to ready their subject for his inquisitor. "Hello!" he yelled again much more forcefully, perhaps expecting immediate attention this time. Marmaduke opened the door to the room. Clinton squinted, trying to see in the dim lighting, kept bad on purpose.

"Mr. Crawford, good of you to join us. I'm Detective—"

"I knows who you is," he interrupted Marmaduke. "I want to go home. *Right Now!*" he demanded, slamming his fist on the table.

"Well, Mr. Crawford, we know you have been trying to sue the churches and government for the return of the properties, those where the crimes were committed. How do you explain that?" Marmaduke now sat at the table across from him.

"I don't got to 'splain it 'cause I ain't done it. I ain't killed nobody and I ain't done nothing to no nigga church or no Injun graveyard." The room quieted. Marmaduke sucked at his teeth, staring long and hard at his suspect. He tapped his temple repeatedly, squinting his eyes, as if seeing a crack into his mind. He thought about his interrogation approach.

"Let's see," he said, pulling a piece of paper from the file. He opened it up and placed it onto the table. "Arrested in '81 for breaking and entering and for, what do we have here? Lewd and lascivious acts. My! My! My! And looky here, pictures." Marmaduke unfolded a newspaper clipping. He held it up to his face, blocking it from Clinton.

71

"Let's see what it says, 'A little taste of Midtown in Marietta.' And there you are, all snuggled up in your birthday suit next to your boyfriend. You a switch hitter? You batting for the other team?" Marmaduke lowered the paper, looking at Clinton who steamed. "The colonel must be twisting in his grave."

"I ain't no faggot. Those cops did that," he yelled, turning red.

The door to the room opened once again. Detective Chennault came in carrying a box. He sat it down on the table, rattling the objects inside. He pulled a paint can from the box.

"You know what that is?" Chennault asked, pointing to the can of paint. Clinton said nothing but he stared at the can. "It's paint, the same kind used to write on the water at Indian Springs. Guess where I got it from? Out of your storage. What do you have to say to that?" Chennault gripped his hips, showing his suspicion, still nothing from Clinton. "And this," he pulled a small plastic bag from the box, "is the feed from your barn—triticale. We found the same grain on one of the bodies."

He took the other items from the box, placing them one by one onto the table in front of their suspect, who examined them closely.

"These is my things. What's y'all doing with 'um?"

"Can you explain these items Mr. Crawford?" Detective Chennault asked him. He still did not answer, staring at the items on the table. "Clinton! Tell me about these items," he demanded, pounding the table, palms open. The sound shook their suspect, breaking his focus on the items lining the table, still no answer. Chennault pulled a folder from the same box, slamming it open. He placed a series of photographs from the folder next to the other items spread upon the table. They showed markings and graffiti from the crime scenes resembling the insignias on the items retrieved from Clinton's home. "These are from the crime scene, these are from your home," Detective Chennault explained, pointing to each of them. "Now, do you have anything to say?"

"Okay, enough of this. Bring her in," Marmaduke said. As Chennault left the room, Marmaduke watched Clinton, with teeth clenched, jaw tensioned, wanting to do more than just question him.

Chennault returned with Maggie, Clinton's sister, leading her by the arm, sitting her in a chair next to her brother. A piggish looking woman, she plopped into the seat, flesh splattered everywhere, porky, like her brother, with a mean disposition. Chennault reached into the box he had brought, retrieved an evidence bag and placed it on the table. The items in the bag clanged.

"We confiscated these from the sex club you were arrested in three days ago. The lab says they are consistent with the knife wounds and marks on the bodies," Chennault looked over at Maggie.

"We ain't telling you feds shit! Ain't that right Clinton?" She talked out the side of her mouth, her voice raspy, skin jaundiced—a hag. She threw her hair back and moved her head from side to side as if shaking something loose. She smelled of tobacco and Old Spice, a man's cologne, and a strange mix of scents. They wanted to open the door, but couldn't—regulations.

"Yeah! We're not saying anything to y'all feds. I want to see my—" At that moment, the door to the room was flung open, interrupting his words. In walked Captain Franklin and Dr. Zones, their entry making Clinton jump in his skin, surprising even Marmaduke.

"What's he doing here?" Marmaduke asked.

"Calm down, Detective. I asked him to come when I heard you were bringing them in. Dr. Zones just wanted to examine those items," the Captain answered.

"But Captain!"

"But nothing."

"I'm not talking to no jiggaboos!" Clinton yelled, folding his arms across his chest and puckering his lips tight. Maggie laughed, earning a mean stare from the Captain.

"It gets real dark in here with the lights out. You wouldn't know which one of us gave you the beat down," the Captain told him in a murderous tone.

Zones walked over to the table, moving his hand over the items, just close enough not to touch them. He looked over at the suspects but cut away to hide his face when he saw Maggie. It couldn't be—but, the same piggish face peered back at him, a glimpse of the red, leather get-up she wore peeked from between the slits of her jail issue jumpsuit. He remembered her from their lock-up together after his arrest at the club. Zones shook his head, trying to focus. Clinton certainly fit the physical attributes of one of the perpetrators but the south was swelled with morbidly obese people.

"Don't I know you?" Maggie asked him. She leaned forward in her chair, staring up at Zones, a thinking look on her face, as she tried to remember.

"No," he lied, looking over at Marmaduke and Chennault, who watched him suspiciously. Zones looked away quickly. He continued to run his hand along the objects on the table.

"Don't you touch my things, nigga," Clinton demanded, still seated at the table.

"Watch your mouth," the Captain rebuked him.

"The blood drop MIOAK." Zones lifted from the table a patch with a cross and a red blood drop in the form of a tear drop.

"The MI what?" Marmaduke asked, both confused and surprised to hear the name.

"M.I.O.A.K. It stands for Mystic . . ."

"Insignia Of A Klansman," Clinton interrupted, angered by Zones' recital of the words.

"The Othala Rune, a pagan Norse symbol for the god Odin." Zones moved to the next item. He lifted and then lowered the object, its heaviness striking the table loudly. The sound echoed through the small room.

"Careful nig—boy with my stuff." Clinton caught himself as he and the Captain locked eyes.

"The Udjat—the eye of Horus, surprising, given its African origins. But I guess they didn't teach you that at Klansman U. And finally, what do we have here? Ah yes, the inverted pentagram. But what is a good old cross burning racist Christian like you doing with the devil's symbol?" He stared at the suspect hard, hoping his eyes would reveal some dark secret. Clinton turned away. Zones looked over at Marmaduke and Chennault, who still watched him closely.

"Well?" Marmaduke asked.

"Are you sure I don't know you boy? 'Cause I never forget a face, specially a niggra's. Give me a minute and I'll figure it out." Maggie still stared hard at Zones.

"He is not your killer," Zones said, turning to the Captain.

"*WHAT!*" Marmaduke shouted, leaping from his seat.

"HA! I told yah." Clinton shouted.

"Captain, you can't be serious. He didn't even question them."

"Listen to the nigga! Listen to the nigga!" Clinton shouted, banging his fist on the table. Maggie joined in, forgetting about trying to recollect Zones.

"Outside," the Captain ordered, snatching the door open. They each filed out of the room, closing the door behind them. The muffled shouts of, "Listen to the nigga!" drifted through the door.

"Captain, the same symbols found at the crime scenes were retrieved from his home and the same type of paint. He has no alibi for the time the bodies are thought to have been placed at the scenes. She was in possession of knives like the ones the M.E. said were used. They're suing to get their land back; that gives them motive and they're Klansmen which should have sealed the fucking deal for you, Doctor." Marmaduke clenched his teeth and thrust his forefinger at Zones.

"Those things don't grow back," Zones warned.

"Cool it, both of you," the Captain said.

"And why did the old hag think she knew you, hah Doc? 'Cause she seemed pretty sure. I pulled her sheets. She got busted down in Midtown at some freak club a few nights ago. Aren't you staying Downtown? You got a sweet tooth for the soft and fluffy kind?"

"Well, Doctor, he makes a point—"

"I ain't no chubby fucker?" Zones growled.

"—about the evidence," the Captain continued.

Zones pulled a file from his oversized briefcase, slapping it onto the table.

"These are the files from the last fifty years of reported Klan vandalisms in the state. In each one of them, there are symbols depicting swastikas, KKK and some reference to a derogatory racial term. This has been the pattern over the last hundred years. Not one of the photos taken at the four crime scenes has any of these symbols in them. Listen, these guys are as predictable as shit stinks. Now why would that change all of a sudden?"

"To throw us off, that's why," Marmaduke answered.

"Those bubbas in there might be bigoted sons-of-bitches and I would like nothing more than to see their kind locked away, but these crimes are not Klan related and that Klansman and Klanswoman in there didn't do any of them."

"Well, Detectives. Have either of you done this research?"

"Well no, but—What about that 'Sieg' and 'Lieh' written in their hands, isn't that Nazi shit?"

"Actually it's Sieg Heil or, 'Hail Victory'. I believe the 'Lieh' is a dysgraphic spelling. The phrase actually has an ancient Roman origin which would support the other Romanized motifs found at the crime scenes. After the fascists in Italy resurrected it, the Nazis adopted the phrase as a salute to Hitler."

"What about the paint we found that matches the paint we found at the Springs?"

"Oil based, you can find it in any paint store. Just add the right amount of thinner to get it to float."

"Is there anything besides circumstantial evidence, anything found at the crime scenes that connects your suspects to these crimes—fingerprints, DNA, hair samples, anything?"

"Well . . . no Captain, but we're still digging." The Captain opened the door to the interrogation room, poking his head inside.

"Mr. Crawford, Mrs. Alford, you're free to go."

"Hallelujah! For once a nigga is right!" Clinton hollered.

"But Captain—"

"But what, Marmaduke?" The Captain gave him a puzzled looked before turning to Zones. "You better be right on this, Doctor or you can kiss that prison contract goodbye."

"But Captain—"

"Cut them loose, Detective." The Captain walked away from them. Marmaduke stood there, watching him disappear down the hall, along with his best hope of solving these killings.

"Well, Doctor, this is your case now." Marmaduke stepped back into the room. He packed the rest of Clinton's things, throwing them with some force into the box, mumbling angry words under his breath. He looked at Clinton and Maggie, frowning, with a growl he said, "Let's go."

Detective Chennault patted Zones on the shoulder, a southern gesture for good luck and hope you didn't just fuck up. The two detectives hauled Clinton and Maggie out of the room and down the hall. Clinton turned back to Zones, shaking his head.

Zones knew he needed to develop a suspect now more than ever. He, however, didn't want to sacrifice the prudent for the expedient. Prudent in this case meant capturing a heinous killer, one who terrorized this southern metropolis. He had no leads except for some bogus story from a jailhouse con. Zones knew he must start from the beginning and that meant a reexamination of the crime scenes.

"Detective Marmaduke." Zones hurried down the hall after him, their one-time suspect still in tow.

"You still here, Doctor?"

"Listen, I need access to the church crime scenes, can you get me in?"

"Sorry Doc, but we've turned those scenes back over to the churches. Isn't that right, Chennault?"

"Yeah, that's right. The only way to see them now, Doc, is to have your own little 'come to Jesus' moment." They both laughed and continued on their way.

Zones wandered down the hall, coming to a room where a TV played. The councilwoman was holding a news conference.

"We have been notified that the police made an arrest in the murders," she began, surrounded by Deacon Pike, Reverend Gainer and others. "They are Ku Klux Klansmen who have been trying to steal the land of black folk and native people, just as I suspected . . . ."

"SHIT!" someone shouted. The sound carried through the halls. The Captain bellowed the expletive. Zones knew his "SHIT" anywhere.

THIRTEEN

When Zones reached the Bethel Primitive Baptist Church, the sounds from the service shattered the quiet morning into full-blown gospel ecstasy. He paused briefly at the covered stoop, placing his ear up to the door. He listened to the hymn being banged out on a tuneless organ. Tambourines rattled, rustling up spirits. Washboards scratched an irritating sound. Drums tapped a rhythm to dance by and hands clapped in praise. He tried to enter unnoticed, but the doors squeaked and the floors creaked with his every step, making it difficult. The smell of fresh paint and strong cleaner lingered in the air, masking the natural odor of the place.

The small congregation all huddled close to the front. They swayed back and forth to the music. Suddenly, it stopped.

"Welcome, brother!" a man from the podium shouted. Reverend Gainer addressed him; Zones recognized him from the TV. Those sitting in the pews turned to greet Zones, who rushed in to find a seat near the rear of the sanctuary. "There are plenty of seats up near the front, brother. Come, please join us," the reverend entreated.

Zones eased up from his seat, walked down the narrow aisle, and slid into an open space at the end of a long wooden pew. They greeted him with nods, pats on the back and a chorus of welcomes.

The congregation hummed and moaned their song. Zones peeked at the time on his phone—midday and still no sermon. For this southern Baptist congregation, when it came to praise and worship, time had no meaning. Reverend Gainer still stood at the large podium, thumbing through scripture, looking for inspired text. An old woman continued to bang away on the organ and the congregation sang from tattered hymnals. Finally, the reverend belted out an, "AMEN" and the music mellowed to a stop.

Many years had passed since Zones last attended church services. He worshipped faithfully until he turned eighteen. He hoped, through church, to find the answer that eluded him everywhere else he searched—why his mother had been taken from him. A young child needed its mother more than anyone, he reasoned. Why then would God take her away from him? Not only that, what kind of God would serve a child a double dose of tragedy and take away his father as well?

His prayers went unanswered. He thought that God should have worked as expeditiously answering his prayers as he did causing his pain. Many nights he pored through the same scriptures he now heard, searching for a divine answer to the pain he still felt. When no answer came, he abandoned the church and its teachings, relegating them to no higher esteem than a criminal psychological tool like operant conditioning or differential association.

"And now unto him who is able to keep you from falling . . . ." the preacher cried out from the podium, the rich, southern texture of his voice carrying through the small chapel. Zones checked the time again, looking at his cell phone. He found watches hard to keep track of, losing one every other month or so.

"And let the people say, Amen," the reverend implored the congregation. A chorus of "AMENs" filled the sanctuary, signaling the service's end.

He approached the podium, a line had formed. Others watched him as he stood there. Eyes that witnessed many things for many years now bore down on him. He smiled as his eyes locked with theirs. He glanced around the sanctuary, looking for signs of the terror that had gripped this space only days ago. He found none. The parishioners had wasted no time cleansing this temple.

The sanctuary emptied out. Zones approached the preacher.

"Welcome, brother, glad to have you visit with us. Are you new to the area? We don't get many visitors your age. Do you have a church home?" The reverend grinned, grabbed Zones' hand, and shook it.

"Well, sir, I'm looking for Reverend Gainer."

"I'm Pastor Gainer, and you are?"

"Zones, Dr. Zones."

"Who?"

"Dr. Zones!" he said a little louder.

"Dr. Zones, it's great to have you worship with us. What kind of

Doctor are you?"

"I'm a criminologist. I'm here about the body you found," he whispered, leaning in close, trying not to be overheard. The reverend's eyes widened. He no longer shook Zones' hand.

"I had hoped the memory of that day had been erased with the freshly painted walls." The reverend looked around the sanctuary at those who still remained. "Come with me." He escorted Zones to the rear of the church, into a small, poorly lit room. "I thought the police were through with me. They turned the church back over to us—said we could go back to normal."

"Yes sir. I'm just following up on a few things."

"A few things, like what? I told the detectives all I know."

"Could you show me where you found the body?" The reverend led Zones back to the sanctuary. All the people had emptied out, giving them freedom to speak openly.

"There were writings and drawing on this wall here," Reverend Gainer pointed out.

"Only this wall?" Zones shined a penlight onto a now clear wall.

"That's right."

"And the body?"

"Over here behind the podium." They made their way over to the podium. The platform, elevated above the main sanctuary floor, gave slightly when walked upon. The reverend stood near a large wooden chair, ornately carved to give it grandeur, matching the grandness of the podium.

"Here?"

"Right here." The reverend pointed to the chair. Zones examined it, shining the small penlight on and around it, hoping to detect some small, missed thing.

"I smell a strong odor of cleaner here."

"Yeah, we cleaned the chair and the floor around the chair."

"The floor. Why?" Zones shined the light where the reverend pointed, catching the outline of a faint image beneath the chair. "Can we move it?" Zones gave the chair a nudge but it did not move.

"Sure can, give me a moment." The reverend disappeared to the rear of the church and returned with a metal toolbox. He placed it on the floor near the chair. The toolbox rattled. He unlatched it, flipped the lid wide open and pulled out a screwdriver.

"Let me help you," Zones offered, seeing Reverend Gainer struggle.

He grabbed beneath the reverend's arm, helping him to the floor.

"Thank you," he said, now on his knees. "Little children like to play over here before the services. I was afraid they would tip over in this chair, so I anchored it." Reverend Gainer struggled to unfasten the bolts. When he removed the last of them, he rocked the chair to check its stability. He braced himself against its sturdy arm, pushing himself up from the floor, grunting. Together they lifted the chair and placed it to the side.

Zones knelt on the floor to examine the area. He placed the light flush, turning it in small degrees to illuminate a spot beneath where the chair rested. He pulled out a digital camera and photographed the area.

"What yah see, Doc?"

"I don't know yet—perhaps nothing, perhaps something. Let me help you put this chair back."

"Ah, don't mind that. I'll get one of the brothers to help me. You just catch the SOB who did this."

"I'll try reverend. You have a good day now." The reverend smiled in agreement as Zones darted toward the door.

"If yah looking for a church home, we'll be happy to have yah," the reverend said as Zones exited.

FOURTEEN

Zones raced to the other side of town headed toward the First Iconium Baptist Chruch. He hoped to arrive in time for the end of services. The authorities had returned this second crime scene back to the congregation as well. Law enforcement didn't dare keep good, church-going southerners from their bible thumping hallelujah time. The people in the south didn't take too kindly to having their worship services interrupted.

"Excuse me, sir, I'm looking for a Mr. Pike," Zones asked the first parishioner he saw.

"Deacon Pike, he's probably in the office." He pointed through the sanctuary.

Zones pressed against the small wave of worshippers exiting the chapel and headed toward a door marked, "office". He tapped on it.

"Who is it," someone shouted through the door.

"Dr. Zones. I'm here to see Deacon Pike." The door started to open, but got stuck. A hard pull dislodged it and the door flung open, making a grating sound as it rubbed the jamb. A short bespectacled old man peered up from behind the thick lenses of his glasses, his body still tucked safely behind the door.

"I'z Pike. What can I do yah for?"

"Mr. Pike, I'm Dr. Zones. I'm working with the authorities regarding the body found here. I was told that you found it." Deacon Pike gathered himself, taking a hard swallow, tugging at his tie.

"Yes sir, I'z finds it right over here." He pointed as he removed himself fully from behind the door. He led Zones over to the pulpit where a stately chair, like the one at the first church, rested. "Right here," he pointed. "And that writing was over on that wall."

Zones opened his case, pulled out a crime scene photograph, held it up and compared it to what he now saw.

"This chair was turned," Zones said.

"Yes sir, it was facing that writing on the wall."

"Which direction is that wall?"

"Let me see . . . that's . . . that's east, yeah east."

"East." Zones pulled out the other photographs, spreading them onto the floor. He picked up one from the Kolomoki Mounds site. The picture showed the view taken from the rear of the body, facing the cryptic symbols. He flipped it over, the writing saying, "looking east". Zones picked up another photograph with the same rear view of the body facing the symbols. He recognized the Indian Springs site from the body resting in the water. He flipped the picture over and written on the back of it as well were the words, "looking east".

"May I move this chair?"

"Sure yah can." They each grabbed an arm and slid the chair to the side. Zones pulled the small penlight from his coat and, just as he had done at the first scene, examined the area beneath the chair.

"Has anyone cleaned this area?"

"We cleaned all this and painted that wall over there."

"Was there anything written or drawn here beneath where the chair was?"

"If I'z recollect right, Sister Parker did have some time with a spot over here."

"I see. May I take some pictures?" Zones took a digital camera from its case.

"I'z don't see why not."

Zones photographed the area beneath where the chair rested, still unsure if there was anything there that was evidence-worthy.

"Thank you, Mr. Pike." Zones gathered his things and prepared to leave.

"Don't mention it, happy to help. Just hope yah get this fella."

Zones smiled and exited the sanctuary. The parking lot emptied out, leaving tire tracks crisscrossing the freshly cut lawn and graveled parking. He wondered why they targeted poor black churches for such a grotesque act. The only common denominator between these two churches and the Native-American burial sites was the previous landowner—a long dead confederate colonel whose progeny he had cleared of the killings. *What if I am wrong?* The media dined on such incompetence. The headlines would read, "Black FBI Consultant

Responsible for Release of Psycho—Racist Mutilator". Zones slumped in his seat, sighing deeply. He caught a glimpse of himself in the rearview mirror, eyes red, color flushed, a heavy burden hovering about, one not to be borne on an empty stomach.

. . .

The diner, tucked into a small building that hosted a number of other eating places before it, served up a steady helping of southern cuisine. A "hole-in-the–wall" in the south, or a "greasy spoon", everywhere else, Zones acquired a taste for the artery clogging delicacies of the southern diet. The food served here, as they say, "stuck to your ribs". He found a small empty table for two near the rear, just the way he liked it. In the past, he had shared larger tables with complete strangers, especially on crowded days. He abhorred forced conversations and crowds, for that matter.

"What'll you have?" the waitress asked.

"What's your special?"

"Smothered pork chops, mashed potatoes and collard greens."

"With sweet tea?"

"Always, Sugar."

"That sounds good."

She scurried off to place the order. He watched her. His eyes surveyed her legs down to where they ended, at her shoes, bronzed pillows holding up a healthy sister—big-legged and thick in all the right places. Her uniform hugged her like a fifteen-year-old overweight Latina's gown on her Quinceanera. She looked back, expecting to be surveilled. She twisted her hips more. A round mass moved beneath her uniform. She knew what she had and how to use it. Zones tried to conceal his gaze, snapping his head around, their eyes met. She clenched the tip of her finger between her teeth, giving him a smile and a wink.

Zones snatched his laptop and the digital camera from his bag and uploaded the crime scene pictures he had taken. He did not see anything at first. He adjusted the pixel quality and ran the image through a series of filters. An image appeared slowly, a geometric pattern, a circle within a square, as if drawn by a child.

The image was from the first crime scene, the Bethel Baptist

Church. The pastor did say that the children sometimes played in the area. Could these forms be the result of child's play? He loaded the images from the second site and filtered them. To his surprise, the same pattern appeared. Thinking he had made an error, he reloaded the images, pulling them up side-by-side. Again they matched. Zones fell back in his seat, still focused on the two images. He sketched the pattern on a pad over and over, retracing its outline, his eyes moving between the pad and the screen, contemplating the meaning of the shapes.

"Here you go, Sugar." The waitress returned with his food.

"Thank you." He hid his face, only partially acknowledging her.

"Anything else?" He shook his head, sheepishly looking up from the computer.

"Okay, just holler if you need anything." She walked away, looking back at him. This time, however, Zones buried his face into the computer screen, trying to hide his lust.

The diner began to fill with the usual souls. A good southerner ate supper at one of the local haunts on Sundays. Many were heavy hitters, professional eaters who devoured "all you can eat" buffets like a biblical swarm of locusts.

Zones finished what remained of his food and darted toward the cashier. The same thick-legged waitress waited at the cash register. He handed her the bill and his credit card.

"T.O. Zones. Does that stand for Take me Out?" She giggled, smiling as if she had thought of something naughty. She handed him back his card.

"Thank you." He took the card.

"Do you have a pen?"

"Sure." He reached into his coat pocket and retrieved one.

"Let me see your hand."

"What?"

"Your hand, let me see it." He stretched forth his hand, a little at a time, not sure of her intensions. She grabbed hold of it gently, writing something on his palm.

"Um," he started to speak.

"I'm Candi. Call me." She placed the pen back in his hand.

"You couldn't write that on my receipt?"

"Our parking area is littered with discarded receipts. But I bet you won't wash that hand until you get home." She flicked his chin with her finger, batted her eyes and flashed him a big smile.

Zones took her in fully, then walked toward the exit. He looked back at her just like before. Their eyes met but this time he did not try to hide his staring eyes. He, however, must be cautious. Pursuing his passions in this conservative town had not served him well. Besides, he didn't need any distractions while trying to find a suspect.

FIFTEEN

Zones pushed the pile of clothes, strewn across his bed, to one side, irritated that he'd forgotten to remove the "Do Not Disturb" sign from his door. He plopped down onto the bed and clicked on the TV. Once again, the councilwoman had decided to hold a news conference concerning the murders.

"Councilwoman Grudges, what do you say to those that thought you were premature, blaming the Klan for these heinous crimes?" a reporter asked.

"I stand behind what I said. Just because the police have failed to do their job proving it doesn't mean it's not so. Besides, if they didn't do these killings, and I doubt that they didn't, there are plenty of other deaths they haven't been brought to justice for—my daddy's death, for one."

"Dr. Hyde, you represent the Inter-Faith Council on the civilian task force, how does this hurt the credibility of the council and the task force working together with law enforcement to capture this killer or killers?"

"We will continue to work with law enforcement to bring the perpetrators to justice . . . ."

Zones lowered the volume on the TV and grabbed his legal notepad. He booted his laptop and logged onto the internet. His search led him to the School of Theology at Howard University; the school housed a database of symbols from indigenous world religions. He had helped compile the list as part of his Doctoral dissertation, traveling extensively throughout the African Continent, working closely with other eminent scholars. Many more researchers covered other continents and their indigenous religions.

"Circle inscribed within square", he typed, searching the compiled database. A number of selections appeared. He scrolled through them, hoping that one matched. He read:

> *The symbol, an ancient one that could be traced through many cultures, has survived into the present. In the Old Turkic religion of Asia, the earth was represented as a square covered by a circumscribed dome. The Buddhist stupa itself was said to be based on a square earth and circular heaven.*

The Buddhists practice passivism so our killers are probably not Buddhists. Now the Turks, they brought this symbolism with them into the Islamic faith so there may be a possibility there. He continued to scroll through the database. He continued reading . . .

> *From the classical world, Plutarch recounted the slaying of Remus at the hand of Romulus, his brother, for violating the pomerium, a sacred circular boundary within Rome's square walls.*

Here we go. This fits with the other Romanized motifs. He downloaded a copy of this information and continued to read . . .

> *The medieval alchemist sought to solve the mystery of the, 'quadratura circuli,' the squaring of the circle. There were even tenth century 'Altars to the Gods' in Tel Beersheva in Meggido formed from the circle and square motif.*

He searched through many of the images; one in particular drew his interest, the circle in square motif of the LDS Nauvoo Temple in Las Vegas Nevada. He retrieved the photographs he took at the crime scene and compared them to the image from the database. He read the caption which described the symbol. It read:

> *This is a great symbol of the Mormon Church, also known as the Church of Jesus Christ of Latter-Day Saints. The circle inscribed within a square represents the earth and heaven combining. It is said to form the throne of God.*

"Throne of God," Zones said softly. He recalled his conversation with the inmate. He pulled the files he received from the FBI from his briefcase and studied each of the photographs.

"Antiochus! Hadrian! Zeus! Sieg! Heil! And now Throne of God!" These all screamed out from the images. The answer felt close, if he could just find some missing piece of vital information. He did not put much trust in the rants of a crazed inmate but he felt compelled to follow-up this clue, if for nothing else than to exclude it. He knew what he must do.

"Hello, Detective Marmaduke. This is Zones."

"Yes, Dr. Zones, what can I do for you?"

"Wanted to let you know that I'll be out of town for a couple of days."

"Vacation time already, Doctor?"

"No, just some research on your case. I have a theory."

"More research, huh? Well, while you're out chasing theories, I'll be looking for real evidence."

"Okay, Detective." He hung up and booked a flight, destination—Utah.

Zones, still sitting on the edge of his bed, thought long and hard about his next move. He wrung his hands as if awaiting some terrible news. He stopped momentarily to notice the name and phone number written in his palm. His nervousness somewhat gone, he picked the phone receiver up. A dial tone sounded as he held the phone to his ear. He dialed the number.

"Hello, this is Candi," she answered, her voice sultry like black silk as the words rolled from her tongue. He said nothing at first, cupping his hand over the phone to block his heavy breathing. "Hello!" she answered again, this time her voice a little stronger.

"This is Zones. I met you earlier at the diner."

"Hello, Sugar, how are you? You know how to keep a girl waiting, don't you."

"It's only been a couple of hours."

"Ah, I'm just kidding with you, Sugar. You're the uptight kind, I see. Where are you?" she asked, taking control.

"I'm at the Westin Downtown."

"Oh, fancy, fancy now. What room number?"

"2210."

"I'll see you in a minute Sugar. Bye!"

"But . . . Hello! Hello!" he shouted into the phone, no one answered.

"Whatever happened to slow and easy? The South sure has changed."

As Zones waited, he ordered room service, a bottle of Riesling and shrimp cocktail—booty food. No black woman could resist the stuff. In a pinch, he'd substituted White Zinfandel, but only got half the freak.

Sitting in the room, dead silence, he heard the ticking of the clock's second hand as it swept around the dial. He jumped at every noise from outside. Zones decided that a good hot shower would calm his nerves. Turning the water on, the bathroom quickly filled with steam. He liked his water hot. He eased himself under the shower and soon all the tension he had felt moments earlier washed away, flowing with the water down the drain.

A knock came at the door. He rushed to dry himself.

"Just a minute," he shouted. Another knock sounded, this time much more forcefully. He made his way through the steam-filled room, in his rush he'd forgotten to close the bathroom door. Opening the door slightly, he raced to the other side of the room and sat on the edge of the bed.

"Come in," he bid her. The door swung open.

"Where are you?"

"Over here. Just keep walking straight." In the meantime, he grabbed his pants, stepped into them, two legs at once, and zipped them up. From his luggage, he snatched a shirt, whipped it on, and shoved the tails inside the pants waste band. As he dressed quickly, an image appeared through the clouds of steam. Candi stepped through the haze wearing a full length trench coat and a wide smile. Clothes seemed a sin to such a form. She ripped the coat open, tossed it to the floor and presented the body of a goddess dipped in dark chocolate to him. Zones gawked and moved to free her of the black laced lingerie that remained.

. . .

The next morning, Zones headed for the airport. As he slumped in his aisle seat for the flight west, he thought of the goddess he had left back in his hotel room. Picturing Candi lying butt naked in bed distracted him from his hatred of flying over the Rocky Mountains and the turbulence they created. He always chose an aisle seat. Seeing the ground from ten thousand feet in the air just reminded him of how great the plunge would be if they didn't make it.

Passengers packed the plane, although the seat next to him remained empty. Shortly a young boy, the pudgy type, the one always picked last for any team, sat next to him. Other similarly dressed characters marched past Zones, taking seats nearby.

With everyone seated, the plane prepared to depart. Zones closed his eyes and said a prayer, not out of belief, but from habit, something he did every time he flew. He settled in for a nap, it came to him when the plane cleared the clouds and reached its flight altitude. Pray first, then nap, he never deviated from this routine.

The plane leveled off once it reached altitude. Zones reclined his seat. His eyes flickered closed, delivering him into a near sleep.

"Excuse me, sir." A voice said. At first Zones ignored it. The words melded with all the other background noises that made an easy rest difficult.

"Excuse me, sir," the voice said again, but this time with a slight nudge. Zones opened his eyes. A pair of thick, horn-rimmed glasses jetted out from the boy's face.

"Yes. What's up?" he asked, still drowsy.

"May I share something with you?" He turned in his seat, looked over his shoulder, creasing his well-pressed, white shirt. A clip-on black tie and slacks completed his ensemble. Zones followed his gaze and saw other similarly dressed young men urging the boy on.

"Have you heard of The Church of Jesus Christ of Latter-Day Saints?" He shoved a small book with the name emblazoned on it at Zones.

"Yes, I have." He sat up in his seat, showing some interest.

"May I read you some scripture?"

"Sure, why not." Zones looked over his shoulder to see the other young men smiling. The boy opened the book and began to read a passage. He listened, leaning in to see the words he read. He heard whispers from behind him. He turned to see the same young men following along in another Book of Mormon, their smiles even wider. They nudged and patted each other on the back. One whipped out a form and began to scribble.

"What can you tell me about the Gadianton Robbers?" Zones asked, interrupting the young boy. His head popped up, ending the reading of the passage. He stared at Zones and then snapped his head over his shoulder, scanning the nervous faces of the others.

"We aren't allowed to talk —"

"Only the elders are allowed to speak about that," one of the young men interrupted.

"Can you show me where they are mentioned in your book?" The young boy looked at the others who nodded in approval. He turned to the scripture. The heading read, "Helaman 2". He handed the book to Zones.

"You may keep it."

"Thank you." He took the book. He hoped reading made the long flight to Salt Lake City more tolerable. He began to read:

> *1 And it came to pass in the forty and second year of the reign of the judges, after Moronihah had established again peace between the Nephites and the Lamanites, behold there was no one to fill the judgment-seat; therefore there began to be a contention again among the people concerning who should fill the judgment-seat.*
>
> *2 And it came to pass that Helaman, who was the son of Helaman, was appointed to fill the judgment-seat, by the voice of the people.*
>
> *3 But behold, Kishkumen, who had murdered Pahoran, did lay wait to destroy Helaman also; and he was upheld by his band, who had entered into a covenant that no one should know his wickedness.*
>
> *4 For there was one Gadianton, who was exceedingly expert in many words, and also in his craft, to carry on the secret work of murder and of robbery; therefore he became the leader of the band of Kishkumen.*

Zones, seeing the first mention of the Gadiantons, thought back to his conversation with the inmate. He hadn't gotten much information from him. Questions about this group still remained. He continued to read. By the time the plane landed, he had read well into the Second Book of Nephi. A curious passage caught his attention, Chapter 5 verse 21 read:

> *And he had caused the cursing to come upon them, yea, even a sore cursing, because of their iniquity. For behold, they had*

*hardened their hearts against him, that they had become like unto
a flint; wherefore, as they were white, and exceedingly fair and
delightsome, that they might not be enticing unto my people the
Lord God did cause a skin of blackness to come upon them.*

Zones glanced over at his seat mate, trying to reconcile what he
read with the affable young boy sitting next to him. He questioned, to
himself, how the Mormon religion might tie in with the crime scenes,
if it did at all. He knew Joseph Smith claimed The Book of Mormon
to be a biblical testament of Jesus Christ by the Native-Americans,
which would explain the Indian mounds and springs connection. He
had read scripture here referencing cursed black folk, which would
explain the black churches' connection. These alone, however, did not
add up to murder.

The plane landed safely in Salt Lake City. It emptied out; Zones
and the young missionaries were all that remained. They hovered like
predators over a carcass, waiting for an opportune time to dine. Zones,
too preoccupied with his reading to fully notice them, remained
seated.

"So what do you think?" one asked, interrupting him.

"Well," Zones raised his head from his reading. "I think that it's
interesting."

"If you're going to be in town, we want to invite you to our church,"
the young boy who sat next to him said, getting a nudge from one of
the others.

"Sure, where is it?"

The young boy reached into his pocket. "Here's our card." He
handed it to Zones. It read, "Salt Lake City Utah Temple."

"Is this near Welfare Square?"

"Why do you want to know about Welfare Square?" one of them
asked sharply. Another nudged him. "I mean, do you need food?"

"Listen, do you think I could speak with someone there?"

"Probably, it's not that far from the church. We can show you
where it is."

. . .

They all piled into a cab heading toward town. The first impression of the place brought to mind the barrenness of the Middle East. The city rested in a valley, framed by snow-capped mountains and the lake from which it derived its name.

The church's hand weighed heavily here. The temple spires rose above the plain like a great colossus. Anywhere else, people might have gawked with suspicion at the young men accompanying Zones, but not here. They were the drones that worked to keep this religious hive alive and the locals knew it.

They pulled into the parking lot of a non-descript building, Deseret Industries in large letters above the door. Other buildings of similar architecture made up the complex. Zones flung open the door to the cab and hopped out. He looked completely around, shaking his head. Upon first glance, what he saw looked normal but how many other religions had a doomsday stash of victuals? *What could this place possibly have to do with this case?* He had questions and the possible answers led him here.

SIXTEEN

They approached the door to the building. A much older man met them.

"Hello brothers," he greeted them each with a firm handshake and a tug on the shoulder, welcoming them inside.

"Hello, Elder Ansen."

"I'm afraid I don't know you." He turned to Zones.

"Zones, Dr. Zones." He reached out to shake his hand. Elder Ansen reluctantly grabbed hold of it.

"We met him on the plane. He'll be attending services with us this Sunday," Joseph, the youngest of them and Zones' seat mate, said with a wide grin.

"Oh yeah, and he would like to speak with the bishop," Gordon, the oldest added.

"The bishop, what for?"

"Well, I'm working on a case for the FBI and—"

"FBI. I thought you said you were a doctor."

"I am. I'm a criminalist."

"A criminalist. Whoa! Did you know this, brothers?" He looked over at the young men who accompanied Zones.

"No!" they all said, shaking their heads.

"What's the crime?" He turned his attention back to Zones.

"I'm not at liberty to say just yet, but if I could speak with the bishop it may help." The elder excused himself, disappearing amid the rows of shelves that stretched from one end of the building to the other.

Zones walked about the facilities. He headed for a point in the distance but turned around when he seemed to have gotten no closer after walking quite a bit. What he did see impressed him. They appeared to offer everything from clothing to foodstuffs, all without cost to those in need. In exchange for these gratuities, those receiving them volunteered in the various work programs offered by the church. No freeloaders here for sure, the religion's potentates held dear the scripture, "If you don't work, you don't eat."

Zones strolled down one of the aisles until it ended at a wall with large windows in it. Through them he saw the inner workings of the organization. A bakery and cannery churned out breads, canned goods and other products. The workers, dressed in white uniforms and hair nets, worked in unison to make sure that production of foodstuffs kept pace with the growing demand. A huge warehouse flanked the main entrance; it was filled to its end with pallets, some stacked so high they must be tied off with rope.

"May I help you?" a worker asked, appearing from nowhere, his foreign accent thick as if too much of something filled his mouth. He gave Zones a familiar look.

"Do I know you?" Zones stared the man in his piercing, blue eyes.

"I don't believe so. Is there something I can help you with?"

"I was just admiring the ties in your rope. I do a bit of sailing myself. What do you call it? It seems intricate."

"It is my invention." He reached up and grabbed a section of rope, his Popeye-like arm pulling it taut. He slipped a blade from his side and began to cut, slicing with little effort through the rope. "I call it the Gordian Knot, named after—"

"The Phrygian fable. Yes, I know it well." He raised his brow, looking at the knot and then back at the scarred face of the man, questioning his claim, having seen the knot before. "May I?" Zones grabbed the portion of rope with the knot in it.

"It is yours to have."

"Mr. Zones," a voice called out. He turned, seeing Elder Ansen, along with another. "Mr. Zones. Ah, there you are. This is Bishop Wadley, a revered church leader and Bishop of Welfare Square Cannery."

"Mr. Zones." The bishop extended his hand.

"Dr. Zones—It's Dr. Zones." He grabbed his outstretched hand, shaking it firmly. His grip made the other hand do all the work, soft and lazy like a breast-fed baby.

"Okay then, Dr. Zones. I see you've met Brother Allard."

"Yes, I was just admiring his rope work and sharing with him my own passion for the sea."

"Brother Allard is quite talented, he can impersonate anyone. Show him, brother." The man began to recite their conversation, but in Zones' voice. He stood there, amazed.

"That's some trick."

"And without a hint of an accent," the bishop chimed in, a wide smile of amusement across his face. "But you didn't come here to be entertained. How may I help you?"

"Well Bishop, I'm investigating a case for the FBI and some of the evidence has led me here to Salt Lake City—The LDS Church to be precise."

"Oh! And exactly what was the crime?"

"Murder."

"Murder!" The bishop and the elder looked at Zones. "Excuse my surprise, Doctor, but murders are rare here and it's not a term we hear often. The biggest problem we run into is trying not to burn the bread or overcook the pot roast."

The bishop stood there haughtily, tilting his head back just enough to make sure his nose rose above another's. He gave the air of being well-bred, rolling his words and showing all his teeth and tongue when he spoke but, despite hyper-correcting, his non-rhotic accent betrayed him. Elder Ansen, on the other hand, nervously rubbed his chin and dry white lips; he soiled his crisp, white shirt sweating. *If they are hiding something, he will be the first to crack.*

"What can you tell me about the Gadiantons, Bishop?"

"The Gadiantons? Why there hasn't been a Gadianton in almost eighteen hundred years."

"So, are you saying they no longer exist?" The bishop looked bashfully at Elder Ansen, hanging his head briefly. He looked back up at Zones, clearing his throat as if to unstick a word.

"Have you seen our facilities Dr. Zones?"

"I didn't come here to take a field trip."

"Let me give you a tour. Excuse us, brother." The bishop placed a hand on Zones' shoulder, gently encouraging him along. He remained guarded, fearing the bishop was stalling. "Our work here is important, Doctor. In these tough economic times, the faithful need the hope we offer. You see, the bread that we bake, the canned goods and the clothing are all symbols of that hope. Without it, people stop believing."

He picked up a newly baked loaf of bread and carved a slice. The smoke rose from the loaf as he carved another. He offered a slice to Zones who gladly accepted. The breakfast he'd had, the only food he'd eaten, no longer satiated him.

Zones took in the voluminous, noise-filled space, the clanking of the conveyors as they moved their cargo along, the churning of the mixers as they concocted their rue and the ovens billowing the sweet aroma of whatever was baking within them.

"And this is our granary, Dr. Zones. We store up to sixteen million pounds in this location alone. That's equivalent to 720 million one-pound loaves of bread, enough bread for every American man, woman and child to have two loafs each. And we empty them out every four to five years. We've expanded it many times to keep pace with the growing demand of the church's welfare and business needs." A caravan of trucks came and went, interrupting their stroll. "As you can see, the demand has never been greater."

"What types of grain do you store here?"

"Oh, we store barley, wheat and rye, mostly."

"What about triticale?" The crime lab had identified the grain he'd discovered at the Indian mounds crime scene as such.

"Triticale. That's a forage and fodder crop. We feed that to our livestock, pigs and cattle mainly."

"Where do you purchase this grain?"

"We buy some from the local farmers and grow some ourselves."

"Do you have any farm operations in Georgia, Bishop, or do you purchase triticale from any farmers in Georgia?"

"Georgia? I don't think so. We purchase many things from many farmers, Doctor."

"Well, I assume you keep records of those purchases right, for legal reasons."

"For legal ... Are you somehow implying that the church is involved in your murder, Dr. Zones?"

"I'm not implying anything, Bishop. I just want to know if you have a triticale supplier in Georgia."

Bishop Wadley's face grew stoic. He was sweating for the first time, even in the shade. He patted the beads away with a kerchief and tugged at his collar. He gulped hard, a visible lump appearing in his throat. He cut his eyes to the left where Elder Ansen had disappeared, then back at Zones, smacking his dry mouth and pasty lips, needing a drink of water. Zones hoped the bishop would want to satisfy a dog's smell rather than its taste and give him what he wanted. If not, he hoped the church could not afford the media glare a murder investigation would bring.

Bishop Wadley flicked his finger, summoning Elder Ansen over to him. Zones turned, he was startled to see the Elder beside him.

"Brother, bring me the list of all our suppliers in Georgia." He rushed away as quickly as he came, disappearing into one of the buildings. "You will see, Dr. Zones, the church has nothing to hide."

"I will go wherever the evidence leads me, Bishop. But while we wait, can you tell me about the Gadiantons?"

"Oh yes, your Gadiantons." He threw his hands up in the air. "Well, you see, Doctor, the Gadiantons are lying, thieving, robbers and murderers, the likes of which the world has never seen before and, I hope to God, will never see again."

"You said 'are', as in present tense."

"As I told you earlier, Dr. Zones, there hasn't been a Gadianton in nearly eighteen hundred years."

"What about the Masons?"

"The Masons?"

"Yes, you're a Mason, right? The pinky ring you try to conceal, the secret handshake between you and old boy there. Some say that the Freemasons are modern day Gadiantons."

"Dr. Zones, you can't believe everything you hear or read for that matter. As for my affiliation with the Freemasons, there is no crime in that. May I remind you that George Washington was a Mason as well."

"What does the church say about that?"

"The church has no official position on the matter."

"So, what about—"

"Ah, here we are," the bishop interrupted him, seeing Elder Ansen approach with papers in hand. He took the papers and thumbed through them. "No, Dr. Zones, I'm afraid we don't have any triticale suppliers in Georgia. So I take it that we are done here."

"If you don't mind, Bishop, may I see that." He extended his hand slightly. The bishop handed the papers to him.

Zones looked through each page. The bishop and his assistant stood nearby, exchanging words in the shadow of the tall, white granary. The constant production of foodstuffs and the ever present sound of stored goods releasing into awaiting receptors drowned out their conversation.

"Deseret Development and Holding Corporation, is this an affiliate?"

"It's a real estate development company, Doctor, among other things."

"So they buy and develop large tracts of land."

"And invest in other real estate holdings."

"May I keep this?"

"Yes, you may. Now, if there is nothing else, Elder Ansen will show you out."

"Thank you, Bishop."

Bishop Wadley disappeared into a building off the square. Zones followed his assistant back through the bakery. The young men who accompanied him were still at the front of the store building.

"Which one of you is the lucky one who gets to give me a tour of your temple?" he joked. The young men scanned each other, unable to respond, the assuredness that once draped their faces now gone. "You said it was nearby," pointing to Gordon, the eldest.

"It's a couple miles—that away." He pointed with some hesitation. "And . . . um . . . you're not allowed inside the temple."

"What do you mean, I'm not allowed inside? It's a church, isn't it? Everyone is welcomed into a church." He pushed past them and out the door he went. The sun bathed him, his hand raised to his brow shielding his eyes. "Now, how do we get a cab around here?" No one answered. He turned to see the young men perched on bikes, dressed in the proper attire. "You've got to be kidding me." Zones walked over to his ride and hopped on. Joseph handed him a helmet and off they peddled, in formation, like five horsemen riding into battle.

They peddled a short distance, winding through the streets of the city. The black and white Mormon uniform they wore drew no undue attention. After all, Salt Lake City was considered their mother ship. They dispatched these young men throughout the world like soldiers, espousing the creed of the Latter-Day Saints, exalting their beloved founder, Joseph Smith, declaring a pearl of great prize, and extolling the magic power of the thing.

Monuments to the fathers of this religion filled this place. Its high rising church spires and granite sculptures to their saints made this the Vatican City of the west. The Mormons laid claim to this land, their stake placed deeply into, not only the soil, but the very minds of the people who inhabited it. The memory of persecution still fresh, they built religious strongholds, guarded by their holy men—the potentates of this dogma. They did not readily tolerate dissent. Everything seemed controlled, from the exacting dress of the young men who accompanied Zones to the soft falsetto voice of the women, void of any threat or malice.

They arrived at the temple. Its spires peaked over the city. Its great size commanded the large square, an alabaster behemoth that gave notice of its dominance. They stopped some distance away, pausing as if they awaited permission to approach.

"What are we waiting for?" Zones asked. They looked at him, needing that final nudge to reach the temple. They peddled the short distance up to the entrance, dismounted and approached the temple doors. Gates protected them but this day they were open. Zones followed the boys as they climbed up the steps to the temple. Joseph knocked softly, trying hard not to awaken anyone.

"Man please," Zones said. With his fisted hand, he pounded the door forcefully. The young men stepped back, shocked, amazed even, at his aggressiveness. The large, heavy doors cracked open and a small, woman poked her head out through it. The young men stepped back again, cowering at the sight of her.

"May I help you?" she asked in the same soft voice seemingly innate to the city.

"Yes ma'am, I'm Dr. Zones and I was hoping to speak with one of your church leaders." The woman stared at him. She moved her eyes along the full length of his body, frowning, with a puzzled look on her face. She turned her gaze toward the others who stood behind him.

"One moment, please." She disappeared back behind the door. Zones looked at Joseph and the others, they still stood behind him, erect, hands to their sides, well mannered. He flashed them a smile of reassurance. The door to the temple opened once more, this time a much older gentleman emerged.

"I'm Doctor—."

"Zones, yes I know. The bishop called to inform us of your visit." The man surprised Zones.

"Yes, I—"

"It was my understanding that he gave you the information you sought, and now you're here," he continued, interrupting him again.

"I was hoping to ask the head of your church some questions."

"I'm sorry but the president isn't available to answer any questions. Good day, Dr. Zones." The man glared at the young men and, with that, he moved back behind the door, closing it quickly with a thud. Zones stood at the closed door for a moment, not sure of what to make of the encounter.

He turned to the young men. "So what's our next move?" They all wore the same expression. Then, as if of one mind, they turned and ran down the steps onto their awaiting bikes, disappearing into the vastness of the square complex, all but one.

Only Joseph remained. Perhaps he did not fully appreciate the displeasure of the church father. He motioned for Zones to follow him, which he did, down the steps and across the plaza to an elliptically-shaped building. Joseph tried the first door but found it locked. He tried another door and it opened. They entered, immediately hearing the sound of music and song. Joseph and Zones eased their way past the auditorium and down a flight of stairs where they came upon two large doors. They opened them and walked stealthily down a long, well lighted hall. Joseph led the way.

"What is your name?" Zones asked him.

"Joseph, my parents named me after the prophet," he whispered.

"Of course," Zones muttered to himself.

"What did you say?"

"Where are we going?"

"This tunnel leads into the temple. Only the elders and the choir are allowed to use it but I use it all the time."

"I thought you Mormons did everything you were told." He looked down at him with some confusion.

"Not me, I'm different." Joseph rolled up the right sleeve of his shirt, exposing a small, but pronounced tattoo.

"What do you have there?"

"You can't tell? It's a girl's left breast. By the time I'm old enough, I'll have an entire body tattooed on my arm." He strained to see the tattoo himself.

"What do your parents think about that?"

"Nothing, they think it's a birthmark."

"Oh. Well you keep at it."

They came to another set of doors and eased their way through them. They passed other doors off the hall, all alike. Zones tried one, turning the knob a degree at a time, inching the door open, peering inside, careful not to alarm anyone. No one there, only tables and chairs filled the space. Zones closed the door and moved on.

"Shhh!" Joseph said, throwing up his hand, coming to a halt.

"What is it?"

"Someone's coming. Quick, hide in there." Joseph pointed at the door nearest him. Zones tried the knob but found it locked. Joseph ran to another on the other side of the hall, yanking on the knob, finding it locked as well. Zones scurried back to a door they had passed, holding it open for Joseph; he managed to squeeze inside just as a group of people rounded the corner. Zones pushed the door closed slowly, trying not to make noise. He and Joseph pressed their ears close to the door, listening to the soft patter of shoes moving past them.

"Let's go," Joseph whispered, sensing the coast was clear. He eased the door open, peeking out, looking around before fully exiting. Zones stayed hidden behind the door, waiting for the all-clear from Joseph.

"Why, hello there, young Brother Joseph." Through the crack between the door and the jamb, Zones saw Joseph turn toward a smiling young woman. Her buckteeth shot from her mouth like cave stalactites and her bug-eyes exploded from their sockets like two pinched grapes.

"Hello, Sister Ann."

"What are you doing? Were you in there?" She looked at the door.

"I wasn't doing anything, just on my way to scripture—You look awfully nice today, Sister Ann."

"Why thank you, Brother Joseph." She smiled and patted her hair, fashioned in a school teacher's bun, making her look older. "Okay then, run along." She looked the door over once again. Zones stayed still, trying to remain invisible.

Joseph backed up, using his body to block the doorway as she walked off, her bible tucked tightly to her breast. He waved and smiled when she turned. He eased back from the door, pretending to go on his way. With her out of sight, Joseph said,

"Okay, it's all clear now."

"That was close." Zones emerged from the room, looking around before fully leaving the door opening.

"Yeah, we'd better go." They walked a short way down the hall, Joseph leading the way. Just as he rounded a corner, he ran into a church elder.

"Young Brother Joseph, what are you doing down here? You haven't seen Sister Ann, have you?" Zones, hearing the man, stopped short of the corner, ducking into a closet stacked with bath and other supplies.

""Um . . . I um . . . passed her on the way here."

"Well, you know this area is off limits to children. What do you have to say for yourself?"

"Um . . . um . . . um."

"Well, go on, spit it out." Joseph said nothing. "What are you looking at? Is there someone else here with you? Annie? Wait right here." Zones heard the hard stomping of feet. "You come with me."

Minutes passed before Zones opened the door and emerged from the bathroom closet, not certain whom he may encounter. Without his young guide, he moved even more cautiously than before. He listened and watched as he wandered through the maze of walls and rooms. He opened doors and peered inside, determined not to be discovered.

Zones stumbled upon a room bisected by a blue, purple and scarlet curtain made of very fine linens. Cherubim embossed the curtain which hung by golden rings from four wooden pillars, overlaid with a gold colored metal. He ran his hands along the tapestry, thinking that he had not seen anything this fine in any church he had ever worshiped in.

Burnt incense filled the air; its thick smoke obscured his vision. Zones rubbed his eyes and nose, the smoke irritating them. His allergies had gotten worse since moving to Atlanta, breathing this stuff couldn't be helping them. He looked around. On one side of the divide stood a table centered in the space and set with wares. A smaller table rested against one wall and a large, seven pronged candelabra rested opposite it on another near the divide. Candles, enclosed in crystal, set within golden holders, illuminated the room.

Beyond the veil stood a golden cube adorned with winged cherubim, their visage that of Native-Americans. A natural light source, the origin of which he could not determine, illuminated the cube. He moved closer to it, running the full of his hand along its intricate carvings; he spied the hieroglyphic text inscribed into its sides—cryptic, just like the images from the crime scenes. The connection between the murders and the Mormons had just grown a little stronger.

He walked around the cube to examine it fully, feeling like Indiana Jones discovering the Ark of the Covenant. He had never seen anything this beautiful before. He tried to lift the cube to test its weight—substantial despite its size. A seam ran along the top of the cube. He pushed against it, forcing the top ajar slightly. The lid grinded as it moved along the cube's edge. "Shit! Hope I didn't scratch it," he mumbled. Light now flooded the cube's void and revealed the gold tablets within. He retrieved one; the inscription matched that written on the cube's side.

As Zones examined the tablet, he heard voices from the hallway. He hurried to return the tablet and replace the lid, finishing just as a light came on and a voice shouted, "Who is in here?"

Seventeen

"Who is in here?" the man asked again, looking around the room. Zones remained hidden, peeking from behind the curtain. The man went about his preparations. Zones saw him lighting candles on the large candelabra, placing a basket of fruit upon the table resting against the opposite wall and placing white garments upon twelve chairs set-out. Five chairs faced each other and two chairs sat at the head. Soon others entered the room, gathering on the other side of the veil. They disrobed. Beneath their clothing they wore strange undergarments.

Their prophet stood at the closed veil as others formed a line on the other side.

"What is wanted?" the prophet asked the first apostle in line, standing stiff and erect like a nutcracker, wearing tightly bound undergarments, emblazoned with images resembling those left at the crime scenes.

"Adam, having been true and faithful in all things, desires further light and knowledge by conversing with the Lord through the veil."

"Present yourself at the veil, and your request shall be granted." The apostle stepped closer to the veil. The prophet reached his hand through an opening made in the veil and clasped the apostle's right hand, placing his thumb over the apostle's first knuckle.

"What is that and what is its name?"

"The First Token of the Aaronic Priesthood."

The prophet now moved his thumb between the first and second knuckle of the apostle's hand for the second token. He asked for and received that token's name from the apostle as well.

To receive the third token, the apostle extended his hand with fingers tight together, and the thumb extended straight up. The prophet placed the tip of his forefinger in the center of the apostle's palm, and his thumb opposite it on the back of the apostle's hand, delivering the token.

"The 'Sure Sign of the Nail' of the Melchizedek Priesthood," the prophet announced.

They continued in this way until the prophet delivered the last token of the Patriarchal Grip. The apostle received it upon the Five Points of Fellowship through the veil, as they still held the grip.

Zones watched as the apostle and prophet placed their left hands through the marks of the compass and the square which were cut through the veil. The prophet placed the inside of his right foot to the outside left foot of the apostle. They placed knee to knee and breast to breast. The prophet and the apostle placed their left hands to the other's back and then mouth to ear.

"This is the Five Points of Fellowship: Health in the navel, marrow in the bones, strength in the loins and in the sinews, power in the priesthood be upon me, upon my posterity through all generations of time and through all eternity." The apostle repeated the token and they relaxed their embrace.

The prophet parted the veil and pulled the apostle through with his right hand. He repeated the ritual for each of the apostles until none remained outside the veil.

"Apostles, take your proper stations and be clothed," the prophet commanded. Zones watched as they took their place at the chairs. They put on the all-white garments, marked with the mystic symbols. Once dressed, they took their seats.

Zones remained hidden in the room, this sanctuary within a sanctuary that gave refuge to the prophet and the apostles. The priesthood retired to this Holy of Holies to commune with their god. His presence, undetected for now, he listened, hoping to hear something that would help his case.

"I understand that we have a visitor," the prophet said. "What exactly does he want?"

"Yes, a Dr. Zones," said the Senior Apostle. "He inquired of triticale and . . . Gadiantons."

"Gadiantons!"

"Yes, apparently there have been a few murders."

"Lord, help us," someone said.

"I ask you, brothers, has anyone here resurrected the old oaths and secrets?" the prophet asked. Each looked around at the other for acknowledgement. No one, however, said anything.

"As your Senior Apostle, brothers, I urge you to speak plainly. There might be someone from the forbidden order working the dark craft unbeknownst to us. We must query our ranks but with circumspect and care. We need not bring undue alarm to the body."

"So what do we do about Dr. Zones?" the Junior Apostle asked.

"Leave him but look to our brothers in Georgia to see what they may know. If they can be of assistance to his investigation, they must do so. If there is a rogue in our midst, he must be purged," the prophet instructed.

"Yes, Worshipful Master."

"What about our work in Zion?"

"Zion? I don't see the connection."

"Well, he found his way here, what if Zion is next?"

"Contact the Temple Lot, but be gentle, brother. Do not give them cause to worry."

"Yes, Worshipful Master."

"Now let us prepare to close this quorum. Is the east guarded?"

"The east is guarded, Worshipful Master."

They closed the quorum with a prayer and filed out of the sanctum, all except the prophet who remained behind. Zones, still hidden, moved along the wall, feeling his way with his hand until he came upon a door. He turned its handle, twisting the knob a few degrees at a time, silencing the tumbles of the lock. He pushed the door open. The hinges squeaked and he went through it.

"Brother?" the prophet called out at the sound. Hearing him, Zones glanced back to make sure no one followed.

Zones hurried through the maze of walls and rooms, just as he had navigated the temple halls earlier. He walked on his toes, fearing that too heavy a step might give him away. He emerged from the tabernacle, into the afternoon sun, still trying to understand what he had just witnessed.

The forbidden order? The dark craft? They sounded clandestine and bewitching, something right out of Harry Potter. The information he had gathered seemed weirder by the minute, the more he thought about it. Zones didn't know quite what to make of it. He knew the psychological characteristic of the ectotonic personality included a proclivity for mystical orders. An introvert by nature, someone with this personality may find solace in secret societies, desiring little but holding deeply attached personal loyalties and belief systems. Carrying these beliefs to their extreme posed no problem for this personality type. The ectotonic personality made the perfect soldier for those wishing to remain in the shadows. *Might he also make the perfect Mormon?*

Zones surveilled the square for signs of Joseph, his young friend, but did not see him. He headed for the nearest square exit, looking for a library or an internet café. He hoped to confirm his new information.

"Dr. Zones! Dr. Zones!" someone cried out. Zones looked back to see Joseph running toward him. "Dr. Zones! Didn't you hear me call you, Dr. Zones?"

"What are you still doing here? I thought they sent you home."

"They can make me go away but they can't make me go home. So where are we going?"

"What do you mean, we?" Zones looked at him perplexed.

"You're black right, or do you prefer African-American? Anyway, we don't get too many of your kind around here, except for the athletes who come up from the university. So you're going to need a frontman."

"A frontman?"

"Yeah, you know; someone to translate, to make it go down smooth with the white folk, a wingman."

"You, my wingman?"

"Yeah, this is my city; there ain't nothing that goes on here that I don't know about. Go on, ask me anything."

"Okay, where's the nearest Starbucks?"

"Starbucks? Coffee? Mormons don't drink coffee."

"Really!"

"Nah . . . I'm just messing with you. We drink that shit like water. Not supposed to, but we do. Follow me." They walked down the street, the oddest of couples. Joseph bounced to a tune only he heard as he led the way. Zones, the sleuth, tried to navigate this place quietly but he stuck out like a third tit.

"Are you sure you're a Mormon?"

"Not really. I don't believe in all that God stuff. I just go to temple to keep my parents off my ass. As soon as I'm old enough, I'm out of here. I'm moving to L.A. I'm gonna be a rapper."

"A rapper—You?" Zones cast a long stare at Joseph, doubting

his rap pedigree. The radio stations played only a steady rotation of Goodnight Annabelle or a medley of Celtic music from the time he had arrived in Utah. Rap music seemed as foreign to this place as good vocals to Bob Dylan.

"Yeah, Doc, I got some serious rhymes. Want to hear my flow?"

"Well, actually—." Before Zones could say no, Joseph broke out into song.

"Doont, Da Doont, Doont, Da Doont, Doont, Da Doont, Doont, Da Doont,

Tie me up, lock me down, and throw away the key. Five-O
on every exit, I'm determined to be free . . . ."

His rap lasted for some time. As he sang, Zones caught a glimpse of two men shadowing them. When he turned, they ducked behind a post or whatever else gave them cover. Zones stopped in front of a storefront, seeing the reflection of his pursuers in the glass. Joseph continued, rapping, walking alone down the street. Zones ducked into a haberdashery. He ran through the shop, looking back to see the two men dash across the street. He found a back door leading to an alley. He ran down the gritty passage, stopping at an open door near the end of the alley. Zones calmly walked through the ice cream shop and out the front door, exiting right behind Joseph; he still sang.

When he finished, pleased with himself, Joseph let out a huge, "WHAT!" accentuated with a fist pump in the air. "Homey got skills," he declared, looking to Zones for confirmation.

"Okay, okay, lil' man got some flow. How long have you been working on that?" Zones glanced over his shoulder but didn't see the two men who chased him.

"Man, I laid those licks down overnight."

"How do your parents feel about your rap career?"

"They're too busy working in the temple, trying to become gods or owning their own planets to notice." This struck a chord with Zones. The inmate at the prison ranted on about this same thing. His crazy rant did not make sense at the time. If Mormon theology played a part in these murders, it may explain some of the symbolism and imagery at the crime scenes. He needed an Internet connection. He glanced behind him again, this time his pursuers approached quickly.

"Right here," Joseph said. They darted into the café.

. . .

"What are you looking for?" Joseph asked. They sat at the rear of the coffee shop, using the free wi-fi. Zones raised his eyes above the rim of his glasses, his head still buried in the computer screen as he absentmindedly sipped his coffee.

"You really read that thing?" Zones asked, seeing Joseph rifle through the pages of the Mormon Bible. His gaze moved between Joseph and the door.

"Every day, all day."

"Does it say anything about Zion in there?"

"Sure, but if you're so interested in Zion, why not just go there?"

"To Jerusalem? I don't think so."

"No! The prophet says they're building Zion here in America."

"What? You mean Zion is here? Where?"

"I don't know, he never said."

He pulled up a new internet search, entered in "Zion + Mormon + America". A familiar phrase popped up on his screen, "The Temple Lot", but so did a location—Independence, Missouri.

EIGHTEEN

Zones, puzzled by this new information, thought he might be on a wild goose chase. None of the dots connected precisely as he predicted. He searched through his case file for any hint of evidence that tied the murders to Independence, Missouri. He had traveled all this way out west to find the answers he sought. Perhaps the answers were closer to home?

Looking up from his computer screen, he peeked outside a nearby window. Hours had passed. The sun no longer hung at its apex. The coffee shop had quieted. The once bustling crowd now slowed down to a trickle. The afternoon caffeine junkies had thinned out, their noise no longer a nuisance. Joseph, meanwhile, slept against the wall.

"Lil' man. Lil' man, time to go." Zone kicked Joseph's chair from beneath the table, waking him.

"I'm up, I'm up."

"You say this is your city?"

"Yeah, I run this," he said, rubbing his eyes, yawning.

"Well, I need to find a hotel for the night, near the airport."

"I got the perfect spot. We'll need a cab."

. . .

"Pull right here on the right," Joseph told the cabbie. "Come on Doc, we're here." The cab slowed to a stop, the right rear door popped open and out hopped Joseph.

"Where? This is no hotel."

"I live here. You can stay with me tonight."

"Listen, kid, I appreciate your help and all but this is where we part company."

"My parents can tell you all about Zion."

"Zion?"

"Yeah, you know, the one that's in Missouri."

"I thought you didn't know where it was."

"I didn't back at the shop. My memory gets better as I get closer to home."

Zones stared at Joseph angrily as his pudgy body rested halfway inside the cab. His anger gave way to hesitation, not knowing what to think about the invitation or what to expect if he accepted it.

"How do you know what your parents know?" Joseph eased fully back into the cab. He motioned for Zones to come closer.

"I know that they know about the Gadiantons in Missouri," he whispered into Zones' ear. He needed no more convincing. Zones opened his door, grabbed his things and exited the cab.

"The fare is fifty dollars for the two of yous."

"Fif . . . Aah here!" Zones took another twenty dollars from his wallet and handed it to the cab driver.

He closed the door of the cab. It streamed slowly away. Smoke billowed from underneath it, momentarily clouding Zones' view of Joseph, who skipped along the walk to a large house with a well-manicured lawn.

A pleasant woman with a stern look on her face met them at the door.

"Well, there you are young man!" she said to Joseph as he pushed past her through the door and into the house.

"Oh, this is Zones, I mean, Dr. Zones. He's staying with us tonight," he told her, reemerging from the house. He grabbed Zones by the hand, led him past the woman, presumably his mother, and into the house.

She stared at him with some surprise.

"I'm Thelonious but everyone calls me Zones. Listen, I don't mean to intrude. I was on my way to a hotel, but . . . ."

"No! No! I understand. Joseph can be quite persuasive. I've always said that if he doesn't become a lawyer, he will be a preacher." She threw her hands in the air, laughing. "I'm Ruth."

She led him into the front room, a vast space filled with memories and images of lives living and those long dead. Every whatnot and trinket, pillow and chase had its own place. Nothing seemed out of order. Not even the wind that gusted through the open window dared

113

disturb the tranquility of the room. Zones roamed around the well-kept room. He contrasted the caring hands that saw to its making with the young Mr. Joseph, would-be rapper and future outlaw. He shook his head, finding it difficult to reconcile the two.

A picture resting on the mantle of a very large fireplace caught his eye. He moved nearer to get a better look.

"The Quorum of the Twelve Apostles," a voice said from behind him. Zones turned to see a man bearing a strong resemblance to the young Mr. Joseph.

"I'm sorry?"

"That picture—it is The Quorum of the Twelve Apostles, the very first one actually after the founders settled here. That's my great, great, great-grandfather there, Herbert Kindle," he pointed, politely taking the picture from Zones. He placed it back on the mantle exactly as before. "You must be Dr. Zones." He extended his hand.

"Yes I am and you are?"

"The guy who pays the bills, of course," he joked. "I'm William-Henry, but you can drop the Henry, only my mother calls me that. Please, have a seat. I see that you've made quite an impression on Joseph."

"Well, he's some kid." Zones sensed that the man knew little of his son's aspirations.

"Yeah, takes after his grandfather, that one. He would make the seventh generation of Kindles in Utah. His mother and I want him to become a church historian, like me, and teach at the university. Something tells me though, he has other plans. I don't imagine he would have shared that with you?" Zones said nothing. "Well, enough about us. Tell me, Doctor, what brings you to Salt Lake?"

"I'm a criminalist consulting on a case with the FBI."

"A criminalist. I haven't heard of any crime here that would warrant the FBI investigating."

"I'm working with the Atlanta office."

"You're working on a crime in Georgia here in Utah? What's the crime?"

"I'm not at liberty to say. But what can you tell me about the Gadiantons in Missouri?" William gave Zones the same stare the bishop gave him when asked about this elusive tribe. He began to think of them more as a fable than flesh and blood.

"Well, Doctor, you've come to the wrong place. You've come to my home demanding answers to a crime you can't tell me about but you imply that it may implicate the church. I don't mean to be rude but we've seen your kind around here before, 'anything wrong, blame it on the Mormons'. Well, not today. It might be best if you left."

His wife, hearing raised voices, rushed back into the room, her clothes and hair dusted with flour.

"Is everything okay?"

"All is fine, dear. Please leave us." She backed out of the room.

Fearing he may have to leave without getting any information, Zones decided to try a new approach.

"This is your ancestor, right?" He walked over to the same picture on the mantle, grasping it again firmly. He held it and pointed to one of the men in the picture.

"You know that it is." William rubbed the palms of his hands together and stared at the picture, instead of Zones.

"And you wouldn't want to see any bad press come to the church, tarnishing the legacy your family has built, would you?"

"No, of course not!"

"I'll make you a deal, William. I'll tell you as much about my case as I can; in return, you tell me what you know about this group and how they relate to Zion."

William appeared to mull over Zones' proposition, looking up at him with uncertain eyes.

"William, do we have a deal?"

"Hello father." Joseph appeared at the door of the room as if from out of nowhere. Zones turned, surprised to see him there, looking like a young English gentleman.

"Hello son." William turned his hand inward, motioning Joseph over to him. He strolled over to his father where he received a tidying up and a pinch on the cheeks. "How was your trip? Did you convert many souls?"

"The harvest is still plentiful, father," he answered properly. The jive talking, streetwise, gonna blow up the joint if y'all don't let me out of this mother-fucker, gangster rapper Master J had gone, replaced by Little Lord Fauntleroy. He looked over at Zones who shook his head and smiled, knowing, as he did, Joseph's true identity.

"Well, that's okay. Jesus couldn't do it all when he was with us either."

"Are you helping Dr. Zones with the Gadiantons in Missouri?

115

Because I told him that you were the best church historian in the whole world, and if anyone could help him, it would be you. I tried, but I haven't been to university yet." Joseph stood there, eye to eye with his father, occasionally looking at Zones over his shoulder.

"You, church historian?" His father beamed, sitting a little taller in his chair. "Why, you never . . . ."

"Dr. Zones told me how important it was to know church history and how it ties in to what he does, so I figured I should know it too." William looked over at Zones, then back at Joseph, still smiling, as if he saw himself in his son for the first time.

"And he's right. It's always good to know where you've been, so that you'll know where you're going." William ran his hand through Joseph's hair, keeping his part straight and every strand exactly as he would have it. He beamed, the tips of his smile seemingly touching his temples, splitting his face in half. Tears swelled as he fought to contain them. From his reaction, you would have thought the lad was shipping off tomorrow. "You run along now," he told Joseph, kissing him on the forehead. "Dr. Zones and I have some things to discuss."

Joseph walked past Zones, head slightly bowed, looking up with his eyes. He flashed him a smile, pleased with his manipulation. When Joseph cleared the room, William asked,

"You will tell me what this is all about, right?"

"Yes, as much as I can. Now, tell me all about the Gadiantons and Zion."

NINETEEN

"The Gadiantons are believed to be murderers, thieves and robbers, a part of LDS biblical history."

"Yeah, I get that. What's their connection to Missouri?"

"Missouri, Independence County exactly, is prophesied to be where the Lord will establish his kingdom on earth—Zion. In the early history of the church, some of the saints accused the church of forming secret combinations—"

"Secret combinations?"

"Secret societies. They were known as Danites, but some said they were Gadiantons. They were charged with driving out dissenters from the church and infidels from Zion."

"How would they have done that?"

"By any means necessary: Threats, arson, murder."

"Is there anything in their history regarding mutilation?"

"Mutilation, why do you ask?"

Zones hesitated, careful, not to disclose too much information.

"Doctor—remember our deal." William reminded him.

"My case involves bodies that were mutilated."

"Bodies!" he shouted. He sprang from his chair, rolling it across the room as he pushed back abruptly. "You mean this is a murder investigation? I didn't sign on for that!"

"Now, hold on, you remember our deal! Mutilations—were there any? Were there?"

"Yes! During their raids they . . . mutilated . . . hacked up some of their opponents."

"Tell me about that."

William took a deep breath. "The year was 1831, eleven years after the Sacred Grove," he began, now sitting back in his chair.

"The Sacred Grove, what's that?"

"The place of the prophet's first vision, somewhere near Wayne County in western New York." He paused for a moment, grabbing two glasses from a shelf, pouring himself and Zones a drink of water from a nearby pitcher.

Zones took the glass. "Thank you, please, continue," he gently encouraged him. William took a sip of water and continued, exhaling loudly.

"The prophet, Joseph Smith, had designated Jackson County, Missouri to be the new Zion," he began, his voice trembling and hesitant. "Soon, many of the saints began to gather there. In the beginning, all went well, until the church began acquiring property and, along with it, power and control. Their beliefs, our beliefs, the gentiles found strange; that was the beginning of the conflicts."

"The conflicts? I read that there were skirmishes with local authorities, Mormons were driven from parts of Missouri."

"Yes, but there was also growing dissent among the church members. The elders formed the Danites, some called them Gadiantons, as I've mentioned before. They used the tactics we spoke of earlier to drive out church dissenters and retaliate against the locals."

"Is that when the extermination order was issued by the Governor?"

"Yes. Their expulsion from the state and their eventual westward move is the reason why we find ourselves here today." William's eyes grew sullen, as if the events had happened yesterday. He took a moment to gather himself. "And that, Dr. Zones, is the story of your Gadiantons in Missouri."

He took another deep breath, expelling all the air from his lungs. His story, however, satisfied Zones' inquiry only slightly. His case had many moving parts, all orbiting the same body—the Gadiantons.

"Does this symbol mean anything to you?" Zones showed William an image he retrieved from his briefcase.

"The inscribed circle. It's a temple symbol. It represents the heavens and earth—the throne of God. Where did you take this picture?"

"If I found this symbol in, on, or around another religious site, what would that mean?"

"When you say religious site, do you mean a church?"

"Yes and Native-American burial grounds."

William reclined in his scat, saying nothing for a moment. He entwined his fingers across his belly and twirled his thumbs, one about the other. The guise of deep thought draped his face while he rested comfortably in his chair.

"This symbol, the inscribed circle . . . where did you find it at the scene?"

"On the floor, near the podium."

"And the Indian grounds?"

" . . . On top of the mound in one and in the water at another. Why? Is that important?"

William rose from his chair and walked over to a large bookcase. He pulled a book from the shelf. He opened it, thumbing through the pages.

"Do you have images of the body, Dr. Zones?"

"You mean bodies and I do."

"May I see them?"

"Now hold on, I don't think you are prepared for that."

"Please, Doctor," he said, his hand extended, expecting his request to be honored.

"I hope you know what you're doing." Zones handed the pictures to him.

"These are all in black and white."

"Yes, that's all I have."

"Do you have a description of the bodies?"

"Yes. There were different body parts sewn together and painted different colors."

"I need the exact description, Doctor."

"Okay, I have that in the report."

"Read it to me," William requested. Zones retrieved the report from his file and read from it.

"*The corpse appeared to belong to a male white, six feet . . . . The head of the body is covered in a gold substance, torso and thigh in silver, legs are coated with an iron material, feet reddish clay . . . .*"

"That's enough, Doctor. Now read this, please." He handed Zones the book he had pulled from the shelf, the pages opened, text marked for him. He read:

> This image's head was of fine gold, his breast and his arms of
> silver, his belly and his thighs of brass . . . .

Zones stopped reading abruptly, closing the book to see its cover. He was reading from the Holy Bible. He continued to read:

. . . His legs of iron, his feet part of iron and part of clay.

He compared what he just read to that written in the investigator's field report. Seeing their similarity, he closed the book.

"That passage from Daniel, Dr. Zones, describes an image in the dream of the Babylonian King, Nebuchadnezzar. It was interpreted by Daniel as the coming of future kingdoms that will foretell the ushering in of God's kingdom on earth—Zion."

"Yes, but I thought another event took place that signaled this."

"In 167 B.C., Antiochus Epiphanes sacked Jerusalem and set up a temple to Jupiter or Zeus, as he's known by the Greeks, in the Holy of Holies. He also suspended the Sabbath, the practice of circumcision and called for the sacrificing of swine in the temple. These actions were considered an abomination."

"So these crimes appear to be trying to replicate the imagery of this dream."

"More than that, your perpetrator seeks to establish Zion by bringing about the abomination of desolation."

"The defiling of the Holy of Holies."

"Yes, or in your case, any holy place."

"But why Georgia, I thought Zion, for Mormons, was in Missouri?"

"Your perpetrator is certainly a follower of LDS doctrine, although misguided. Some in our flock believe that all of America will become Zion."

"Will there be a connection with Gadiantons?"

"Perhaps, but that's where I get off this train, Doctor."

"About the Holy of Holies, the church has such a place in the temple here, do they not?"

"Yes, it's for the prophet to commune with God."

"Have they ever had anything happen like this?"

"No, I mean, not to my knowledge. The prophet controls all access to it. There are only a few who know where it's located."

"I see. One more question. You all keep a database of your members' ancestry, right?"

"You mean their genealogy? We do."

"Where would I gain access to it?"

"There's a link from the church's website. Why do you ask?"

"Just want to follow a hunch."

Having found some of the answers he sought, Zones no longer

thought of his visit to Salt Lake as a wild goose chase. Sure, questions still needed answering and theories needed to be proven but the veil was slowly lifting; what was truly behind these crimes was coming to light. Finding the culprits who committed these crimes was still paramount and for this his search would turn from the physical to the virtual.

TWENTY

Discomforting rushes of heat struck Zones' face. Humidity draped him like a sloppy kiss. The air was stagnant, the wind voided; the trench coat he wore was now a burden upon his return. The weather, a cool summer breeze the day he left, had changed into a sweltering midday arrival. He was back in Atlanta.

Zones wiped the sweat from his brow, cursing the heat, but happy to have returned. The south so vastly different than out west, had spoiled him with its easy way of life. The people here forgave even the most egregious carelessness. One found tranquility here in the midst of the big rush as scurrying souls relaxed in their wandering, aided by the soothing sayings of street poets conjuring up new rhymes and the phonetic sounds of jazz music playing to prosodic lives.

Sam met Zones at the airport. He stood outside the terminal next to his car. He wiped his brow with a kerchief, a once dry, crisp white cloth now soiled and drenched with sweat pouring in a steady stream down his face.

"Monk man," Sam called out, as Zones emerged from the terminal. He hugged him, took his bags and tossed them into the trunk along with his own charcoal grey trench coat. "How was your flight?"

"It was long."

"Yeah, I hate those west coast trips. Your aunt does too. She bugged the shit out of me about taking her to Hawaii for our fifteenth wedding anniversary. Now, I didn't want to go—shit too damn high and all. But she bitched and she moaned about it. So I said okay. Made the reservations, got to the airport, got onto the plane, it took-off and she threw-up all the way there and all the way back. I never have to worry about going to Hawaii ever again, or to Europe, Africa, any of those bitches. Now I tease her and say, 'Baby, let's go to Istanbul,' or some other far off ass place and she looks over at me with the evil eye. That shit's funny as hell." He laughed, amused at his own storytelling.

"So where do you go for vacation then?"

"We have discovered the relaxing, unrushed, tranquil—"

"And cheap."

"Yes, and cheap, pleasures of cruising. The moral of the story is, be careful what you wish for. You might just get it and then not be able to handle it." He looked over at Zones, a wry smile on his face.

"How does she like it?"

"Just fine, we're cruising over to Europe and then taking a cruise to the Mediterranean."

"Must be nice."

"Not as nice as Utah. What was her name?"

"No name."

"Come on boy, you can tell your old unc. I told you about those Mormons or Latter-Day Saints. That shit has always confused me. But those Mormon girls are freeeeaky! Now it may take you some time. Their daddies keep that stuff on lockdown and you got to get her out of Utah. They won't do anything there. That damn church got spies everywhere. But once you do, it's like Christmas come early, if you know what I mean. And whatever you do, don't join their church. That owning your own planet and spirit wives is some strange shit."

"Really now, is it any stranger than Catholicism?"

"You watch your mouth! Your mother was a Catholic."

"Yeah, some good it did her."

"You need Jesus, boy."

"Cut the crap, unc. You know damn well why I went to Utah. I know you know about my work with the FBI. I also know that you sabotaged my job with them."

"Whoa! Hold up there partner," Sam tossed his fedora, his "brim", as he called it, onto the dashboard. "Now maybe I did know about your side thing. I don't like it but it's on your own time so I can't do much about that. As for the FBI, all I told them was that it may do you some good if you were to get some practical experience working with psychopaths and killers before bringing you on as a profiler. They agreed that once you've gotten your feet wet, they'd bring you on."

"They said that?"

"Sure they did. I ain't fucking with you."

"But Agent Rose said they didn't have any more money in the

budget for the position I wanted."

"Rose wouldn't know a budget from a bingo chip. His ass is so low down the totem pole that Al-Qaeda would get the memo to a staff meeting before he does."

"You're saying he's lying?"

"I'm saying he doesn't know what the fuck he's talking about. Okay? Okay!" Sam plucked the fedora from the dash, tamped the top and dropped it back atop his head. "You niggas will make me get my gators stained fucking with y'all. They're already two-toned."

Zones gave Sam a hard gaze. He distrusted his words. He'd heard questionable stories from Sam for many years, the innocence of his father was perhaps the biggest. To his jaded ears, Sam spewed more lies, more stories.

"What has it been, an hour? Can you drive any faster?" Zones glanced at the dashboard clock. The drive to Downtown took twenty minutes. The daily commuters and the workers had long gone. The button-down suits, fancy cars, the movers and shakers, potentates of glass and steel empires had escaped the city for their suburban castles. They left their kingdom to those who wandered its streets and alleys to eke out a living.

Zones and Sam arrived at the hotel, pulling into the porte-cochere.

"I'll call you to go over the business presentation for the warden. And you may want to look into an apartment . . . ," Sam shouted through the open passenger side window. Zones glanced back, barely acknowledging him. " . . . and get off my dime in that expensive ass hotel," he muttered.

Zones disappeared into the hotel entrance. He rode the glass-enclosed elevator up to his room, enjoying its compelling view. The city glistened. Lights shone in the distant darkness like southern jewels, until extinguished by resting souls tired from the day's labor. The moon and stars hung like ornaments on a celestial tree, dressing up the pitch dark night. He took the scenery all in, preparing for a restful sleep.

. . .

The next morning, Zones rose early. The mystery of the crimes had invaded his sleep. The elusive "who done it" missing clues remained unearthed. Unable to solve the murders within his dreams, but undeterred, he flipped open his computer and began his search for the perpetrators.

He scoured the internet for "Gadiantons" and "Missouri", but found little except a few benign discussion groups. He added "Danites" to the search, but this restricted the results even further. Next he searched "Missouri" and "Danites" and came across information that pertained to an account which gave rise to them.

The story recounted an 1838 Missouri event told to him in Salt Lake regarding the Danites or Gadiantons. Church philosophy invented the group but some speculated they grew from a remnant of the occult of money diggers; Joseph Smith belonged to the same group. A band of swindlers, the Gadiantons claimed to possess the ability to locate gold by using a seer stone. In fact, they arrested Smith and charged him with violating the Vagrant Act, which outlawed such deception. The remnants of this cult remained with the church and their membership was highly guarded.

His reading revealed a number of purported Danite members and those victimized by them in a skirmish between church dissenters and church leaders. A letter sent by the Danite leaders addressed to Henry Chowder, David White, James Winter, William Peters and Lynwood Jones, threatened them with bodily harm, even death, if they did not leave the county. Next, Zones searched the genealogical database for relatives of these men. To his surprise, they all had relatives living in the Metro Atlanta area. He had a hunch.

"Good morning, Captain Franklin's office."

"James, this is Dr. Zones."

"Well, aren't we the eager beaver this morning. What can I do for you handsome?"

"You're not only smart but you have excellent vision as well."

"That's beautiful and smart, get it right now."

"Okay beautiful, I need a favor."

"I'm your genie, baby. What's up?"

"I have a list of five names and I need to know if any of them have filed a missing persons report lately."

"Okay, give me the names." Zones gave her the five names. "Let's start with Charles Chowder. He didn't file a missing persons report but his wife did, on him. Collins, she filed a report on her son. Curry . . .

I don't see a George Curry, but I have a Marc. Peters and Jones . . . I have reports filed by both of them."

"You said Mark Curry?"

"Yes, M.A.R.C," she spelled out.

"You have addresses for them?"

"Yes, I'll email them to you."

"Thank you, beautiful."

"And you better not forget it."

Zones took a moment to contemplate his findings. The odds of relatives of the five people whose names appeared in a letter from 1838 living in the same metropolitan area, also having filed missing persons reports had to be astronomical. Zones knew that he needed to interview the descendants.

He slipped out into the early morning. The first address lay northwest of the city, Marietta, back where Marmaduke started. He approached the door to the house. It flung open and a middle-aged woman poked her head out.

"Have you found my husband?" She sounded desperate. The depth of despair showed on her face, belying the layers of makeup she had troweled on.

"I'm sorry." Her demeanor startled Zones.

"My husband, have you found him? I filed a report almost a month ago. You are with the investigator's office, aren't you?" She glanced down at the temporary FBI identification hanging from Zones' coat pocket. "When I filed the report, they said someone would come by when they had something."

"No ma'am, I'm Dr. Zones, a consultant. But I am here regarding your husband Charles. May I speak with you?"

"A consultant—oh." Sadness moved over her face. "I guess so." She opened the door, stepping aside to let him in. "Please have a seat. May I get you something to drink?"

"Yes, please." She disappeared into the kitchen, the smell of freshly brewed coffee lingered in the air. He didn't drink coffee and wasn't especially thirsty. He accepted, sensing that keeping her busy would calm her.

"Is decaf okay? Ever since Charles went missing the caffeine made me so nervous. The doctor stopped me from drinking it." She walked with both cups balanced precariously on saucers, measuring her steps to keep from spilling them.

"Yes, that's fine. Let me help you with that." He took one of the cups from her.

"Thank you, cream or sugar?"

"Honey, if you have it."

"I do and I'll be right back." Once again she disappeared into the kitchen, behind a wall adorned with pictures and a collection of angels.

"You have a lovely home."

"They are Charles' family. They go back to the eighteen hundreds," she offered, seeing him browsing the images.

"Do you know much about his ancestors?"

"You mean his parents?"

"I mean his great, great, great-grand parents."

"I don't understand. What would they have to do with his disappearance?"

"Maybe nothing. What about Lisa Collins, George Curry, Robert Peters or Sarah Jones, any of those names ring a bell?"

"No, I can't say that they do."

"When was the last time you saw your husband?" Zones took a sip of his coffee.

"About three and a half weeks ago. He was on his way to meet a client to show him a property he had listed."

"Your husband is a realtor?" She nodded. "Do you know who this client was?"

"No. Charles really didn't discuss his business with me. I told all this to the detectives; it should be in their report."

"Who was his broker?"

"Harry Norman but the detectives said that the person he met with used a false identity."

"Do you know what property he was showing?"

"I'm not sure, but I believe it was a church. At first I found it strange that he would have a church listed. But ever since the market went bad, he hasn't turned down any business. His office should have that information. I have his card around here somewhere." She searched the junk drawer of a nearby table, rummaging through the items stored away in it. "Yes, here you go."

"Okay. Well, thank you, Mrs. Chowder."

"Is that it? What about Charles?"

"We're still working on his case."

"I've been waiting for over a month!"

"No one has contacted you since—"

"Since I filed the report? No."

"Do you have any personal effects of your husband's that I can take with me?"

"What do you want, his clothes, papers, his wallet?"

"Do you have a tooth brush?"

"Tooth brush. You want his DNA?" She grew sadder than before. Zones said nothing, allowing the revelation of his request to sink in. He feared that more words and more explanations would compound her grief. Mrs. Chowder stared distantly, perhaps into a future her mind had fashioned for her—one without her husband. She hung her head. Zones placed a hand on her shoulder, partly to comfort but mostly to hasten her to the task. She looked up, her dismal eyes meeting his encouraging ones. She disappeared once again behind the same picture-lined wall, reemerging with a tooth brush and a lock of hair. She eased the items to him, holding them in her cupped hands as if they were an offering, not knowing if the sacrifice had already been made.

"Thank you. I will let you know if we get anything."

"Thank you, Doctor."

"One more thing Mrs. Chowder, what religion are you and your husband?"

"Baptist. Why?"

"Nothing, just curious. Good day, Mrs. Chowder." He walked back into the still early morning, hoping he had brought some solace to her. He checked his list for the next location. The name Sarah Jones popped from the page. She lived in Marietta as well. A short drive, he soon arrived at her residence.

"Mrs. Jones, I'm Dr. Zones. I called earlier."

"Yes, please come in. And it's Sarah."

"I know that you've given the detectives a statement but I have a few more questions for you, if that's okay."

"Sure, ask me anything. We were beginning to worry that nothing was being done."

"How much do you know about your ancestry?"

"What do you mean?"

"I mean, do you know how your family came to be in Georgia?"

"I'm not sure how this could possibly help you find out what happened to my sister, give me one moment." She left him and returned with a frail-looking elderly woman.

"This is my grand-mother. She's the story-teller of our family. If anyone would know, it would be her." She led the woman by her arm, gently lowering her into a chair. "Nana, this is Dr. Zones. He's here to help us find Susan. He wants to ask you some questions, okay?" The old woman looked attentively at her, mostly at her lips as if reading them. "Go ahead, Dr. Zones."

"Hello Mrs . . ." He paused, looking over to Sarah for help.

She softly said, "Lillian."

"Mrs. Lillian, I'm Dr. Zones. How are you today?" She nodded her head and smiled. "I want to ask you some questions about your family, if it's okay. Can you tell me about your relative from Missouri, Lynwood Jones?" She said nothing; she worked her mouth as if chewing something. She dropped her head slightly and squinted her eyes.

"Yes, they moved here from Missouri."

"Do you know why they moved here?"

"My grand-mother said they were run out of Missouri after a falling-out with Joseph Smith. They were Mormons back then."

"Now, do you know the other families that left with them?"

"Yes. Yes." She worked her jaws as if loosening them up. "There were the Chowders, the Whites, the Winters and the Peters. They all moved to Georgia together. Don't know their people's whereabouts now though."

"Do you know the people who ran them out?" Once again she searched her memory for stories passed down through generations, now perhaps the key to solving the mysteries of their missing loved one and these murders.

"No, all I know is that my grandmother said the other Mormons ran them out. And she said something about a salty preacher or something like that. I forget what that is though."

"Okay, thank you ma'am."

"Come Nana." Sarah helped her from the chair and back to her room.

"I don't understand what my ancestors have to do with my sister missing," Sarah said as she walked back to Zones.

"Well, it's just a hunch that I'm working on. What can you tell me about your sister? Who were here friends? Where did she work?"

129

"She worked at a bar in Atlanta. Her friends, I wouldn't know. We are ten years apart so we didn't have much in common, including friends."

"When was the last time you saw her?"

"About eight days ago. Susan worked the evening shift at the bar. I spoke to her the night she went missing. She lived alone so I convinced her to call me every night as soon as she got in. I didn't receive a call that night so when I couldn't reach her I went to her apartment. Susan wasn't there and no one had heard from her. I called the cops that day and of course they said that she had to be missing for seventy-two hours before they would initiate a search."

"Has she ever gone without contacting anyone for any length of time?"

"Never this long. Besides, she loves Nana and would never put her through anything like this."

"Has anyone asked you for a DNA sample?"

"DNA? What for?"

"Listen, the police may need a sample to compare to any remains they may come across." Tears welled up in her eyes as she hid her face within her hands. "I didn't mean to upset you but you must prepare for the worst."

Sarah wiped the tears from her eyes. "Do you need my DNA or her DNA?" she asked, now partially composed.

"If you have any personal items belonging to her, those would be preferable."

"She should be in your system. Susan's had her share of run-ins with the law. A while back she fell in with the wrong crowd, got caught up in drugs and spent some time away. She had to provide a sample then."

"Thank you, I'll have them check the system. Here's my card. If you think of anything else, please call me. You take care."

Zones visited the other three families, asking similar questions and collecting DNA samples from them as well.

. . .

Back in Atlanta, Zones found a local coffee shop and sat down with his laptop to search for information based on what he had learned from the old woman. He entered "Missouri + Salty Preacher" for his search. It revealed nothing useful. He revised the search to "Mormon + Salty Preacher", but still no useful results. He tried a number of combinations before finally coming upon another story from 1838 about the "Salt Sermon" and a name, "Sidney Rigdon". A genealogy search revealed that he, like the others, had descendants living in the Metro-Atlanta area.

TWENTY-ONE

"Dr. Zones, this is Sarah Jones."

"Hello, Sarah."

"After you left, my Nana remembered another family who fled Missouri."

"Another family. A sixth?"

"Yes. Their name was Whitfield."

"Did they settle in Georgia as well?"

"Yes, they all arrived together, she says."

"Does she have any more information other than that?"

"No, that's all she has."

"Thank you, Sarah."

This name had not come up in the initial research. He searched the internet again, this time for, "Mormons in Georgia". He came across a story from 1840 about a Mormon family, the Reddings, and their flight from Missouri. They lived in Whitfield County. *Could the grandmother have been confused and remembered the county's name instead of the name of the family?* He searched the genealogical database for the Redding family name, none appeared. He retrieved a phone directory from beneath the night stand next to the bed and looked for the name, Redding. Many Reddings were listed but only in and around the city of Atlanta. He decided to search the Whitfield County directory online, hoping that the family still maintained roots in the county. It contained fewer names. He began to call them, starting with the first.

"Hello, Alfred Redding?"

"Yes."

"I'm with the FBI. I'm trying to reach the Redding family from Missouri."

"FBI! The feds, I can't help yah." The phone went dead, followed by the dial tone. If all his calls ended like that, he would need a ruse.

He moved down the list, calling each name and inquiring about their family history. He neared the end of the list without finding the Missouri Reddings'.

"Hello, Mrs. Redding?"

"Yes, this is she." The voice, that of a young girl, much too young to know anything about early Mormon history, piped back.

"I'm looking for Margret Redding. I'm Dr. Zones with the FBI."

"The FBI! Is everything okay?"

"Do you know how to contact her? It's important."

"She's visiting with my sister down in Atlanta." She gave Zones the number. He thanked her and then dialed.

"Hello!"

"Margret Redding, please."

"This is she."

"Ms. Redding, I'm a consultant with the FBI and I'm trying to locate the Redding family that settled in Whitfield County from Missouri."

"Yes, that's my mother's people."

"Ms. Redding, I really need to speak with you. Can we meet somewhere?"

"You say you're with the FBI? What is this about?"

"Just some routine questions concerning a case I'm working on. What is your address?"

"My niece, Patricia, would have to give you that. We're about to go to supper, but hold on, I'll put her back on."

"I live in Virginia-Highland, do you know where that is?"

"I'll find it. What time will you be back from dinner?"

"Eight or later. Tomorrow might be better."

"Patricia, this is extremely important. Is there any way you could postpone your diner?"

"You're scaring me sir. Why can't you tell me what this is about?"

"It's best if we discussed this in person, Patricia."

"Then it'll have to be tomorrow."

"I'll see you tomorrow morning, around eight," Zones said. He flipped his phone closed, shoved it into his coat pocket and slapped the table, his coffee spilling over the rim.

He had a whole day before their meeting. One more name remained for him to investigate—Sidney Rigdon.

Once again searching the internet, Zones realized that Rigdon had counseled Joseph Smith and preached the infamous "Salt Sermon". Based on the New Testament gospel of Matthew 5:13, "The Similitudes", Rigdon declared:

> *Ye are the salt of the earth: but if the salt have lost his savour,*
> *wherewith shall it be salted? It is thenceforth good for nothing,*
> *but to be cast out, and to be trodden under foot of men.*

He used this passage to justify threatening church dissenters with death and to drive them from the county and from Missouri. Rigdon eventually found himself targeted by the church. They excommunicated him and drove him from Missouri.

Zones had to find Sidney Rigdon's progeny in the event that they might also be targeted. Once again, he turned to the church's genealogical database and found members of the Rigdon family living in Georgia. One, in-fact, headed Deseret Holding Company, the business holding company of the Mormon Church. *How did the descendent of an excommunicated leader of the early church end up as the chief executive of the business arm of the church?* If his theory held up, the Redding and Rigdon families might be targeted by the killers. No one knew when or where the killers would strike next. Tomorrow could not come soon enough.

TWENTY-TWO

He watched from behind a wall of hedges, enjoying the cover they provided as he lay in wait. A blue Toyota Celica pulled into an empty bay of the Qwik Clean twenty-four hour car wash. The driver, a slight young girl, had just finished her shift at a local diner, her second job.

The young girl slung open the car door, sliding across the black interior, her baby-blue-eyes matching the car's exterior. She had purchased a compact, no doubt, to accommodate her small statue and perhaps her equally small budget. She tried to put money into a coin changer but it did not work. She returned to her car and searched for exact change for the car wash. When she found them, she put the coins into the machine, turned the knob to activate it and began to wet the car down with the handheld sprayer. The car sparkled with only a few spots; she obviously took pride in its appearance. The young girl continued wiping and spraying her car, unaware that someone was watching her.

He continued to observe her from behind the hedge, enjoying how her body cloaked the car's hood. She stretched to clean every inch of it, one foot planted firmly on the ground while the other was balanced in the air. Her twiggy legs poked through the bottom of her swing dance dress. He fornicated in his mind, thinking ravenous thoughts, wanting her. His lust boiled over to rage. He could no longer contain himself. He turned to the brute who watched with him, stalking and surveilling her moves as well.

"Bring her to me," he ordered him.

Shortly, another vehicle pulled into an empty bay beside her. The van rattled and blew puffs of black smoke into the air; its rusted frame bearing only a hint of paint. The brute lumbered from the vehicle, his wide, massive frame proportionate to the van he drove. The van squeaked, rising up a few inches as he relieved his great weight from it.

She washed the undercarriage of the car, kneeling down close to the ground. His domineering frame hovered over her, a small creature in his presence. His wide body blocked the light from a lamp, casting a broad shadow over the bay, reducing the young girl's vision. She stopped and turned slightly. His master still watched from the hedges, knowing that she would lay bound and captive very soon. His brute just needed to take her. The possibility alone aroused him, frustratingly so. He tried to relieve his pent up desire by masturbating but relief did not come. In his anger he yelled,

"Take her, now!"

She sprang up and turned around fully. Before the young girl could say or do anything, the brute reached out and wrapped his large hand around her face, lifting her from the ground. Her legs dangled in the air for seconds and then she kicked violently to try and free herself. She screamed out but her shrill voice went unheard, muffled by the hand covering her mouth. He carried the young girl over to the van and placed her in a large trunk fashioned especially for this purpose. He tried to close it but she fought him. She flailed and kicked at the lid, fighting for her life. He beat her back and closed the trunk. She knocked and banged from the inside but the padded lining dampened her efforts.

TWENTY-THREE

"The car, a blue on black, is registered to a Carolyn Armstrong, a white female, approximately five-feet-one-inch tall, nineteen years old, dark-brown hair and blue eyes, occupation, waitress." Detective Chennault read from the case file.

"Did you say waitress?" Zones asked.

"Yeah, down at the Waffle House on Ponce. Why?"

"Was she left-handed?"

He flipped through the pages of the report. "Umm, she was a southpaw. Why do you ask, Doc?"

"Probably nothing, but the M.E. matched two of the arms from the same victim, a white female. They had significant differences in bone development and arm strength, similar to what we would see when one limb is used more than the other. Waitresses tend to favor their strong side when carrying trays; in the case of our victim, the left side. Depending on when she went missing, you may want to have medical records pulled for possible DNA matching."

"That's the first sane thing you've said all day, Doc. You have any more bright suggestions like that?" Marmaduke asked.

"In due time Detective." He gave Marmaduke a little of his own medicine.

They continued to walk through the site of the Qwik Clean car wash. Paper, discarded cups, cans and other debris littered the ground. Zones moved along the perimeter of the lot where a hedge, about eight-feet high, screened the site from view.

"Over here, Detectives," Zones called out to them.

Chennault ran to Zones. "What is it, Doctor?"

"Right there—that is where he stood." Zones pointed down toward the ground with his head. Footprints and candy wrappers littered the area.

"How can you be sure, Doctor?" Marmaduke asked, now joining them.

"He could have stood here, watching her, perhaps eating candies, picking up the wrappers, looking at them. These deep foot impressions are similar to what we saw at the Native-American sites. I'm not sure, however, if he chose the victim or if he chose the site and waited for a victim."

Zones pushed his way between the hedges, careful not to disturb the ground around him. He walked a short ways along a side alley.

"Here, he parked here until he was ready to make his move."

"Get CSI over here! We need tire and foot casts made!" Chennault shouted over the hedges.

"And how do you know this?" Marmaduke asked sarcastically.

"The profile suggests that one of the perpetrators would avoid interacting with the victim, except by proxy. He's a voyeur, perhaps due to his sexual dysfunction. He stays in the shadows and watches as others perform the act that his psychosis prevents him from being able to do." Zones paused briefly, staring off into the distance. He squinted and bit down on his bottom lip, envisioning the killer in his mind. "He's the husband who hides in the closet and jerks off while he watches his wife's paramour ravish her, in your perps case, ravage her. These shrubs make a good closet, Detective. Now I don't claim to know these things for certain. Profiling is an art, not a science. But isn't that why we investigate?" Zones walked away, leaving Marmaduke to question the validity of his analysis.

. . .

"Chennault, let's get the rest of this scene processed," Marmaduke said.

"Sounds good, I'll round them up."

The other investigators assembled around them and Marmaduke started issuing orders. "All right, everyone, listen up!" he barked. "We're going to do a grid search of the entire area, starting at the victim's car. Everything is evidence. We'll sort it out at the lab. Let's get something on this fucker."

The crime scene investigators fanned out. They walked the site, shining their flashlights on the ground, at the victim's parked car and behind the hedge where Zones thought the perpetrators may have stood.

"You think you'll get good impressions?" Chennault asked an investigator as he and Marmaduke stopped behind the hedged wall.

"I'll run these photographs through TAD, see what we get," he answered. He poured a white slurry from a plastic bag into the foot impressions on the ground. Minutes later the slurry hardened, forming a cast.

Working together, Marmaduke and Chennault sketched the scene and measured distances. All points intersected at the abandoned car. Two technicians were busily dusting it for fingerprints, the black powder had peppered over the once shiny exterior.

Marmaduke found no signs of blood or a struggle. "It's like this girl went quick and easy," he told Chennault. "Like she just got snatched right up."

"You think she might've known the guy?"

"I don't know. Seems like a great place to go for a date."

"You see that convenience store?" Chennault gestured to a dumpy cinderblock storefront selling cheap food and cheap gas. A crowd of locals were huddled around a large drum with charred wood sticking up from it. They ignored the "No Loitering" sign on the wall above. "We ought to check and see if any of those guys saw anything. Maybe that store's got cameras."

Marmaduke nodded; the two set off across the parking lot. Chennault headed into the store, Marmaduke approached the three men standing around the drum.

"Anyone know about that car left in the carwash?" He got no response. One man hung his head, looking down to the ground. He swung his foot back and forth, clearing some unseen thing from his way. He kept lifting his hands from his pockets to his mouth, blowing hot air into his clenched fists as if he was cold in the early summer. The three men were unshaven with matted hair and eyes crusted over— feral children of an urban jungle.

Chennault pushed open the door, a bell clanging against glass. "The clerk in the store said the cameras on the building didn't work, that one of you would know what went down. I got twenty dollars for the first cat that can tell me—"

"I seen a van, a hooptie drive away. That's all I seen," one said, barely looking up.

"Describe the van." Chennault readied his pen to write.

"I did. I said it was a hooptie!"

"Look, if you want these two dimes, you better shake those crack webs loose and give me better information than that." The man scratched at his head, his eyes closed tightly, saying nothing.

"Ooh! Ooh! There was some writing on it," one of the others said, hopping in the air like a jester. "Dessert, that's what it said. And it was white," he added, eyeing the twenty dollars strongly.

"A white, beat-up van with 'Dessert' written on it?" He paused in disbelief. "A Dessert van?" Looking disgusted, Chennault ripped the twenty, handing each of them half. He and Marmaduke walked back to the carwash. A crime scene analyst dashed toward them.

"Detective, I believe we have a semen specimen."

"Hot damn!" Marmaduke said. "Now that's the kind of break I'm talking about! Look, Chennault, I've got to head to the office. You process that semen sample and keep making sure they check every inch of this place. I'll see you there shortly."

TWENTY-FOUR

"Dr. Zones, this is Detective Marmaduke. Captain wanted me to give you a courtesy call. We got a hit on the DNA at the carwash site. We're going to pick up the guy for questioning. Captain wants you to be there."

"What's the address?"

"It's in Buckhead, on Peachtree Street."

"Buckhead?"

"Yeah. What's the matter, not ritzy enough for you, Doc?"

"Is that a home address or a work address?"

"Home, why?"

"I'll see you there, Detective."

Zones slid out of the coffee shop, eager for the short drive to Buckhead. The address surprised him. It didn't fit the first perpetrator's profile. The sleek, urban landscape of high-end shops and five-star dining fit the second perpetrator better. Zones pulled up to the high-rise in the middle of a business district. The area was filled with people as they dashed in and out of shops and stores. The area beat with the energy that his mesotonic personality sought, but a high-rise lacked the privacy for him to play or the space for perp one, his ectotonic partner, to work. Perpetrator two must play. He had little inhibition and had to spend time with his victims, proven by the length of time from them going missing to the discovery. Zones remained open to the possibility of a second location. Every time the evidence conformed to his theory, another piece of evidence contradicted it. He wondered what this new information held in store for him.

The residence, a steel and glass tower rising above the city, shimmered and glistened, a glass sculpture honed from the imagination of a master architect. Buckhead sat north of the city, a wealthy enclave of homes, businesses and shopping malls. The city's elites, the peddlers of influence, the merchants of luxury, the political and business strongmen who guarded their stations and treasures at all cost, made their homes here. The wealthy lived and played in Buckhead while the poor came here to sip from their ruby slippers and live a life temporarily that many would never know.

"Dr. Zones," Marmaduke greeted him as he entered the sparsely decorated, modern inspired lobby.

"Detective."

"We are just about to go up."

"I can't let you up without a warrant," a woman said from behind a large wooden desk.

"Chennault." Marmaduke motioned to him, whereby he presented the woman with the warrant.

"I need to call the resident," she told him, raising the phone up to her ear, preparing to call.

"No! No calls! Officer, make sure no one does anything foolish," he instructed, looking hard at the woman.

The detectives, officers and Zones all piled into the elevator with the building's security officer. They watched the elevator pass each floor, rapidly ascending to the penthouse level. They eased quietly out of the elevator, the building security officer leading the way.

"Mr. Rogers! Mr. Rogers! Building security, Mr. Rogers!" he shouted through the door. They waited briefly for a reply but none came.

"Open it," Marmaduke instructed. He unlocked the large, heavy wooden door, unexpectedly quiet for its size, welcomed by those who wished to enter unknown. Marmaduke moved the security officer to the side, they entered, guns drawn.

"Mr. Rogers! Atlanta P.D. We have a warrant," Marmaduke shouted. They moved stealthily through the maze of rooms, looking for anyone hidden or otherwise, but they found no one.

"It's all clear!" an officer shouted.

Zones entered and began to look around the home. He gazed out over the city from a window with a spectacular view. He continued to look around the well-kept, artfully decorated, expensively furnished space. An opened Architectural Digest lying on a coffee table caught his attention. He picked it up, reading the caption below the photograph of a well-dressed man standing in front of the very building they just invaded.

"Detective Marmaduke!" he called. The detective soon appeared at his side. "Meet your perp." He held the magazine up to him.

"Architect of the year. Still doesn't mean he can't be a crazed killer. Well Doc, what do you and your Ph.D. think?"

"I don't see this as the lair of your killers, certainly not perp one. Look around you, Detective." Zones turned with him, looking at the space. "You see a finely decorated space with contemporary paintings, fine tapestries and sculptures. Your second unidentified subject loves physical adventure and courageous combat. He would have a space filled with images of his high-risk adventures and extreme exploits. He's a hockey player or a mixed martial arts enthusiast. He may even be a hunter. We see none of that here."

"How come every time we have a viable suspect, you come along with your double-barreled theories and shoot them down? Seems to me you're stretching this thing out like you and your uncle stretch out those consulting contracts. Oh yeah, I had my boys to check your uncle out. He bids on six-month contracts that magically get extended to five years. Whatever kind of hanky panky y'all pulling with those prison boys, it ain't gonna work here. And besides, you're trying to say that rich folk don't kill? I tell yah, you college boys and your theories."

"No, I'm saying that the last place you'll find a sociopathic killer is a high-rise condo in the middle of Buckhead. Where would he dismember a body? From the looks of this guy, he would no more soil his freshly pedicured hands cutting up bodies than you would use yours flipping through the pages of a twelve-step program manual."

"What are you trying to say, college BOY?"

"Oh! So we're going there!"

"We can go here, there or anywhere!"

"Okay, you're a drunk, a functional one, but a drunk none-the-less. You probably have a stash either on you or in your car. Try as you might, the mouthwash you down every half-hour can't mask that hundred-proof breath you exhale or pour from your sweat. I take it your Captain doesn't know or else you'd be behind some desk while you dry-out. Should I go on, Detective?" Zones knew all the signs of being a drunk; he had learned it the hard way. He witnessed his father beat his mother unmercifully, killing her in one of his stupors.

"Why, you little shit!" Marmaduke shouted, moving toward Zones, his hands fisted and ready to strike. Chennault and another detective standing nearby rushed over to pin his arms.

"You better leave, Doctor," Chennault said.

"I don't care what the Captain says, I'm not gonna work with a prick like your motherfucking ass!" Zones turned to leave. "Let me go, damn it," Marmaduke demanded, throwing Chennault and the other detective off his tightly held arms. "Where does this asshole work?"

"Who, the Doctor?"

"No! Who gives a shit about him? This faggot ass guy!" He waved his hand around in the air.

"He's an architect with Portman."

"Okay, have the A.P.D. go down and pick him up and bring him to our station."

"What about the Doctor?"

"What about him?"

"The Captain ain't gonna like you not working with him."

"I'm working with him just fine. We got DNA and a match from a site he identified. Let the Captain try to deny that. And let the good Doctor try to debunk it. Now let's go get this guy. The good Doctor can continue to chase ghost theories."

TWENTY-FIVE

Nestled on the outskirts of the city's business district, the harsh steel and glass towers gave way to the tranquil charm of Virginia-Highland's southern bungalows. An eclectic mix of hair-dyed punkers and well-suited executives strolled along its European-styled ways. The history of the place spilled from weathered pub signs and old ladies and gents sipping tall glasses of sweet tea from the coolness of their porch swings.

Virginia-Highland bustled with people in the streets, tasting, touching and experiencing Summerfest—a time for street parties, the Parade of Homes and Taste of the Highlands. Late into the evening, people still invaded the streets in search of hedonistic pleasures. In this carnival-like atmosphere, Zones slowly made his way to the home of Patricia Redding. Red and white barricades with black and white patrol cars blocked-off the streets. He drove around looking for a place to park, finally finding a gypsy spot some distance from his destination. He waded through the mass of people celebrating whatever fancy crossed their minds. The scent of southern barbeque, apple pie and peach cobbler lingered in the evening shade. Young women and young girls Riverdanced to the sound of Bluegrass music. The tap of their heels, as they leapt into the air, scuffed up the blacktopped road. Artists and clowns entertained the young, giving them their fair share of balloon hats and painted faces, their parents delighting in their children's good time. This activity filled Zones' senses with a lust so palatable that he lost his bearings in the mash of people. Now lost, he stopped a reveler and asked for directions to set him back on his path.

Zones soon came upon a small bungalow. He stopped in front of it and stood near the curb at the edge of the street. He snatched the paper with the address written on it from his pocket. He looked down at the curb edge, the address matched. A well-manicured lawn exploded with color from the spring tulips and calla lilies. Birds, even with the sun long past setting, still chirped from a nearby magnolia tree. Lights illuminated the walk leading up to the cottage-styled home, set back off the street, drawing no undue attention to itself. Zones approached the door of the dimly lit house, ringing a bell that sounded irritated with him pressing it. No one answered after several tries. He peered through the glass pane of the door but saw nothing. He moved to a window at the front of the house, careful not to look too suspicious.

"Ms. Redding!" he called out to her loudly, still no answer. He crept to the side of the house; he found a van parked there rear first in the driveway with its doors open. It looked quite out of place but workmen often practiced their craft well into the evening hours at the request of their patrons. He continued down the side of the house, peering through each window. He came upon one with its curtains drawn, parting from the breeze flowing through its partially opened sash. A light illuminated a form lying still on the floor. Movement from the corner of the room toward a bed drew his attention. He saw a woman bound and gagged. She struggled to free herself but to no avail. Zones stepped back from the window, shocked and confused. He retrieved his phone from his coat pocket and dialed 911.

"911, what is your emergency?"

"There are two people in immediate danger. I need the police and an ambulance here right away," he whispered, trying not to reveal himself any further.

"Where are you located sir?"

He took the paper with the address written on it out of his pocket. He gave it to the dispatcher.

"Is there anyone hurt on the scene?"

"There's a woman lying on the floor, not moving."

"Can you check for a pulse?"

"I'm outside and I think someone is still inside."

"Can you have them check?"

"No! They may be burglars."

"Burglars? Oh, I see. Stay where you are. Help is on the way. I'll remain on the line until they arrive." Zones thought for a moment, peering into the room again, seeing the struggling woman, fearing that little time remained to rescue her from the fate that awaited her.

"I'm going in."

"Sir! Sir! Don't go in the house. Remain where you are, I have help coming."

Zones rose from his crouched position outside the window. He pushed the cracked sash up, looked around the nearly darkened room and eased himself through the now wide open window. His approach startled the woman on the bed. Their eyes met, hers widened with fright. He raised his finger to his lips, motioning her to keep quiet as he reached down to check the body on the floor. He rounded the bed where she lay and began to untie and disentangle her from the restraints. Zones had seen this unique knot three times before. As he dug his fingers in between the strands of rope, twisting and tugging at the knot, she began to move wildly.

"Remain still," he warned her in a whisper.

The rope pinched the young woman in half, squeezing where it wrapped around her. Even breathing drew the rope taut. Zones looked around for something to cut her free. He found a small pocket knife attached to a key ring resting on top of a table near the bed. He clutched it tight to keep the keys from rattling. The tiny blade proved difficult to open. He bit down on it with his teeth, the hard steel stinging them. With the blade partially out, he extended it fully and began to cut at the rope. Slowly the edges frayed. He worked the dull knife furiously to cut her free.

She continued to struggle against her restraints. This time, however, her eyes widened even more than before. She mumbled through her gag. He reached to remove it. He sniffed the air, smelling a foul odor of rotting garbage and decomposition. Just then, the floor creaked loudly. Zones turned. A heavy hand, in the form of a fist, struck him on the side of the head. He glanced off the bed and landed with a thump on the floor.

. . .

Zones popped his head up from the floor of the bungalow. Sirens blared in the distance. He lay stretched out, grabbing and rubbing the back of his neck and head, aching like never before. The room swirled around him when he sat up. *Whatever hit me really got me good.* Zones looked over to the floor near the window. Seeing the body still there, he struggled to his feet, and stumbled over to her. He felt along her neck for a pulse. A faint throb pressed back against his finger. The sirens outside grew louder and soon the small bungalow was swelled with police.

"What the hell hit me?" Zones moaned, still rubbing his head. He struggled to sit up.

"Just hold still sir," the paramedic said, wheeling Zones out of the house.

"What is this, an ambulance? I'm not going to the hospital." He struggled to the edge of the gurney.

"Are you sure you don't want to see a doctor?" the paramedic asked, trying to bandage Zones' head.

"No. I'm fine. Will the old woman be okay?"

"Yeah, got wacked pretty good though. She's still out. Tough old bird, taking her over to Grady now."

"What about the other woman?"

"What other woman? We only saw you and the old lady."

"There was a van! They must have taken her in the van!" Zones hopped out of the back of the ambulance, heading for a detective inside the home. He took a few steps, stumbled and landed hard on the green grass.

. . .

Zones woke up the next morning in Grady Hospital to the unwelcomed questioning of an officer.

"How did you come to be there? Did you know the other victim?" he asked. Zones explained some of what he knew without going into the details of his case. He didn't want to muddy his investigation. Satisfied with what he heard, the officer had no more questions.

"Officer, could I get a ride back to my car?"

"Sir, I haven't released you to drive," a doctor said. "The meds I have you on can cause drowsiness."

Zones turned to see a familiar face, one from the television.

"You're with the Inter-Faith Council and on the task force with the councilwoman, Doctor . . . ?"

"Hyde. And you are," he looked at his chart, "Mr. Zones."

"Actually it's Dr. Zones. I'm consulting on the case for the FBI. So you really are a doctor?"

"I'm afraid so, my church ministry is an unpaid position." Zones nodded, but questioned this. "So what are you consulting on?"

"I'm helping them profile the un-subs . . . the perpetrators."

"I see. And what does your profile say about our killers?"

"Unfortunately, Doctor, I'm not at liberty to say."

"I understand. In that case, Dr. Zones, you're cleared to go but not to drive." He scribbled on a pad, ripping away a sheet. "Here's your prescription. You can fill it on your way out." He handed Zones the paper. "Follow-up with me in a couple days."

"Can you give me a lift to DeKalb County P.D.?" The officer looked at Dr. Hyde for approval. He nodded in agreement.

They stopped at the hospital pharmacy. Zones shoved the prescription at the young woman behind the counter. She took it, punching into her computer.

"I'm afraid we don't have this prescription, sir."

"What? But the Doctor just wrote it." Another woman, a little older, joined her, taking the paper.

"You saw Dr. Hyde for a concussion?" she asked.

"Yes, but now I've got a headache." She excused herself, disappearing behind a wall.

"I just spoke to Dr. Hyde," she said, now back at the counter. "The prescription is for Elavil, not Livale. Transposition—he'll do that now and then. Just ask him when you suspect that," she told the young woman.

. . .

The drive ended soon after it began. They traveled against the morning rush hour traffic and traversed the city in a way only an officer of the law could.

"Thank you, officer." Zones eased from the squad car, his head still wrapped and aching. He popped one of the pain capsules into his mouth, hoping it would kick in soon and relieve him of his discomfort. He climbed the steps to the entrance and made his way inside the building, toward the Captain's office.

"Doc, over here," James called, seeing him walk through the doors. Zones sluggishly headed over to where she stood. "What happened to you? Never mind, I don't even want to know. They're down in interview room five, straight down the hall."

"I need the DNA from these tested and compared against our five victims." Zones reached inside his coat pocket, handing James the small plastic bags containing the samples he had collected from the families. He stumbled down the hall, bracing himself against the walls as he wandered from side to side. Soon he stood in front of interview room five. The walk took longer than normal. He rested outside the door; he unwrapped his head bandage, tossing it in the trash and collected himself before entering.

"We have your DNA, Mr. Rogers!" Marmaduke shouted from within the room. "If this girl dies you get the needle, you prick."

"Dr. Zones, where the hell have you been?" Captain Franklin asked, seeing him as he pushed through the door. "James has been trying to reach you all morning." He looked at Zones' ruffled appearance, frowning. "You look like shit! What happened to you?"

"Listen, Captain—"

"You know who that is in there? That's your perp, one Frank Rogers. We got his DNA from the carwash scene, right where they said you told them to look. Good work, Doctor." He slapped Zones on the back. A rush of pain shot to his head. He tensed up, the discomfort showing in his face, the medication not yet working as it should. "We might be able to close this case and then I can get the councilwoman off my ass," he said, observing their suspect from another room.

"Captain."

"What?"

"He's not the perpetrator."

"What do you mean? We've got his DNA."

"I don't care, he's not the one."

"Don't you fuck with me, Doc! If he ain't the perp, then who is?" The Captain squared up to Zones, hands on his hips, mean-mugging him, like an aging prize fighter flexing before the fight.

"I don't know but I know it's not him; I got a concussion to prove it."

"What do you mean?"

"I was following a lead, when I went to investigate, I was attacked and the perp took another victim."

"Hold on, you went to investigate? You don't investigate, Doctor." He thrust his index finger at Zones. "We investigate, you consult. Come with me." They left the observation area and entered the interrogation room.

"Detective Marmaduke, Dr. Zones here seems to believe that we have the wrong guy."

"We got hard evidence, Captain, evidence he pointed us to. Don't you see what's going on, Captain? He's more concerned about lining his pocket than solving this case."

"Well Doc, is he right? Is this about money?"

"I'm not even going to dignify that."

"See! What I told you?"

"May I, Captain?" Zones asked, wanting permission to question their suspect. The Captain motioned for him to go ahead.

"Mr. Rogers, can you think of any reason why your DNA would be at our crime scene?" He did not respond.

"He hasn't said a thing since he got here. That's because he's GUILTY!" Marmaduke chimed in.

"Listen, I'm the only one here who believes you are innocent. If you don't help me help you, then it's just going to be you and the three of them." Rogers looked around at each of them. They stared back like a pack of wolves. His face grew long.

"How do I know this isn't some good cop, bad cop routine?"

"You don't but you have to weigh your options here."

"You're just concerned about murders right—nothing else?"

"All we care about are murders, right Captain?"

"That's right, just murders. Now let's hear it."

Rogers cleared his throat and swallowed hard, preparing to speak, still looking uncertain.

"I was in the area . . . I have a reoccurring appointment with . . . I see . . ."

"Are you trying to say you were buying pussy?" the Captain interrupted. A long pause passed between them. Finally,

"Yes."

"What was your DNA sample?" the Captain asked Marmaduke.

"Semen."

"What patrol works vice in that area?"

"That's Johnson's beat," Chennault answered.

"Okay, give him a pen and paper. Write her name down, the corner she works and the dive she hustles out of," the Captain commanded him. Rogers took the pen and paper. His hands trembled while writing the information the Captain requested, unlike the steady hands of a master architect. When he finished, the Captain snatched the paper from the table, handing it to Chennault, saying, "Call this in." Chennault took the paper. Sometime later, he returned to the room. "Well?" the Captain asked.

"They found her and she remembers Romeo here. Said he insists on bringing her roses. He likes to pretend they're on a real date. Apparently he's a regular."

"Good thing your wifey has a 24-hour drive-in," Marmaduke joked.

"She added something else. Said some pervert offered her two bills for a sperm sample. Said it could have been his' she gave him."

"Everyone get out, now!" The Captain yanked the door open. They all piled out of the room. "Didn't we just go through this with the redneck?" he bellowed. "Now you bring me some fancy pants with a thing for prostitutes! Time is running out here—Well?" He got no reply. The Captain banged his fist against the door. "Somebody, tell me something," he demanded, throwing up his hands almost in defeat.

"If I may, Captain."

"What do you have, Doctor?"

"I need you to contact Atlanta, have them look for a second missing woman."

"A second missing woman?"

"Yes, she was abducted from a home in Virginia-Highlands."

"And how do you know this?"

"I was there; that's how I got this bump on my head—when I followed up on a lead."

"Oh yeah. Well, I have my own case load to worry about. I don't need to get involved in anyone else's."

"I believe she's victim number seven."

"You mean she's connected to my murders? Okay, all of you in my office. And cut him loose." They followed the Captain, stomping back to his office. "James, no calls and no interruptions." He slammed the door behind him and paced back and forth, rubbing his clean-shaven head and taking deep breaths. "Okay, Doc, give me what you have and don't leave nothing out."

"I've identified five missing persons who matched the M.E.'s description of the five bodies. I've spoken to their relatives and collected DNA samples—"

"Spoken to their relatives! Collected DNA! Captain, he's interfering with our investigation. None of that DNA is any good without CSU collecting it!" Marmaduke pounded his fist on the Captain's desk, rattling the objects on it. He stood with his mouth agape. A menacing frown draped his face and a vein on his neck noticeably throbbed.

"Quiet, Detective, we can always recollect if we have to. Go on, Doctor."

"As I was saying, I'm confident that the DNA will match."

"No one told me about any DNA. Where is this DNA now?"

"I gave it to James to have it processed."

"Figures. Go on."

"During the course of my investigation, another potential victim came up. I was at her home to meet with her when someone knocked me unconscious."

"And this potential victim?"

"I believe the same people responsible for the other murders abducted her."

"And how did you figure out who these victims were?" Marmaduke asked. He folded his arms and leaned back in his chair. A soft tap from his shoe marked the time between his asking and Zones' answering. To cap off his disdain he smirked.

"**Shit, Marmaduke, I'm asking the questions here!**" the Captain shouted, looking hard at him. "Answer his question, Doc." Zones opened his mouth but no words came out. He sighed, reluctant to share his theory, fearing it made his evidence less credible. He looked over at Marmaduke, now resting comfortably in his chair, all pleased with himself as if full from some fine meal.

"First of all, they are all legitimate missing persons. I had James cross-check them in the database. Secondly, whether you agree with my methodology or not, you can't argue with the fact that there is a missing woman out there."

"Was there an answer somewhere in there, Captain? I didn't hear it."

The Captain, like Marmaduke, folded his arms and tapped his foot. When he puckered his lips and cocked his head, Zones knew that he had to explain.

"All of these victims, including the most recent one, had a Mormon ancestor who was forced by the church to leave Missouri in the early nineteenth century."

"So you're still on this Mormon thing. I thought you said it could be any of them—religions that is," the Captain said.

"I did but now I'm confident of the link."

The Captain thought for a moment. He plopped in his chair and grabbed his head.

"Alright Doctor, I'll go with your theory. But, as I warned you before, my job isn't the only thing at stake here. If shit goes sideways for me, POOF to those perky little contracts of yours with the prison system. And I will make it happen. Do we understand each other?"

"Yes, Captain, but what about the call to Atlanta?"

"I'm on it now. If there's nothing else, I suggest you two get to work."

"There is one more thing—the possibility that the CEO of Deseret Holding Company may be linked to this case."

"CEO of Deseret Holding! Tanner Rigdon? Didn't we run security for that big swank he had last year down at the convention center?" the Captain asked, looking over at Marmaduke. He nodded. "Linked how?"

"I don't know yet. He or someone in his family could be a victim—or a perpetrator."

"Perpetrator! What the hell, Doc, I must have too much hair left on my head; you want me to pull the rest of it out!"

"Deseret Holding does over a billion dollars' worth of business in the state," Marmaduke added.

"Yeah and Rigdon makes campaign contributions to over half the state's politicians, including the mayor, the governor and the councilwoman. So we're not going to even go there. I don't want to hear anything about Tanner Rigdon associated with this case. This conversation never happened; it doesn't leave this room and that's an order."

"So that's it, just like that?"

"How about this, you said all your other possible victims had missing persons reports filed, right?"

"Yes."

"Did Rigdon?"

"No."

"Then case closed, Doc."

"So you're protecting this guy?"

"Guy! What guy? I wasn't talking about any guy, were you, Detective?"

"No, no guy here."

"See Doctor, no guy. Now, get out. And Dr. Zones, remember what I said," the Captain admonished him as he walked out the door.

"Where to now, Doc?" Marmaduke asked him sarcastically.

"Where is Deseret Holding located?"

"You heard the Captain, mums the fucking word on Rigdon."

"Excuse me, Dr. Zones, there's a call for you, your Uncle Sam. You can take it there," James told him.

"Damn!"

"Business calls," Marmaduke teased.

"Hello."

"Monk! Where the fuck you been? I've been trying to reach you since last night!"

"Hey unc. I um . . . lost my phone."

"Damn boy, they're gonna be some lonely bitches around tonight, not being able to get a hold of your ass. You better get back online quick, or ole unc may have to do his civic duty and re-enlist into the motherfucking player's club god-damn-it! Cause you know, back in the day—"

"Is there something you wanted?"

"What? Oh yeah, we have a 9:00 a.m. appointment. It's a presentation in the city so I'll pick you up at 8:00 a.m."

"Okay, I'll see you in the morning."

Just as he hung up, James rounded the corner, coming from the Captain's office.

"Dr. Zones. Good, you're still here. Atlanta wants you to come back over for a statement. Marmaduke will give you a lift."

"A statement! They want to meet with me while two women's lives are in danger? They need to be dragging the area for that van."

155

TWENTY-SIX

Patricia worked the frayed section of rope until it broke. She scrambled, fumbling through the darkness of the cramped trunk for the lighter she kept in her pocket with her cigarettes. She felt the van sink down; she halted her search. Her captor had returned after making a long stop. The van pulled off. She hurried to find the lighter. Patricia flicked it and a flame illuminated the space, revealing some of its contents.

She moved the flame along a pile of things toward the rear of the trunk. When she reached the back end, a face broke through the darkness, mouth and eyes bound tightly. This startled Patricia and she dropped the lighter. She searched hurriedly for it, found the lighter, struck it once again and discovered another girl's body.

Patricia placed her trembling hand up to the exposed nose, feeling a slight breath. She touched her. The girl, bound like a rodeo steer, began to cry.

"Shhhh! Please be quiet." She tried to silence the bound girl. Patricia removed the tape from around her eyes and mouth. Their captor groaned loudly. The girl let out a scream. She shoved her hand to her thin lips, muffling her cries. Her big, blue eyes, bat-like in the darkness, grew wider with fear.

"Help me! Help me!" she begged. Patricia reached behind to untie the girl's hands and feet. The rope pinched down tight around her boney arms and legs. She moved her hand along the crisscrossing paths of rope, trying to find a knot to untie. The rope's path led her along the girl's wrists and ankles, around the back of her neck and around her waist. She came upon a knot.

"I'm going to try and untie you," Patricia whispered. "I need you to stay still."

"Okay," the girl said, whimpering.

Patricia put down the lighter to work the tight knot loose. She dug her fingers between sections of rope abutting each other, trying to separate them. She worked as fast as she could in the confined space. The urgency of the moment showed on the bound girl's face.

"Is it loose?" She twisted her neck and head behind her. Patricia still struggled. The knot battled against her. Intricate, not your ordinary bow tie, her attempt to unravel it failed. She felt around the trunk, looking for something, anything to help loosen the rope. When she found nothing, she plucked the lighter from the floor, struck it and brought the flame up to the rope. She watched as it charred the fine twine and burned away the woven threads one at a time. The rope slowly unraveled but the flame dimmed, losing its strength before finally going out. She flicked it over and over, trying to light it. One hard flick and the lighter lit again but by then the van had slowed to a stop. The trunk's lid flew open, flooding the space with light. The brute stood before them, grunting. He reached for Patricia, slinging her over his shoulder.

"Help me!" she screamed, striking the brute about the head and back. He hauled her inside a desolate farmhouse. They had reached the place where their captor worked his evil.

TWENTY-SEVEN

Zones did not share all he knew with the officer at the hospital. He didn't want to muddy up his investigation. However, a young woman's life depended on his willingness to provide more information. On the way to the Atlanta Police Department, he rehearsed his story, what to say and how to say it. Zones had to convince them of Patricia's abduction, without getting into the details of his analysis. He decided to keep any stories of Gadiantons to himself, along with tales about Mormons, abomination or ancient religious feuds. Besides, he'd had enough trouble trying to persuade the DeKalb authorities, especially his escort, to follow his evidence to its end.

Marmaduke barreled down the highway, trying to keep the bottles of Wild Irish Rose and Thunder Bird from rolling beneath his seat. The bottles clanked as they collided with the other empty ones he kept there. Zones had already revealed his vice to him but he did not want to be the one who confirmed it. The two didn't speak much at first; each hugged their door handles, one leaning as far apart from the other as possible as if some unseen barrier separated them.

Zones looked around the interior of the car, its tattered finishes a symptom of old age and neglect. Marmaduke caught Zones' smug look and gave him a hard look back. He asked,

"What?"

"What do you mean, what?"

"I saw that look."

"What look?"

"That turned-up nose look."

"I don't know what you're talking about."

"If you got something to say, say it."

"Okay then, is this the best you can do?" Zones looked around the interior again.

"Oh! Well I'm sorry that the transportation doesn't meet your highness' standards. I'll request use of the Bentley the next time I'm to chauffeur royalty around."

"Well, you asked."

"That I did. We'll see how your highness likes sharing his transportation with fifty of his subjects on a bus."

A car approached the passenger side of the vehicle traveling extremely fast. The driver swerved into their lane.

"Watch this guy," Zones warned.

"What? You're Drivers Ed. now? I was driving while you were still riding Big Wheels."

They said nothing for a while and then Marmaduke asked,

"How does this psychoanalysis thing work anyway? Not that I believe it, just curious." Zones glanced over at Marmaduke, certain that eight years of rigorous study could not be watered down into a thimble's worth of explanation. To pass the time, he tried.

"What makes us who we are, Detective, is our life experiences. You've lived a different life than I have." He paused to let that sink in. "And that's what makes you, you and me, me. If I wanted to know how a hard-driving, experienced Homicide Detective would react to his environment, I would study you."

"And for a know-it-all, 'I'm gonna show the man', psych-cop, you would study you," Marmaduke shot back.

"Touché, Detective." Zones smiled. "Your perpetrators are no different. We may not know them but we know of them. We've studied them before. We know their signature."

"Signature?"

"Exactly as it implies, an identifying mark. Their criminal 'John Hancock', if you will."

"And what signatures do you see in these crimes?"

"The psychological signatures, other than those I've mentioned already, would be that one perp is a thinker, the other is intuitive. One's an extrovert, the other is introverted. They attract each other because they are opposites, each finding in the other what they themselves are lacking. They come together to make a whole."

"Sounds like a fucked-up pair, if you ask me, some evil sons-of-bitches."

Zones nodded in agreement. Just then, Marmaduke slammed on the brakes, avoiding the speeding vehicle. A loud clank sounded. Bottles rolled from beneath his seat. He thrashed his feet, trying to corral the stampeding bottles.

"Damn it! These people can't drive."

Zones, seeing the bottles roll and Marmaduke's attempt to conceal them, said nothing, he continued . . .

"Now there's an interesting word—evil."

"What do you mean?"

"It's an ancient concept. In fact, as long as there has been the notion of good, there has been the notion of evil. Their origins, however, come from man's interaction with man rather than man's interaction with God. Therefore, for me, the concept of evil is derived from man's need to explain the absence of good in man. Now, as far as there being an 'entity' called evil, this is purely sociosomatic."

"Explain this sociosomatic, Doc." Marmaduke corralled the last of the bottles back beneath the seat.

"If we lived in a society where there was no crime, no misdeeds, no trials and tribulations, then there would be no concept of evil or no reason to rationalize the misfortunes that we experience as a society. Therefore, the concept of evil is manifested into an entity for the sake of pacifying society's fear of itself."

Marmaduke cut his eyes to Zones, saying nothing. His head spun. Zones sensed he did not understand any of what he had just heard but he did not want to appear ignorant.

"Any more questions, Detective?" He looked down toward Marmaduke's feet; Marmaduke followed his eyes to the bottles peaking from beneath his seat.

"Tell me, where does a black man get a name like Thelonious?" Zones smiled, accustomed to the question.

"My grandparents. Our family's tradition demands that the grandparents name their grandchildren. My great-grandfather was a fan of the jazz composer, Thelonious Monk, and my great-grandmother was enamored with Othello ever since she saw Paul Robeson in the Shakespearean production. They named my father Thelonious Othello Zones and his parents named me the second.

"Oh!" Marmaduke said, without giving the answer another thought.

Zones pulled out the knotted rope he had gotten from Utah and studied it.

"What is that, Doc?"

"A puzzle—one I'm finding very hard to solve."

"You know how I solve a puzzle?" Zones gave him his undivided attention, expecting something profound to help him solve the knot problem. "I look at the answers in the back first." Zones' face dropped.

They arrived in Downtown Atlanta moments later. The streets were filled thick with morning traffic. Cars jostled for position, weaving in and out between lanes. Tires screeched to a sudden halt or raced to beat the change of the light. Pedestrians moved blindly amongst this chaos, an intersection where man met machine. In this way they traveled, sticking out like a fat woman in the Sudan amongst all the cleaner, newer cars. The drive frayed Zones' nerves, hectic but civil. Southerners, polite in their road rage, said nothing. They made no menacing gestures or brandished or used firearms. Instead, they stared, steely, cold, piercing gazes felt deep within the flesh, lasting well past the drive. This killed you.

. . .

"So Dr. Zones, how do you know the missing woman, Patricia Redding?" Detective DuBoise asked, sitting pretty in his chair like a little girl having tea. He looked to be of dubious heritage, high yellow with light eyes. He glanced at his writing pad from behind wire rimmed glasses, his hair slicked back, good hair, they called it, a toothpick tucked securely in the corner of his mouth.

"I was scheduled to meet with her on the DeKalb County mutilation case I'm consulting the FBI on."

"And how was she connected to the case?" His look grew intense. "And should I be concerned that your case may have spilled over into my city?"

"I wasn't sure. That's what I wanted to meet with her about."

"You're a profiler. How did your profile determine that she was a possible victim?" Zones paused, glancing over at Marmaduke who sat quietly next to him. He kept to himself about how he truly developed the missing woman as a victim. He needed to end the Detective's questioning, or risk being here all day explaining himself.

"I never said that I profiled her, Detective. But to answer your question, her name came up when following other evidence. Now there was a van parked on the side of the house, an old rusting one, a crew van like the ones you see on construction sites."

"Okay, thanks, Doctor. We'll get a BOLO out on that."

"So is Atlanta P.D. joining the task force to help find her?"

"No, but we would like a copy of your case file. We'll assign our own detectives."

"You'll have to get that from DeKalb County. Detective Marmaduke could help you with that."

Zones spent just over one hour being questioned before heading to the crime scene. He held back the knowledge of his analysis but not the knowledge that her disappearance may be connected to the other murders. The revelation disturbed them.

"Where's Marmaduke?" Detective DuBoise asked Zones.

"He already left."

"I'll have an officer give you a lift back to DeKalb."

"That's okay. I left my car parked close by."

"Oh yeah, Doc, you said you lost a phone. Is this it?" He pulled a plastic bag from his coat pocket, tugging at it to free the phone, showing it to Zones.

"Yes. That's it."

"Got it before the crime boys, so no paperwork. Thanks, Doc. We'll be in touch."

Zones stepped off the curb and into the street, departing the bustling scene, heading for his car. He walked much the same path he had walked when he first visited the home, a path that only hours before overflowed with the festivities of a community in celebration and revelry. Shopkeepers and street vendors swept and wiped in preparation of the masses returning to indulge in all they offered, most unaware that a monster lurked among them.

. . .

Zones flopped in his car seat and flicked on the radio. "This is the jazz of the city 91.9 FM, WCLK," the DJ announced. *"A Love Supreme"* flowed through the tenor saxophone of John Coltrane. He turned up the volume. Sax blared through the car's small space. The music put him into a thinking mood. He fired up the engine and headed for Midtown. Zones had one other piece of business he needed to take care of—an audience with the great Tanner Rigdon.

The Captain may have been intimidated by Rigdon's power and influence, but Zones had grown up on the rough streets of Compton. What was a Wall Street white boy compared to a tangle with the Crips and the Bloods? Gaining entrée to Rigdon would not be easy, however. He needed a ruse.

TWENTY-EIGHT

The Peachtree Starbucks played host to an eclectic mix, a popular haunt even during the middle of the day. Atlantans never let a little thing like work get in the way of a piping hot cup of coffee and a sweet roll. People came here for the same reasons—to see what's going on and to be seen. No one knew why rational people would erect such lavish monuments to such a small bean or why other rational people made pilgrimage to them on a daily basis. But build they did and come they did, each finding no wrong in the insanity of the other. Zones found himself drinking and eating with his fellow devotees—bacchanalians all of them.

He took a sip of his coffee. Steam from the hot libation rose from the warm cup. A headline from the Atlanta Journal-Constitution he was reading captured his attention. *"Deseret Holding to Break Ground on New Development in Midtown"*, it read. Rigdon's company invested millions of dollars into a new luxury, mixed-use development. The wheels began to churn in Zones' head. He had an idea.

"Brullinni's. How may I help you?" someone answered. It was the diner where Candi worked. He never noticed the name before—Italian, selling soul food.

"Candi, please."

"Hold please." A loud noise echoed through the phone. Zones heard the clank of pots and pans, the background noise of what seemed to be a busy day at the diner.

"This is Candi."

"Candi, it's Zones. I need a favor. Could you meet me? I'm at the Starbucks in Midtown."

"Is this you Sugar? I don't get a break for another hour. What is this about anyway?"

"I'll explain when you get here."

Candi arrived over an hour later, her entry noted by the turning of heads. She sashayed through the shop, looking bodacious as ever. Zones looked up from the paper he still read, just in time to see her approach.

"Thank you for coming."

"Now what was so important that you had me come all the way to Midtown on my lunch break?" She sat down in her tight, form-fitting dress. The buttons on it desperately clung to their loops, some on the verge of pulling through.

"I need you to call this guy and pretend you're my secretary from *Developer Magazine*. Tell him that we want to do a full page spread and cover of him and their new development in Midtown. Get him to make an appointment today. Okay? Here, I've prepared a script."

"So all I have to do is pretend I'm your secretary and read this script."

"That's all."

"I've never been a secretary before but I'll try."

"Here's the number." Candi took the paper with the script and number written on it and began to dial, calling out the numbers as she pressed the buttons on her phone.

"Is this Mr. Rigdon's office? I'm calling on behalf of our editor, Mr. Zones. He would like to write a feature article on Mr. Rigdon and your company's new development in Midtown. He has a few openings today and would like to schedule time with Mr. Rigdon . . . Okay." She moved the phone from her mouth, placing her hand over it. "She just put me on hold," she whispered to Zones, popping gum and shaking her crossed leg as if she were gossiping with a girlfriend. Zones smiled and nodded in approval.

"What magazine am I with?" she repeated, looking over toward Zones again. "I'm with LGBT Community Magazine." Zones' eyes widened in disbelief.

"No! No! No!" he said softly, shaking his head rapidly back and forth in disapproval.

"It's L.G.B.T. and it stands for Lesbian, Gay, Bi-sexual and Transgender and we cater to that community."

Zones felt his plan falling apart, his ruse sabotaged. He covered his head with a newspaper, fearing the worst.

"Not interested, huh! So Mr. Rigdon has no problem taking our money but he has a problem talking to us? Who does he think will be buying those homes and shopping in those stores, Tony Perkins and Michelle Bachman? You tell Mr. Rigdon that, just in case he doesn't know it, he's building right in the middle of gaydom. Also tell him that Mr. Zones wishes him good luck trying to sell those condos with a big fat 'NOT GAY FRIENDLY' sign at the entrance."

"Give me the phone," Zones said, grabbing at her. She slapped his hand way.

"Well, I don't know, Mr. Rigdon. I've spent two hours just trying to make an appointment with you, but let me see." Zones stopped trying to take the phone. "You know, Mr. Zones is very busy and we've got other interviews lined up: the Mayor, the Governor, President Obama, the Pope, but I'll see." She playfully pretended to search through a schedule. "I'll have to move some things around but he'll be there. You have a good day, Mr. Rigdon." She hung up, her role well portrayed. The look of defeat was wiped from Zones' face. "How did I do, Sugar?"

"You did great, a little off script but great."

"You care to tell me what that was all about? You're no magazine editor. Lucky for you, I flipped the script. The gays have all the juice now. If you want to shake up these stuffed shirts nowadays, you got to threaten G-bombing them."

"Well, it has to do with a case I'm working on and you don't want to know the details."

"If you say so. Can a girl at least get a kiss?"

He leaned over and kissed her. She was happy to have helped.

Twenty-Nine

"Mr. Rigdon will see you now," his secretary said, appearing from behind two very large wooden doors. She escorted Zones back to another set of large doors. "You may go in." She left him at the entrance to Rigdon's office. He hesitated for a moment then pushed against the door. Rigdon was sitting at his desk, finishing a phone call. He rose from his chair, extending his hand out. Zones shook it.

"You must be Mr. Zones."

"And you must be Tanner Rigdon."

"Please, have a seat."

"Very nice office, love the view."

"We bought this building right at the height of the real estate collapse. It sold two years prior to that for twice what we paid for it. Goes to show you the price of patience in this business." Zones nodded in agreement, looking around the spacious office, adorned with all the self-aggrandizing trophies of someone full of himself. A series of large images hanging on a wall captured his attention.

"You climb?" Rigdon asked, seeing Zones' interest in the pictures taken of him rock climbing.

"No, but I love sailing. Not a lot of opportunities for that around here though. Say, that's an interesting knot, what do you call it?" Zones asked, seeing an enlarged image of it.

"I call it the Gordian Knot, named after the Phrygian fable. Are you familiar with it?"

"No, can't say that I am. So this is your invention?"

"Yes, developed it while climbing the Matterhorn."

"I see." Zones knew he had lied.

"But you're not interested in that. You know, I was surprised to hear from your organization. I don't get many requests for interviews from you people. It was refreshing to hear that you weren't another one of those development magazines trying to sell ad space by disguising it as an interview." Rigdon smiled. "So, ask away."

"Thank you for your time. Now your company, Deseret Holding, it's actually owned by the Mormon Church, isn't it?"

"We are the business arm of the church," he answered nodding. "Off the record, I don't have anything against your type. That little dustup with your people and the church over that marriage thing was a call made by the robe wearers in Utah. Live and let live, I always say."

"Thank you," Zones smirked, moving around in his seat. "What other types of businesses are you involved in?"

"Well . . ." he sighed, taking a deep breath, pausing, "we have agricultural operations, manufacturing, financial services and, of course, real estate."

"And how much control of the business operations does the church have?"

"Like most corporations where there is a CEO, there is a Board of Trustees providing oversight. It's no different here. But I'm responsible for the day-to-day operations."

"How has Deseret managed to prosper in an economy that has been quite hostile to most businesses, especially real estate?"

"That's called minding your 'Ps & Qs', Mr. Zones. We have operations in every time zone so we must stay abreast of all markets. Our business forecasting is the best."

"Tell me about your agricultural operations."

"Yes, we have cattle ranches in Florida and Nebraska, farming operations in various states and throughout the world."

"What kind of crops do you grow on your farms?"

"The typical: vegetables, fruits, grains—"

"Tritical?"

"I'm not sure what that is."

"It's a forage and fodder grain for feeding livestock—cattle, pigs. It's not important, just thought you may be familiar with it. Now, do you own any farming operations in Georgia?"

"Not at the moment but Georgia is a possible expansion area."

"Are you currently scouting for locations and if so, where?"

"Now Mr. Zones, if I told you that, the price of land in the area would double overnight."

"Fair enough, Mr. Rigdon. Perhaps you could answer this. Do you find the job demanding?"

"It can be but I take command and get things done."

"So you're the take-charge type? Have you always been this way?"

"Absolutely, only way I know how to be. I love having the reins in my hands." He thrust his hands forward, clutching the air, shaking them and clenching his teeth. "I've been this way forever. The best time of my life was my early childhood, when all the other kids, even those older than me, followed my lead."

"What bothers you most about the job?"

"Other than the small hotel rooms they make me stay in," he quipped, "the times when I'm not in control."

"And when is that?"

"Let's just say rarely." Rigdon answered questions without reservation. He rocked in his chair relaxed and confident, just the way the trap maker liked it. The questions Zones posed were not merely small-talk, but rather a well-designed way to assess his personality.

"Now, we know about the Midtown development. Does your organization have any other major real estate acquisitions or developments planned for Georgia?"

"Midtown is our only major development in the state."

"Really!" Zones thumbed through pages of his notes. He buried his head in them, searching for information he already knew the answer to. "What about the Bethel Primitive Baptist and Iconium Baptist Churches sites? And didn't you also bid to acquire the Kolomoki Mounds and Indian Springs sites?"

He looked up from his notes for Rigdon's reply, watching his eyes turn from receptive and gleeful to steely and withdrawn.

"Who are you really?" he asked.

"I'm Thelonius Zones, editor of LGBT Community Magazine."

"You're no magazine editor. Who are you?"

"Tell me about these properties and whether or not the church knew of Deseret's interest in them."

"This interview is over unless you tell me who you really are."

"My name is Zones and you're right, I'm not from a magazine. I'm a consultant.

"A consultant for whom, one of my competitors?"

"I'm not at liberty to say."

"Listen, I don't know anything about the properties you've

mentioned. Our company has no interest in them; I'm sorry, but you're sorely mistaken. But I do have a proposition for you. Come to work for me. I like your resourcefulness, how you schemed your way into my office. I can use a man like you. I'll pay you twice what they're paying. You can be my double agent—what do you say?"

Zones ignored his proposal and continued his questioning. "You had ancestors in Missouri that split from the church in the early nineteenth century. When did they reconcile with them?"

"What! Now you've really lost me! I don't understand any of this. This discussion is over."

"What do you know about the mutilations at these sites and what do you know about Gadiantons?"

"I don't know anything about mutilations and I don't know anything about Gadiantons, Mr. Zones, if that's even your real name!" He sprung from his chair and walked to his office door. "You can leave now!" he demanded, holding the door open. Zones remained seated, not moving, confident, assured that he held the upper hand.

"Sit down, Mr. Rigdon," he told him. Zones looked forward in his chair, his back to him.

"Call security!" he directed his secretary.

"If you don't know anything about these crimes, how come a vehicle registered to your company was seen leaving two, not one, but two of the crime scenes? Call me crazy but I would say that's as close to knowing about something that one could get." Zones now faced the door Rigdon stood near, seeing a guard approach.

"See this gentleman out." The guard rushed toward Zones. He stood up, gathered his things and calmly marched past Rigdon.

"I'll see you around—soon. Oh yeah, smile." Zones took Rigdon's picture with his cell phone, surprising him.

"**I'll rip your fucking head off if you show your face around here again!**" Rigdon yelled. He followed Zones out with his eyes, certain to see him again.

Rigdon had reacted like someone who had something to hide, a guilty person. Unlike the other families Zones had questioned, he became defensive and uncooperative. If he was involved in these crimes, what did the church know about them, if anything? *The Captain's unease, if he knew Rigdon had been questioned, would turn into downright fear if I implicated an entire religion. This, however, might be my course if the evidence pointed that way.*

. . .

After his interview with Rigdon, Zones arrived at the architectural firm of John Portman and Associates, located just blocks away from Deseret Holdings in Downtown Atlanta.

"I'm here to see Frank Rogers," he told the receptionist.

"Is he expecting you?"

"I'm his frat brother from college, thought I'd surprise him while I was in town."

"He doesn't normally see anyone without an appointment."

"He'll see me. Just tell him I met a very sweet girl who lives in Decatur; she loves roses and intimate dates and I'd like to introduce him to her."

"Oh! That's so sweet. Mr. Rogers works so very hard. He should meet a nice young girl, you know, to help relieve the stress. Some of the girls here are such floozies," she whispered.

"Oh don't worry; she's a professional at stress relief." She dialed his extension, conveying to him what Zones said. Rogers rushed from his office, walking briskly down the corridor, looking straight ahead. He approached the receptionist who directed him to Zones. A magazine was shielding his face.

"Hello Frank!" Zones greeted him as if old friends.

"What are you doing here? I thought I was through with you. And what's with the sweet girl in Decatur business? Are you trying to get me fired?"

"Calm down. I'm not trying to get you fired, I need a favor."

"A favor! Why should I do you a favor after everything you put me through?"

"If you remember, you'd be facing kidnapping and murder charges, not working in some fancy building, had it not been for me. Now think about that before you say no."

"What's the favor?"

"Our Decatur friend, I need you to introduce me to her."

"What!" he said loudly, drawing the receptionist's attention.

"Is everything okay Mr. Rogers?" He smiled and raised his hand.

"After everything that's happen, you now want me to go back down there? No! I refuse."

171

"You refuse?"

"Yes. I refuse. As you said, you've already cleared me so you can't hold that over my head." With that said, he headed back down the corridor toward his office.

"Okay," Zones said. He walked over to the receptionist. "Frank is joining me in his boss' office later; how do I get there?" She pointed him in the direction opposite Rogers' office. "One more thing, is there a costume shop nearby?"

"Yes, downstairs in the mall." Sometime later, Rogers left his office and headed that way as well, reaching his boss' office.

"I'm here to see—."

"Come in Frank," his boss said, seeing him outside his office. He entered. "This is Dr. Zones."

"Shalom, brother." Frank's mouth hung open, seeing Zones in this get-up. He cut a glance to his boss who looked puzzled.

"Are you all right, Frank," he asked. He nodded. "Dr. Zones is with the Temple Shanahnah. They're looking to build a new sanctuary and he asked for you specifically."

"Yes, brother, our rabbi requires that the new temple not be defiled, so we need an architect that is pure so I was referred to you. You are pure, no?" Zones asked smiling, yamaka on head, Bible in hand.

"Pure?"

"Yes, nothing has defiled you like drunkenness, gambling, cavorting with roundabout women."

"No."

"So if we were to ask law enforcement, say for example DeKalb County, where we're located, if you have been charged or suspected of any of these things, they would say no?"

"No! I mean yes!"

"You confuse me, brother. Is it yes or is it no?"

"It's no! You won't find anything."

"Great! Now are you free to visit the site with me?"

"Well, actually, I'm . . . ."

"Of course he is, Doctor. Frank, take a long lunch," his boss said. They left the office. Rogers stared hard at Zones, thinking him ridiculous in his get-up.

"Are you kidding me, a black Jew?"

"Read your history, we were the first Jews." Rogers again stared hard at him.

"What's next? Are you going to want me to do anything else after this—like testify? You promise me that all I have to do is point her out?"

"Yes, just point her out."

"I'm driving," Rogers insisted as they reached the parking garage. They piled into his candy apple red convertible Benz sport coup, black leather interior with stained hickory wood inlay, personalized plates, chrome whips riding on twenties—the kind of car that attracted the attention of raunchy women.

They reached DeKalb County quickly. Graffiti was scrawled across the support of the overpass, it read, "The Belvederes". They pulled off the interstate and onto a street where a bevy of young girls strolled the area for no apparent reason. They turned into a motel parking lot, its sign leaned badly. The name of the place was deteriorated to unreadable. Rusting metal ornaments hung loose from their supports and tattered cloths waved in the wind. The place was a dive well-suited for broken souls.

"Right there, room ten." Rogers pointed to the door.

"Room ten?" Zones confirmed, looking at him strangely, trying to reconcile this well-bred from Buckhead with the shit-hole place he found himself in. "What's the knock word?"

"The what?"

"The knock word. The word you give her to let her know that it's you and not some nigga trying to jack her. Listen, I know the game."

"It's . . . it's the name on my tag."

"Your license plate? HA, HAAAAA." Zones clapped his hands together, amused by the revelation. Rogers sat there, obviously embarrassed having to tell him that, and angry that he found the name amusing.

"I shouldn't be long or do you want to come in for a little reunion?" Zones teased. "Wait right here."

He popped the door, eased from the cramped car and walked to the room. He stood there, staring. Zones walked to the rooms on his left and right. Their doors did not have numbers either. Whores learned that ploy quickly to confuse the police in the event of a raid. He walked two rooms down to find a number and then counted. He tapped lightly.

"Who's there?" a voice shouted.

"Tinker Bell," he replied, barely able to contain his laughter. The door to the room swung open. A woman dressed in black lingerie with a huge smile on her face stood before him.

"Tinker . . . Why you're not my Tinker Bell." Her wide smile shriveled to a pucker and her once outstretched arms gripped her hips. The sound of tires squealing came from the parking lot. Zones turned to see a candy apple red streak tearing out, disappearing down the street.

"Son of a bitch!"

"Was that my Tinker Bell?"

"Are you Marilyn?"

"Yes. Who's asking?"

"I'm Zones. I need to ask you a few questions. You told the police that someone paid you money for a sperm sample." She looked Zones up and down, hands still on her hips, doing a slight Mae West shake.

"You paying me for this time? I talked to them because they're the popo. It's gonna cost you." Zones frowned and sighed, reached inside his wallet and handed her twenty dollars. She took the money and stuffed it inside her bosom. "Yes, he offered me two-hundred dollars for it. I thought it was weird and shit, but two hundred dollars is two hundred dollars. You feel me?"

"Did he specifically ask for anyone in particular—their sperm, I mean?"

"Nope. Just said sperm."

"Was this the guy that asked you?" He slipped his phone from his pocket, showing her the picture of Tanner Rigdon.

"No. The guy that asked me had darker hair, beady blue eyes and a scar right here." She ran her finger down the side of Zones' face.

"Okay, thank you, ma'am." Zones flipped his phone closed. He turned to walk away, fearing he'd lost his final chance to implicate Rigdon.

"That was the guy who picked it up and paid me."

Zones flipped the phone back open. "This guy? This guy paid you?"

"Yes! Yes! He tried to disguise himself and all but that was him."

"If he was in disguise, how can you be so sure?"

"Honey, in case you haven't noticed, all I do all day, every day is see men. He could have put on as much makeup as Little Richard and I still would have recognized his ass. Besides, the chump came back later trying to get a freebie, dropping his pants, showing me his thang like I've

174

never seen one before. It took him some time though, had to get out of this white girdle—called them his protective underwear. Strangest damn thing I've ever seen, a man in a girdle but I ain't judging."

"What happened?"

"What happened? I tried to break him off a piece, you know, a little pro bono, as they say. But the damn fool couldn't get it up. Got mad and ran off. Never saw his face again until you showed me that picture."

"Okay then, thanks."

"One other thing, if he tries to say that I'm lying, ask him about the birthmark he has shaped like a jellyfish on his ass."

. . .

Zones got what he wanted from Marilyn—Rigdon in possession of evidence found at one of the crime scenes but he feared he needed more. Captain Franklin needed more. He dialed Marmaduke for an update.

"Detective Marmaduke, this is Dr. Zones. I was calling to see if you had any luck tracking down where those pig appendages came from?"

"No, Doctor, not yet. Apparently there's a place that can check animal DNA now. When they compared our sample to that of the pigs at the Crawford place, they didn't match. We're still looking though. But your DNA results did come back; all five are a positive match to our corpses. Looks like you're ahead this inning, Doc."

"That's good news, Detective, means we're on the right track. But if we don't want a sixth or a seventh victim, we need to find the farm where those pig limbs came from."

"I'm afraid you've got other problems too. Captain got a call from the councilwoman, the mayor and the bishop of Rigdon's church concerning your visit to his office. He ain't happy."

"Why did he call them? I didn't even say who I was working with." Zones was worried that this might happen, Rigdon throwing up roadblocks by calling his political cronies. The last thing he needed was political influence injected into his investigation.

"Not sure, he must have called around."

"Maybe he'll feel better once he hears that I can connect Rigdon to that DNA sample gathered at the car wash."

"Connect him, how?"

"Apparently he paid for it."

"Wait a minute. I thought Rogers' hooker got paid for that."

"Her name is Marilyn. And she remembered him too."

"That's your proof, the word of a hooker? His lawyers will have a field day." Marmaduke chuckled, almost laughing. "Whore truth is worth whatever you pay for it."

"All I need is to get him to come in for questioning."

"Good luck with that. He's too politically connected for that to happen. Unless . . . ."

"Unless what—unless what, Detective?"

"Unless the media gets wind that he's wanted for questioning. That may loosen up his lips."

"And who would provide that wind?"

"Leave that to me, Doctor."

"I thought you didn't believe my theories."

"Let's just say that, so far, your theories have gotten us closer to solving this case than we've ever been."

"So you admit that I can investigate."

"No, you're still a college boy . . . I mean man."

"That's okay, Detective, understood. I guess I'll go and see what the Captain wants."

"I'll see you there."

When Zones got back to his car, he headed straight for Rigdon's office. Just as he parked, he saw Rigdon walking up Peachtree Street, entering a car. Zones waited as long as he could then pulled out into traffic and followed Rigdon through Downtown. He dodged both cars and people who left the use of a crosswalk to little old ladies and children.

"Where are you going, Mr. Rigdon? Somewhere incriminating, I hope."

Rigdon parked at a small office building populated with doctors and other healthcare service providers. Rigdon entered one of the offices. Zones followed, making certain that he remained unseen. He peeked inside one of the offices through a glass opening in the door. Rigdon was seated in the waiting area until called by the nurse. The name on the office read Susan Sloan, Ph.D. Zones returned to his car and waited. An hour passed before Rigdon reemerged from the building. Again Zones followed him.

They approached Midtown, turning onto Twelfth Street. He knew the area. It looked less menacing during the day. Rigdon pulled onto Piedmont Road and parked right outside of *Heels*. Zones watched him exit his car, scamper across the road and approach the same non-descript door he had entered through eight days ago. He observed Rigdon knock and then disappear inside. His company built their Midtown development on the same block so Rigdon being in the area didn't surprise him. But going into a sex club before opening hours, however, that raised questions. He remembered the conversation between the clerk and the officer at the jail during his release. He called James.

"I got an address for you." He stretched his head out the window, looking for the address to the club. "1080 Piedmont Road. Who owns it?"

"It says here that it's owned by The Gabriel Corporation."

"Any directors or executives listed?"

"The corporation is held in a trust. I have the registered agent's name, Mizrah Coen. Would you like his contact information?"

"There's a reason why people have trusts and registered agents. What do you have on two dead crackheads found at that address? It used to be a florist back then."

"Just that, two dead crackheads, nothing suspicious was found. By the way, aren't you supposed to be meeting with the Captain?"

"Damn! Tell him I can't make it."

"Now you know that's not going to fly. Give me something better than that."

"Uhh . . . ." Zones couldn't think of anything.

"That's okay, leave it to me." James grumbled something about always covering his ass under her breath.

"I heard that. Thanks anyway," he said relieved. "One more thing, what do you have on a Susan Sloan, Ph.D? She has an office on Peachtree Street."

There was a pause as James typed.

"Says here that she's a psychologist; her specialty is obsessive compulsive disorders, pretty blonde too."

"Your system keeps all that on file?"

"I Googled her."

"Thanks. Gotta go."

Zones waited until Rigdon left the club. He followed him to a gated community north of Atlanta. He remained there, not returning to his in-town condo.

"*What are you up to Mr. Rigdon?*"

THIRTY

Zones arrived at the DeKalb precinct and headed straight for the Captain's office to find James. He stopped short of her desk, peering around a corner, out of sight. He drew her attention with a wave of his hand. James looked at him wickedly, wagging her finger as if he had done something naughty. She checked around her and then waved him over.

Zones eased his way to her desk. "I need a favor," he said in a low voice.

"You know that you're in a world of trouble with the Captain, don't you?"

"He hired me to solve these murders and that's exactly what I'm doing. I can't help it if the evidence takes me in a direction that he's uncomfortable with."

"I hope you know what you're doing."

"That's what my first girlfriend in high school said."

"Well, did you?"

"Got her pregnant that night."

"You're so full of shit. What do you need?"

"You have access to the tax records database?"

"Why?"

"I need to know if Tanner Rigdon owns any property in Georgia. If you can't find any, check his parents and his siblings. You can get their names from their family Facebook page. I'm looking for rural property, farm land, somewhere they can keep livestock. If you find anything, cross reference that location with feed stores that carry triticale."

"You're sure you want to do this? Captain's already talking about pulling your contract and kicking you out of here."

"Then you better find me something or you won't see my pretty little face around here anymore."

"Gone, get out of here."

"Dr. Zones, may I see you please?" the Captain bellowed from down the hall, about to enter another room.

Zones watched as the Captain disappeared into the room. He looked back at James. She laughed but tried to hold it. He moved to the door the Captain had entered. The sign read, "Gentlemen". Zones stepped inside, wondering why the Men's Room and not his office.

"Over here, Doc," he called. He moved closer, toward where the voice emanated. Sounds he heard echoed off the tiled walls and floor. Zones peeked beneath a stall where a pair of pants rested on the floor with two legs growing out of them. He stopped in front of it.

"You a military man, Doctor? 'Cause if you're a military man, you may appreciate what I'm about to explain to you."

"No, I'm afraid not, Captain. But we have two missing women that—"

"In the military, you have what we call a chain of command. Say that with me, Doctor."

"Listen, Captain—"

"Doctor! You're not saying it." A loud sound came from within the stall. A pungent odor filled the air.

"Chain of command," he repeated, trying not to breathe the stale, malodorous air.

"There you go. Now what that means is that I have someone who is responsible for directing my actions. I'm responsible for directing others' actions and so on and so on. This is how the universe works, somebody or something being responsible for and being responsible to somebody or something else. Since the dawn of fucking time, shit has worked this way. So what makes you think that it's going to change for you?"

"If this is about Rigdon—"

"Who? Because I distinctly remember saying that name was not to be mentioned again."

"I have evidence that he purchased that semen sample and I have an eyewitness who can identify him as the one who purchased it. That places him at the scene of one of our crimes."

"And just how did your witness identify him?"

"I showed her a picture of him."

"Was it a photo array?"

"A what?"

"Photo . . . Did you show this witness other images of similar individuals of like physical characteristics?"

"No."

"Then you don't have a witness, Doctor." The door to the stall swung open. The Captain squatted there, looking up at Zones from his reading. "And I thought that I told you not to question Rigdon. Now I got the councilwoman and the mayor on my ass over your little stunt. Chain of command, remember, Doctor? It's all moot anyway. Rigdon's attorney called; they scheduled a time to come down and talk."

"An interrogation?"

"No, not an interrogation, a conversation. You got that, Doctor?" The Captain lowered his paper, giving Zones the stink eye.

"Yes, Captain, I got it. So when do we get to . . . converse with Mr. Rigdon?"

"They want to come in tomorrow."

"I have an appointment early tomorrow morning but the afternoon should be good."

"Who the hell said you were going to be there?"

"If I hadn't lit a fire under his ass, he wouldn't be talking to you at all. Now Captain, you hired me to solve these crimes—let me do it." The Captain looked up at Zones from his toilet seat, a grimace on his face.

"I'll see you tomorrow at noon, Doctor, but we're not waiting."

Zones felt relieved that the Captain now seemed onboard with the way he was handling things.

"What about the search for the two missing women, Patricia Redding and the one from the carwash? Are they still searching?"

"The dogs tracked her from the carwash for a while but lost the scent. For the Redding woman, you'll have to check with Atlanta."

"Is that it? We don't have much time. They've both been missing for five days now. We're right at the kill window."

"What do you want from me, Doctor, to form my own personal search party? We're doing all we can do. You need to bring me a viable suspect. Until then, I don't want to hear your condescending bullshit. Now close my damn door—let a black man shit in peace." The Captain snapped the paper he read taut and resumed his reading. "And Doctor, you keep your child support up or they'll haul your ass to court and lock you up again. Georgia doesn't play that shit. Don't let that be the reason you miss another one of my meetings."

Zones tore out of the bathroom, gasping for air. The Captain's last comment didn't make much sense but he felt better about the direction of his investigation, particularly the chance to interrogate his prime suspect. With his money and influence behind him, Zones knew he had only one opportunity to prove that Rigdon's hand lay all over these murders. Perhaps, more importantly, he had one chance to find out where they hid the missing women.

THIRTY-ONE

Zones and Sam wound through the Benteen Park neighborhood on their way to the prison. They passed a large clearing bearing the area's name, void of any park amenities, used more like a large cut-through. They turned down streets where patches of grass sprinkled lawns overgrown with weeds and brush. They dodged potholes and jockeyed with people for space in the road. The community was in transition, from poor to rich, they hoped, but there were no guarantees—life here was more chess than checkers. Like most impoverished communities, development came slowly. Very few conveniences existed for families living in this enclave of mostly small post-Civil War homes and some newly built bungalows.

The community struggled to stay alive, fighting to remain relevant. While their closest neighbors in Grant Park and Little Five Points thrived with the newest amenities, Benteen Park lay dormant with only patronizing attempts to provide services. This crime-laden area enjoyed, at best, an old drive-in theatre and a few mom and pop establishments. Although predominantly black, whites and Hispanics carved out a piece of the American dream for themselves here—buying homes for less, those that fell into disrepair; they restored them as best they could to some semblance of livability.

In this backdrop, the United States Penitentiary rose above the horizon. It lay nestled like a big baby in a litter of small ones. The prison sat as a landmark to all who visited this community, a community that Zones and Sam hoped would be fruitful someday, monetarily.

As they arrived at the prison, Sam went over the details of their meeting.

"Now, as a part of the presentation, I've agreed to give them a demonstration of a counseling session," he told Zones.

"Don't you think that's a little risky? We can't control what may happen with inmates."

Don't worry about that. I've handpicked the inmate personally. But you have to maintain your cool, no matter what happens."

"What do you mean?" Zones grew suspicious.

"Nothing. Nothing. Just keep your cool in the event he's a ringer trying to throw us off, you know, seeing how we'll hold up under pressure."

"Okay, I hope you're right."

"Always baby, always."

They walked through the doors. The granite façade of the impressive federal architecture emanated a sense of permanence as well as security. Guards perched high in towers and miles of fence and wire circled the vast campus grounds. Just the sight of this place stirred up fear in Zones' heart.

The warden, a friend of Sam's, greeted them. They embraced, then headed across campus to another building, this one less stately but well-guarded. He led them to a room with an observation area. The lights flickered with every breath taken. The white painted walls sterilized the space visually. The loud clank of heavy steel doors heard in the distance, echoed throughout the building. Uncomfortable chairs bruised the body, causing pain. They set the stage for failure.

"Here's the file on the inmate. I'll give you a minute to review it before I have him brought in," the warden said before leaving the room.

Zones and Sam reviewed the file together, preparing for the consultation. The warden reentered the room, dimmed the flickering lights to nearly dark, and drew back a curtain covering a window that looked into another room saying,

"This is inmate 925376, aka Steven Tyler, aka The Finger, labeled by the media because, after leaving the country with his investment clients' money, he sent them a postcard with his middle finger drawn on it. The feds recovered the bulk of the monies but they think he's stashed the rest pending his release."

"I don't understand. He made it before sentencing reform and has done almost thirty years; why not just make recovery of the remaining funds a condition of early parole?" Zones asked, looking briefly through the inmate's prison file.

"Can't, paperwork has gotten lost and what we do have is dated after November 01 of '84. Besides, cat figures it's worth riding out the last ten years. You would too for ten million dollars."

"Got to admire the SOB," Sam added. Zones looked at him strangely. "I'm just saying. Ten million dollars—Shit!"

"So what do you want us to do?"

"Talk to him. See what you can get."

"We don't do interrogations, Warden."

"What? But Sam you—"

"We don't call it interrogation. It's not exactly the clinical thing to say. But we get similar results. Ain't that right, Dr. Zones?" Zones looked at Sam uneasily. He had played these same old tricks before, bending the truth to his liking, making unethical promises, skirting the lines of justice just enough to keep him out of the very places from which he now profited. "You see, Warden, Dr. Zones is a master at making an interrogation look just like two old friends having a conversation."

Zones rolled his eyes, taking in a huge breath, and then releasing it. "Motherfucker!" he said under his breath.

"You say something, Doctor?" the warden asked.

"No sir."

"Well, let's go in." Zones followed the warden into the next room where the inmate sat in his bright orange, prison issued jumpsuit. He smiled, placing his palms flat on the table. He drummed his fingers, relaxed, having been questioned by the authorities many times during the many years he'd been incarcerated.

"Mr. Tyler, this is Dr. Zones." He sat straight in his chair with both feet planted squarely on the floor. "He's going to talk with you for a moment, please give him your undivided attention. The guard will be right outside, Doctor."

"Thank you, Warden. Oh guard, could you please bring us two of those chairs from the waiting area, you know the ones with the cushions?" The guard looked at the warden. He nodded. "And something to drink too, I'll take a Coke. What would you like Steve? May I call you Steve?" The inmate stared at Zones. He turned to the warden. His pumpkin-shaped head bobbled on top his skinny neck. Looking back at Zones, he nodded.

"A Mountain Dew," he answered with a strange accent, a mixture of northern aristocracy and southern poor white trash. It forced you to listen attentively or risk thinking he'd just insulted you.

" . . . And one Mountain Dew for my friend Steve here."

"A honey bun would be nice too," Steve added, taking advantage when and where he could, as all cons learned to do. The guard, once again, looked toward the warden, this time with some disdain. Zones knew the look, had seen it many times. The warden whipped his head to the side, giving that okay as well. He then left with the guard.

While they waited, Zones scanned the file, shaking his head and humming sounds of agreement. Steve stretched his neck. His head snapped uncontrollably to his right shoulder. He leaned forward, trying to see what Zones was reading. Zones chuckled, drawing Steve's attention even more.

"Ingenious."

"Is that my file?"

"Our snacks have arrived." The guard had returned with two chairs, two drinks and a honey bun. He placed the chairs on the floor, the drinks on the table, tossed the honey bun down next to them and left the room with a hard stare at the inmate.

"I said Mountain Dew. This is Sprite." Steve eased over into the cushioned chair.

"They were out," the guard shouted, smiling cunningly.

"Here, take my Coke." He took it. Zones closed Steve's file and placed it in his briefcase. He retrieved another file, much thinner than the previous one. He opened it and placed it on the table, flipping through the pages. "I see that you're from New York. You could have requested one of the federal facilities there. What brought you to Atlanta?"

"I don't like the cold. Only stayed there because my wife—ex-wife, didn't want to leave her family. Figured since she was divorcing me, I might as well stay where I wanted to." He tore through the honey bun package, popped the top off his drink, chugging it.

"I see. So you have no contact with your ex-wife?"

"The bitch."

"You had no children with her?"

"Tried for years, Doc said I shot blanks."

"Okay, Steve, that's all I have. Guard!"

"I haven't finished my honey bun and my drink."

"You can finish it back in your cell. Guard!" Zones called out. The inmate rushed to eat and drink his snack. Inmates prized honey buns. If not shared upon demand, a finger, an eye or a life could be lost. "Mr.

Tyler is ready to return to his cell," Zones told the guard appearing at the door. He snatched him to his feet. Honey bun filled his cheeks and spilled from between his lips. He used his hands to hold the chewed mush in. The warden and Sam rushed into the room, having observed the interview.

"What the hell was that?" the warden asked. His already oversized muscles puffed up even more. "You didn't ask him about his case. And what's with the file switch?" Sam stood next to him, shooting Zones a look that showed he was none too pleased, that his chance to land this contract might have just slipped away.

"He's been here how long, damn near thirty years, and hasn't given up where he hid the money? You think my asking him about it directly was going to change that? As for the file switch, it's called angular transaction—a kind of psychological mind game."

"Is this the consulting you're offering, Sam? 'Cause I got a prison full of twelve-dollar-an-hour babysitters that could do better than this. And I don't want mind games, I want results."

"Now, hold on. Hold on. I'm sure Dr. Zones has a reason why he did what he did and a theory about where Tyler could have stashed the money—a damn good one. Ain't that right, Dr. Zones?" Sam stretched his eyes wide, a crazed look came over his face.

"I do."

"Let's have it then."

"For starters, if he wanted to be in a warm place, he could have requested Florida. So there has to be another reason why he wants to remain in Atlanta. Next, his wife didn't divorce him, he divorced her. He's named as the plaintiff in the divorce decree. Also, a semen analysis done a year ago, as a result of a sexual altercation with another inmate, showed his sample to be vital and motile; he's not sterile. Finally, they captured him in Ireland which didn't have an extradition agreement with the U.S. Unfortunately for him, one was pending so they sent him back in good faith. I'd bet that the money has been laundered back into the states, most likely from Ireland and is in Atlanta. I suspect someone close to him has it, a relative perhaps or a woman with whom he has sired children; it keeps her loyal to him. Has he had any visitors, Warden?"

"No, but every May 5th he receives a birthday cake that's delivered here. It's two days before my wife's birthday—helps me remember."

"May 5th? His file says his birthday is on November 15th."

"Maybe it's the day he will be released."

"No, that's in October. But it does say here that he fled the country in May of '83. I suggest warden that you find out who's sending those cakes. Money laundering laws were pretty lax before 1984; he could have moved the money back into the country as a business investment."

"Hmmmm," the warden said, stroking the hair on his chin. Sam watched him closely. "Good work, Doc, gives me somewhere to start."

"Hot damn! We're in business now!" Sam shouted.

"Send the contract to my office, Sam. I'll see that it gets signed." The warden left the room, leaving them behind. Sam slapped Zones on the back, still smiling.

"I got one more for you, Monk."

"Why? We've already closed the deal."

"And a good deal it will be. But this one is a favor for a friend looking for some answers."

"You're going to have to give me a minute." Zones stepped outside the room to make a phone call.

"Captain Franklin's office."

"James, this is Zones, I need a favor. I need to know if Rigdon took any international flights recently, and if so, where. I'm looking for countries that don't have an extradition agreement with the U.S."

"That may take a minute if I need a warrant."

"See you soon."

Zones wondered if Rigdon, like the inmate, could have been embezzling monies from his company and needed the murders to somehow cover it up. He may have been grasping at straws but he needed something in order to go to battle with Rigdon. A trail leading to countries with secretive banking laws, lax money laundering oversight and no extradition agreement with the U.S could all spell embezzlement.

"Is there a file?" Zones asked, returning to the room

"Thought you would never ask, here you go."

"This is it? The other file was much more detailed."

"Yeah, I know. He's a new inmate, all his records haven't arrived. Just do what you can. I'll have the guard bring him in." He headed out the door and down the hall. Zones read through what few pages of the inmate's file he had. He looked for a name, but found only a number. Moments later the guard delivered the inmate to the room.

"Inmate 999621!" the guard called out.

"Have a seat. I'll be right with you," Zones said, not looking up, his head buried, reading the file. The inmate pulled the chair out from the table. Its legs dragged on the floor, making an irritating sound. The inmate plopped down hard into its cushioned seat.

"Hello son."

Zones snapped his head up. "What the fuck! Sam, you son-of-a-bitch!"

"Now just hold on. Don't blame Sam for this. I asked him—"

"Where the hell . . . this is a federal prison. What is your murdering ass doing here? Sam, you fucker!"

"If you would just listen—"

"I don't want to hear a thing you have to say. **GUARD!**"

"Just give me five minutes. I promise you I'll never try to contact you again."

"You said all you needed to say to me twenty-four years ago when you left my mother to die on a dirty kitchen floor. **GUARD!**" He appeared at the door. "Please take this inmate back to his cell."

"I have something for you that your mother wanted you to have!" he shouted as the guard moved in to take him.

"One moment," Zones told the guard, interested in his father's words, but cautious. "This better not be any more of your bullshit." He nodded at the guard who then released his grip on his father.

"I didn't kill—"

"This is bullshit."

"Okay! Okay!" he pleaded, sitting back in his chair. He closed his eyes, sighed deeply and took a moment to gather himself. "Sam!" he called out. Zones looked over toward the one-way observation glass, knowing that Sam was watching from the other room. The door opened. Sam walked in carrying a box that he placed on the table in front of them. Zones cut him a harsh look.

"What is it?" Zones looked at the box resting on the table in front of him, not knowing if he should open it. He distrusted the gift bearer but desired to possess something of his mother's. His only remaining memory was the image of her huddled and dying on the floor.

"Go on, open it," his father encouraged him, breaking Zones' gaze on the box. He removed the lid, unwrapped the tissue paper crudely enclosing what lay within. He lifted the well-worn book, a Bible, from the box and up to his face, kissing its cover.

"It belonged to her mother; she said she got it from her grandmother. It's believed to have been in five generations of her family before her. She made me promise that if anything—." Zones shot him a look, causing him to pause.

"Thank you." He gathered his things.

"I'll be here for a week if you're ready to hear the truth."

Zones walked to the door, stopping short to glance over his shoulder. Part of him wanted to stay. He reached for the door.

"One more thing—Sam tells me you're working with the FBI, says there's a young girl missing."

"Yeah, two, a college student and a waitress."

"Don't know what use it could be but I got a guy who may be able to . . . you know . . . help find her. He's looking into some things for me, with my—"

"Who is this guy and where can I find him?"

"Sam knows how to reach him."

Zones went out the door, down the hall and out into the court. He crossed the wide field where the inmates played, through the impenetrable looking walls and out to Sam's awaiting vehicle. At that moment, he experienced a freedom he hoped his father never would.

THIRTY-TWO

"What is this place?" Zones asked Sam as they pressed down a long hall filled with more shadow than light, echoing their every step.

"Used to be an old cotton mill. Now, like everything else, they've converted it into lofts." Sam stopped at a door, the old industrial type. He knocked. The sound reverberated throughout.

"Who's there?" someone shouted through the door.

"Sam. T.O. sent me." A loud clank sounded as the large, steel door slid open, rolling along a rail with a roar.

"You say T.O. sent you?" Sam nodded. The wiry young man moved backed from the door and they entered.

The space buzzed with activity. Computers, servers, hi-definition screens and various other electronic devices filled every corner. Several people manned stations, staring into monitors as streams of data raced across their screens.

"I'm Chip, everyone calls me Stats. What can I do for you?" He led them over to a desk overrunning with computers. "Don't answer that!" he said, hearing Zones' phone ring. "They can track us through those." He rushed to a table near his desk, ripped a sheet of foil from its roll, snatched the phone from Zones' hand and wrapped it in the foil.

"Hey!" Zones reached out to take the phone back but Stats raced to the other side of the room. He waved a device over the foiled wrapped phone, eventually returning it to Zones.

"It's secure now."

Zones looked at Sam, bewildered. "Is this the guy T.O.," Zones made quotation signs with his fingers, "thinks can help me? Psst! I'm out of here." He turned toward the door.

"Now hold on, Monk. All the nut jobs you deal with in the joint and you can't put up with geek boy for a minute or two?"

"I don't have time to pussyfoot around while there are two women in the hands of killers."

"I feel you but we're already here. At least see what he can do."

Zones sighed and turned back toward the desk. "So what do you do anyway?"

"Many things, what is it you need?"

"There were two women abducted five days ago and I need to find them."

"Do you have the details of the crimes or know anything about who did it?"

"I have the crime scene report and a psychological profile of the perpetrators."

"That's good, that's good," Stats shook his finger in the air and paced the floor. "We can run a geographic profile algorithm using a density analysis by kernel estimation. We can then calculate the standard deviation using the Spatial and Temporal Analysis of Crime." He plopped in his chair, pulled up to his desk, whipped out his keyboard and switched on the power. The devices lit up, beeping, flashing and grinding until they powered up full blast.

"Can you help or not?"

"Did you not hear me? Now, where were they abducted from?"

"From a home in Virginia-Highlands and a carwash in DeKalb County." Stats typed away at the keyboard.

"Tell me about the victims."

"One is a twenty-one-year-old college student."

"Where?"

"Emory."

"It's not Tech, but okay." Stats rolled his eyes and turned up his lips. "And the other girl?"

"Eighteen, waitress, worked the second shift at Waffle House."

"Any boyfriends, husbands?"

"These are not familial abductions." Zones pounded his desk. "I have a pretty good idea who's behind them. I just need to know where they're being held."

"Then tell me about your suspect, not who, but the profile."

"There are three." Zones scanned the room, seeing what looked to be a Department of Defense internal network site on one of the monitors. "The leader is adventurous, an extrovert, athletic, duplicitous—."

"Sounds like a mesotonic personality."

"Yes." Zones' attention snapped back to Stats, surprised by his understanding of body-temperament types. "And one of the other two has an ectotonic personality."

"What about socioeconomics?"

"The leader is upper middle-class and runs in a highly exclusive social circle. The other two are most likely lower class."

"Anything else you can tell me?"

"We believe they're being held in a rural area, somewhere that can accommodate livestock—like a farm."

"Your suspects, where do they live and work?"

"The leader lives in Atlanta, the Buckhead area and works Downtown. I don't have a residence or a workplace for the other two."

Stats continued to work away at the computer, entering the data given to him. Zones moved closer to the desk, leaning forward, trying to see the screen. Stats turned, grabbed the edge of the monitor and shielded it from Zones' view.

"You say you do many things. Is one of those things hacking government networks?"

Stats spun in his chair. He leapt from his seat and darted to a printer shooting out paper across the room. He snatched the paper from the holding tray, thrusting it at Zones,

"Your kidnappers are located in this area."

Zones took the paper, his eyes still locked on Stats before focusing them on the circular, shaded area on the map he held.

"Here?" He pointed down at the map. "You believe my victims are being held here?"

"My analysis is ninety-seven percent accurate, much better than the eighty-five percent you'll get from the FBI."

"How much area does the shaded circle cover?"

"Fifteen square miles."

"That's still a large area. Can you get any more accurate than that?"

"That kernel density area is twenty percent smaller than what you'll get from the FBI."

"What area is this?"

"South DeKalb."

Zones continued to study the map, not knowing how much good

it would be, if any. Just then the alarm from his phone sounded. Zones threw off the foil and flipped the phone open. His scheduler reminded him of his interview with Rigdon back at the station.

"What is that? What is that?" Stats shouted, bouncing around from station to station. "They're coming! They're coming! Go to def con five," he continued to shout, running between computer stations.

"Calm down, junior, it's just an alarm!" Sam tried to grab hold of him.

"An alarm?" he questioned, slowing down enough to listen.

"Yes, an alarm—Jesus, son, you need a vacation and a Valium."

"We need to go." Zones folded the map and shoved it into his coat pocket. He headed for the door, stopping short, turning to Stats. "Tell me, what are you helping T.O. with?"

"I guess it's alright to tell you. I'm helping him find who killed his wife."

Zones thought for a moment, cutting Sam a harsh look, thinking this charade was all for his benefit.

"Don't waste your time."

Zones spilled back out into the approaching midday. He headed for a showdown with Rigdon and his gaggle of lawyers. Just as he exited, shots rang out, whizzing past him, striking the fluted red brick of the building behind him.

"Shit!" Zones shouted, stooping and then hitting the ground as bullets flew past him.

"What the fuck!" Sam ran toward his parked car, crouching behind it. He ripped open the passenger side door and crawled inside. Seconds later, Sam sprang from behind the car, returning fire, the air swelling with cannon-like gun fire. The click of the gun's trigger did not stop until he spent all his bullets. A van peeled off down the street, disappearing into the noonday sun.

"Shit Monk! What cat have you pissed off?" He spun the barrel of the gun around, tossing it to Zones, handle first.

"What am I supposed to do with this?"

"Use it. Apparently you got issues with someone. Now let's get out of here; that piece ain't exactly legal."

THIRTY-THREE

Zones arrived at the DeKalb precinct just in time to witness Tanner Rigdon and his battery of lawyers approach the entry to the precinct— the media fast in pursuit.

"Mr. Rigdon, Mr. Rigdon, did you have anything to do with the mutilated bodies found in those churches?" a reporter asked him. They walked quickly toward the entrance.

"My client has nothing to say at this time," the oldest attorney said.

"Do you expect your client to be charged or arrested today?" another reporter asked.

"I expect him to sleep soundly in his own bed tonight," he snapped back. They came to the entrance of the building. Guards posted at the door kept the media from entering.

Zones slipped in through another entrance, unseen by the cavalcade of reporters and lookie loos impeding normal traffic. The Captain paced outside his office, wringing his hands, sweating profusely.

"Where have you been? They've just gotten here."

"Picking my ass off the ground after dodging bullets!"

"Someone shot at you?"

"Yeah, and I got a pretty good idea who was behind it."

"Now don't go jumping to conclusions. It could've been a gang-related drive-by or a mistaken identity."

"Gang-related, my ass! That chump tried to have me wacked! And if you think I'm going to let him just sit in there and hide behind some mouthpiece, you're crazy. I'm about to put some magic on it now."

"Listen, Doctor, if you want this questioning shutdown before you've had a chance to get one in, then go in there and start accusing your prime suspect of trying to have you killed. Now let's just go in there and have that nice, peaceful conversation we agreed to." The Captain continued to wring his hands and sweat.

Zones thought about what the Captain said, knowing he was right; the attempt on his life pissed him off.

"For a man who saw combat, you sure are the nervous type."

"That's because, over there, you knew when they were coming and death was swift. These guys kill you slow just when you least expect it."

"Where are they?"

"Only if we understand each other, Doctor." Zones gave the Captain a quick nod. "Interrogation room one with Marmaduke. Now what's the game plan?"

"Do you know how the Umbou hunters of Cameroon catch a large snake?"

The Captain rolled his eyes. "I don't have time for this shit, Dr. Zones."

"They wrap animal skin or cloth around one of their legs as bait. Then they stick that leg into the snake's burrow, allowing it to be swallowed. When the snake is sufficiently engorged the hunter is pulled from the burrow, snake firmly affixed to his leg, then the snake is easily cut away from the leg. We have our big snake. I've set the bait. Now we just need to cut the snake away."

"I hope you and those brothers in West Africa have a plan in case that snake goes too far up that leg."

"Who is his attorney?" They stood outside the interrogation room.

"Some slick suit, Mizrah Coen."

"Mizrah Coen?"

"That mean something to you?"

"We'll see."

They entered the interrogation room.

"Good evening, gentlemen; I'm Captain Franklin and this is Dr. Zones. I'm sure you know Detective Marmaduke. Thank you all for coming down to answer a few questions. I'm sure everyone can appreciate the seriousness of the crimes we're dealing with and will act accordingly. If all goes well, we won't keep you long and you'll be out of here in time for your next round. I'll defer to Dr. Zones, who has a few questions. Dr. Zones . . ."

"Thank you, Captain." Zones turned to his suspect. "I'm sure you're surprised to see me, Mr. Rigdon."

"Let's move on, Doctor," the Captain said. Zones stared hard at Rigdon, ignoring everyone else. He clenched his fists and bit down on his teeth. The tension showed in his face. "Doctor," the Captain said again.

Zones scanned the room. "Dr. Hyde, what are you doing here?" he asked, seeing him mixed in with Rigdon's battery of lawyers.

"My client asked him to be here. He's his spiritual advisor," Mizrah answered.

"You're with the church?"

"I'm a bishop in the LDS Church. Mr. Coen is here to protect Mr. Rigdon's legal interest and I'm here to make sure his—."

" . . . and the church's."

"Yes, and church's spiritual interest is protected. I must say, Dr. Zones, I was surprised to hear that Brother Rigdon was suspected, in any way, of these crimes. He is an outstanding member of the community."

"I see. Mr. Rigdon," Zones switched his attention quickly, "your company, Deseret Holding, had an interest in purchasing the properties where the Iconium and Bethel Baptist Churches are located. Is that correct, sir?"

"My client was unaware that those properties were being considered for acquisition by Deseret," Mizrah answered.

"The question was for Mr. Rigdon."

"You have your answer. His answer would be no different." Zones looked over at the Captain, who twirled his finger, motioning him to move on.

"Your company was also interested in the Kolomoki Mounds State Park in Southwest Georgia and the Indian Springs in Central Georgia, isn't that correct?"

"Again, my client was unaware of these company interests."

"Is your client the CEO or the copy boy?" Zones snapped, growing irritated.

"I'm the CEO."

"Oh, look, he talks. Okay, Mr. Rigdon, why was a van registered to your company seen at two of the crime scenes?"

"We've had a number of vehicles stolen over the years. I'm sure that if you checked with the Atlanta authorities or others in the area, you'd find reports filed."

"So you have no explanation why or how four properties your company expressed an interest in happened to be the same sites where those bodies were found or how a vehicle registered to your company happened to be at two of the crime scenes?"

"No." Rigdon leaned back in his chair. The back of his head rested on the palms of his hands, one leg crossed over the other.

"How about this, could you tell us how DNA recovered from a crime scene was in your possession at one point?"

"I need a moment with my client." Mizrah, Rigdon and the other attorneys gathered in a corner of the room conversing in a whisper. They returned to their seats.

"Are you saying that his DNA was found at the scene or that DNA alleged to be in his possession was at this crime scene?"

"The latter."

"Well, I would argue, Doctor, that the DNA belonged to the person who left it at the scene."

"And I would argue that my witness, who provided him with the specimen, will testify that he paid for it and picked it up. My witness can describe him right down to the jellyfish-shaped birthmark on his ass." Once again, they gathered together.

"My client is willing to plead guilty to a misdemeanor solicitation. We'll pay the fine and be on our way." Rigdon glanced uncomfortably at Dr. Hyde, obviously embarrassed. "As for DNA, he knows nothing about that. Now if there's nothing else, my client would like to get back to his duties." Mizrah looked around the room for confirmation. "Captain?"

The Captain sat quietly, shooting stares at Rigdon, Zones and Mizrah. He fidgeted with his hand, as if rolling something with his fingers. Taking one deep breath, he stood up.

"Thank you for coming down, Mr. Rigdon." With that, the Captain ended the questioning.

"Now that you know Mr. Rigdon has counsel, please contact my office should you have any further questions. Good day, gentlemen." Mizrah handed them his business card and headed for the door.

"One more question. This one is for you, Mr. Coen." Mizrah turned, looked straight at Zones, crossed his arms in front of himself and huffed. "What could you tell me about the Gabriel Corporation? You are its registered agent, are you not?"

"I agent for many companies, Doctor. And I'm not at liberty to discuss my clients' privileged business."

"Could you tell me why Gabriel Corporation runs a sex club out in Midtown on the same block where your client is developing a condominium project?"

"I believe our time is up here, Doctor." Rigdon appeared rattled, fidgeting with his watch and brushing back his hair, avoiding eye contact with Zones and Dr. Hyde. Rigdon's crew all filed out of the room, exited the building and ran into the crush of media that awaited them.

"A sex club in Midtown, is it?" Dr. Hyde asked Zones. He lingered behind Rigdon and his entourage, watching them press on through the mob of reporters.

"A very popular one at that, from what I hear," he answered.

"Dr. Zones, I think it's about time for your follow-up visit. I'll see you tomorrow in my office, okay?"

Dr. Hyde joined the cavalcade, leaving Zones to believe there was something more behind his invitation. As they pressed through the crowd, Rigdon held back, allowing Mizrah to make the first statement.

"We've just concluded a meeting with the authorities. Mr. Rigdon cooperated fully, answering all their questions. He does not know anything about these crimes but has extended an invitation to cooperate with the authorities should they have need of his expertise. And now, Mr. Rigdon, would like to read a statement."

Rigdon pulled out the statement Mizrah prepared for him. "As my counsel has just said, I've cooperated fully. I know nothing about these crimes but the authorities have brought transactions to my attention that were carried out on behalf of Deseret Holdings, completely without my knowledge, involving properties where these crimes occurred. I will launch a thorough investigation of these actions, no matter where they lead. Thank you."

"Mr. Rigdon! Mr. Rigdon! Exactly what is it that was done without your knowledge pertaining to the crime scenes?" a reporter asked.

"Apparently, the four crime scenes were part of a land acquisition purchase by Deseret; it was not made known to me."

"Isn't Deseret the business arm of the Mormon church? Who, other than the church leaders, would be able to authorize these transactions, if not you?"

"We are the business arm of the church. And, other than myself, the church leadership would be the only persons with the authority. But this is highly unlikely. Before we jump to conclusions, we must conduct a thorough investigation. And, with the support of my bishop, Dr. Hyde, that's exactly what we will do."

As they continued their news conference, Zones received a call.

"Tell me something good, James. I'm watching a killer go free."

"I got bad news and not so bad news. Which one do you want to hear first?"

"Given my choices, it doesn't matter."

"Okay then. I didn't find any other properties listed in Rigdon's parents or siblings names, except for their personal homes. I also checked for properties in their spouses names as well—nothing there either."

"Shit! Nothing?"

"Not even an outhouse. I ran a search of all the feed companies in Georgia that sold triticale, there are many including small, local distributors."

"How many?"

"Eighty-seven wholesalers and one hundred twenty-six distributors, not counting the little mom and pop's."

"Damn! It'll take time and forever to run all those down. Time we don't have." A long pause passed between them. Zones patted himself down, looking for something. He reached into his inside coat pocket, snatching the geographic analysis.

"Dr. Zones—You still there?"

"I'll be right in."

Zones dashed up the steps to the precinct, appearing at James' desk.

"That was quick."

Zones unfolded the geographic analysis, slapping it down onto her desk. He smoothed out the creases in it.

"You have the addresses of those companies, right?"

"Yeah, right here." She tapped at the keyboard, pulling up the database of feed companies.

"Okay, I need all of the ones that are located within this area." Zones followed the circular outline on the paper with his finger.

"That's between Williams Drive in Atlanta and Marshall Boulevard in Lithonia going east-west and Sentry Drive in Tucker and Brannen Road in Atlanta going north-south. That gives us ten." She printed the list.

"Let's call each of them. I'll take five and you take five." Zones took the printed list and tore it in two. "We need to know about any deliveries or orders for triticale."

"How far back?"

"The first of the five victims went missing almost two months ago. Let's start there."

. . .

"I have six deliveries for triticale for the last two months. What do you have?" Zones asked James.

"I have eighteen."

"How many of them fall within our geographic profile?" James compared the addresses, marking them on the map.

"Eight." She grabbed a pen, circling areas on the paper. "These addresses here."

"Damn, that's still too many. We'll never cover all these in time without a team."

"Yeah, good luck getting the Captain to okay that."

"Who owns these properties?"

James banged away at the keyboard again. "I have Southern Farms, Peach State Farms, Taylor Family Land Trust, The Gabriel Corporation—"

"Stop! The Gabriel Corporation? We linked them to that club in Midtown?"

"The registered agent is—."

"Mizrah Coen! Where's Marmaduke?"

"He's in interrogation room one." He raced down the hall, slipping, sliding and hitting the wall. "But he's in there with someone," she shouted at him. Zones burst through the door of the room, startling those inside and interrupting the interrogation.

"Have you lost your mind, Doc?"

"Listen to me, can you get a few officers together, I believe we got a location on our missing women."

201

"What? Where did this information come from? And have you run this by the Captain?"

"A very reliable source and if you haven't noticed, the Captain isn't exactly feeling me lately."

" . . . And for a good damn reason. You haul one of the most powerful men in the state down here accusing him of multiple murders with no evidence other than the fact that he enjoys slutty women."

"Yeah well, we can make up for all that if we hurry."

"You think your info is good, huh? If your perp is there, we may need SWAT."

"Can you get that?"

"The commander owes me one. Besides, if this is good, he'll look like the hero, his narcissistic ass."

"Can we go?"

"Sure, I'll have someone else finish up in here."

They hurried out of the room and back down the hall. Zones felt good, real good about this new information. If the evidence led to the whereabouts of the victims and their captors, it would be ironic—a big lead from a small grain. He only hoped they weren't too late.

THIRTY-FOUR

In a deteriorating farmhouse in rural South DeKalb County, weathered wood, with barely a hint of ever having been painted, fell from its frame. Many years of neglect and the many creatures that dined on it contributed to its decline. Its tin roof sat on top of its frame like an old man's fedora tilting over his brow, rusting like a can left outside in the rain far too long. Windows with broken panes did little to ward off insects or the elements and both moved freely throughout the old structure. If the visual unpleasantness was not enough, the house and property reeked with the stench of pigs and other animals, garbage strewn about, food spoiling in the open air; human bodies, some whole and some in parts, festering in the summer sun. Flies swarmed everywhere, covering the walls, moving as one along everything they invaded, crawling in and out of every orifice. But none of this bothered those who butchered the bodies.

In the dim light, three menacing forms moved about the horror they created. They worked their craft as cries for help went unaided and wounds inflicted were given no balm. The dread they brought hovered above, a dark shadow masking the atrocities they birthed. They worked where only the damned could—in the belly of the beast.

They said little as they worked, treading through the thick, slime-covered ground. One of the butchers was so massive that he sank deeply, getting stuck. They sharpened their knives and blades, sparks flew from the wheel as steel met stone, their tools readied for the grim work they had to do. They were not alone in their task, however. A kettle of vultures circled above, ready to apply their talons to flesh, their constant presence a foreboding to the horror that was to come.

One of the perpetrators moved about the filth and grime with ease, surprisingly at home, not surrounded by the rich tapestries and fine linens to which he was accustomed. He watched as the others executed his plan. His brute tried his hand at sculpting his master's work, pounding and crushing bone and flesh into an unrecognizable heap. His master preferred to direct, only occasionally touching his captives.

He found a particular fondness for Patricia who laid his captive, bound and restrained a long way from where she ought to be. As he prepared to leave with the other two perpetrators, he derived a certain pleasure from checking her restraints himself, making sure there could be no escape for her. She kept her eyes closed tightly, faking sleep. She caught her breath when he lightly fingered her impaled ankles where the gambrel protruded from her flesh. He shifted the lifting block and chain at her feet, just to see if she squirmed. He had cauterized her wounds to stop the bleeding but they still felt tender. He checked the knot, his favorite knot, that bound her to the table. Lastly, he gathered her tied hands, taking her fingers in his mouth, biting them. He ran his finger just under the edge of the cloth that gagged her mouth, daring her to bite him in return or to scream or both. He turned away, disappointed when she did neither.

They took the shortcut through the woods, heading for the nearby town. With the old, rusted van gone, burned to its steel skeleton, their journey took longer. Still, he was certain the knot binding her to the table was solid. With a wave of his hand, the other two fell in line behind him as they made their way into the deep shadows of the woods.

All three spilled out from the other side of the tree-line next to the small, country town, on their way to market. In town, their master was suddenly aware of his minions' appearance. They made the oddest of couples, one an overlarge brute with little mental faculty, donning a child's Porky the pig mask; the other, a slighter figure of some intelligence, bowed legs and sailor's arms, piercing blue eyes and a scarred face. He placed him in charge of carrying out his schemes.

"Where's yah van, didn't see yah drive up?" the clerk from the market asked.

He said nothing to the store clerk and moved straight through the disarrayed shop, packed with stacks of stuff piled high literally to the rafters and near to toppling over, except for the bracing of some unseen restraint. The slight one answered.

"Had to scrap it, cost mo' to fix than it was worth."

"Yeah, know what yah mean. Had an old Chevy like that." The

clerk grabbed a rusting tin can from the counter, spitting the liquid from his chewing tobacco into it. "If yah looking for those knives yah like, we moved them to the other side the store."

The larger of the two traversed the aisles gingerly, there was nary a space between him and the unsteady shelves. The slight one loaded the brute up with the things they desired. He carried the supplies in his arms, clutched to his large belly, things equal to his weight.

"Yah got a lot of stuff there. Yah sure yah don't need a wheel barrow to tote all that away?" The clerk strained his neck to try to see the large man towering over him eye to eye. "Why yah friend wear that thing on his face?"

"How much?" the slightly built one asked, ignoring his question.

"Let yah have it for ten dollars." He counted out ten more ones to add to what he placed on the counter as the clerk placed their things in a bag. "Yah sold many hogs lately?" The slight one shook his head. "Yeah, but times is tough. Old man Walker had to slaughter a few of his cows. No grass is growing in this heat and he couldn't buy hay and gas both, so he sent them to the slaughterhouse. Get something off 'um, yah know. I see yah must be slaughtering too. Them buzzards been over yah place a long time." They loaded up their things into the wheel barrow and started on their way. His oversized partner pushed the heavy load.

Now, as their master prepared to depart this place, to leave his work to the others, his concern about leaving a scent for the hounds that pursued him grew stronger. Back through the woods they went, the exact same way they came. Not long into their journey, a call came in. He answered it.

"You two need to leave now. And only you two," the voice said over the phone. "We must sacrifice the brute." The master motioned for his brute to proceed on while he and the slight one reversed their path, returning the other way.

. . .

Never in her life had she felt so far from the haven she once knew in Virginia-Highland. The young woman, Patricia Redding, found herself stored amongst the strewn body parts, filth and flies, held captive to a fate she felt was certain. She existed on the same sustenance afforded the swine, kept alive this long only for the impending pageantry and spectacle of her death.

The day passed and her captors prepared to leave, as they often did. The refined one, the one who wore the Rolex watch and gave the orders, checked her restraints before leaving. She closed her eyes, pretending sleep, willing herself not to give him the satisfaction of crying out when he prodded her. She squinted as he left, waiting until they disappeared into the woods, knowing that enough time had passed to fully open her eyes. They walked this time, unlike before, their van gone for some reason. She hoped this gave her more time to free herself than before.

Patricia had tried and failed to escape before. She believed this time, however, that she'd figured out the intricate knot; now, with more time, she expected to be freed of her restraints this time. Using the fingers of her bound hands, she pulled the gag from her mouth and sank her teeth into the knot. She pulled and tugged, but it was too well-made. Losing hope and time, she surveyed the dark space looking for something to aid her. One of her captors had made a most fortuitous error, leaving a blade on the table next to where she lay secured. Patricia struggled to reach it. The knife rested perilously near the table's edge. At every attempt, it inched closer to falling, spinning over the edge and back like a high wire performer, delightfully teasing the crowd below. With one final attempt to grasp it, she lunged forward. The blade fell; she managed to grab it, sharp end up, cutting her hand. She dared not let it go, enduring this pain. It was not worse than any pain she had endured previously.

Working quickly, Patricia sawed into the rope, cutting it from her hands, freeing them. She rose up, pulled her legs to her chest. The pain from the heavy gambrels clinging to her flesh bit into her with every move. She reached down to her foot, grabbing the hook, working it loose from one of her Achilles. Blood began to ooze from the wound, now reopened, the pain so great she barely remained conscious. She wanted to scream, but she couldn't, she would have to do this again. Patricia looked around constantly, thinking that every sound she heard was that of her captors approaching. She dreaded coming this close to freeing herself only to, once again, be bound and gagged.

She freed her other foot from the restraint. In her haste, she leapt from atop the table, landing firmly upon the slurry ground. She took two steps, adrenalin her only support. She fell, crashing face first, her weight too great for her weakened feet. Patricia tried to lift herself up using the table for support, overturning it when it could not support her weight, falling back onto the ground, passing out from the pain.

Patricia awoke to the sound of grass and leaves being trampled underfoot. For a moment, she believed that she lay in her bed at home, waking up from a bad dream or a bad hangover. She raised her head up out of the mucky slime and saw her surroundings. The pungent odor of death and decay filled her nostrils; it quickly reminded her of the peril she faced.

In the distance, she saw her captor approaching, pushing a loaded wheelbarrow along the rough, isolated path. The barrow swayed and the wheel pressed into the dry earth. The brute emerged from the wood. He neared the farmhouse. Patricia's heart raced, panicking as fear set in. She looked for a place to hide, finding only the pig sty nearby. They used the sty to dispose of the remains not used for their macabre purposes—hands and feet stuck out from the ground and faces stared up from the murky mire. Patricia raised her head, staring at the sty. She stretched out toward it, clenching her hand, grabbing nothing but air. Her hand fell limp to the ground. She mustered the strength to drag herself through the muck. Behind her, she left a trail, a sure clue to where she hid. The chance was worth risking. Inch by inch, Patricia moved herself toward the pig sty, looking up constantly to see her captor pushing his load closer.

He drew closer, moving faster than she could crawl. Finally, she reached the sty, opened its gate and crawled inside. The animals stirred, moving about as she wove her way between their legs. Some escaped through the open gate of the sty, covering the drag trail she had made. Patricia's body sank into the mud, burying herself, her face all that showed, along with the lifeless ones strewn about.

The brute dropped his load short of the house and ran toward her. She lay still, not even battering an eye, thinking that he saw her scurrying about. She prayed silently. The words, "Please Lord! Please Lord!" kept playing in her head. When she saw that he had run to corral the pigs, she exhaled, her body relaxed and her constant prayer ceased.

Patricia watched as he rounded the pigs up, chasing them back into their pen. The brute stepped all around her body as she lay still, buried beneath the murky mire; he avoided crushing her as the edge of his boot touched her cheek. He grunted loudly. That sound frightened her, gave her the creeps even. Of all the other horrid things surrounding Patricia in this hellish place, his grunting disturbed her the most.

The brute went to retrieve the load he had left near the house. Looking through gaps in the slats of a screen wall, he noticed the overturned table and that his captive was missing. He searched franticly for her, tossing and scattering things, grunting as he did when corralling the pigs. Not able to find her, he then did a remarkable thing. He sniffed the table where she had lain, sniffed the length of the path she had dragged herself through and into the sty. Seeing him approach, Patricia lay still, submerging her face entirely, closing her eyes and holding her breath. She neither saw nor heard him, entombed, as she was, in a slurry grave.

She felt vibrations as he stomped around the pen. The slurry shifted as the pounding vibrations grew stronger, partially exposing her face. With one eye peeking out through a breach in the mire, she saw him looking around, sniffing, coming closer. He hovered right over the spot where she lay buried, but saw nothing. He stuck his massive hand into the muck, grabbing hold of her, lifting her up from the floor of the sty and into the air. He tossed her over his shoulder, grunting as before but now with a laugh. She screamed and cried for help; there would be no rescue.

THIRTY-FIVE

Zones, Marmaduke and Chennault raced through the South DeKalb countryside. The SWAT team they hoped for did not materialize—too risky for the commander's career for a SWAT team to get involved without the proper approval. They were on their own. The paved roads they so easily traversed turned into bumpy, pothole-filled, graveled paths, tossing them violently into the air and bringing them crashing to their seats.

Zones had convinced Marmaduke that the place where they were now headed held two doomed women captive as they awaited rescue. The evidence they needed to convict Tanner Rigdon would also be there, he hoped. He sensed that Marmaduke did not fully buy into this, however, he merely played the odds. Zones had identified the victims based on his theories. The DNA he gathered matched the dead bodies or their body parts. Marmaduke's investigation had not produced any suspects, at least he had one. Besides, should all this house of cards come crashing down, the majority of the blame would be on the Captain's head; he would carry only a marginal load.

Zones, on the other hand, had no such option. He did not have the same police responsibilities but he knew that solving this case, with the national attention it had garnered, meant the difference between a position with the FBI's Behavioral Analysis Unit and remaining a prison consultant with Sam's firm. As they drove, he replayed all the evidence and information he had collected in his mind: The symbols at the crime scene matched those important in the Mormon faith. The victims, all five, descended from 19th century Mormon Church dissenters. The prime suspect descended from a 19th century Mormon who tormented the ancestors of his victims, only to find himself excommunicated by the church. The prime suspect's company had an interest in acquiring the properties where they had discovered the bodies. Now a grain delivery to a farm, the same type of grain that was discovered at one of the crime scenes, was connected to his suspect's attorney. In his mind, these were not coincidences, they were bonafide pieces of evidence.

As they continued on, the bottles beneath Marmaduke's seat clanked, ringing through the tattered interior of the two twenty-five. A half-filled bottle rolled out, stopping at the heel of his shoe.

"We're not going to have a problem are we?" Zones asked, seeing him push the bottle back with his foot.

Marmaduke held out his hand, fingers spread wide apart and said, "Steady." It jittered in the air as they drove over the pockmarked path. He grabbed for the steering wheel, gripping it tight when the car veered off course.

"Shit!" Zones yelled.

Marmaduke spun the steering wheel from left to right. The Deuce fishtailed, whacking high grasses and brush, sending birds, insects and small creatures scattering, before coming under control.

"Steady, my ass! Perhaps Chennault should drive." Zones turned to see Chennault lifting himself from the floor of the car.

"Nobody drives Shirley but me." He ran his hand over the dash, patting it. Zones stared, shaking his head. He pulled the rope he had brought back from Utah out of his briefcase. "You still haven't figured that out yet?" Marmaduke asked, seeing Zones wrestle with the rope.

His phone rang. "Zones," he answered, still cutting Marmaduke a distrusting look, trying to steady the phone to his ear. "Ahaa—I see— Okay, thanks, James."

"What did she want? Has the Captain found out about our little field trip?"

"No, the Captain is meeting with the councilwoman and the mayor, he still doesn't know."

"What was she calling for?"

"They discovered a burned out van matching the description of the one I saw at the Virginia-Highland home."

"Where? What part of town?"

"Decatur."

"That's an awful long way from here. You're sure about this place, Doctor?"

Zones said nothing. He did not know for certain if they were headed in the right direction, but why would there be triticale deliveries to a farm owned by a shell company that's controlled by Rigdon otherwise? He had to find the missing women and this clue gave him the best chance of doing that—preferably alive.

"We are two miles out," Chennault said, trying to read the map as it bounced around. They had taken a wrong turn before and didn't want to get lost again.

"Two miles. We need to prepare," Marmaduke said.

"So how does this work? What do we need to do?"

"What do you mean by 'this' and 'we'?"

"This raid we're doing."

"You don't do a damn thing. The last thing I need is a dead civilian on an unauthorized raid. But Chennault and I pull up, we go in, get these motherfuckers and then get the hell out of there. Comprende!"

"No negotiations?"

"Negotiations! What for? Do you really think the perps who cut those bodies up are gonna want to negotiate? Besides, you saw how much good talking did with your Klansman."

"Look, you should know by now that Rigdon is one slippery motherfucker. He may not have even been there. That means no fingerprints, no DNA, no victim witness, nothing. A live perp may be the only way to get Rigdon."

"So you're asking us to try and talk these guys out?" Marmaduke turned to Zones, taking his eyes off the dusty road briefly. He caught a glimpse of Chennault in his rearview mirror shaking his head. Zones did not want to leave this place without the evidence to implicate Rigdon. Marmaduke, on the other hand, just wanted to go in, kick butt—all John Wayne-like—take these characters down, and get back to base before the Captain figured out what happened.

They pulled up to the old farmhouse. Their vehicle disturbed the dusty dirt and gravel road when Marmaduke slammed on the brakes, throwing a cloud of dust and rocks into the air. The structure leaned in many directions. Weathered and weakened, its bones swayed. The house suffered from paranoia—not sure if it wanted to be charming or evil.

They all eased from the car and gathered at the trunk, their eyes locked onto the farmhouse. Zones spun around, surveilling the area, not seeing another house or person anywhere. He heard the grunting

211

of pigs, their smell permeated the still air. He looked up, seeing a kettle of birds circling and sounding off.

"Now this is the lair of a killer, Detectives."

Marmaduke scanned the area as well, cutting Zones a look, agreeing with his eyes. "Let's get this party started," he said, pulling open the trunk, grabbing the bullhorn.

"You're expecting a war?" Zones asked Marmaduke, seeing an arsenal of weapons in the trunk.

"I pity the fool," he quipped, whipping the bullhorn to his mouth. "This is the DeKalb County Police. We have the place surrounded. Come out with your hands up." He called out, secured behind his car. He waited for several seconds, getting no reply. "All occupants of the house please come out with your hands up. This is the DeKalb County Police," again he announced, again with no reply. "Well, what do you want to do now, Doc? This is your show. They could be in there destroying evidence, or worse."

Zones thought for a moment, staring at the old farmhouse, then back at Marmaduke, not even sure if they had the right place.

"Let's do it."

"Now you're talking." Marmaduke and Chennault converged on the house. They kicked in the front door, whipped out their guns and breached the home's interior.

They moved through darkness, navigating hordes of trash and furnishings strewn about. The stench nearly overwhelmed them, it also spurred them to continue on, checking rooms and checking around corners.

Zones, meanwhile, crept up the stairs to the covered porch, nearly falling through a weakened board. "Damn it!" he said, regaining his footing. He hadn't stayed in the car as he was told. His curiosity got the better of him and he entered the farmhouse anyway. The eerily quiet space and the awakening stench shocked his senses. Zones whipped a kerchief from his pocket and thrust it to his nose. He walked a short ways down a hall, passing in front of a door. He reached for its handle, preparing to open it. Just then, a hand broke through the door, leaving a large hole. The knife it wielded protruded from the wall just above Zones' head.

"Shit!" He ducked. Zones looked up at the knife above him, then back at the door, seeing the large man move from the closet, splintering the door and retrieving the knife from the wall. Zones ran down the hall shouting, "Detective Marmaduke!"

The noise drew the attention of Marmaduke and Chennault; they came running from different parts of the home. They met Zones standing at the bottom of the staircase, breathing hard, gesturing wildly.

"We told you to stay in the car!" Marmaduke yelled, looking around him, his gun still drawn.

"Calm down, Doctor, calm down," Chennault said, patting the now doubled over Zones on the back. "What did you see?"

"The biggest mother . . . motherfucker I've ever seen." he told them, finally catching his breath.

"Which way did he go?" Marmaduke asked. Zones pointed ahead of him, down a hallway. They started in that direction. "Hold it—I heard something." Marmaduke stopped in his tracks.

"Did you hear that creaking upstairs?" Chennault asked. Just then, lathe began to fall from the ceiling.

. . .

Marmaduke led Chennault up the stairs, spreading out once they reached the top. Seeing a figure move in the distance, they followed, rounding a corner with their guns drawn. They came to a room filled with stuffed animals, hundreds if not thousands of them, neatly displayed as if for a small child.

"What the—" The scene surprised Marmaduke. This room, void of the filth like the rest of the house, sparkled with lace and soft chiffon. "Check that closet," he instructed Chennault. He grabbed the handle of the door, holding his gun steady. He ripped the door open, and shined his light into the dark void, prepared to fire.

"Clear." He eased the door closed.

"I know we saw him come in here." Marmaduke looked around the room. He lowered his gun, scratching his head.

Chennault walked over to an area where the stuffed animals neatly rested. "What do you make of all these?" Marmaduke shrugged. Toy animals of all kinds, some still wrapped in plastic, filled the room. He moved closer, leaning in to get a better look. He shined his light over the toys and gazed into their marbled eyes when one of them blinked—the pig head. "Shit!" Chennault tried to jump away but it was too late.

A hand latched onto his throat. He gasped for breath. The brute rose from his hiding place. The stuffed animals, once neatly arranged, cascaded from their resting place, falling to the floor. He lifted Chennault by the neck, dangling him in the air.

"Drop him!" Marmaduke shouted. He aimed his gun but did not have a clear shot. Chennault continued to struggle, flailing and gasping. The brute drew a knife, raised it and flung it at Marmaduke with deadly accuracy, striking him in the chest. The force knocked him to the floor where he lay bleeding.

The brute then drew another knife. Marmaduke struggled to regain his footing, trying to reach his weapon only inches away. He screamed, "NO!" and stretched out his hand as if to grab the blade from across the room. The brute grunted and laughed. He raised the knife and prepared to thrust it into Chennault, who he still held by the neck. Just as he started to lunge the knife, shots boomed at close range, striking him in the arm. Chennault fell to the ground, the hand still clasped firmly around his neck. Blood dripped from the large man's nearly severed arm. He bellowed and turned toward where the shots had been fired.

Zones, holding a police issue, Remington pump shotgun, trained its light and scope on the brute. He fired center mass, still the large man came, grunting menacingly, blood dripping, knife hanging to his side, a pig mask covering his face.

"What the fuck are you, man or beast?"

Now close enough to strike, he raised his knife in the air. Zones fired once more at his head and he dropped without taking another step. He lay dying. Blood drained from his body and stained the old wood floor. Zones rushed over to Marmaduke where he lay injured. He knelt next to him.

"Are you okay?"

"Yeah. Check on Chennault." Zones went over to him, placed his hand on his neck and felt for a pulse. He reached for his phone and called 911. Later, the old farmhouse was swarmed with police, paramedics and crime scene analysts.

. . .

"What in hell is all this shit? Looks like the pigs took over this place. Anyone got boots? Fuck!" Marmaduke looked over at the corralled pigs and the human remains that littered the ground. His wound was not life-threatening so he refused the hospital trip. They patched him up and let him go.

"We may have a couple of extra pair in the van," an analyst offered.

"I'd appreciate that." He hurried away and soon returned with two pairs of black, rubber boots. Marmaduke and Zones placed them on their feet, stuffing their pant legs into them, trudging through the thick slime, heading for the spot where their victim was hanging. "Sorry we couldn't get you a live witness, Doc."

"Well, you tried. We won't get much of anything from this mess, that's for sure." Zones turned to look at the filth they stood in. "We have body parts all over this place. This guy must have been a mad man."

"Mad man is right. Let's go take a look at our guy upstairs." Marmaduke led the way past other investigators and crime scene analysts. "Let's see what we have here."

"He was one tough son-of-a-bitch. Took damn near everything I had to bring him down."

"Good thing you found that Remington in my trunk and ignored me when I said stay put."

Zones smiled. "What's that over his head?"

"Some kind of pig mask. Let's see what we have here." Marmaduke knelt down beside the body. He reached over and removed the pig mask from the face. "What the fuck!" he yelled, jumping back to his feet.

"Damn!" Zones said, startled by the grotesquely deformed face. Marmaduke dropped the mask back in place.

"Detective Marmaduke!" Someone shouted. He and Zones raced down the stairs. A detective pointed back toward the pig sty when they reached the last step.

"Over here, Detective. This one is alive." They lowered her body from the gambrel, her face unrecognizable from the muck covering it.

"Do we have a bus here?" Marmaduke asked.

"They're all gone. Be a while before another can get here."

"Okay, let's load her up."

"Are you kidding? Those roads are bumpy as hell. The ride alone may kill her," Zones said.

"If she stays here she'll die anyway."

"Can we get life flight?"

"Call it in," Marmaduke told the other detective. "Ma'am—Ma'am, stay with me. Help is on the way," he continued to tell her as he wiped the mud from her face.

"She looks like the Virginia-Highland woman, Patricia Redding."

"Patricia, stay with me, dear," he comforted her, trying to keep her awake.

"It'll be here in twenty minutes," the detective said, returning to where they tended to her.

"Any sign of the other missing girl, Carolyn Armstrong?" Zones asked.

A shout came from the other side of the farmhouse. "Over here, Doctor."

Zones tramped through the muck, lifting his legs high in the air, reaching Chennault; he had also refused the ride to the hospital.

"What do you have, Detective?"

"We're too late for this one." He stepped to the side, revealing the body of a young girl carved into pieces on a table.

. . .

Soon the life flight helicopter landed. They loaded Patricia Redding into it, still alive, barely. As the helicopter lifted off, the Captain pulled up to the scene. He walked tough and looked mad. Marmaduke and Zones, seeing him storm toward them, their clothes waving violently in the wind, turned and headed back into the farmhouse.

"OH, NO YOU DON'T. MARMADUKE, DR. ZONES; STOP RIGHT THERE!" the Captain shouted over the roaring sound of the propeller blades. They stopped in their tracks and turned toward the Captain. They felt certain they'd hear his fury for the clandestine, unauthorized raid. Fearing he would say something wrong, Marmaduke said to Zones,

"Let me do the talking."

"Marmaduke!"

"Before you say anything, Captain, please follow me." He led him through the house.

"Good God! What is that smell?"

"Here, you're going to need these." Zones handed him a mask and boots. They continued through the house and out to the pig sty. With all the animals removed, only the human remains littered the ground, strewn across the muck and mire. The Captain stopped short of the sty. His mouth hung open beneath his hand. His eyes widened with every glance.

"And we found one of the missing women still alive. She was on that life flight that took off right before you got here. The Doc found information that led us to this place." The Captain said nothing, only stared out across the carnage.

THIRTY-SIX

Patricia Redding lay in a hospital room in a semi-conscious state, among a Baghdad grid of machine wires, crisscrossing each other in no particular order. The hospital staff kept her secluded from the media and everyone else, except her relatives and those close to the investigation. Captain Franklin did not want anyone to know that any living person had been taken out of the farmhouse. The world knew only that something vile, brutal to every sense and hard to envision or comprehend, showed its face through the acts it perpetrated on a rural Georgia farm. They contained this information for now but must learn all they could quickly before the perpetrators found out about her.

Zones paced the floor in a Grady Hospital ICU waiting room when Dr. Hyde approached Patricia's family. Before he could even speak, Margret, her aunt asked,

"Will she be okay, Doctor?"

"Right now she's stable. She's been through a lot. Her infection was bad and deep but we think we have it under control. Rest is the best thing for her now."

"When do you think she'll awaken?"

"Hard to say. The brain tries to preserve itself at all cost; sometimes to do that it shuts itself down. I know you and everyone else are anxious." He glanced toward Zones who tried to look casual and pretended not to eavesdrop on their conversation. "I have the FBI and Homicide Detectives asking me every five minutes when they'll be able to speak with her. But right now we just don't know."

"Okay, thank you, Doctor." She grabbed his hand, shaking it. The expensive looking watch he wore jiggled. It clashed with his rumpled scrubs and tanned arm.

"Dr. Zones, my office, please." Zones followed Dr. Hyde down a hallway. "You know, Doctor, when I asked you to come to my office, I didn't mean under these conditions."

"When do you think we'll be able to question her?"

"As I told her aunt, it's best that she rest for now—right here." He pointed to his office. "She has had a very traumatic experience. I wouldn't be surprised if she didn't remember anything right now, given what she has been through." Dr. Hyde threw off his lab coat. He hung it on a hook and plopped in his chair. He flung open a desk drawer, pulling out a file and opening it.

Zones wandered around the spacious office, it was extremely neat and filled with all manner of photographs. Dr. Hyde joined him near a wall lined with images.

"That's Afghanistan, 1980—just after the Soviets invaded. That's me treating a Mujahideen fighter. Little did I know that would turn out to be a bad thing." He grabbed Zones by the head, feeling it all over. "Any pain or headaches?"

"No, not since those pills kicked in."

"Yeah, you got the good stuff." He pried one of Zone's eyes open, shining a light into it and then doing the same with the other. "And that is Central America, 1985, during the civil war. I'm treating a villager right after her home was razed by the Sandinista Juntas. That's Sri Lanka, 1986, civil war, Liberia, Somalia, Bosnia, war, war, and war, you get the picture."

"Seems like you've found your calling."

"What can I say; it's where I want to be. Open wide." Zones' mouth sprung open. "Say Ahh." Zones complied. He moved to his ears, shoving a scope into one and then the other. "Close your eyes." He moved in front of him. "Now, lift your left leg out and touch your nose with your right index finger—now the other way—great."

"All good?"

"Like new, although I recommend you get a follow-up exam with your PCP." Zones gave a big exhale. This little exam reminded him why he hated doctors. He didn't want to become anyone's 'patient'. "So tell me, Dr. Zones, you really believe Tanner Rigdon is behind these killings?"

"No. I know he's behind them and soon I'll prove it."

"Well, the church president has instructed me to aid you in any way that I can. I understand you paid them a little visit last week."

"Yes, but he wouldn't meet with me. What's the matter now? He

219

and the Quorum afraid this will blow back on them, muddy up those pristine white robes they like to prance around in?"

"What do you mean, Doctor?"

"Nothing. Are we finished here?" Dr. Hyde nodded. "You can tell your president I said thanks, but no thanks."

Zones returned to waiting and pacing. He joined Marmaduke who carried two coffees, clenched a donut between his teeth and tucked a newspaper beneath his arm. The smell of a freshly smoked cigarette lingered on his breath—he seemed ready for the day. He no longer felt the pressure of needing to find a perpetrator for these crimes now that they killed at least one of the sick bastards. He walked a little different now, not his usual woe-is-me gait.

Zones reached for one of the coffees.

"Here you go, Doc." Marmaduke handed him the coffee, pulling the other one back. "This one's my own special brew." He smiled. Zones took the cup, lifted its lid and stuck his nose to the rim, savoring the smell of the brew. He often tried to quit the stuff, it raised his heart rate and consequently his blood pressure. His life, however, demanded it. Shit was too hectic for him to run off of adrenaline alone.

"Smells good. Thanks, Detective."

"Got it black—figured you liked it like you liked your women."

"That's what gives me my glowing complexion."

"Black coffee?"

"No, black women."

"Then damn, maybe my pale ass should try it."

"I don't know. It may be too strong for you. May want to start out with a little cream first, lighten it up some and then work your way up to the darker stuff."

"You're full of shit." Marmaduke laughed. He took a sip of his coffee and a bite of his donut before unfurling his paper. "You heard anything on our vic?"

"They're not letting anyone see her except her relatives. They just took her Aunt Margret in there with her now."

"Isn't that the old lady that was attacked? Why don't you just ask her to take you in?"

"I would if she'd come out when a doctor wasn't around. But what good would it do if our victim is still in a coma. I need them to wake her up before Rigdon learns that she survived and concocts a story or an alibi."

"Hopefully, Chennault is locking down the crime scene and keeping everything under wraps."

The two of them waited in the lounge of ICU, just like all the others waiting to hear of their loved one's condition—in limbo—not knowing if the hand of fate had been kind or cruel. They stayed the night, trying to rest as comfortable as possible. They stretched their legs out across the chairs or lay on the hard, concrete floor. They got up every twenty minutes or so to stretch out the tight spots. They stayed there hoping to be able to question their lone survivor.

"Are you okay?" a grandmotherly-looking woman asked Zones. She had slept there all night, cuddling up on a couch. She would get too close when she spoke to you but her kindness made the intrusion alright. "They have blankets if you need one. Is your loved one doing okay? I'm waiting to see my daughter. She was robbed and they roughed her up bad. I'm on my way to see her now."

"Robbed? You say that your daughter was robbed?" She nodded. "Well, I have a detective right here." He grabbed Marmaduke by the arm, interrupting his reading, eating and drinking. "He'll be happy to help you."

"What's going on?" Marmaduke sat up from his slumped position, nearly spilling his coffee.

"This kind, kind lady has suffered the most unfortunate thing." Zones held her hand, patting it. She stood there, the cookie-baking type with a beehive coif and a perfect set of dentures. "Her beloved daughter was mugged and her assailant got away. I told her that, as one of the city's finest from Major Crimes, you would take it upon yourself personally to hunt the scoundrel down and bring him to justice."

"But I'm not City of—"

"Fantastic! We should hurry while the information is still fresh to her." Zones snatched Marmaduke up from his seat.

"Oh really! Come on then." The old woman pulled at Marmaduke who went easily. She brushed donut crumbs from his coat and all three headed to the nurse's station. They followed behind a nurse to the ICU.

Zones slipped through the door of Patricia Redding's room. Her Aunt Margret was sitting there reading quietly. She paused to see him enter. He flicked her a smile, then turned his attention immediately to the young woman he had, only hours before, helped rescue from the farm. The maze of wires and machines hooked up to her freaked him out a little.

"Patricia," he softly called her name, leaning down close to her, grabbing her by the hand. She gave no response, not even the flicker of an eye.

"I haven't seen much change. Will she be alright, Doctor?" Margret asked.

"We hope so," he answered, not wanting to say more than that to her. "Have you tried talking to her? Sometimes a familiar voice will awaken the brain."

"Yes I have, but I got no more than you did."

"Patricia, do you know where you are? Do you know how you got here? Can you tell us what happened to you? If you hear me, squeeze my hand." She still gave no response. Zones thought for a moment, trying to come up with a way to awaken her. "Is there a song or a poem that she is particularly fond of or a word perhaps?"

"Well, she's a music major at the university and she loves jazz. Said she wants to teach deaf people how to hear music, something or other about vibrations."

"Who's her favorite artist?"

"Oh, I don't know, but she played this one song all the time in the car, at home, everywhere. Now, what was that song title?" She clasped her hands, closed her eyes tight and lowered her head. "I believe the singer's name was Monkey or something like that."

"Monk?"

Margret lifted her head up abruptly. "Yes! Yes! That's it, Monk. And the name of the song she played was a real pretty name. I even told her that when she had children, if it was a girl, she should name her after that song. Let's see, I know it began with a 'P'."

"I think I got it." Zones whipped out his phone and logged onto his Apple music site. He downloaded Thelonious Monk's 'Pannonica'. He knew the tune well as he did all of his music; he was Monk's namesake after all. He was partial to 'Round Midnight' himself. He placed his phone close and hit play. Music exploded into her ear. A sweet piano lullaby with melancholy riffs accompanied the blaring sound of the brass section.

As the song played, Patricia's eyes moved beneath their closed lids. Her head shook, slowly at first, but then rapidly. She moaned. Her whole body now shook. The once pleased look on Zones' and

Margret's faces turned into concern. Zones took the music away, hoping that would calm her.

"No! No!" she repeated. Lights on the machines flashed and data on their displays changed rapidly. Alarms sounded, attracting the attention of the nursing staff.

"What happened?" a nursed asked, bursting through the door. Zones stood back from the bed, trying to blend in with all the other fixtures in the room.

"I don't know what happened. The Doctor was playing her some music, trying to wake her up and she started doing that," Margret told her. The nurse looked back at Zones standing behind her while she struggled to calm Patricia. She injected a solution into her IV, that quieted her.

"May I see you outside, Doctor?" the nurse asked Zones. He followed her out of the room and they walked down an out of the way hall. She stopped in an alcove in front of the staff restroom.

"Who the hell are you?" she demanded. "I know every surgeon in this hospital and your face does not come to mind. Now if you don't give me some answers, I'm calling security."

"Okay. My name is Dr. Zones—"

"That's it, I'm calling security."

"Let me finish. Let me finish. I am a doctor, but I'm a Ph.D. I'm a consultant with the FBI and I helped find her. I know she's been through a lot but the man responsible for doing that to her is still out there and she's the only one who can help us find him. I just had a few questions for her, that's all."

"How do I know you're not the one who did that to her? FBI consultants don't go around impersonating doctors."

"There's a Detective Marmaduke interviewing another one of your patients, he can vouch for me." The nurse looked him over. Her eyes moved the length of his body. She rolled her eyes, snapped her hands to her hips, and, with attitude, said,

"Give me thirty minutes. If the doctor and family say so, you can speak with her if she's awake."

"Okay, fair enough."

Zones walked back to the waiting area. Marmaduke sat slouched in his chair, back from his visit with the old lady. He read his paper and finished his coffee. The crowd thinned and the hospital quieted. The scent of death, however, still lingered. The ICU, by its very nature, ministered to those standing at the precipice of life or death. The tilt of the balance in their favor often fell to the skill of the surgeon, the care of the staff, the luck of the draw or to fate. Those who waited found comfort in their shared suffering. They asked each other about the status of their infirmed constantly. They practiced a sadistic ritual of unloading their grief onto others, hoping to lighten their own burdens. They were hoping the coffers of the dead were filled and unable to fit another soul into its chest.

Zones spied the clock on the wall. The hands ticked at a pace beneficial only to those near death. He had bargained with the nurse for thirty minutes but the wait grew longer. Zones needed to speak with Patricia. He knew Rigdon had committed these crimes. He felt it in his bones. He just needed someone other than himself to say so. He considered donning a disguise and returning to her room, but thought better of it. A second arrest in the same city would mean bad news for him. The good news was that Patricia had stirred from her coma, responding to her favorite song. He only hoped that he hadn't harmed her by doing so but the success of this case rested in her hands.

Even though the Captain and the city elites saw no problem allowing this case to die, along with the brute and all those bodies, the criminologist in him could not. He fought hard against allowing conspiracy to triumph over logic and reason, reminding himself of something his college professor once said: "The effervescent mind is the stuff of reality, fable, illusion, dreams and yes, conspiracy. And so, do not think it imprudent or simplistic to believe that this same mind could also be evil." An evil conspiracy fitted the nature of these crimes.

THIRTY-SEVEN

"Yes, these are nice." The Captain kicked back in his office chair, smoking a fat one. He spun the cigar between his lips, wetting the end. His feet rested comfortably on his desk, crossed at the ankles, his argyle socks exposing his penchant for flare. He blew puffs of smoke in the air, cool-like, as if he had the world all figured out. Captain Franklin exhaled, letting out a huge puff of smoke. He was relaxed for the first time since this case landed on his desk. He no longer held all the tension inside him, the pressure of trying to get these crimes solved quickly.

"You know this is a non-smoking building, don't you?" James asked rhetorically, puffing on a stogy herself.

"Fuck it, I deserve it. I just closed the biggest case the state has ever seen in record time and with the least amount of expense."

"You mean Dr. Zones closed the biggest—"

"Yeah, yeah, yeah, I guess he did do a little something. But it was my idea to hire his ass. I'll throw him and Marmaduke a bone or two. But the accolades are all mine, baby. Hell, they may even make some up just for me."

Captain Franklin continued puffing on his stogy, the office filling with clouds of sweet-smelling smoke, some escaping from beneath the door. He focused his eyes toward the window, through the billowing clouds of smoke. He squinted at the set of golf clubs resting in the corner of his office—Taylors with a Big Bertha driver.

James saw him focus on the clubs. "It has been a while since you've played a round."

"Not much longer. Me and my boys will be hitting the links on Saturday, soon enough. I can smell the greens now." He tooted his lips, taking a deep breath.

He reminisced about being out there, closing his eyes, smiling, leaning even further back in his chair. Suddenly, the imagery in his mind turned dark. He no longer saw the lush greens of a golf course; he saw the fields of a desolate farm littered with decaying bodies, reeking of death. He swung his feet from atop his desk, planting them onto the floor. Captain Franklin sat erect in the chair, his eyes now wide open.

"What's wrong?" The Captain said nothing. He discarded the cigar. It no longer tasted sweet in his mouth, no longer holding any flavor. His thoughts of summer mornings on the links morphed into a horrid night on a rural farm, looking out over the fields of hell.

He rose from his chair, washed his face with his dry hands, loosened the tension from his neck, shrugged his shoulders and gathered himself. The City Council and the areas' respective mayors wanted a briefing on the case. They wanted the details, how the investigation had unfolded, what profiling techniques his investigators had employed, what evidence they had extracted, a thorough accounting of the case. For this he needed to be fully briefed.

"Get me Dr. Zones and Marmaduke," he told James.

. . .

Marmaduke answered his phone on the first ring, hearing James barking.

"When, now?—Okay," he told her, hanging up with a sigh.

"That was James. Captain wants us in."

"But we haven't spoken to our victim."

"Then you better do something quick. He's meeting with the suits shortly and you're supposed to be the one with all the answers." Zones retrieved his phone and dialed. "Who're you calling?"

"James, this is Zones."

"Did you get my message?"

"Yes, I did, we'll be there soon. I need a favor. Can you send a photo array to my phone?"

"Sure, who's the subject?"

Cupping the phone with his hand, he said softly, "Rigdon."

"You city boys just don't know how to leave well enough alone. Does the Captain know about this?"

"No. And let's keep it that way."

"What's your plan, Doc?" Marmaduke asked as soon as Zones hung up. He didn't answer. An image on the TV captured his attention.

"Turn that up! Turn that up!" he demanded, rising from his seat, pointing at the TV. Someone increased the volume slightly. He stood there, transfixed on the screen. Images of Rigdon flashed across the screen. " . . . . Tanner Rigdon, CEO of Deseret Holding, one of the largest businesses in the state, is leaving for the United Arab Emirates to open their first office in the Middle East, this after being questioned in the brutal deaths of five people. When asked if this was an inroad for the church, he responded that it was, 'Strictly business.' In other news . . . ."

"He's running!" Zones said. "God damn it, that son-of-a-bitch."

"What?"

"Rigdon, he's running. The U.A.E. has no extradition agreement with the U.S. If he gets on that plane, he's not coming back. Call the Captain and tell him that our victim just identified Rigdon, and have him to stop that plane."

"But she hasn't. You know that and I know that."

"She will. She will. Make the call." Zones ran over to the nurse's station. He found the nurse he'd spoken to earlier. "Nurse, I really need to speak with Patricia Redding. This is very, very, important. A very dangerous man could be getting away if—"

"Sir, I was just looking for you. She's awake and the doctor and family have given their permission for you to speak with her."

Zones tore down the hall, only slowing just before bursting through the door to Patricia's room. Marmaduke huffed behind him.

"Oh, there you are, Dr. Zones," Dr. Hyde called out, stopping him short of entering the room. "I was just looking for you."

"Why? I was just about to go in to speak with the victim."

"Didn't the nurse tell you? I want to be present when you question her."

"Suit yourself." Zones entered to a surprised look on Margret's face.

"Please let me explain," he pleaded before she could say anything. "I'm Dr. Zones and—"

"Dr. Zones? You're the man who called to meet with me about my family," Margret said, pointing her finger at him.

"Yes ma'am. I'm working with the FBI."

"He's the one who found you in your home and he also led us to where Patricia was being held. If it wasn't for him, she wouldn't be here today," Marmaduke interjected, joining Zones in the room.

"This is Detective Marmaduke with DeKalb County." Zones turned to Patricia who rested upright in the bed. "Do you remember what happened to you?" She closed her eyes, rested her head back on her pillow, and frowned painfully.

"I don't think she's ready to talk right now," Margret intervened.

"The man responsible for doing this to you and doing worse to others could be getting away. You're our only survivor," Zones explained, sitting beside her bed, holding her hand, looking into her eyes. She squeezed her eyes closed, focusing a little harder, but still struggled to remember. Patricia shook her head—she couldn't remember a thing.

"If I showed you pictures, do you think you could identify any of them?"

"I could try." Zones scrolled through the photo array James had sent him. Rigdon's image was photo number four. When she got to him, she stopped, much longer than she had with the others. He saw the mechanics of her mind working in her face.

"Does he look familiar, Patricia? Is this one of the men who abducted you?"

"Doc." Marmaduke interrupted, cautioning him not to help her identify Rigdon.

"Is this the man, Patricia?" he asked again, ignoring Marmaduke's caution.

"I don't know. I just don't know," she cried, covering her face.

"I think that's enough for today, maybe tomorrow," Margret said. Dejected, Zones walked out of her room. He feared his last chance to implicate Rigdon had disappeared with Patricia's memory.

"Don't get so down on yourself, Doc. You win some and you lose some. If Rigdon's the psychopath you think he is, he's got his just desserts coming. If he tries that shit over there in sand land, he'll pay with his head, literally. I'm just glad I didn't have the Captain to stop that plane." Zones knew that he would not have done it, not without some evidence. They walked a short distance from her room when shouts spilled into the hall.

"IT'S HIM! IT'S HIM!" someone shouted, causing doctors and nurses to race toward the screams.

Zones and Marmaduke turned to see them running into Patricia's room. They raced back to her room as well.

"What happened?" Zones asked Margret.

"I don't know. While the Doctor was examining her, she was watching the news and when this fella came up on the screen and started speaking, she just lost it." Zones turned to look at the TV. "That's him. That's when she started to scream, when she heard his voice."

"That's Rigdon," Marmaduke said.

"I need to speak with her," Zones demanded, fighting his way through the mash of doctors and nurses trying to sedate her.

"Who are you? Get this guy out of here," one of the doctors shouted as he, Dr. Hyde and others tried to restrain her.

"Patricia, is that the man?" Zones shouted at her, ignoring the Doctor's demand for him to leave.

"His voice!" she said, fading as the drugs set in. Zones looked back at Marmaduke for approval.

"We need more."

"Can you remember anything else, Patricia? I need something more," he pleaded. She dozed off, her fight with her caregivers waned. Her eyes rolled back into her head. She pointed wildly, her hands gestured. She ran her finger over her palm before it fell limp onto the bed.

They herded everyone out the room.

"She needs to rest," Dr. Hyde told Margret. "The stuff we gave her should keep her out until the morning. I suggest you get some rest as well."

"Could someone call me a cab?"

"We can take you, Mrs. Redding. Where to?" Zones offered.

"Virginia-Highlands, I'm her only family—raised her and her sister since they were children. I'm staying in Atlanta until Patricia recovers and is well enough to take care of herself."

. . .

They pulled onto the street where Patricia's Virginia-Highland home was located. Margret got out and disappeared into the house. The place showed no signs of the crime or the resulting investigation that took place over a week ago. It looked pristine like all the other yards on the street, better even. As they pulled off, Zones noticed two women standing out in their yards. They protected themselves from the sun with light airy clothing, big floppy straw hats, shades and gloves. He noticed them only because of the way in which they spoke—with their hands. They drove a short ways past them when Zones shouted,

"Stop!"

"What now?" Marmaduke slammed on the brakes, screeching the wheels and marking up the road. He brought the car to a sudden halt. Zones leapt from the car, leaving the door open behind him. He raced toward the two women, startling them. They readied the gardening tools they held in their hands, preparing to strike.

"No! No! No!" he pleaded, throwing his hands in the air. "I just have a question." One looked puzzled. He turned to the other repeating, "I just have a question to ask you." She looked him up and down, tools still at the ready.

"What do you want?"

"You speak sign language, right?"

"What of it? You're not deaf."

"Can you tell me what this means?" He pointed with his right index finger then raked the finger across the palm of his left hand. He waited for a reply but she gave none. He repeated the gesture again, slower this time, just in case he had moved too fast the first time. Again he waited, but got no reply. "Do you understand?"

"I understand, just waiting for you to sign a complete sentence."

"That's all I have."

"What little you have said was, 'Something scratch'."

"Something scratch . . . something scratch," he repeated, thinking aloud. "So if I pointed at you, I would be saying—"

"That you scratched me, yes."

"Thank you." He walked briskly back to the car, leaving the women confused, still holding their tools.

"Who processed Patricia Redding?" he asked Marmaduke, hopping back into the car.

"CSU I'm sure. Why?"

"She scratched him. And if we find his DNA underneath her fingernails, we got him."

"How do you know this?"

"She told me."

"It can take a long time to process crime scene evidence, especially DNA. Rigdon could be well on his way to the U.A.E. before the results are back." Zones looked at him disappointedly. "I know you're on a roll, kid. I don't mean to burst that optimistic bubble growing inside your head."

THIRTY-EIGHT

They arrived at the CSU lab or the dungeon, as Marmaduke called it, a windowless basement cave painted white and void of noise—the occasional gunfire from the ballistics testing was the only exception. To spot the people who worked there you only needed to look for the pasty white complexions. They looked like ghosts, paler than the lab coats they wore. The brass made vitamin D testing mandatory to ensure that all dungeon staff were not Vitamin D deficient. Some, however, still appeared to be deficient.

They took the elevator to the basement. The doors opened and they stepped out into the world of the crime scene investigator. Zones' eyes widened. He peered in every door or through every glass wall he came to, marveling at the inner workings of a crime lab. He had dissected brains for a neuropsychology class as a graduate student but nothing more than that. The crime lab was something totally different.

They had equipped each lab with the latest in crime fighting tools: powerful microscopes for physical and trace evidence analysis, blood and blood splatter labs whose experiments painted the walls like abstract works of art, a firearms and explosives lab, and a state of the art computer forensics lab with electronic parts strewn about.

They met with the Assistant Commander who took charge of the evidence processing for their case himself. He rearranged the whatnots and plaques displayed on a bookcase in the corner of his office when Zones and Marmaduke entered.

"Hello Marmaduke. And you must be Dr. Zones." He drew the blinds covering a window. Light flooded his office. "Come, I'll walk you over to see the lab director." They filed out of his office and followed him down a dark hall.

"Are you this hands-on with all your cases?" Zones asked.

"I took charge of this one because of its high profile. Didn't want any slip ups; other labs around the country have come under scrutiny in these types of cases. The last thing I want to see is a headline reading something like, 'Hick Town Crime Lab Bungles Evidence: Menace May Go Free'."

"Is that why the Georgia Bureau of Investigation is processing the evidence?"

"Some, but not all of it." They came to a door. "This is it here." The AC reached for the knob. The door flung open before he could grab hold of it.

"Oh hey," the man standing in the doorway said. The AC squared up, surprised by his sudden appearance. They stared at each other for a moment. The title stitched into the white lab coat he wore read, 'Director'. He stretched his neck to look around the AC. "Who do you have there?"

"This is Dr. Zones, a consultant with the FBI and you know Marmaduke. They want to know about any DNA from that victim at the farmhouse."

"From beneath the nails," Zones added.

The lab director scratched his head and looked off into nowhere. He took a bite from the bologna sandwich he held in one hand and clutched a clipboard tightly with his other hand, tucking it beneath his arm.

"Well?" the AC asked.

"We did take finger nail samples but we sent those over to the GBI. The samples were very contaminated from the site. They had the only equipment that could extract the DNA."

"I'll call ahead, let them know you're coming," the AC offered. They turned to leave, following the AC down the hall.

"Or you can just ask me, save you a trip." They all stopped and turned to look at him from halfway down the hall. The AC stomped back to him.

"Where's the report?" He looked him straight in the eyes. The director stuffed his sandwich in his mouth, clenching it between his teeth, mayonnaise oozing from between the bread. He ripped the report from his clipboard and shoved it at the AC.

"I was just on my way to your office with it." The director chewed a bite of his sandwich. He fumbled with the thick glasses falling from his face, pushing them back up on his nose.

"Here you go." The AC handed the report to Zones. He opened it and read.

"They did find DNA. Now all we have to do is match this to Rigdon's."

"Where would we get that? His attorney wouldn't let him give us a sample, and we're running out of time. His plane will be out of U.S. air space soon," Marmaduke said.

"First we need to see if the Captain can stop that plane." They turned, rushing once again, heading toward the stairs and Captain Franklin's office.

"I have it." They stopped from halfway down the hall, turned and approached the director.

"You have what?" the AC asked, leaning in close to him. He stretched his neck, curled his lip and bugged his eyes. "Stop trickling the information to us."

"Tanner Rigdon's DNA," he answered, in a matter of fact tone.

"You have Tanner Rigdon's DNA?" Zones asked. He nodded.

"And just how did you get this DNA?" The AC stood erect, folding his arms across his chest, squinting at the director.

"I collected it."

"When? His attorney wouldn't let him near a swab," Zones added. The director took another bite from his sandwich. He chewed it, smacking his mouth.

"Give me that!" The AC ripped what was left of his sandwich from his hand, tossing it into a nearby trash can. The director froze with an aghast look on his face. He stopped chewing and then slowly continued, finishing up the pieces of sandwich left in his mouth. "Answer the man's question."

"Follow me." The director turned to look at the discarded piece of sandwich and then looked back at the AC. They walked into a room where a large, oversized cabinet sat against the wall. He opened one of the drawers and retrieved a small metal box. He unlocked it and thumbed through a number of glass slides before stopping at one. He pulled the slide from the box, held it to the light, placed the slide beneath a microscope and examined it. He peered down the lens, adjusted the focus, stepped back from the table and said, in a weird French accent, "Gentlemen, I present to you Monsieur Rigdon." They each stepped up to the microscope to view the slide. The director pulled another bologna sandwich from a nearby drawer and ate it, the ire of the AC as plain as day on his face.

"Where did you get this?"

"I told you, I collect them. I collect the DNA of all powerful and famous people, all that I can get. I have the Mayor of Atlanta's, The Governor's, Hank Aaron's, plenty of people. It's my hobby."

"So let me make sure I got this right. You go around collecting the DNA of famous people—"

" . . . famous and powerful."

"Whatever. And you store them here?" the AC questioned.

"Yes. Isn't it neat?" A big smile grew on the director's face.

"Is that shit even legal?" The AC turned to Zones and Marmaduke. They shrugged.

"There's nothing illegal about collecting discarded material. Besides, some people collect autographs and pictures of these people; I collect their DNA."

"You actually follow these people around and collect their trash?"

"Or trade for them with other collectors."

"So there're more of you freaks out there?" The lab director frowned at the AC.

"I, for one, don't give a damn. How soon can you run an analysis and compare it to the samples in here?" Zones asked him.

"I've already run the analysis. We typically do that soon after collection to make sure the sample is good."

"Using department owned facilities and equipment. That's why you store that shit here," the AC snipped. The director ignored him, continuing his explanation.

"All I would have to do is compare the profiles and . . . ." He held the profiles side by side, handing his sandwich to Marmaduke, who took it reluctantly. He moved his finger from one paper to the other, comparing the lines of DNA code. The director spun around in his chair, retrieved a book from a nearby shelf and opened it, placing it on the table. He thumbed through a few pages, reading, moving between the book and the DNA profile. He peered back through the microscope and then at the profile. Finally he concluded, "They're a match."

"The samples taken from our victim and the one you just compared are a match," Zones confirmed with him.

"Uh-huh," he answered, his mouth filled with sandwich.

"Don't get too excited, Doctor. There is no chain of custody here. Rigdon's attorneys will have a field day with this, especially after they find out how his client's DNA was acquired. You're talking invasion of privacy here. They can make this federal," Marmaduke said.

"Only the four of us know about this, right? I have an idea. We need to meet with the Captain."

"You know the Captain won't fall for this, don't you?" Marmaduke whispered to him so the others wouldn't hear.

"We're not going to tell him, at least not this version." They left and headed upstairs, straight to the Captain's office.

"You two can go on in. He's in there sweating like a virgin about to get him some for the first time," James told them as they approached. They entered the Captain's office cautiously. He was spraying air freshener around, trying unsuccessfully to cover up the smell of cigar.

"Where the fuck have you two been? I called your asses over an hour ago. Have a seat," he commanded them, still spraying the office. "Now I need all the details about how we cracked this thing and don't leave nothing out. Whatever you know, I want to know. Now give it to me." He sat at his desk, waiting for whatever they had to share. Zones looked at Marmaduke, thinking that he really didn't want to hear all they knew.

"Well Captain—"

"Hold it. James, get in here," he called to her through the closed door. "Take this down." James pulled up a chair. "Okay, go ahead."

"Before we start, Captain, we need to stop a plane from leaving the country."

"Plane. What plane?"

"The plane that Tanner Rigdon is taking to the U.A.E."

"Tanner Rigdon? I thought we were past this, Doc. Now we're back to Rigdon? The mayor and councilwoman have made it clear that Rigdon is off limits. So unless you have something more than a theory, I don't want to hear his name mentioned again."

"Our surviving victim positively ID'd him." The Captain started to take a sip from the coffee cup he held but stopped abruptly. His eyes peeked over the top of his glasses at the two of them. Marmaduke sat stoically, quickly cutting his eyes toward Zones, his lie written all over Marmaduke's face.

"Is that true, Marmaduke?" The Captain lowered his cup from his lips.

"Well . . . I . . . Yes." The Captain stared at him intensely, trying to read his face.

"You're a lying sack of shit, Marmaduke. But you must have something and it's not an ID, that's too easily disproved. It's something you can't use, something you acquired illegally perhaps but it's proof nonetheless." He thought for a second. "I don't know if I should risk everything on your obsession with Tanner Rigdon—but okay. James, call it in."

"Now we're talking." Zones hopped from his seat.

James exited the office. The two of them tried piling out right after her.

"Sit down!" the Captain yelled, pulling a pen and pad from his desk drawer. "I still need that information—Go."

"First, we developed a profile of our perpetrators. We then identified the five victims through the missing persons database and DNA typing. The profile indicated that the crimes were religiously based, a genealogical analysis showed a historical Mormon connection between all the victims—"

"Hold up Doc, we don't want to go there."

"I'm just giving you the facts, Captain, you can spin it however you want."

"Yeah, keep going."

"We linked trace evidence found at the crime scene to a shipment of grain to a number of locations. We narrowed our search, using geographic profiling, to an old farmhouse where we found one of the perpetrators and one of the missing victims alive. We traced ownership of the property to Tanner Rigdon."

"Is that it?"

"That's it."

"Okay then, you can go." Zones and Marmaduke rose to leave. "Hey! When are you two going to learn? Don't think I fell for your victim ID bullshit. The AC down in the crime lab is my frat brother. We chased tail together all up and down the east coast. You didn't think I would get a call about you two pricks' scheming, did you? Get out and close my door. And this better not go sideways either."

They hurried from the Captain's office, appearing at James' desk.

"Are they going to turn him around?" Zones asked her, as he and Marmaduke hovered. Hearing only one side of a conversation frustrated him, like a child impatient with their mother for not dipping the ice cream fast enough.

"Okay—thank you. They're turning it around." Zones pumped his fist, thinking his prey would soon be caged. "They should be landing within the hour."

"I'll drive," Marmaduke said.

. . .

Zones and Marmaduke met Rigdon's plane at the airport, along with a throng of reporters. Marmaduke led him away, hands cuffed behind his back, with no heed taken for his station in life. Zones stood at a distance; he relished seeing the smirk Rigdon wore like a crown being wiped from his face. Their eyes locked onto each other, Zones tipped his tan Kangol cap to him. His face now wore the smirk.

Despite feeling satisfied, Zones knew that his work had just begun. The DNA evidence would not hold up in court. He needed a confession.

"Hello James. Marmaduke is on his way to the station with Rigdon. We're going to question him but first we'll give him a few days to stew. I need you to put him in the smallest interrogation room you have available."

"I got one that we're kind of using as a storage area. It's about the size of Marmaduke's two twenty-five."

"Perfect. The small space should give this mesotonic bastard a bit of the fits."

THIRTY-NINE

Once again, Tanner Rigdon found himself waiting in an interrogation room at the DeKalb County Police. Mizrah, Dr. Hyde and his battery of attorneys prepared him for questioning. Looking less confident than before, he buried his head in his hands. His attorneys tried to console him.

Marmaduke walked into the room carrying a small brown box and a ton of confidence. He said nothing at first, deciding instead to allow the evidence to speak for him. He dropped the box onto the table, rattling the objects inside. Rigdon watched as Marmaduke dug into the box, taking items out and putting them on the table in front of him. Rigdon's gaze moved from Marmaduke to the objects on the table. The small space was split down the middle, a sense of dread filling half the room and confidence and conviction filling the other half. Marmaduke emptied the box of the objects. He whipped out a folder and opened it onto the table. He placed the crime scene pictures from the farmhouse in front of him, saying nothing. He looked up briefly to gauge Rigdon's reaction. When he placed the last of the photographs on the table, he took a seat and stared at his suspect sitting across from him.

"Let's see here. Tanner Rigdon, CEO of Deseret Holding. How long have you held that position? Oh, I see, five years," Marmaduke read through the report. He began to whistle the theme song from Perry Mason.

"Is that necessary, Detective?" Mizrah asked.

"Oh, I'm sorry. Am I disturbing you?" he asked with an exaggerated look of apology on his face. "I see you rose through the ranks pretty quickly. A little help from your old man, no doubt?"

"I'll have you know that I started as a laborer digging trenches and hauling lumber, Detective." Rigdon leaned forward in his chair. Marmaduke sensed he had hit a nerve.

"Well, there's nothing like hard, get-your-hands-dirty, sweaty-ass-work to whip a silver-spooned, born-half-way-to-home-base brat into shape." Rigdon leaned back in his chair, looking over at Mizrah and then at Dr. Hyde.

"Do you have real questions, Detective, or are we going to sit here and play games?" Mizrah asked.

"And why are we in this small ass room?" Rigdon chimed in.

"Yes, Detective, a little more room would have been more accommodating," Dr. Hyde added.

"Don't like our accommodations, do you? Don't worry, the cells are a little larger. Now tell me, Mr. Rigdon, why are your juvy records sealed?"

"We have no records concerning that matter." Mizrah answered.

"Well, it's funny because I knew that would be your answer." Marmaduke pointed his finger and whipped his arm out at Mizrah. "So I pulled the crime reports from the neighborhood where your parents still live—perfectly legal. It appears that your childhood neighbors, over a period of five years, reported their small animals turning up dead. Now that got me curious so I tracked down a necropsy report on several of the animals and I found out that they died of cardiac arrest with abnormally high levels of potassium in their blood. Now, to a country boy like me, potassium chloride might as well have been nuclear fusion. Shit, I don't know the difference."

"It's hot in here." Rigdon pulled at his shirt collar, loosening his tie. "Is this legal? Isn't this against the Geneva Convention?" he asked Mizrah.

"Could my client get some water, Detective?" Marmaduke motioned to Chennault to bring a pitcher of water and cups.

"I'll help you, Detective." Dr. Hyde leapt from his seat and bolted for the door ahead of Chennault.

"Now, where was I? Oh yeah, potassium chloride. The M.E. determined that at least two of the victims died of cardiac arrest and also found elevated levels of potassium in their blood. Do you see where I'm going with this, Mr. Rigdon?"

"I don't see what dead animals from twenty plus years ago have to do with my client."

"Well, perhaps you'll see this. Remember that flower shop your client had been trying to buy for the longest time? No? Oh right, it was that shell company you set up that wanted it. But the old biddy who owned the shop wouldn't sell. That is, until she opened up one morning and found two dead bodies inside. She sold it to you days later. Sounds vaguely familiar, doesn't it? That's how you were able to build that swanky place in Midtown, without that one property the city wouldn't allow you to build it. What type of business is located there now?" Marmaduke asked, turning to Chennault.

"A sex club," he answered before leaving to get water.

"A sex club," Marmaduke repeated, shaking his head and sucking his teeth. "I wonder what the church would think of that?"

"Old news. I still haven't heard anything that says murder, Detective," Mizrah said. "And I'm sure as hell not going to let you clear cold cases using my client."

"How about this, you are a patient of a psychologist who specializes in OCDs—Dermatophagia and others. That's finger biting, isn't it? Because the M.E. found bite marks on the victim's fingers." He shoved the report across the table, spun it around right side up and thumped it with his finger for emphasis. They looked over the report. Rigdon squirmed in his seat.

Chennault returned with a pitcher of water and cups.

"Oh, your Bishop?" he asked, seeing Rigdon gawk at the door until he closed it. "He's sucking up air out in the hall." He sat the water and cups in the middle of the table. Rigdon grabbed one, poured himself water nearly to the rim and chugged it down.

Dr. Hyde returned to the room visibly distressed. Rigdon's eyes followed him to his seat as Marmaduke continued his questioning.

Marmaduke began with the items placed on the table, holding the blades up, showing them to him. "These are only a small sample of the knives found at your farmhouse; they were used to cut up five bodies matching those at the four dump sites." He dropped the bag back to the table. "This is a picture of the body parts strewn about the property, given no more care than the slop you threw on the ground to feed your pigs."

"I don't know what you're talking about." Rigdon turned away from Marmaduke.

"This is a picture of the burnt out van you used to transport your victims. You went to one of those fancy universities, didn't you Mr.

Rigdon?" Marmaduke waited for the reply he knew wouldn't come. "Yeah, you went to one. So you may know what Eddy-Current Magnetographing is." He read from the forensics report, smiling.

"Is there a point to this, Detective?" Mizrah asked. Marmaduke ignored him, focusing instead on Rigdon. He eyeballed him the way two alpha-males of any species might before challenging each other for the leadership position.

"You see, Tanner, may I call you Tanner? Good. In these older model vans, the VIN number was stamped into the metal, even when subjected to intense heat, a VIN number could be retrieved from the metal using the Magnet thing. So when our lab boys looked at this VIN, we found it registered to your company."

"We've already explained that, Detective. This is old news," Mizrah said.

"You've already explained that the vehicle could have been stolen and that's a plausible explanation. But what isn't plausible is this." Marmaduke pulled a piece of paper from his file and slid it across the table toward Rigdon. He just stared at it. "Go on, you can touch it. But I can't promise that it won't bite."

"What is this?" Mizrah asked.

"What you're looking at is a DNA analysis comparing your specimen to those collected from the fingernails of your last victim, Patricia Redding. You see what it says right there?" Marmaduke leaned across the table, pointing to the paper. "It says 99.99 percent match. That means the DNA is yours. Can you explain how your DNA got underneath the nails of a woman found close to death, hanging by her legs and bound with rope in a filthy farmhouse?" He lifted the plastic bag holding the rope off the table and slammed it down.

"I didn't kill anyone and I don't know anything about a farmhouse and dead bodies." Rigdon slammed his fist on the table. His face turned bright red. Veins became more pronounced in his neck, visibly throbbing, feeding blood to his face.

Tears swelled up in his eyes, his first sign of sincere emotion. Marmaduke was taken aback. He expected the same smug, cocky, hiding behind his lawyers asshole that they had encountered the first time. This softer Tanner Rigdon was a little difficult to take.

"If you didn't do this, who did, your evil twin? Is there someone else running around out there with your DNA? Do you have an identical impersonator, Mr. Rigdon?"

. . .

Zones watched from the observation room along with the Captain and the District Attorney. He knew how the scene would play out. As Marmaduke continued to make accusations and present the evidence to support same, Rigdon and his attorneys would deny, deny, deny. This charade served only to unsettle the suspect and allow him to see what challenges he faced trying to defend himself. Neither party expected to see a Perry Mason moment.

Zones leaned in, getting closer to the one-way mirror, peering through it, looking for something specific. He honed in on the rope, in particular, the knot.

"Dr. Zones, what is it?" the Captain asked, seeing him pressed close to the mirror, looking intently. "I've seen that look before."

"Impersonator," Zone said aloud. He stared at the Captain, but actually through him. His eyes widened and his mind spun with thoughts he knew the Captain wouldn't want to hear. "Bishop Wadley said impersonator." He rushed from the room and into the interrogation room. Rigdon, seeing him enter, shouted,

"This is your fault! You did this to me!" He leapt from his seat. His attorneys restrained him.

"May I see that, Detective," Zones asked him before he placed the rope back in the box. He held it up, looking at the intricate knot.

"What is it, Doc?"

"I've seen this knot in only three other places." Actually it was four, but he couldn't tell them about the one he saw in the bondage room of the sex club.

"Where's that?"

"In Utah, in his office, and wrapped around Patricia Redding in her home." He looked over at Rigdon who sat, still steaming. A look that said he wanted to do Zones some serious harm was on his face. "Who, other than the brute, was your accomplice?"

"My accomplice? I had no accomplice and I don't know anything about a brute."

"Marilyn, the whore you paid for the sperm sample, told us about another man with a scar who asked her to get the sample. Who is he?" Rigdon looked at Zones, dumbfounded. He gripped the table tightly.

His eyes grew menacing. "Listen, you're not going to convince me that you're not good for these murders. I don't care if you do your time alone or share it with your friend. We have a live witness and your DNA. That's all the evidence we need to convict you. Ask your mouthpieces here what that means."

Mizrah rose from his chair. "We're out of here. Our client isn't going to answer any more questions."

"Your client hasn't answered any questions, at least not truthfully," Marmaduke snapped back.

"You tell the DA, when he's ready to deal he knows where to reach us. Come on, Tanner."

Zones took the photographs of the symbols painted on the wall and stacked them in front of Rigdon.

"What is this?" Zones slammed the picture to the table. Rigdon said nothing, just stared down at the picture. "The Nauvoo Pentagram," Zones said. "And this? The compass and square, the eye of Horus, the inscribed circle. And here, the white painted walls, a sacred color to Mormons." Rigdon hung his head, shaking it. "You don't know what any of this means, do you? Your bishop knows." Zones cut a glance at Dr. Hyde, still suffering from some unknown distress. "But you know who did this, don't you?"

Rigdon, perhaps seeing an opportunity for a way out or at least to minimize his involvement in these crimes asked,

"If I told you everything, what kind of deal could I get?"

"Tanner, I strongly suggest—"

"Suggest what? You going to do my time?"

"Tanner, you may want to listen to your attorney. There's more than you at stake here," Dr. Hyde advised him.

"I need a moment with my client. That means the ears in there too," Mizrah said, looking at the one-way mirror.

They left the room and turned off the electronic listening device. A few minutes passed and Mizrah appeared at the door.

"We're ready" he said. They all returned to the room and took their places. "Before we start, I need the DA's okay on this."

"You got it, Mizrah," a voice said over the intercom.

"Now let's hear it," Marmaduke said.

Rigdon scooted his chair closer to the table, resting his arms on it, looking down at his fingers, fumbling with them as if examining something.

"Stop stalling, Mr. Rigdon."

"I know nothing about a fat man, a brute or a farmhouse," he started. His voice was stern and angry. His eyes cocked, a finger pointing at Zones. "But the other guy you're looking for, Allard, or some shit like that. I call him the Norseman. They sent him from Utah."

"They who?"

"The church but I don't know who specifically."

"Now, just a minute," Dr. Hyde interrupted. The church is not—"

"Quiet, Doctor." Marmaduke threw up his hand, cutting him off. "Continue."

"He just showed up and said he was sent from Utah. They sent him to take care of a little problem I was having with this woman."

"You want us to believe that the Mormon Church is involved in this?" Marmaduke gave Dr. Hyde a quick look. "What kind of problem?"

Rigdon glanced at Mizrah. He licked his lips and rocked in his seat as if it was filled with pins. He moved in closer to Mizrah, consulting before revealing his problem.

"She accused me of raping her. Said she was going to report me to the police and go to the media if I didn't pay her. So Allard devised a scheme to plant the semen of someone else on her things. He arranged it and I paid just like the whore said. We used some and threw the rest away; I guess you found it."

"The church had nothing to do with this, Detective. Whatever scheme those two cooked up cannot be attributed to the church," Dr. Hyde said.

"I think this is where the church bus pulls in to throw you under it, Mr. Ridgon." Marmaduke gave him a moment for Dr Hyde's disclaimer to sink in. "Was it you or Allard who discarded the semen?"

"It had to have been him. I've never been to that side of town."

"So if we're to believe this story and you didn't rape her, why not just let her prove her case in court?"

"Let's just say my client has had similar accusations lodged against him in the past and he couldn't afford another claim of this nature," Mizrah answered.

"And what is the name of this woman?"

"Margret Mitchell," Rigdon said after a long pause. Zones and Marmaduke looked at each other, a side-splitting laugh on the verge of escaping their mouths. They turned their attention back to their subject, sensing the name was too fictional not to be true.

"Margret Mitchell. That's the name of this woman?" Marmaduke laughed then pushed a pen and paper across the table to him. "Her address and phone number." Rigdon scribbled the information down. "I'll be back." Marmaduke took the paper and exited the room, giving Rigdon a hard stare, one that said, "If this is a wild goose chase, you'll regret it".

"What about the vehicle? That was your vehicle, wasn't it?" Zones asked.

"I had him burn it right after you left my office that day."

"Why? If you weren't trying to hide any evidence from these crimes, why bother?" Their quietness signaled an incriminating story.

"I had him to burn it because Allard used it to . . ."

"To what, damn it."

"To transport her."

"What do you mean, transport her? You're not talking about a body are you?"

"She was alive when she left my home. But . . ."

"But she wasn't conscious. Are you trying to say that you drugged her and then raped her? So you had the van destroyed to cover up any evidence of her being in it."

"Listen, when you came to my office alluding that the van was seen at places connected to those murders, I didn't want to be caught up in anything Allard was doing on the side."

"So your first inclination was to help him cover it up, not call the authorities?"

"My client isn't admitting to helping anyone cover up anything. Now whatever someone else used a company van for cannot be attributed to Mr. Rigdon."

"Let's say I believe you; I'm not saying that I do, not by far. But say that it's true, how then do you explain the DNA underneath her nails—your DNA? They've got you dead to rights with your own DNA as evidence."

"I can't explain that. I've never met the woman. Look at me. I have no scratches on me anywhere."

Zones thought hard about what he said. He saw no visible scars on Rigdon. A woman fighting for her life would have left deep scratches, not the superficial kind that healed overnight. The lack of scratches didn't mean he wasn't a killer but their absence did bother him.

"All I know is that your DNA was found beneath her nails."

"You don't believe me? Here, I'll show you." Rigdon stood up and disrobed, surprising all of them. Seconds later, he was completely nude. He turned around, arms extended into the air. He then bent over and spread his cheeks. "Is that proof enough for you?" At that moment, Marmaduke returned to the room.

"What the—" he started, seeing Rigdon standing there in nothing but his birthday suit. "What the hell is going on here?"

"Did you check out his story with the woman?"

"Yeah, she said he drugged and raped her—denied blackmailing him of course. The last thing she remembered was having a drink at his home and then waking up back at her place. She doesn't know how she got there though." Marmaduke watched as Rigdon put his clothes back on.

"Excuse me." Zones left the room.

"Where're you going, Doc?" He did not respond. He re-entered the observation room where the Captain and the DA still looked on.

"What's going on in there, Doc?" the Captain asked.

"I don't know yet, maybe something, maybe nothing. Do you have the DNA analysis report?"

"Yeah, here it is. Why?"

"You don't want to know." Zones looked through the report, coming to a section explaining the type of sample analyzed. They were oral mucosal skin cells from the mouth. He lowered the report, looking concerned.

"What is it, Doctor?"

"You don't want to know," he told him, quickly exiting the room.

"What do you mean, I don't want to know?"

Zones re-entered the interrogation room. He pulled a penlight from his coat pocket and walked around to the other side of the table where Rigdon and his attorney sat.

"Stand up."

"For what?"

Zones said nothing, just gave him a, "Get your ass up before I get you up", kind of look. Rigdon rose from his chair.

"Face me and open your mouth."

"What is it you want, Dr. Zones?" Mizrah asked.

"You can instruct your client to open his mouth now or submit to a full body cavity search by the thickest-fingered guard I can find." Mizrah nodded. Rigdon opened. Zones clicked on the penlight and shined it into his mouth. "Wider." He moved the light around inside his mouth, examining it for any signs of trauma. "Okay, you can have a seat." He walked back to his seat. "Detective Marmaduke, could you please get me a cup of coffee." Marmaduke frowned. "Would you like something Mr. Rigdon?" He shook his head.

"What's going on, Doc?"

"Just thirsty, Detective." Zones took his seat back across from Rigdon. Marmaduke left the room, looking skeptical. "Detective Chennault, there's a file James pulled for me, could you get it for me?"

"Sure, Doc."

Zones walked over to the door after him. He placed a chair behind it, wedging the chair beneath the handle and preventing entry. He returned to his seat, leaned forward close to Rigdon and said,

"If you want to walk out of here and not spend the rest of your life behind bars, or worse, you'll tell me where I can find Allard."

"What the fuck are you doing?" Captain Franklin shouted over the intercom. Moments later, someone banged hard at the barricaded door.

FOURTY

"Open this door, Doctor!" Captain Franklin yelled from the other side of it. "You're not going to get him off like you did the other two."

"What did he mean by that, you getting two others off?" Rigdon asked.

"Just what he said, I got two others out of here when the evidence pointed to them. So unless you give me something, I can't help you. Now where is Allard? If he committed these crimes, it's in your best interest that we find him."

"Dr. Zones, you open this door now. I'll have you arrested for interfering with an investigation."

"I don't know where he is."

"You said he was sent from Utah. Could he have returned there?"

"I doubt it. They would want him as far away from them as possible."

"I can no longer listen to this, I'm leaving," Dr. Hyde said.

"Sit down, Doctor. No one is going anywhere. Now you called him the Norseman. Why?" Zones already knew he was from the Netherlands.

"Because he is from Finland or Norway, one of those countries."

"Do you think he would have gone back there?"

"He told me he was wanted there—Interpol was looking for him." Zones rose up and headed toward the door. "What are you doing?"

"If that's all you got for me, I'm not going to stand in between you and that pit bull out there." Zones motioned to remove the chair from the door.

"Okay! Okay! There's a house outside of Macon. You will find him there."

"Here, address and directions." Zones slid paper and a pencil in front of him. As before, he scribbled on the paper. Zones took it, read it and scanned the drawing. Looking back at Rigdon, he said, "This better be good." He moved closer to the door, the Captain still outside, banging and shouting. Zones removed the chair lodged behind it. The Captain and two uniformed officers burst through the door.

"Officers, arrest him. This is the last time you'll interfere with this investigation. Make sure you pat him down too." They took hold of Zones and rushed him from the room. "This meeting is over, gentlemen." He took hold of Rigdon.

"Captain, you and the DA must remember our deal. My client has cooperated fully, giving you the true perpetrator of these crimes," Mizrah said as the Captain removed Rigdon from the room.

"That's between you and the DA."

. . .

They hauled Rigdon into a cell, separating him from the others. He stood there, looking down at what would now be his bed—a cot.

"Your second hot is at one," the guard said. She slammed the barred door behind him. "Turn around, let me uncuff you." He stuck his hands through a space in the bars. The handcuffs fell from his wrist.

Rigdon plopped down hard onto the cot. The ends of the worn mattress curled beneath his weight, its sparseness a far cry from the cushioned beds he laid on each night at home.

He turned to the guard. "Do you know when I'll get out—my bail? The guard looked down on her charge sheet.

"Get comfortable. These charges ain't for parking tickets or a drunken bar room brawl. You've hit the big times now."

"I want to see my attorney."

"You just did. Besides, ain't no amount of fancy legal talk gonna make these charges go away. You need to be calling on Jesus." She turned and tore down the hall.

Zones convinced Rigdon to give him the information he sought. This information would either save him, as Rigdon hoped it would or send him to the gallows. He had explained away all the circumstantial evidence against him. The DNA, however, was the stickler that he could not explain. If Rigdon thought that by giving up Allard the District Attorney would somehow ignore the DNA evidence against him, he was mistaken. If his strategy failed, his attorneys would have to come up with some way of explaining his DNA underneath the nails of the victim, found bound, gagged and hanging by her feet in a human slaughterhouse.

Rigdon placed his face in his hands. His elbows rested on his knees. His head stayed buried there for a while, perhaps praying, but more than likely he was thinking about how badly he had fucked up this time. He rose up and leaned back across his bed, his eyes closed, his head resting on the wall separating his cell from the next one. He took a deep breath, expelling it in one big whoosh. He opened his eyes, seeing Zones occupying one of the cells across from him, watching him closely.

FOURTY-ONE

A caravan of armed law enforcement vehicles barreled down a desolate road, just like the time Marmaduke, Chennault and Zones assaulted the old farmhouse. This house also sat back off the main road on a large tract of land. The nearest house was at least one mile away, same as the first farmhouse.

"We are staged here at the old general store and Miller's farm is here," the local sheriff pointed out on the aerial map, unfurled across the hood of a vehicle.

"Is there anything between here and here?" Marmaduke asked, circling a large swath near the farm with his finger.

"No, this is all open land."

"That doesn't give us much cover."

"If you approached the house from the road, he may see you coming and make a run for it into the woods before you get there. Now, if you come up through Brown's farm from the rear, you can get right up on him and he'll never see you coming. The drive is a little longer but it'll save you the hassle of having to chase him through the woods if he gets wind of you."

"What do you think, commander?" Marmaduke asked.

"That sounds good. We'll set up stations here and here, team one there and team two there. Team three will approach from Brown's farm and when they're in position, I'll give the signal for teams one and two to move in and flush him out." They all agreed. "Everyone check your fire."

The commander and his men were not at the first farmhouse raid. They fist bumped each other, pounded their chests and shouted,

"Hooaah!"

"My boys don't want to miss out on the action this time," the commander said.

"Just one more thing, Sheriff, do you have something for these gnats?" Marmaduke swatted away the swarming bugs, they irritated him as much as the waiting did.

Team three took a side road to Brown's farm, the abandoned property was a casualty of drought and a bad real estate market. Where crops of corn, onions, and tomatoes once grew, the tracks of armored carriers crisscrossed the vast open fields. They came to a wooded area along the backside of the property. The SWAT teams stormed from their vehicles and marched through the woods. They hiked at least five miles through thick brush and weeds before coming upon the home. They took their positions along the rear perimeter.

"Team three in position, over" the team leader called over the radio.

"Team three in position, copy. Any sign of subject, over?"

"That's a positive commander, got a visual on subject, over."

"Hold position and maintain visual, over."

"Copy, holding position."

The commander positioned the other teams.

"Let me see that thing." Marmaduke took the team leader's radio. "Commander, this is Marmaduke. Remember, we need this one alive."

"Alive, or as alive as you and Chennault left the other one?" the commander quipped.

"We didn't have a choice in that one, Commander."

"Copy, Detective—you hear that boys, this is a catch and release. I repeat, a catch and release."

"Copy that, Commander."

They stormed the small house, launching concussion grenades, bursting through the door, guns drawn and readied to fire. This time there would be no negotiations, no time for the perp to prepare for the onslaught about to be exacted upon him.

Allard ran through the house and out the back door, toward the woods. Seeing him approach, Marmaduke and team three emerged from their secure place in the woods, surrounding him.

"On the ground!" someone shouted. Allard complied, lying face down, arms stretched out at his side. Two commandos moved in while the others covered them. They handcuffed and pulled him up from the ground.

"I will tell you everything Tanner Rigdon has done," Allard said, his rich accent comingling with a nervous smile.

FOURTY-TWO

"Zones! Thelonious Zones!" his jailer called out, harkening back to the day when he first arrived in Atlanta and got caught tasting its home cooking. They held him that time for more than four hours. He stared across his jail cell at Tanner Rigdon but said nothing. They played this cat and mouse game throughout the investigation, each taking a turn as the rodent. Who would come out the victor, neither one knew.

"Right here!" Zones called out. He leapt from his resting place, pressed his face to the steel bars and waved his hand.

"Step back," the guard demanded, before placing the key into the lock and opening the cell door. "Come this way." Zones complied, walking through the cell door, on his way to his release. Rigdon rushed to the door of his cell, looking through the bars as Zones approached.

"Did they get him? Did they get Allard? When will I get out of here?" Rigdon asked as Zones passed by. He said nothing, just stared at him, seeing the despair on his face. *This guy won't survive this.*

Moments later, Zones walked toward Captain Franklin's office. The usual station noise fell silent to the squeaking wheels of a push cart as the cleaning crew tidied up the place. He looked around but saw no one at first. He rounded a corner seeing James; she sat at her station shuffling papers.

"Go on in, they're waiting on you. Hope your accommodations were to your liking."

"Let's just say that Rigdon isn't the only one who wouldn't make it on the inside." He poked his head in the door.

"Dr. Zones, come in," the Captain greeted him. Gone were the harsh words of arrest he had spewed hours earlier. The DA stood near the corner swinging a golf club. "Now Dr. Zones, please tell me why we put on that little charade for Mr. Rigdon, not that I didn't enjoy seeing you locked up for four hours."

"Well, Captain, as you know, Rigdon's DNA sample we used to compare with that recovered from our victim was obtained by less than legal means."

"Yeah, the District Attorney and I expressed the possible challenges that might be brought up at trial earlier—the fruit of the poisonous tree and all."

"And all the other evidence we had against him, the van, interest in the properties, the sperm sample and the historical connections were purely circumstantial so we needed Rigdon's remaining accomplice."

"This Allard character."

"When Rigdon didn't bare any scratches, this concerned me. The DNA sample was from the mucosal skin tissue of a body cavity—more likely from the mouth, which heals quicker than other skin surfaces."

"That's why you examined his mouth."

"Right. When Detective Marmaduke brought in the rope from the farmhouse, I recognized the knot in it as one identical to another I saw in Rigdon's office and another one from a trip to the Mormon Church's Welfare Square facility where I met Allard. They both told me it was their own invention so I knew they had to be accomplices. We just needed to get Rigdon to tell us where Allard was."

"How did you know Rigdon would give him up, especially with his attorneys present?"

"This was where the profile got tricky. The crime scenes suggested a religious zealot of sorts but Rigdon showed no such tendencies. He wasn't that religious and other than his job, he held no particular allegiances to the Mormon Church. I confirmed this in my first meeting with him. His motive in this crime was purely profit-driven. He embezzled money from Deseret Holding through a shell company he set up. People who commit profit-driven crimes will make profit-driven deals, so we setup a scenario for him to make such a deal."

"What about his accomplice, this Allard fella?"

"Mr. Allard, unlike Rigdon, who displays signs of a narcissistic personality disorder, is a zealot. He believes in his cause."

"And what is that?"

Zones gathered the things taken from him during his staged arrest. He noticed a Bible on the Captain's desk. He walked over, grabbed it and flipped through its pages until coming to the scripture he sought.

Zones took a pen from the desk and marked a passage. He placed the Bible down in front of the Captain and then turned to leave. Zones looked back to see the Captain frown with a bewildered look on his face.

"Matthew 24:15?" He picked the Bible up and read:

> *"When ye therefore shall see the abomination of desolation, spoken of by Daniel the prophet, stand in the holy place, (whoso readeth, let him understand:)."*

"What the fuck does that have to do with my question? Dr. Zones! Dr. Zones!"

Zones continued walking out the door, saying nothing, leaving the Captain with even more questions.

"Good bye, gorgeous." Zones passed James sitting at her desk.

"And."

"Smart."

"And don't you forget it."

Zones walked out of the DeKalb County Police station and into a late southern evening, this case and the horror it brought was behind him. Just as he left, his phone rang.

"This is Zones."

"Dr. Zones, I see that Mr. Rigdon has been arrested," the voice on the phone said. It was the Bishop of Welfare Square.

"Yes, Bishop, he has."

"We're happy this issue is behind us, Doctor."

"The church fathers don't fear this could soil the Mormon Church? After all, Rigdon was the CEO of your business arm."

"Which would be like a mere footnote in the next couple of years, Dr. Zones. In any event, I will convey his arrest to the, 'church fathers', as you say."

"Just one more thing, Bishop? There was a gentleman working at the Square in your storage area tying down crates, he had a foreign accent."

"Yes, Brother Allard. Unfortunately, he returned to his home country, somewhere in the Netherlands, I believe. Why do you ask about him?"

"I shared with him that I did a bit of sailing; he promised to teach me to tie a knot he invented. He called it the Gordian Knot. Are you familiar with it?"

"I'm afraid not, Dr. Zones. I don't get to fraternize with the help very much. As you probably noticed, we are very busy here. There are always those in need of the church's help. We can always use new hands, Doctor. You may want to consider joining us."

"I'm sure that we'll meet again, Bishop." He closed his phone. Zones pulled the collar to his trench coat up and buttoned it. Rain trickled from the sky. He walked through the drizzle toward the Marta station, clearing his mind, pondering his next move, pleased with himself. His phone rang again.

"You miss me already?"

"Just spoke to the M.E. She said the body parts Chennault found on the table at the farmhouse did not come from Carolyn Armstrong. And the bite marks on Patricia Redding's fingers and the others' didn't match Rigdon," James told him.

"What! Whose were they?"

"Many donors. DNA matched them to the five other bodies used at the four dumpsites. None of the bite marks matched the victims or the one dead perpetrator."

"So we still have a missing person and one more dental impression to take. I'll be right there."

FOURTY-THREE

"What did you do with the other girl?" Zones asked Rigdon, sitting across from him in a small room with bad lighting. He said nothing, perhaps still mad about the harsh questioning he had gotten earlier and about being accused in the killings. "Why not help yourself? Give me the girl and I'll let the DA know that you cooperated." Rigdon yawned and passed the time by cracking his neck, trying to work out the stiffness in his body. "You could possibly save yourself from a needle prick."

"Save myself from a needle prick! Are you fucking kidding me?" he scowled. "How many times do I have to tell you that I had nothing to do with these killings? So if you're depending on me to help you save this girl from the guy who did put those bodies in those places, then you can just add her to the body count. Now I'm ready to go back to my cell."

The guards hauled him out of the room. If Zones did find the missing girl, it wasn't going to be with Rigdon's help. He needed to find another way. He must find what he missed in his initial investigation—a second slaughter farm.

· · ·

"Okay, James, I got nothing out of Rigdon. We're going to have to retrace our steps. Let's see—we're missing something," Zones paced the floor. "Why would Rigdon not stash Carolyn Armstrong with all the other bodies?" He pulled the geographic profile from his pocket, studying it. "When I first met Rigdon in his office—"

"You mean when you impersonated a gay magazine editor?"

"Yeah," he answered with a straight face. "He said Deseret had plans to purchase land for farm operations but he wouldn't say where."

"And I didn't find any land holdings for the company other than the Midtown development and their Downtown corporate office."

"Rigdon said that he couldn't tell me about their land purchase because, if made public, the land prices in the area would double. Do you have access to real estate sales prices?"

"I can access the NAR and Tax Assessors databases."

Zones smoothed the map out onto James' desk. "Let's check the sales prices in these areas." He marked them with a pen. "Start from one year ago today. I'm looking for any area where the sale prices jumped significantly."

James pecked away at her keyboard. "Okay, the areas with the greatest increase in sales price are here in the Lithonia area."

"Now look at each area and see when the prices started to increase."

"You have an increase along the I-20 corridor but Stonecrest Mall is mostly responsible for that. Right here, along Covington Highway, these started to increase around May of 2011."

"Now which properties where sold right before that time?"

"I have twelve parcels."

"That's still too many. Go ahead and pull the sales and transfer documents on those. Let's see who purchased them. Where's another computer I can use?"

"Sandy's office, she's gone for the day."

Zones began to review his notes and retrace his research. He combed back through the information on Mormon history to see what he may have missed, if anything. He revisited the "Salt Sermon" and the Danites and the various other tales of this sect. Zones clicked on a link to a webpage that read, "Additional Information". Scrolling through the data he came across a familiar last name. He ran it through the genealogy database.

"James!" he shouted, leaping from his chair and dashing to her desk. "Let me see the names."

"Here they are, I've printed them, but—" Zones ripped the paper from her hands, thumbing through each page with great interest.

"None of them are Deseret?" he said, coming to the last page.

"No shit, Sherlock, that's what I was about to tell you before you went all greedy man on me."

"What about addresses?"

"I'll have to read those off to you. This printer is acting up again."

"Okay, shoot." He snatched a pen from her desk, getting ready to write.

"128 Covington Highway, 3498 Browns Mill Rd., 1006 Old Man James Rd., 65 Edyh Rd—"

"Spell that."

"E.D.Y.H., 27 Stanton Farm Rd—"

"Hold it. Where's the map?"

"Right here." Zones compared the map to one of the addresses. His eyes moved back and forth between the two. He flipped through his notes, pulling out the paper on mesotonic personalities, scanning it. He pulled the investigator's report, reading the crime scene notes on the appearance of the bodies.

"Where's my medication?" He rummaged through his briefcase, finding the bottle of Elavil. He thumped the map on the desk saying, "Gotcha!" Zones scooped up the papers, stuffing them back into his case. "Where's Detective Chennault?"

"He's back at the farmhouse, processing it, and Marmaduke is bringing Rigdon's accomplice up from Macon"

"Get hold of Chennault and tell him to meet me at the Edyh Rd. location. And I need to borrow your car."

"My car? My baby!" She got real serious. "Now that's my Mary Kay baby. She ain't used to being handled by no man."

"I'll be gentle." James gave him a hard stare. "I promise." She reached for her keys, handing them to him.

"And what do I tell the Captain?"

"Tell him that Rigdon is guilty—but not of murder."

"WHAT!"

FOURTY-FOUR

Zones barreled through the South DeKalb countryside, much the same as before, only this time the roads drove smoother and he traveled alone. James' GPS made getting lost much less likely, unlike with Marmaduke and Chennault. He stopped just outside the gate to a sprawling, heavily wooded area. Zones stepped from the car, looking around for any sign of Chennault. He saw no structures of any kind, leading him to believe there were only trees. He paced for a moment, hoping that someone would come soon.

His patience got the better of him. Zones went to open the gate but found it secured by a chain and lock.

"Shit!" He walked back to the car, tossed all manner of things around in the trunk, looking for something to pry the lock. "Women!" he said, finding nothing. Zones climbed back into the car, cranked up the engine and tore through the gate, making a loud noise, leaving it dangling from its supports. The front bumper dragged the ground and scratches marred the pink color of the Cadillac Escalade.

The long, winding road meandering through the forest of trees led him to a clearing where a very large house stood. This farmhouse, unlike the first one, resembled a stately mansion. He parked just short of the drive and walked up to the house. A void, soulless abode on first perception, the house loomed like a menacing overlord about to exact retribution on his subjects. Zones ascended the stone steps, prepared to run rather than charge, if need be. Keeping on his toes, he moved stealthily along the slate stoop. He reached the double wooden doors, two huge slabs of hewn wood that dwarfed him. He grabbed for the lock, pausing, then pulling back to retrieve his phone. He whipped it out to call James. He was prepared to dial but no bars showed, no signal.

Zones turned the lock, hearing the tumbles as they fell into place inside the cylinder. The knob stopped turning and the door popped open with a loud creak. He pushed it open just enough to squeeze himself through, closing the door behind him. The space, large, like a castle, swallowed him up. He moved toward faint sounds he heard coming from a distance away. With the wall to his back, he crept down a grand, circular staircase. The sounds he heard grew stronger as he descended. When Zones reached the end of the stair, he came upon a narrow, dimly lit hall framed by a maze of rooms. At the end of the hall, in one of the rooms, he saw a faint shadow moving violently on the wall. The weak sounds became very distinct moans. Zones moved forward into the large room, finding a young girl tied to the wall with rope using a familiar knot.

He rushed toward her. She screamed.

"Shhhhh!" he said, trying to quiet her. "Are you Carolyn Armstrong?" She nodded. Her earth-colored mane spread violently over her face, interfering with her streaming tears. "I'm here to help you. I just need to find something to cut this rope."

"Bravo, Dr. Zones!" a voice chimed in to an accompanying, measured clap. The sound echoed throughout. Zones turned to see none other than Dr. Hyde, imagine that. He smiled and posed atop a stair tread, hand on hip as if he were some duke or an earl. "It would seem that I underestimated you." He stepped down the stairs.

"And I you, Doctor."

"Do tell, Doctor Zones, what gave me away?"

"No one thing but to start with, your mesotonic personality—the so-called humanitarian trips to all those war zones—adventure-seeking, the classic profile for perp two. Your dysgraphia, the backwards spelling of 'Heil' on the palms of the bodies, the prescription 'Elavil' you wrote me, and finally, this place. Your dysgraphia for 'Dr. Hyde' is 'Edyh Rd.'. Then there's the Mormon thing, of course, your ancestor, Orson Hyde, was an apostle in the church and a close contemporary of Sidney Rigdon. I missed him initially in my research. The genealogy, however, confirmed it."

"And how do you account for your victim, Ms. Redding, identifying Tanner Rigdon as her assailant, finding his DNA underneath her fingernails?"

"You were in the room as well when she tried to tell me who her abductor was, perhaps that's why you were so quick to sedate her.

As for his DNA, you're Rigdon's primary care physician so getting a sample wouldn't have been very difficult."

"Touché, Doctor, but do you know why I do what I do—my work, Doctor?"

"Zion."

"So you have done your homework." Dr. Hyde paused in his descent from the stairs. "Zion is the only hope for this world," he said, reaching for the heavens. "The government throws dollar after dollar into programs, to no avail. Poverty! Crime! War! Famine! Since our sorry asses first populated God's green earth, we have been hell-bent on turning it into a cesspool. But now they will have to bow to the power of the church."

"So you kill to save the world?"

"Is that not what the Lord had to do?"

"The way I read it is that he gave his own life."

"Semantics!" he said, his chiseled face contorting whereby his brow dipped far into his eyes. He continued to ease down the stairs, reaching the main floor. "Did you forget the flood, Doctor?"

"We can end this right here. No one else has to get hurt. Let this young girl go and call it quits."

"Quits! Quits! Why, I've only just begun!" He moved slowly, parallel to Zones, on the other side of the large room. Zones moved away from him and past Carolyn; she was still tied to the wall. Neither took their eyes off the other. "You, of all people, should understand what I do, Dr. Zones. Isn't cleansing the world of its filth the reason why you joined the FBI? You should be joining me."

"Serial killers and terrorists, yes, but tell me what the five innocent victims you and your minions slaughtered have to do with any of what you've just said."

"Innocent! **THEY WERE THE PROGENY OF THE APOSTATES, THERE SPILLED BLOOD WATER FOR THE SHEAVES OF ZION!**" he ranted, shouting at the top of his voice, overturning a table and its settings. The sudden outburst frightened Carolyn, she screamed, drawing Zones' attention. He took his eyes off Dr. Hyde who burst into song. "Bringing in the sheaves, bringing in the sheaves . . ." The sound of gunfire filled the space. Bullets whizzed past Zones, bouncing off the rubble stone walls, striking the floor, the ceiling and furnishings. "We shall come rejoicing, bringing in the sheaves . . ."

Zones dove behind a wooden chest. He landed hard on his shoulder, striking the tiled floor with some force. He grimaced in pain and clutched his arm. Carolyn continued to scream, her high-pitched screeches competing with the low, crackling booms of gunfire.

"Show yourself!" Dr. Hyde shouted. Zones remained hidden, crouched low to the floor. "If you don't, I'll kill her!"

"Shit!" Zones rose from behind the chest, one hand in the air, the other dangling at his side. Blood gushed from his arm. Dr. Hyde stood behind the now untied Carolyn. He pointed a gun at her side.

"Get the other up!" He pointed the gun at Zones.

"I can't. You shot me, you son-of-a-bitch."

"You keep it there then and don't try anything." He moved to the other side of the room, shuffling sideways behind his captive, the gun still pointed at Zones. He waved it sideways, motioning for him to move toward the ropes hanging from the wall.

Zones inched over, taking his time getting there.

"You know why your people will never get ahead, Doctor? Failure to recognize opportunity. With you working on the inside—put your hand in there." Zones stuck his hand in the loop of the rope. "Now tighten it up."

"I can't raise my arm."

"You think I'm one of your asshole homeboys? Use your good hand to secure the other one first." Zones used his left hand to lift his right hand into the loop of the rope. Blood ran in a steady stream down his arm, pooling on the floor. "Now tighten it." He pulled the knot, the same one he had seen many times now and had studied from the very beginning of this case, tightening the rope around his wrist. "Now the other." He lifted his left hand into the loop, hanging it there.

"Now what?" Zones asked, unable to draw the knot.

"Just pull down on the rope." Zones pulled and the loop tightened. "As I was saying, with you on the inside, we could have made a serious dent in the problem. But now—" He plopped Carolyn in a chair, pulled a roll of tape from the drawer of a table and secured her hands to the chair's arms. He placed the gun on top the table but then pulled a large knife out of the drawer. "I will have your head." He charged toward Zones who was hanging tied to the wall helplessly. A wild look in his eyes, Dr. Hyde readied the knife, raising it above his head.

As he neared, Zones dug his finger in between a weak strand of the knot, one that he had found while studying it. He pulled it, loosening the loop just enough for him to free his hand. As Dr. Hyde charged, Zones slipped his left hand from the rope, pulled the black Glock 17 9mm that Sam had given him from his rear pants' waist band and fired five rounds at him. He struck Dr. Hyde center mass. He stumbled back further with every bullet strike, hitting the hard, cold floor.

Zones' hand dropped fast, like a stripper picking up twenties. The gun fell to the floor as his finger released the trigger. He hung there by one arm, blood still gushing from his wound. He passed in and out of consciousness. The smell of gunpowder lingered in the air. Carolyn sat tied to a chair across from him, but she was alive.

Footsteps rushing down the stairs replaced the sound of gunfire. Chennault and a team of officers stormed the room with their guns drawn.

"Cut him down," Chennault said, seeing Zones hanging from the wall. "And call for an ambulance."

. . .

"Well, Dr. Zones, at least the FBI knows you can take a bullet," Marmaduke quipped.

"More importantly, I can give a few too," Zones snapped back, sporting a cast and a sling. "So to what do I owe the concierge service, Detective? Are you feeling guilty that I took a bullet when all you got was a knife prick?"

"There's a slope coming up and these wheelchairs don't have any brakes. I could've allowed that big, ugly-assed orderly roll you up out of here."

"Speaking of ugly asses, how did the Captain take having to tell the DA to drop the charges against Rigdon? I'm sure he was his normal eloquent self."

"Let's just say, shot on not, you would be rolling in between steel-barred doors and not these glass ones if he had his way."

"Well, at least they got him on embezzling money from his company."

"Yeah, at least. May cut a deal though, to keep him from suing."

Marmaduke pushed Zones through the sliding glass doors of the hospital and out into a slight Atlanta night breeze. Hospitals still didn't agree with him, although he appreciated the care.

"Here you go, Doc." Marmaduke stopped the wheelchair at the curb of the sidewalk, locking the wheels in place. "You're sure I can't give you a ride? I cleaned the Deuce and polished up the pleather."

"So, it's date-ready?" They both laughed. "Perhaps next time, the hotel isn't far from here. I'll see you tomorrow when I brief the Captain."

Zones rose from the chair, throwing up his collar and flipping on his Kangol. He looked left and then right, just as he'd been taught to do when adventuring into life. He stepped off the curb and into the night, heading toward a lighted sign that parted the darkness like a flame chasing the bad things away. *"Jesus Saves"*, it read, emblazoning the night.

The walk through town did something that a quick drive could not—it gave him time to reflect. Zones couldn't believe the perils he'd survived: being knocked unconscious and left on the floor to whatever fate awaited him, the farmhouse and his encounter with the charging brute, bringing him down with a shotgun blast, dodging gunfire on the outskirts of town, saved only by Sam's return fire, and finally, finding himself tied to a wall in the lair of the mastermind behind the killings and bringing him down just like he did with the brute.

Zones hadn't signed up for this GI Joe shit. His job description read, "FBI consultant and profiler", not "SWAT commander and gunslinger". He must take better precautions if he wanted to make this a lengthy relationship. He was happy to have been in both places and of some assistance when the shit had hit the fan.

After his briefing with the Captain tomorrow, the memory of this case would fade into history, then on to the next one. He did not like to linger—that relationship thing, he guessed. His job was done here, not perfect, but done well, he thought. Just ask Carolyn Armstrong and Patricia Redding. *Jesus Saves. So do Remington and Glock.*

THE END

www.ingramcontent.com/pod-product-compliance
Lightning Source LLC
Chambersburg PA
CBHW071127170626
46809CB00002B/522